Symbolic of the revolution in transportation early in the 20th century, a Buick Model 10 "White Streak" motors past a team of oxen on a bridge near Standish, Mich., circa 1908.

DAVID BUICK'S MARVELOUS MOTOR CAR

The men and the automobile
that launched General Motors

Revised Third Edition

by
Lawrence R. Gustin
with Kevin M. Kirbitz

FOREWORDS BY BOB LUTZ
AND NICOLA BULGARI

Buick Gallery and Research Center, Alfred P. Sloan Museum

This was cover art for the first Buick Manufacturing Company and first Buick Motor Company catalogs.

For the grandchildren: Grant, Olivia, Zachary, Drew, Ava

First edition, 2006
Second edition, 2011
Third edition, 2013
   Updated, 2016

ISBN: 978-1-943995-01-1

Published by Buick Gallery and Research Center, Alfred P. Sloan Museum.
Produced by Mission Point Press, Traverse City, Mich.
Cover photo of Buick Model C: David Franklin

CONTENTS

A word from Nicola Bulgari

Nicola Bulgari is vice chairman of the Bulgari Group, that very prominent organization of international jewelers based in Rome. He has the world's largest private collection of vintage Buicks, housed in Rome and in Allentown, Pa. Nicola supports such organizations as the Buick Gallery and Research Center of the Alfred P. Sloan Museum in Buick's former home town of Flint, Mich., provides a major trophy for the annual Buick Club of America national meet and supports Buick drivers in such international events as the Peking to Paris and Around the World motor rallies.

He was presented the first annual Buick Heritage Trophy at the Buick Club of America's Buick centennial meet in 2003. In 2016, he hosted the club's 50th anniversary meet at Allentown.

Growing up in Rome at the end of World War II, I was captivated as a child by the Buicks of the late 1930s and early '40s that were so popular with wealthy and important people, including those in government and the Vatican. Also, Buicks were among the first American automobiles imported into Italy after the war. I never lost my passion for these cars.

Here's one example of my enthusiasm for Buicks. Once when I was very young, I saw an advertisement for a 1935 Buick 96S Sport Coupe which absolutely fascinated me. Only 41 were ever built and even though I dreamed of this car for half a century, I never thought I'd see one. But finally Keith Flickinger, my wonderful restorer in Allentown, found the last surviving 96S Sport Coupe. It was almost rusted away, but Keith lovingly restored it and presented it to me at the 2003 Pebble Beach Concours d'Elegance, on the occasion of Buick's centennial celebration there. It was certainly a highlight of my life.

The story of Buick is one of the great adventures in automotive history. I've given you a hint of why I am such a fan. But there's so much more to talk about, including how it all started, and I'm excited to have been asked to help introduce the details revealed here, some for the first time. When your cast of characters includes David Buick, Billy Durant, Louis Chevrolet, Charles Nash and Walter Chrysler, for starters, you know you've got something special. Enjoy the story of The Buick.

Nicola Bulgari

A word from Bob Lutz

Robert A. Lutz, who retired in 2010 as General Motors vice chairman but continued to serve as an adviser to top management, began his outstanding career in senior positions at General Motors in Europe. He progressed to vice president of BMW in Munich, chairman of Ford of Europe and then executive vice president and a director of the parent Ford Motor Co. He later became president and vice chairman of Chrysler Corp., responsible for worldwide car and truck operations. He was persuaded to "unretire" in 2001 to become GM vice chairman of product development and chairman of GM North America. Finally, he served the "new" (post-bankruptcy) GM as its vice chairman.

In the automobile business, the job is always to look forward. New product is everything. What motivates the customer is how the design appeals to the senses, how the car handles, sounds and feels — in short, how it looks and performs.

You can't compromise. When I came back to GM in 2001, this time as vice chairman of product development, one of my first tasks was to approve two new Buicks. Looking at the early renderings, I wasn't impressed. So we stopped their development and ordered total redesigns. The redesigned models were delayed in getting to showrooms, but they did well in the marketplace, and my long enthusiasm for the Buick brand was strengthened. Finally, thanks to the unleashed talents of those in GM Design, we had made an impact — and it felt great to be a part of the marque's long and illustrious history.

As we move forward we're continually making big improvements in every aspect of new Buicks — the look, the ride and handling, engine performance, fit and finish, materials. I have no hesitation in calling Buick's new offerings by far its best ever. This is no place to make a sales pitch, but I merely offer the latest models of the Buick Enclave, LaCrosse and Regal as exhibits.

Having said my focus is always on the future, I must admit I have real affection for and great interest in a marque's history. Heritage can often help shape future design. If you talk to veterans such as Bill Porter, a very knowledgeable Buick design chief, now retired, you'll hear about Buick's "romantic" designs of the past and be reminded of such styling cues as sweepspears, portholes and waterfall grilles. As Porter once said, "Buicks must always be designed with a strong front end." And he was insistent that Buicks must also be very distinctive — you should know it's a Buick the moment you see it, from blocks away.

Knowledge of history can tell you a lot — for example the story behind Buick's recent runaway successes in China. When GM and the Shanghai Automotive Industry Corp. agreed on a $1.5-billion joint venture in the mid 1990s, the Chinese very much wanted the first models out of that new plant in Shanghai to be Buicks, not any other GM brand. Why Buicks in China? Well, prominent Chinese business people and politicians had been driving Buicks for as long as anyone could remember. Even the last emperor bought Buicks — he bought a lot of cars but Buicks were said to be his favorites. With that kind of heritage, it's no surprise that Buicks became the first superstars in the Shanghai joint venture.

Every business story — success or failure — is a people story. And I would say Buick's people story is among the most interesting in the industry, especially in its formative years. It's indisputable that Buick can claim one of the most important and dramatic chapters in U.S. auto history, especially as the foundation for GM. But it's the people who have made the Buick story so fascinating to me.

Alfred P. Sloan Jr. once said that "Buick had the management of stars." Billy Durant, the master promoter and salesman who would found GM, deserves the credit for building Buick from a nearly bankrupt little concern to the industry's sales leader in just a few years. And some formidable fellows named Charles Nash, Walter Chrysler and race driver Louis Chevrolet were all part of the Buick story in its first 10 years — before automobiles bearing their names were being produced.

But this book focuses on the man who gave his name to the car — David Dunbar Buick. Now I'm told his name is on a sprinkling of historical markers in Detroit, Flint and his birthplace of Arbroath, Scotland, and his last name has adorned more than 40 million motor vehicles. And I know he is honored in the Automotive Hall of Fame.

But little had been written about David Buick until recently, when Larry Gustin took on the job. Larry's 50-year writing career has been split about evenly between newspapers — mostly at *The Flint Journal* in Buick's former hometown — and Buick PR, where he was assistant director. He produced the first edition of this work in 2006 and it got a fine review in the *New York Times*. One fellow historian even noted, quite correctly, that it "fills a gaping hole in automotive history." (About 35 years ago Larry wrote the first biography of Durant, and both the Durant book and first edition of this one have recently been translated into Chinese and published in Shanghai. Buick is indeed a star on the other side of the world.)

In reading the manuscript of this account of David Buick, I do understand why other auto historians overlooked him as they searched for dramatic characters. He didn't say much, he left no memoirs and he allowed his money and his company to slide away. David Buick made the kind of mistakes any of us could have made, and maybe a few we never would have imagined. Some would say he was no hero.

But in some ways he was. This was a man who wanted to build automobiles and he overcame every obstacle to make that happen. He had to do it all — organize the business, design and engineer cars and engines and transmissions himself, discover and hire mechanical geniuses to design even better ones, find financial angels for his plants and buyers for his products, then create the factory and hire and train the workers to manufacture the product. In total, a monumental job. But finally he got cars out the door that performed well enough to attract Billy Durant to build the business into a giant. That's impressive enough, because Durant actually hated automobiles until he was given a ride in one of David Buick's marvelous motor cars.

This is not only the first detailed account of David Buick's career, but it's also a very interesting telling of those dramatic times when the American automobile industry was born, with thanks to Larry and his talented technical and research assistant, GM engineering manager Kevin Kirbitz, who provided much of the information for this expanded edition.

I'll always look to the future of this industry, and do what I can to motivate people to build the best products. But to be successful in the future, it's good to know where you have been. And in Buick's case, this is where you'll find the answers. I hope you enjoy this story of how it all began for Buick, the car and the man.

Bob Lutz
June, 2011

David Dunbar Buick

"Mr. D.D. Buick is a gas engine expert and is very largely responsible for the creation of the marvelous motor which bears his name."

—William C. Durant, general manager, Buick Motor Company, in a letter dated May 7, 1906. Durant would found General Motors in 1908 with Buick as the foundation.

"It was Buick that made any kind of General Motors car line worth talking about."

— Alfred P. Sloan Jr., GM's legendary chief executive after Durant, discussing the Buick marque's stature in the early years in his biography, *My Years With General Motors.*

Introduction

In any discussion of automotive history, Buick deserves special attention. That would be true if only for this: Buick was the financial pillar on which General Motors — which became the world's largest industrial corporation — was created.

But that's only part of it. Buick has produced a great deal of automotive lore. There were the innovations, starting early with the "valve-in-head" engine that surprised the auto world with its power and efficiency.

And famous models — Century, Roadmaster, Super, Skylark, LeSabre, Riviera, Gran Sport, Regal, Grand National, GNX, Electra 225, Park Avenue and later Reatta, Enclave, LaCrosse. And, okay, the 1962 Special with America's first mass-produced V-6, which, along with the turbo 1979 Riviera S Type, was proclaimed a *Motor Trend* car of the year.

Buick's show-car legacy begins with the legendary Y-Job, the industry's first "dream car," and includes such concepts as XP-300, LeSabre, several Wildcats, Centurion and up through the decades to the new millennium's gorgeous retro Blackhawk (more show car than concept and unfortunately sold) and then the classic convertible Velite, a model almost everyone wanted produced.

There were notable styling features — boat tails, hardtop convertibles, hood ornaments with goddess and bombsight designs, "sweep-spear" bright metal side decorations, front fenders that swept back to touch the rear fenders, carnivorous pop-art grilles of the '40s and '50s, and — most famous of all — portholes. And great engines after the early valve-in-heads, including the "Fireball" straight 8, the so-called "nailhead" V-8 and the "3800" 3.8-liter V-6, also available turbocharged and then supercharged.

Buick's pioneer-era racing teams led by Louis Chevrolet and Wild Bob Burman won 500 trophies from 1908 to 1910, and Buick's stock block V-6s of the 1990s dominated several fields at the Indianapolis 500. Speaking of sports, golf and Buick linked up with the 1958 Buick Open that pioneered bringing major corporate sponsorships to sports. Later there were more Buick-sponsored PGA tournaments — with the Buick Open spanning more than half a century.

International heritage? Buick's is, in a word, impressive. Before 1910, Buick was the foundation for GM Export and GM of Canada. A Buick in 1914 was the first car to cross South America. Adventurer Lowell Thomas used a Buick in 1923 for the first motor expedition into Afghanistan. Buicks swept speed, reliability and fuel economy awards in tests conducted by the Soviet Union in 1925. Also that year, GM Export sent a Buick Standard Model 25X around the world without a specific driver — passing the car from agent to agent — to prove the reliability of the car and GM's global network.

In the 1920s and '30s, Buick — an "Empire" car because some were built in Canada — was a favorite of British royalty. During King Edward VIII's abdication crisis, his fiancé, Mrs. Wallace Simpson, made her legendary escape to Cannes in a Roadmaster he had bought for her — and Edward himself owned a custom-built 90 Series Buick. In China, such political leaders as Sun Yat-sen, first (1912) provisional president of the Republic; World War II Generalissimo Chiang Kai-shek; postwar premier Zhou Enlai; and even Pu Yi, the last emperor, sometimes either owned, drove or were driven in Buick automobiles. In fact Buick was so popular in China that when GM and China agreed on a $1.5-billion joint venture in Shanghai in the late 1990s, the Chinese insisted Buicks must be the first cars produced. Soon Shanghai Buicks led in the booming Chinese market and concept and production Buicks were being designed jointly in China and the U.S.A.

Also internationally, a 1948 Special completed the second Peking-to-Paris rally (1997). The first was 90 years earlier, but this one went through Tibet. A 1949 Super wagon circled the globe, starting and ending in London, in "Around the World in 80 Days" (2000). That vintage-car rally commemorated the dawn of the new millennium. A 2002 Buick Rendezvous won a silver medal in the 15,000-mile Inca Trail adventure drive (late 2001). Lead driver Pat Brooks collected his award on the evening of a Buick-sponsored reception atop Rio de Janeiro's Sugar Loaf. International jeweler Nicola Bulgari displays his collection of about 50 vintage and modern Buicks in Rome (he has even more in the United States). He cruises in them with journalists for articles in classy European magazines.

The Buick name has been very visible in entertainment. Among many examples: A 1940 Limited Phaeton is in the famous airport scene with Humphrey Bogart and Ingrid Bergman in *Casablanca.* Tom Cruise and Dustin Hoffman drive a 1949 Roadmaster convertible across the country in *Rain Man.* Vintage Buicks are prominent in *Pearl Harbor* and *The Road to Perdition.* Stephen King places a 1954 Buick (but with a '53 mistakenly on the jacket) at the center of one of his horror stories, *From a Buick Eight.* And somewhere out there is the music video, *Aliens Ate My Buick.*

Buick was the starting (and growing) place for auto leaders from the beginning. Among them: William C. Durant, GM's founder; Charles W. Nash, a founder of what became American Motors; Walter P. Chrysler, founder of Chrysler Corporation; and Harlow H. Curtice, a postwar GM chief executive and *Time* magazine's 1955 "Man of the Year." Louis Chevrolet, onetime Buick racing star, helped Durant form Chevrolet Motor Company. Moving to recent times, Lloyd E. Reuss was chief engineer and then general manager of Buick before serving as GM president in the early 1990s.

What about David Dunbar Buick? When the story of the Buick automobile is recounted, its namesake typically is granted his several perfunctory lines of type. David Buick — or Dave, as he liked to be called — is remembered as a successful plumbing inventor. Sometimes he's even praised as a developer of fine gasoline engines in the pioneer days. But usually he comes off as a dreamer ignored and forgotten first by his company, and then by the public, and ultimately by auto historians.

It's true he's listed in the Automotive Hall of Fame. Get your name on roughly 40 million cars and you'll be there. But not much has been written about him. For one thing the slight but hard-edged Scottish immigrant (1854-1929) never recorded his accomplishments in any detail. His family didn't help — it didn't preserve many of his letters and photographs. He himself didn't attract positive attention with his later business ventures. And because he died broke, and therefore was labeled a failure, auto historians generated little energy filling in the blanks.

As one historian, George S. May, observed in his exhaustive 1975 book, *A Most Unique Machine: The Michigan Origins of the American Automobile Industry,* "few aspects of American automobile history have been so poorly recorded as that detailing the movement of David Buick from the plumbing business into the business of developing and manufacturing engines and automobiles."

But this much is known. David Buick led a team that created gasoline engines for motor cars that were truly remarkable. They were powerful, durable and efficient engines that proved formidable on race tracks and in hill climbs. And, more important, those engines provided the power to negotiate the deeply rutted mud, clay and sand roads that often defeated other cars in the early 20th century.

David Buick created one of two big story lines that connected in Flint, Michigan, in 1904. His theme was about a faltering little company with a great engine, Buick Motor Company. The other big story line was that of the brilliant organizer and promoter, William C. Durant. When Durant was introduced to the Buick automobile, it was almost like an explosion in the business world. That combination, Durant and Buick, formed the beginning of General Motors.

In the 1960s, '70s and '80s, it was still possible to learn about David Buick, Billy Durant and their times from a few first-hand sources. David's grandson, David Dunbar Buick II, well remembered the auto pioneer who had once lived with him and his family. Fred Hoelzle, who knew David just a little and who worked on one of the first Buick engines, lived into his 90s in the late 1970s and loved to discuss the early days. Also available in the early 1970s were Flint philanthropist Charles Stewart Mott, a General Motors board member for 60 years, who lived to age 97, and Durant's widow, Catherine, then in her 80s, both of whom had been witnesses to those early days when Durant took over David Buick's company and created a giant.

Aristo Scrobogna, Durant's last personal secretary, remembered in the 1980s that Durant talked about respecting David Buick's abilities. Charles E. Hulse, a Flint vintage car buff from the 1930s, related memories of his interviews with Walter Marr, who built the first Buick automobile, and others who were with Buick Motor Company from the company's earliest days. George H. Maines, a locally prominent public relations man, didn't know Buick personally, but recalled in the 1960s he had interviewed Durant about David.

For a few years now, or a few decades, I've been searching for David Buick. Back in the 1960s, as a young newspaper reporter and automotive editor in my hometown of Flint, I listened to George Maines, Sloan Museum Director Roger Van Bolt and local historian Clarence H. Young tell the true stories of David Buick, Billy Durant and the beginnings of General Motors in hours of fascinating conversations. In the 1970s, I spent many hours interviewing C.S. Mott and Catherine Durant about those early days for a biography of Durant. In the 1980s, I began two decades of employment at Buick public relations, becoming assistant director and semi-official company historian while updating five reprints of a Buick history book co-authored with Terry B. Dunham and first published in 1980.

In 1994, I journeyed to David Buick's old hometown in Scotland to help unveil a plaque near his birthplace. And during Buick's centennial celebration in 2003, and anticipating the 150th anniversary of David Buick's birth in 2004, I applied (while at Buick PR) for a Michigan historical marker commemorating his achievements, and those of his company. The only state marker on the grounds of General Motors headquarters in Detroit, it's positioned along Jefferson Avenue facing Beaubien Street, five blocks down Beaubien from the original Buick engine shop of 1900. That shop was in a building that, at this writing, is still standing.

So in the early years of the new millennium, there were reasons to take a new look at the life of the founder of the Buick automobile. One significant archive became available as the first edition of this book was being written. The research material of the late Charles E. Hulse, mentioned above, was made accessible through the courtesy of Hulse's daughter, Susan Kelley, vintage car enthusiast Jack Skaff and the Sloan Museum's Buick Gallery and Research Center. A number of changes were made based on Hulse's research. Also, new information became available about Charles G. Annesley, a 19th century link between Henry Ford and Walter Marr — and therefore between key figures in the birth, early in the 20th century, of Ford Motor Company and General Motors. This was thanks to Michael W. R. Davis, who shared his unpublished master's thesis on Annesley, an interesting but little-known figure. And I received significant help from the late William B. Close, whose widow Sarah is a granddaughter of Walter Marr, Buick's first chief engineer.

Research for my Durant biography was put to good use. You can't separate Buick's heritage from the incredible Billy Durant. Even the story of how Durant created the Chevrolet needed retelling here because the Chevrolet story is closely tied to Buick's beginnings a few years earlier. The birth of the Chevrolet automobile, and its connection with Buick, were fully explored starting in the second edition, published just before Chevrolet's 2011 centennial.

The first edition (2006) was expected to generate new information about David Buick and that has turned out to be true. The second and third editions contain new information from various sources but mostly from Kevin M. Kirbitz, a GM engineering manager and Buick historian who also contributed to the first edition. He unearthed 19th century plumbing magazines that told of Buick's early career. They yielded three photos of David not seen since the 19th century and ads for his plumbing supply company. Kevin traced David's early homes and documented his Detroit manufacturing real estate – including a recently razed foundry at 290-305 Beaufait Avenue (1067 Beaufait today). Buick's first engines may have been cast there.

Kevin discovered records of a 1904 lawsuit by Buick Motor Company involving Reid Manufacturing Company, Detroit, and its short-lived Wolverine automobile. The transcripts, featuring testimony by David Buick and his boss, James Whiting, provide unique glimpses into David's role in designing, manufacturing and marketing engines in the Buick firm's earliest days. Kevin also found details of David's failed real estate venture in the 1920s in central Florida.

This third edition includes Kevin's new-found California newspaper interview of David Buick from 1910, more on David's Florida venture, the only known Buick Motor Company stock certificate, published for the first time, and photos of new statues of David Buick (late 2012) and Billy Durant (2013).

Terry Dunham, my co-author of *The Buick: A Complete History* and a close personal friend for more than 40 years, was able to view most of the new material, including photos of David's statue, shortly before his death at age 72 on November 2, 2012. His memorial service in his hometown of Howell, Mich., took place December 2, the day after the Buick statue was unveiled in nearby Flint. Terry's enthusiasm for this book was a force that led to completion of all three editions. He felt strongly that this was an important project, a story that needed to be told.

The contributions of Terry, Kevin and the others show up in the following. However, individuals may interpret similar information in different ways. Therefore, it's appropriate to state that while I received plenty of help, which made this book possible, I'm alone responsible for the opinions and errors that may have crept into these pages.

Lawrence R. Gustin
Flint and Lake Orion, Michigan

This statue of David Dunbar Buick, created by sculptor Joe Rundell, was unveiled in downtown Flint, Mich., December 1, 2012. It's adjacent to statues by Rundell of Louis Chevrolet (unveiled in August 2012) and William C. Durant (August 2013).

Kevin M. Kirbitz

Statue of William C. Durant, Buick promoter/ manager who later founded General Motors and then Chevrolet, is unveiled before an enthusiastic crowd in downtown Flint, Mich., on August 17, 2013. In this sculpture by Joe Rundell, Durant appears in motoring outfit as in photo on Page 123. The Durant statue is positioned between those of David Buick and Louis Chevrolet, both installed the previous year. Speakers at the Durant unveiling included GM North America President Mark Reuss, Durant great-grandsons Duke and Gordon Merrick and writer Lawrence R. Gustin, who noted the event was taking place 40 years to the month after he completed the manuscript for the first Durant biography in 1973.

Chapter 1

An interview in Detroit

Maybe he saw too much. Too many people making all the decisions. Too much chaos as the company expanded rapidly. Too much work, too many hours.

"When we were getting the Buick Motor Company under way, there wasn't an executive in the place who ever knew what time it was," David Dunbar Buick lamented in 1928. "We worked until we had the day's job done and were ready for tomorrow and then we went home — and not until then….

"For seven years I didn't have a Sunday or holiday off — not even Christmas or the Fourth of July. I worked 12, 16, 18 hours some days…I tell you, the automobile business was a tough one in those days."

You can debate whether he was complaining or boasting. But David Buick was telling the truth. Said William Beacraft, Buick's first engine plant foreman and master mechanic: "I used to sleep in the shop, but we could never keep up with demand." All of the pressure did leave Buick, in his own words, "a physical wreck." So a little more than a year after William C. Durant, the super promoter, built up Buick Motor Company and then used its success to create General Motors in 1908, David Buick just packed up and wandered off.

Claiming illness from overwork and pocketing maybe $100,000 in severance, he left the company. Buick left Buick. In the spring of 1910, he put Michigan behind him and headed for California. He soon boasted of big wins in the oil fields there. But the success was illusory and short. Over the next several years, he apparently lost most of his Buick Motor Company nest egg. He followed with other business ventures that were also either failures or disastrous failures. When he stumbled back to Detroit, he was close to destitute.

In early 1928, an impoverished David Buick was tracked down at his workplace at the Detroit School of Trades by a young newspaper reporter named Bruce Catton, and consented to a rare interview. The

David Buick through the years

5-foot-5 ½ auto pioneer looked all of his 73 years. He was thin and frail and bent. He had a deeply lined face, coke-bottle glasses and wisps of gray hair barely covering his baldness.

He had not been easy to find. David Buick couldn't afford a telephone (let alone an automobile), so his name wasn't in the directory. "Time was when every city editor in Detroit knew where to find David Buick," Catton observed. "Today not one does." But Catton, a reporter for the Newspaper Enterprise Association, had his sources. He also had a historical bent — he would become the first editor of *American Heritage* and a Pulitzer Prize-winning Civil War historian.

Actually David's arrival as a staff member at the trade school three years earlier had been heavily advertised. But by the time Catton found him he was a low-paid instructor and glad to have the job. Catton arrived eager for the interview because, he wrote, "in all the collection of strange tales that are told in Detroit, the automobile capital, there is no tale as strange as the tale of David Buick."

The tale is strange because Buick's name was famous, his accomplishments were significant and his fortune was nonexistent. That's what captivated Catton, but it was also strange because David Buick was hard to typecast. One acquaintance painted Buick as a rough-talking man, "always chewing tobacco." Another, Detroit businessman and politician John C. Lodge, who has a freeway named after him, labeled Buick "a hard man to do business with." When Enos DeWaters, later Buick chief engineer, arrived at the company in 1905, David Buick startled him with this greeting: "Well, I don't

know what in hell you're going to do, so you might as well start as general foreman in the Assembly Department." In later years, a string of lawsuits in California tarnished his reputation at the same time they depleted his finances.

Yet Benjamin Briscoe Jr., a Detroit auto supplier and manufacturer, and briefly Buick's financial angel, described Buick as "a personal friend and a fine chap generally." His grandson, David Dunbar Buick II, told the writer his namesake was "quiet, a dreamer." Buick's surviving letters reveal a logical mind and a gentle disposition.

Another reason Buick's story is strange is because, for a long time, it was decidedly non-automotive. His 25 patents and successful business enterprises were mostly related to the highly profitable plumbing industry. Then, in the mid 1890s, when Henry Ford and others began building horseless carriages, Buick began to focus on making stationary and portable engines for the farm and industry. But it wasn't long before he was on to powered boats and motor cars. And when he did catch the car bug, it brought him great fame and great pain, almost simultaneously.

Intrigued, Catton sensed Buick was a man whose dimming memory still held a story. And so that day in 1928, they sat across from each other in a small room of the Detroit School of Trades, and began to talk about Buick's career.

3

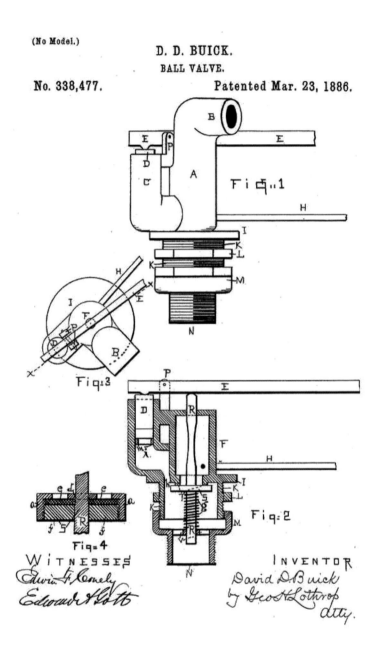

One of David Buick's earliest patents was for a ball valve. He secured at least 25 patents during his career.

Chapter 2

From Scotland to Detroit: The early years

For the true beginning, scroll back to Scotland. David was born September 17, 1854. He arrived in a small row house built of local red sandstone at 26 Green Street in Arbroath, a Scottish fishing, shipping and farming village on the North Sea, the first child of Alexander and Jane Rodger Buik. (Note the spelling, and the footnote.)[1] He was baptized October 15 as a Presbyterian in the Church of Scotland.

All that exists of Green Street 150 years later is a bit of curbing along the front of the former Masonic Hall (sold in 2005 to the British Legion), a building more than a century old, where a plaque commemorating David Buick's nearby birthplace was unveiled in 1994. The street's other buildings were demolished in the early 1970s for a housing development.

But in 1851, when a census was taken, 297 people lived in 62 dwellings along Green Street. Most were employed in textiles. About half were locally born. The rest had come from other parts of Scotland, except for 21 from Ireland.

In 1851, Alexander, 20, was living with his parents on High Street in the nearby village of Forfar. Like his father, James, he was a carpenter. Jane Rodger, 17, lived at the nearby Salutation Inn, where she was a servant. But other Buicks and a David Dunbar lived on Green Street in Arbroath, where the young couple moved after their marriage on May 22, 1853, in the Church of Forfar.

---

1 As another Arbroath native, Eric G. Buick, notes, Eric's ancestors also sometimes spelled it Buik. According to Eric, the spelling sometimes varied depending on what day it was and is of no significance. He said Jane's maiden name of Rodger was also often Roger. Other variants for Buick in Scotland include Bewicke and Bowick. Possible definitions range from bauk or baik, an unploughed ridge or wooden base, or the head rope of a fishing net. Or bouk or buik, which could mean bulk, size, quantity or the touchhole of a cannon. Or buik or buke or beuk, a book, record book or the Bible. A place in Northumberland is named Bewick, from the Old English beo + wic, meaning outlying farm, apparently a station for the production of honey.

David Buick's birth record in Arbroath, Scotland. Note the 'Buik' spelling.

Arbroath was a prosperous community. At the harbor, trade was booming, though ships now faced big competition from a railroad. Some 2,750 tons of flax were landed from ships for processing in 1854 but 6,000 tons arrived by rail. A newly invented stone-cutting machine revolutionized a local quarry industry, according to local historians Eric G. Buick (no relation) and Alasdair M. Sutherland. Paving stone from Arbroath was soon found on the streets of New York and Cologne. Two Arbroath manufacturers had a stand at the Paris Exhibition where they sold one of their new lawn mowers to Napoleon III.

But there were threats. Men were posted on the outskirts of town to check all arriving travelers because a cholera epidemic had broken out in Montrose in 1854. Also the Crimean War was at its height, and recruiting sergeants regularly called on the town.

Ships left Arbroath for destinations around the world. *Storm Nymph,* for example, sailed for Melbourne, Australia, October 19, 1854, with a mixture of cargo and passengers. Cheap transportation out of Leith and Dundee was available to emigrants, who more often chose to travel from Liverpool and Glasgow. In the mid-1850s, favorite destinations were Canada and Australia. The United States was an unusual choice.

Arbroath was not only prosperous but visually interesting with small shops strung out along its picturesque harbor below the impres-

6

Green Street in Arbroath, Scotland, where David Buick was born about halfway up the block on the left on September 17, 1854. This photo was taken 99 years later, with the street decorated for the 1953 coronation of Queen Elizabeth II. But small stone row houses along the street could date back a century. A plaque commemorating David Buick's birthplace was placed in 1994 on the building on left with the seven chimneys.

sive ruins of Arbroath Abbey, where Scotland's Declaration of Independence was signed in 1320. But apparently it wasn't prosperous or interesting enough for Alexander. Two years after David's birth, Alexander took his little family to the United States, settling in Detroit, Michigan. The city was in the middle of a population boom, having grown from a frontier outpost of 2,200 in 1830 to a booming city of 45,000 in 1860. By 1890, Detroit would be a metropolis of 205,000.

In the mid 19th century, Detroit was an attractive and busy city, with impressively big buildings and suggestions of its French beginnings still evident in some of its architecture and its people. The city fronts on the Detroit River, a wide and still beautiful blue-green strait connecting Lake Erie and Lake St. Clair. After the opening of the Erie Canal in 1825, Detroit became a major stop for ships negotiating the St. Lawrence River to Great Lakes ports as far away as Chicago on Lake Michigan and — especially after the locks opened at Sault Ste. Marie in 1855 — Marquette and Duluth on Lake Superior.

When Alexander brought his small family from Scotland to Detroit in 1856, they certainly were not alone. Indeed, while the record

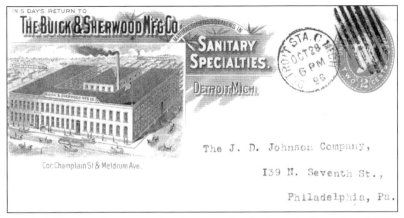

Buick & Sherwood, a major plumbing supplies business in Detroit by 1890s.

is not entirely clear, it appears that not only did all of Alexander's siblings — five sisters and four brothers — also relocate to Detroit, but their father did, as well. (Records are incomplete on whether Alexander's mother had died in Scotland).[2]

It was good that all of those family members immigrated because tragedy struck early. A second son, Thomas A., was born to Alexander and Jane two years after David, but in 1859 Alexander, age 28, died of no recorded cause. Fortunately Jane, suddenly widowed with two small sons, was surrounded by her husband's family. The 1860 census lists not only Jane Buik, 27, and her sons David, 6, and Thomas, 4, but also that they lived in the same house with Alexander's younger brother, David, 22, a machinist, Ellen, 22, probably his wife, both born in Scotland, and a girl, Lavina, 2 (possibly Alexander and Jane's daughter, though she apparently didn't live long). Next door was James, 52, a carpenter, likely Alexander's father.

Still, without his own father, David would have to grow up fast. While he did attend the Bishop public school, he also helped his mother by working two newspaper routes — he delivered the *Detroit Free Press* in the morning and the *Daily Union* in the afternoon. At age 11, David got mad at a teacher, threw an inkwell and jumped out a school window, his grandson told the writer. He never returned.

His mother quickly found work. Detroit city directories reveal that in 1862, Jane was a carpet weaver, living at 162 Columbia East,

---

2 James and Janet (nicknamed Jessie) Buik had 10 children, in order — William, John, James Stook, Alexander Ross (David Buick's father), Elisabeth Cowper, Helen Ross, David Bruce, Janet (Jessie again), Mary Ann and Nillie.

and by 1864, she was a grocer and seller of liquor at the southeast corner of St. Antoine and Elizabeth. On December 6, 1865, Jane, 32, married Daniel Wilson, 28, a machinist. Also that notable year — the Civil War ended; Lincoln was shot — young David left Detroit to work on a farm. In 1867, Jane and Daniel had a child, Jane, David's half sister.

Four years after his departure, David, age 15, was back. Daniel Wilson had died; Jane had been widowed a second time. Maybe David's goings and comings had something to do with Daniel Wilson. (Besides daughter Jane, Daniel and Jane had a son, Daniel, who also died in 1869). By 1871 Jane was again a grocer, at St. Antoine and Columbia, also her home, and her children's. David helped run the store — Jane Wilson & Son. It's been said Jane operated a Detroit candy store for many years and, sure enough, she's listed as a confectioner at 364 St. Antoine by 1885.

For David, helping his mother run a store was part-time work. In 1869 he found a job at James Flower, Bro. & Co., a storied machine shop at Brush and Woodbridge downtown. He became an apprentice brass finisher, then a brass finisher and in 1879 a foreman there.

The timing is remarkable. Young men learned skills at Flower's they would need to prosper in Detroit's great industrial age that was beginning to muscle up. One was Henry Ford. As an apprentice there in 1879, Ford, 16, could have worked under the direction of 25-year-old David Buick. That's a possibility because the record indicates David Buick was a foreman and Henry Ford an apprentice at the same time (1879-1880) in the same shop.

It's interesting there is no record that either ever mentioned knowing the other. Although it was a big plant — with 70 to 80 experienced workmen employed in various departments on three floors — Buick and Ford both apparently worked in the brass finishing operation.

David was well acquainted with one worker at Flower's — William S. Sherwood, who arrived as a brass molder in 1873. Sherwood, born in Lincolnshire, England, October 20, 1851, learned to be a brass molder in London, arrived in New York in 1872 and stopped in Toronto for about a year before arriving at Flower's. Sherwood and Buick became friends and eventually business partners.

The shop's atmosphere was captured by Frederick Strauss, who was a sweeper at age 12 when Henry Ford arrived at Flower's.

Strauss's recollection, related by Sidney Olson in *Young Henry Ford*, was that it was a loud and raucous place: "It was a great old shop. There were three brothers in the company, all in their 60s or more... they were Scotch and believe me they could yell. They manufactured everything in the line of brass and iron...they made so many different articles that they had to have all kinds of machines, large and small lathes and drill presses. They had more machines than workmen in that shop...Everything about the place was as old as the three brothers. The building was so old it was braced up and shored up all over to keep it from falling down."

The booming business of James, Thomas and George Flower encompassed a foundry and machine shops, a pattern shop and construction department, all equipped with machinery driven by a 50-horsepower steam engine. Equipment included cranes, cupolas, lathes, punches, screw cutting machines, steam hammers and planers, most of the machinery of the firm's own invention and construction. Flower's handled big projects, such as fitting up the water works in Detroit, Kansas City, Toledo, South Bend and Bay City, Mich.

In 1881 Buick left Flower's and began working for himself, but he and Sherwood soon joined a small firm that manufactured plumbing supplies and was headed by one Alexander G. Alexander. When David received his first patent, for a stop valve, he assigned one third of the rights to Sherwood and one third to Alexander. David became factory foreman in the firm, which produced water closets and other plumbing fixtures, before he and Sherwood bought out Alexander and established Buick & Sherwood Manufacturing Company in July 1884.

The business quickly blossomed. In 1891, *Detroit in History & Commerce* reported Buick & Sherwood's main plant stretched 162 feet along Meldrum Avenue and 152 feet along Champlain Street, with an 80-foot structure in the rear. By then the firm employed 122 workers producing $200,000 worth of products a year. The company made plumbing woodwork and "sanitary specialties," including bathtubs and toilets. It listed its sales territory as the entire United States and said it had "considerable trade" in Canada and South America. There was a branch office in New York.

Besides his skill with brass, David displayed a talent for invention. Between 1881 and the first several years of the 20th century he was assigned 25 patents, mostly plumbing related — for a lawn sprinkler, flushing device, water closets, valves and the like. His most

David D. Buick,
President & General Manager
of the Buick & Sherwood Mfg.
Co. Detroit.

Wm. Sherwood,
Vice-Pres. and Supt., attends
to the general manufacturing
and shops.

A. D. Babcock,
Secretary and Treasurer,
handling the financial
reins.

C. S. Siddons,
General representative on the
road, giving special attention
to the eastern trade.

In 1894, David Buick and other officers of the Buick & Sherwood Mfg. Co. are featured (above) in The Plumbers' Trade Journal *as hosts of a national plumbers' convention in Detroit. Later that day, the four are pictured again (from left, circled): David Buick, A.D. Babcock, William Sherwood (whose beard was shaved off between photos) and C.S. Siddons.*

notable creation at Buick & Sherwood was said to be for a method of annealing porcelain to cast iron to create white bathtubs and other fixtures. There's no such patent in his name, but one of the company's 1896 ads says its steel bathtub was made from "the finest Bessemer steel, galvanized to make it absolutely rustproof, and instead of a copper lining it is coated on the inside with an insoluble enamel (not porcelain.)" Perhaps this enamel coating was David's big contribution to white fixtures.

Either way, the conventional wisdom is that David could have become very wealthy by capitalizing more on making and selling these desirable enameled fixtures. Indoor plumbing was a very big industry in the last half of the 19th century.

Actually, the company and the man were doing well anyway and David was becoming quite the entrepreneur. In the 1890s he also created, with Albert D. Babcock, the Buick & Sherwood treasurer, a succession of firms — the Detroit Lawn Mower Company, Mutual Vapor Stove Company and Kinney Disinfectant Company.

Buick was 24 when on November 27, 1878, he married Caroline (Carrie) Katherine Schwinck, about 20, born in Michigan of German parentage, in Detroit. They began a family of four children: Thomas David, born in 1879; Frances Jane (Fanny), 1880; Mabel (or Maybelle) Lucille, 1883; and Wynton Rodger, 1898. The 1880 census reports David and Carrie and their first two children were then living at 207 Montcalm in Detroit. It was a cozy arrangement, as David's mother, his brother, Thomas, and 13-year-old half-sister, Jane, lived there as well.

In 1888, with their financial situation now quite robust, David and his wife and children moved into their own home at 373 Meldrum Avenue (today a vacant lot, the address changed to 1187 Meldrum). It was a two-story wood frame house with cedar-shingle roof on the east side of Meldrum between Champlain (now Lafayette) and St. Paul. It may have been of a gingerbread style evident in surviving houses in the neighborhood. It was slightly larger than others nearby, on a lot nearly twice as wide as those adjoining. A two-story barn, also larger than others in the neighborhood, stood at the rear of the property. It's said some of Buick's earliest work on engines and automobiles took place in that barn. David's brother, Thomas, and his wife lived next door at 379 Meldrum. Buick & Sherwood, at the southwest corner of Meldrum and Champlain, was in walking distance, only a half block away.

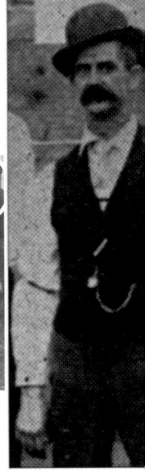

Wives and daughters of 1894 plumbers' convention attendees in Detroit are photographed (above) at the Buick & Sherwood factory on Champlain (now Lafayette) Avenue. This is the only known photograph of the original Buick & Sherwood factory. In 1896 (below), David Buick (right) and William Sherwood (center) pose with the talented Buick & Sherwood "base ball" team. At right, an enlargement of David from bottom photo.

On September 3, 1892, the plant was destroyed in a fire. Buick & Sherwood had to sue the Mechanics Insurance Company to collect as the circumstances were suspicious — the fire occurred only two days after Buick & Sherwood bought a $4,000 policy on the property. Robert J. Allen, a Michigan lawyer who discovered the lawsuit in 2007, observed, "these are suspicious circumstances to any insurance company" in 1892 or today. But it's also hard to believe someone planning arson to collect insurance would set a fire only two days after buying the policy.

By the mid 1890s, David Buick seemed all set. He was regularly patenting his plumbing inventions and the business, newly rebuilt, was doing well. He was raising a family. He was serving as a member of the board of the Detroit Red Cross. He was a prominent member of the Detroit Yacht Club and was racing his sailboat with some success. The Buick & Sherwood "base ball" team could, according to a published report, "hold their own with any amateur ball team in the country."

When Detroit hosted the 12th annual convention of the National Association of Master Plumbers in 1894, Buick & Sherwood provided a grand gesture by inviting all 200 members of the association's visiting Ladies Auxiliary to be photographed in front of its factory. The company provided refreshments and arranged for each woman to receive a copy of the photo. (Instead of speaking to the group, David merely introduced Albert Hyde of Chicago, who explained: "Mr. Buick cannot address you himself for he lost his voice in a severe fall this morning." Maybe so, but he looked healthy enough in a group photo taken later that day).

If David was shy of speaking in public, he still attracted public attention. *The Plumbers' Trade Journal* of New York reported on March 1, 1899, that "the most prominent man in Detroit today is without a doubt David D. Buick, of the well known firm of the Buick & Sherwood Mfg. Co., manufacturers of plumbers' supplies." It didn't hurt that his company was one of *The Journal's* more prolific advertisers. (In those ads, Buick & Sherwood used the trademark "Success" for its products, pointing out, "Success stamped on every article of OUR manufacture is a guarantee that is never questioned.")

Of particular note, the editor was delighted with a suggestion by David that the city create an icon for a planned Detroit 200th birthday exposition in 1901. David envisioned a 160-foot-tall structure that would be shaped to represent Antoine de la Mothe Cadillac, founder

Ads for Buick & Sherwood include (clockwise from left middle) an 1894 "Success steel bath tub," an 1887 listing of its products and an 1894 illustration of water closets. Left, David Buick's design for a statue of Detroit founder Cadillac was published in The Plumbers' Trade Journal *in 1899. The idea never went anywhere.*

Buick & Sherwood 19th century bathtub, a model designed with a small sink attached for apartments with limited plumbing, from a razed California hotel. It was purchased by the Durant-Dort Carriage Company Foundation and is displayed in the company's Flint office building, a National Historic Landmark.

Kevin M. Kirbitz

of Detroit. It would basically be a statue, on Belle Isle in the Detroit River, and so enormous it could house a library and museum. A drawing accompanied the article, made from Buick's original sketches as submitted to a bicentennial committee.

In 1899, *The Plumbers' Trade Journal* was impressed with "this magnificent undertaking." Having conceived it, *The Journal* gushed, "Mr. Buick, who, while a thoroughly modest and unassuming man, has found himself made widely prominent." Buick's proposed statue of Cadillac would have been about nine feet taller than the Statue of Liberty from heel to torch.

Eventually most of the big Detroit bicentennial plans faded. Buffalo, N.Y., pre-empted the planned Detroit exposition when it announced it would hold the Pan-American Exposition in 1901 (largely remembered as the event where U.S. President William McKinley was assassinated). All that has survived of David Buick's statue idea is the 1899 sketch in *The Plumbers' Trade Journal*.

David enjoyed the several Detroit bicentennial parades anyway, commenting particularly on one star attraction, "a very handsome woman of superb figure" who drew acclaim driving a Roman chariot. For the record, the chariot driver has been identified as a Mrs. William Crosby.

But something else was also turning David's head — the gasoline engine. As historian Arthur Pound observed in *The Turning Wheel: The Story of General Motors Through 25 Years*: "To David Buick a bathtub must have seemed a dead and inconsequential thing in contrast with the gasoline engines which had long engaged his eager and inquisitive mind." Or as someone once put it in shorthand, you can't drive a bathtub to town.

16

Chapter 3

Gasoline engines: The obsession begins

David Buick turned to gasoline engines at a dynamic time for inventors and machinists. The world was on the edge of a revolution in transportation. The enormous popularity of bicycles in the late 19th century led to advances in manufacturing of precision metal components, as well as creating a mindset for individual transport via a mechanical device rather than by horse.

Engine technology was rapidly advancing. Inventors and machinists everywhere experimented with steam, electricity and even springs as motive power. Internal combustion engines fueled by gasoline, vapors and natural gas were being invented and improved.

But most of this was happening in Europe. While horseless carriage activity in Detroit was beginning to stir, the city was not yet on the cutting edge of automobile technology — not even close. By the start of the 1890s, Europeans were well ahead of Americans, with some motor vehicle production already under way. The first American gasoline motor car was not driven until 1893. The first in Detroit arrived in 1896.

Actually, the first known automobile in Michigan did not come from Detroit, but from the little farming community of Memphis between Flint and Port Huron. It was steam powered, it was called "The Thing," and it was built in 1884-85 by Thomas Clegg and his father, John. Tom Clegg said The Thing could move along at 12 miles per hour and that he drove it about 500 miles total on 30 trips through farm country in the summer of '85.[1]

---

1 When the writer visited Memphis in 1981 for a newspaper story about a state historical marker being placed there to commemorate The Thing, the city treasurer, Harold Fries, 74, could still remember seeing one of Tom Clegg's ancient steam vehicles rusting on a ridge. That was until one day in 1931, when Clegg's nephew and another man pushed the historic vehicle over the ridge and into a swamp. "The machine disintegrated as it crashed down the hill," said Fries. "Mr. Clegg was mad about that. He said, 'What did you do that for? Henry Ford might have

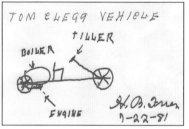

Tom Clegg's Steam Car

While David Buick was patenting his early plumbing inventions, another man a few miles to the north was using his mechanical creativity differently. In 1884-85, Tom Clegg (left) built Michigan's first recorded automobile — propelled by a one-cylinder steam engine — in a Memphis, Mich., machine shop (1880s photo above) operated by his father, John. Son and father are 8th and 9th from left. Tom drove the 12-foot-long vehicle 500 miles that summer. The Cleggs tore it down and in 1886 built a second vehicle, also historic, preceding Ransom Olds' steam car by a year. In 1981, Harold Fries, 74, who saw the second vehicle before vandals destroyed it in 1931, drew a crude sketch (far left) from memory for the writer. Wayne Pickvet drew the original vehicle (bottom) in 1981, basing the details on Tom Clegg's published descriptions.

(Pickvet drawing: *The Flint Journal*, copyright Aug. 9, 1981. All rights reserved. Reprinted with permission).

Clegg once complained, according to Arthur Pound, that his vehicle always returned to the shop under its own power, overcoming every grade and bog in its path, but could not overcome "the sneers and abuse" of public disfavor. In 1885, the people of Memphis and environs were not ready for the automobile.

Auto historians credit two events for accelerating interest among U.S. automobile enthusiasts — the World's Columbian Exposition of 1893 (better known as the Chicago World's Fair) and the *Chicago Times-Herald* auto race, the first American car race, also in Chicago, in 1895.

The Chicago fair was impressive, including, in no particular order, the first Ferris Wheel, a variety of gasoline engines, the "muscle dancing" of Little Egypt and one gasoline-powered vehicle — a quadricycle patented by Karl Benz of Germany. Among attendees were three men whose names would be remembered — Charles B. King, Ransom E. Olds and Henry Ford.

While Olds and Ford were mere visitors, King, a multi-talented 28-year-old Detroit engineer, was very much a participant at the fair. He won its highest award for a pneumatic hammer he had designed. A steam brake beam he had invented was also displayed — it would eventually become a standard item on rail cars. These significant inventions provided money for King's motor vehicle experiments.

King tried to get a vehicle ready for the 1895 *Chicago Times-Herald* race. He was unable to beat the deadline — but he was not alone. At one point an amazing 83 vehicles were entered; but on race day — Thanksgiving 1895 — only six made the starting line.

One was entered by J. Frank Duryea. Historians generally date the first successful drive of a gasoline-powered automobile in the United States to September 21, 1893, in Springfield, Mass., when Duryea drove a machine developed with his brother, Charles. Now, two years later, the Duryeas were about to give it more national visibility. While King had no entry, he wanted into the race. So he signed up as an umpire.

The weather that Thanksgiving morning was abysmal, the roads covered with 4 to 6 inches of snow, as well as 2-foot drifts in places, after a stormy day and night that had seen winds of up to 60 miles

---

wanted it for his museum.' " Actually, Ford apparently did. He is said to have sought to move Clegg's small shop to Greenfield Village, but the request came several months after Tom Clegg had torn it down. Pieces of Clegg's old steam auto may still be sitting in the swamp at the bottom of the ridge.

per hour. As a result the route was abbreviated — instead of from Chicago to Milwaukee, it would now be about 52 miles, from Jackson Park in Chicago to Evanston and return. Had the race not been postponed twice, leading the *Times-Herald* to the edge of ridicule, the organizers might well have delayed it.

But off they went — the Duryea, three imported Benz gasoline vehicles and two electrics. One of the Benz cars was called the Mueller-Benz because owner Hieronymus Mueller of Decatur, Ill., and his son Oscar had made alterations they felt justified the name. The electrics had no chance in the cold weather and retired early. Only two cars completed the race — the Duryea, driven by Frank, the winner in 10 hours and 23 minutes, finishing at 7:18 p.m., and the Mueller-Benz, which arrived 1 hour and 45 minutes later.

The Mueller-Benz finished only because King, who was umpire in the car, took the wheel when driver Oscar Mueller fainted late in the race. Mueller had been driving an open car in freezing weather for about nine hours with almost nothing to eat since breakfast. His passenger, Charles Reid, had fainted earlier and had been taken away by cutter. Under the rules, the starting driver had to be with the car at the end or it was disqualified. King drove to the finish, holding onto Mueller to keep him from falling out. Mueller went to the hospital (and recovered) and King went to the nearby Del Prado Hotel for "the most sumptuous Thanksgiving dinner" he ever had.

King was no doubt energized by the experience. Continuing his momentum, he advertised as a manufacturer of gasoline engines in Detroit late in 1895. On March 6, 1896, King drove a gasoline-fueled horseless carriage along Woodward Avenue in Detroit — credited as the first such drive in what would become the Motor City.

The *Detroit Journal*, which remarked "the connecting rods fly like lightning," described King's vehicle as "a most unique machine," providing George May with a title for his 1975 book detailing Michigan auto history. A friend of King's followed him on a bicycle that night. His name was Henry Ford.

Ford, born in 1863 on a farm in what is now Dearborn, Mich., had a mechanical bent from childhood. In 1891, he took a position in Detroit with the Edison Illuminating Company, eventually becoming chief engineer. When Ford attended the 1893 fair in Chicago, he was particularly drawn to several gasoline engines. Ford began work on the engine for his first motor vehicle early in 1896 and was able to drive it in the early morning of June 4 that year. While King was

Above: Charles B. King (right) and assistant Oliver Barthel in the first gasoline automobile driven in Detroit, on March 6, 1896. Below: Henry Ford and his Quadricycle, which he drove in Detroit three months later, on June 4.

Known all Over the World

THE Buick Stationary Engine has been on the market for the past seven years, and is well known and fully guaranteed. We have a plant capable of turning out (2,600) twenty-six hundred engines per year. We want agents in every town. Write at once for agency.

BUICK MOTOR COMPANY
The Engine Builders   **Flint, Mich.**

Kevin Kirbitz

This 1904 ad in The Implement Age *appears to confirm Buick was marketing its engines in the late 19th century*

first by three months, Ford's "Quadricycle" is seen as a more sophisticated work — a lightweight (500-pound) machine that could travel briskly at 25 miles per hour, a gazelle compared with King's ponderous 1,300-pound carriage that rumbled up Woodward at 5 to 8 mph.

Ransom Olds also benefited from the Chicago fair. He took advantage of an opportunity to ride in the Benz gasoline vehicle displayed there. Three years later, on August 11, 1896, only months after King and then Ford tested their first motor vehicles, Ransom Olds treated a newspaper reporter to a successful test ride in Lansing of his gasoline-powered vehicle.[2]

Meanwhile, back in Detroit, David Buick was becoming interested in gasoline engines and horseless carriages as well. He must have known something about what others were doing. King's drive had been reported, though sparingly, in the newspapers. Buick would likely have seen the stories. Information on advances in gasoline engines could also be found regularly in *Scientific American* and other magazines.

---

2 While he trailed King and Ford by a few months, Olds had advantages in moving from a builder of one car to a manufacturer. Olds was already in charge of a booming manufacturing business in Lansing. Also, he and his company had been experimenting with engines, first steam and then gasoline, for more than a decade. In 1901, Olds, who was lured by financiers to build a factory in Detroit, produced about 425 curved-dash Oldsmobiles — becoming the first volume producer of automobiles in the United States even though a fire burned down his new plant in Detroit in March.

David told his 1928 interviewer, Bruce Catton, that he became interested in gasoline engines in 1895. "I had one horse-drawn dray to take my goods to town, but I needed another. I couldn't afford a new team, although I got my second dray on credit; and I got to thinking about making an engine that would move the dray without horses."

Why this successful businessman couldn't afford a couple of horses is puzzling, but thinking about making an engine and becoming fascinated with engines was apparently a small step for David Buick. Certainly his passion for engines soon surpassed whatever interest he still had in plumbing inventions and supplies. But Buick's first forays into this field were not for automobiles. Buick was building and selling at least a few stationary engines of an L-head design for farm and industry use by 1897. He may have been making and selling engine components a little earlier.

An L-head is a four-cycle engine with valves positioned in the block alongside the piston in roughly an L-shaped design. These engines could be set up for such work as churning milk, cutting feed or running a pump or a saw. Buick's engines were no doubt being hand-built at first, in very small numbers.[3]

A Buick Motor Company advertisement published in *The Implement Age* September 22, 1904, includes this statement: "The Buick Stationary Engine has been on the market for the past seven years, and is well known and fully guaranteed." That ad, in effect stating Buick engine production began about 1897, is one of the few clues about Buick's engine activities in the 19th century. But the recently discovered record of a 1904 lawsuit has David testifying he had been manufacturing motors and gears for automobiles since 1895 and "I built one of the first cars that ever ran on the streets of Detroit…."

Researcher Charles Hulse discovered a news brief buried in the Cleveland-based *Motor Vehicle Review* of October 24, 1899. In its

---

3 The four-cycle engine dates to 1877 when Nikolaus August Otto patented the "silent Otto" in Germany. The engine had four piston strokes per cycle. The first stroke sucked the fuel in, the second compressed it — with an explosion at the end of that stroke, the third or power stroke drove the piston back down, and the fourth exhausted the burned gases. This was an immediate sensation, an important advancement over the two-cycle, which combined the intake and compression functions into one stroke and the power and exhaust functions into a second.

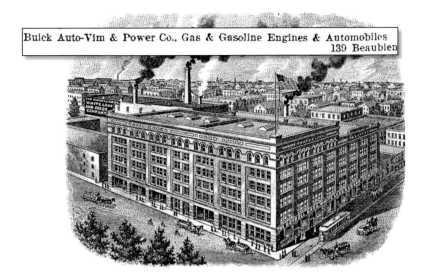

First Buick Auto-Vim & Power Co. listing, in 1900 Detroit telephone book, references gasoline engines and automobiles. Buick Auto-Vim was located in the Boydell Building on Beaubien and Lafayette (then Champlain) in Detroit, to the left in this engraving (above) and likely on the second floor (indicated below). The building was still standing as of this writing. (Kevin Kirbitz collection)

one sentence, Buick is twice misspelled as "Bruick," but the item is the earliest known published evidence of Buick linked to motor vehicles (and reports Sherwood was also his early motor partner). The full text, a dispatch datelined Detroit:

"The Bruick & Sherwood Manufacturing Company, of this city, manufacturers of sanitary specialties, is experimenting in the manufacture of motor carriages, and it is reported that a company will be organized at an early date with Messrs. Bruick and Sherwood as the prime movers."

However, that partnership was short-lived. In December 1899, Buick and Sherwood sold their plumbing supply business to the Standard Sanitary Manufacturing Company, headquartered in Pittsburgh, for $100,000.[4]

At about the same time, in late 1899 or early 1900, David created a firm with the vigorous name of Buick Auto-Vim & Power Company. Now he had a proper center for his engine experiments and production.

Buick Auto-Vim's address in the 1900 Detroit phone book is 139 Beaubien Street. Detroit addresses were revised in the early 1920s; in 1900, that address was at the southwest corner of Beaubien and Champlain (now Lafayette) in downtown Detroit. Buick Auto-Vim was apparently on the second floor, at the front corner nearest to the Detroit River, of the Boydell Building, a six-story red brick structure still standing more than a century later. There were numerous ad-

---

4 The sale was part of a merger of nine plumbing supply companies: Standard Manufacturing Company, Dawes & Myler, Pennsylvania Bath Tub Company and Victor Manufacturing Company, all of Pennsylvania; Ahrens & Ott Manufacturing Company of Kentucky; Cribben & Sexton Company of Illinois; J. Volrath Manufacturing Company of Wisconsin; Sanitary Enameled Ware Company of Indiana; and Buick & Sherwood Manufacturing Company of Michigan. Buick helped organize and manage the Detroit branch of the new firm and was still listed as a director as late as 1901. It is likely Buick could have remained with Standard, as many of the other former owners had done, but he and Sherwood had severed all ties by November, 1901. On October 1, 1902, the name of the Buick & Sherwood Manufacturing Company was officially changed to Standard Sanitary Manufacturing Company, Inc., of Michigan. Around 1906, Standard's Detroit factories were sold to the Detroit Motor Castings Company. Standard would merge in 1929 with the American Radiator Company, becoming the American Radiator & Standard Sanitary Corporation. According to the company's website, by 1948, people came to refer to the firm simply as American-Standard so the company adopted the shortened name as well. The hyphen was officially dropped in 1968, to yield the American Standard known today.

Barn behind David Buick's home on Meldrum in Detroit, where Buick experimented with his early engines and one or more automobiles.

dresses within the large building (including Dodge Motor Works at about the same time). One of them, at 139 Beaubien, was also used in 1900 by, among others, the Hygienic Seat Company, likely connected with Buick's previous line of work.

Buick, with his new-found capital from the sale of Buick & Sherwood, began to accelerate his engine business. He hired a Canadian, W. S. Murray, as his engine foreman (the year is unrecorded but probably 1899). It is recorded that in 1899 Buick hired a Detroit machinist named Walter Lorenzo Marr as Murray's assistant.

Arthur Pound suggested Sherwood's involvement with Buick had continued from plumbing supplies to gasoline engines, noting Sherwood had "an adventurous turn." Certainly the 1899 news item confirms Sherwood's early involvement with the engine business. The two men were close for many years, and Sherwood named his first son David Buick Sherwood. But apparently he became disenchanted with his longtime partner. "Dave, either get down to work or get out," he exploded finally, in the memory of a Sherwood granddaughter. In 1903, Sherwood formed Sherwood Brass Company (sold to Lear-Sigler in 1970).

THE MOTOR VEHICLE REVIEW 31

Further Tests with Mail Matter

DETROIT, Mich., October 23.—Special Correspondence.—Last Friday afternoon a trial in mail collection was made in this city under the direction of Postmaster Dickerson, an electric motor carriage made by the Still Motor Company, of Montreal, Canada, being used for the experiment. The vehicle is a small three-wheeled affair and is driven by electricity. The machine is very compact, and because of this it can be turned in a circle the length of the running gear, something less than eight feet. The motor used has three-horse power, and the vehicle weighs about 800 pounds, having been built for pleasure riding, not for mail carrying purposes. The test was made under the direct supervision of Superintendent of Carriers Burke, and he accompanied the operator of the machine. They covered a route of about 12 miles, and picked up about 70 mail boxes in about an hour and thirteen...

From Cycle Material to Motors

BUFFALO, N. Y., October 21.—Special Correspondence.—John W. Frey, manager of the Buffalo Cycle Supply Company, now located at 895 Washington street, informed a MOTOR VEHICLE REVIEW representative that this winter would see but little cycle material turned out by his company and that almost entire time would be occupied in experimenting with the motor vehicle. The company has almost completed its first motor vehicle, and the vehicle will be soon ready for public inspection. Mr. Frey stated that new capital is coming in to the company, and that there would be an entire change in the plant and its management. As to who is on the point of coming into the company he would not say, but stated that definite developments would soon be reached.

***

> The Bruick & Sherwood Manufacturing Company, of this city, manufacturers of sanitary specialties, is experimenting in the manufacture of motor carriages, and it is reported that a company will be organized at an early date with Messrs. Bruick and Sherwood as the prime movers.

money. Of course this would depend altogether on what it would cost to build or rent them, and concerning this I have made no inquiry."

The Bruick & Sherwood Manufacturing Company, of this city, manufacturers of sanitary specialties, is experimenting in the manufacture of motor carriages, and it is reported that a company will be organized at an early date with Messrs. Bruick and Sherwood as the prime movers.

have been tested, with the most gratifying results, and the firm believes that the claims for the bicycle tires that I have been so well sustained during the past two years and a half should hold good for the motor tires.

***

The Various Lessnesses

And now a motor vehicle factory concern wants to locate in Marseilles, Ill. Pretty soon you may expect to read something like the following, says the Daily Register: About 10 o'clock this morning a horseless milk wagon loaded with cowless milk collided with a brainless rider on a chainless wheel. The luckless wheelman was badly injured and, being homeless, he was taken to the home for the friendless.

***

Invented a New Motor Carriage

Simon Brothers, Webster City, Ia., have invented a new motor carriage, and a stock company with a capital stock of $150,000 has been organized to establish a factory.

Motor Vehicle Review in October 1899 announces the intentions of "Bruick" and Sherwood to enter the motor carriage manufacturing business. This is the earliest known published report linking Buick to motor vehicles.

Within weeks after creating Buick Auto-Vim, David sent Murray off to explore how to manufacture engines. A scrap of information survives suggesting Buick's plans and timing. On February 28, 1900, Murray showed up at the office of C.B. Calder, general superintendent of the Detroit Shipbuilding Company. In his diary, Calder noted Murray, whom he identified as an engineer for Buick & Sherwood, asked "if we could advise him in regard to the best mill for boring out gasoline engine cylinders (as) they are going in the business to make 20 engines a day." Recalled Calder: "We advised his going to the Westinghouse people."

(This may be a reference to the Westinghouse Engine Company of Schenectady, N.Y., which incidentally hired Henry Ford in the early 1880s; for about a year Ford serviced the company's engines owned by farmers in southern Michigan. Also a possibility: Westinghouse, Church, Kerr & Company, another Detroit engine building firm.)

Twenty engines a day was an ambitious schedule. David Buick had clearly crossed the line, at least in his mind, from engine developer and tinkerer to serious manufacturer.

Chapter 4

Buick and boats

By early 1900, David Buick was moving forward with his plan of entering the automobile business. No longer would he concentrate on stationary engines, though he still manufactured them. He clearly stated the direction of the new Buick Auto-Vim & Power Company with this line in its first listing, in the 1900 Detroit phone book: "Gas & Gasoline Engines & Automobiles."

The company would also try motorizing boats. After all, David was a boating enthusiast — even if he did fancy sailboats. By 1898, he was vice commodore of the Detroit Yacht Club and was winning sailboat races with some regularity. That year he was a winner in his class in a big event, the Inter-Lakes Yachting Association (ILYA) Regatta, to this day held annually at Put-in-Bay, on South Bass Island in Lake Erie. He won with his 27-foot sailboat, the *Carrie B.*, named for Caroline Buick. (A small brass cannon used by David as a regatta starting gun has been donated by Buick great-grandson Doug Boes to Flint's Buick Gallery and Research Center.)

Almost nothing is known about Buick Auto-Vim's early engine manager, W.S. Murray, except he was hired for his expertise in marine engines. But Walter Marr is a different story. In 1899, Marr was 34 and newly employed by the Detroit Shipbuilding Company after selling a bicycle shop. Eight weeks into the job, he was working with friends on a powerboat motor when Buick, walking along the dock, observed him with great interest. Buick's attraction to boats and his new work in gasoline engines were no doubt coming together in his mind. David was ready to build marine engines, and Marr must have looked like someone who could help that idea along. Buick immediately hired Marr as Murray's assistant.

In the spring of 1900, Murray struggled at Buick Auto-Vim to build an engine and install it in a boat. Murray was having problems and Marr did him no favors. Marr recalled: "I knew it [the engine] was wrong but he was my boss and during the daytime I had to take

David Buick's innovative 'sprite'

Although he became a builder of marine engines, David Buick, as vice commodore of the Detroit Yacht Club, was earlier an enthusiast of sailboats. On Sept. 25, 1898, the *Detroit Free Press* featured Buick's newly built 27-foot "little water sprite," the *Carrie B.*, named for his wife. It came from the shop of Joseph Poullot, one of the youngest boat builders on the Great Lakes, and its design was described as "a startling innovation." Poullot relied on Buick's idea of building it with no ribs. It depended for strength and rigidity on double diagonal planking. The outer shell was clear cedar shaped and then overlaid with an inner shell of clear oak affixed with small brass screws. This made for smooth inner and outer surfaces. "She presents an unusual and at the same time very pleasing appearance on the interior," the writer observed. In the article discovered by Kevin Kirbitz, the *Carrie B.* was described as stronger than a ribbed boat, and Buick was said to have "spared no expense. She has, besides her cruising canvas, three sets of sails…[and] probably has the most complete sets of canvas of any yacht on the lakes." After much praise of the vessel, the writer noted, however, that *Carrie B.* "is an outcast and cannot race under Yacht Racing Union rules." Maybe not, but as the previous page pointed out, David Buick was in fact a winner with *Carrie B.* in a big race organized under other rules.

4–CYCLE MARINE

GASOLINE.

Buick Manufacturing Co., Detroit, built this overhead-valve marine engine. The image is from a pamphlet circa 1902.

his order… But at night I would take the engine down and build it up again according to my notions. I always had it back the way he built it by the next morning."

Murray was stumped in designing an "elbow" in the drive train to carry power from the engine to the propeller. The elbow had too great an angle, Marr remembered, and "it nearly knocked the bottom out of the boat when we tried to run it." Buick became impatient with Murray and turned to Marr.

"Marr, can you put that motor in there the way it should go?" Buick asked.

Marr did. "All right, Marr," said Buick. "You're the new boss."

According to Marr, Murray was eventually fired over this. It must have been early in the year, because the Detroit City Directory for 1900 lists David Buick as president of Buick Auto-Vim & Power Company and Walter Marr as manager, engines.

Recalling the boat in a luncheon club speech decades later, Marr related: "I built it the way I wanted to and the ship beat any boat on the river" in its class.

This Buick Motor Co. ad for a marine engine was created after Buick had reorganized and moved to Flint.

This was probably the 20-foot boat Buick sold to one Albert Stegmeyer, who in 1899-1901 turned his bathhouse on the Detroit River into a gasoline launch livery. In November 1901, Stegmeyer wrote to David, praising the Buick engine in that launch. The letter mentioned he had bought the boat and motor from the Buick company two years earlier, seemingly dating it to 1899. More likely, work on this first documented Buick marine engine was begun in 1899 and was completed in spring 1900. Stegmeyer probably counted the 1900 and 1901 boating seasons as two years.

As for the engine itself, Stegmeyer praised it as "the best there is on the Detroit River…I can beat every one except a 30-foot launch which has a 12 H.P. engine against my 3 H.P., but it does not beat me very much…." He compared the Buick engine to others in his livery. "Whenever you go down to the livery you will see several owners of the different boats fixing up their engines, and it seems there is always something the matter with them…I have had absolutely no trouble at all with my engine…."

David was so pleased with Stegmeyer's endorsement he had the letter printed in his first three engine catalogs.

Walter Lorenzo Marr, as a young bicycle maker (above) and a few years later as Buick chief engineer.

Walter Marr and his bicycle shop at Grand River and Second in Detroit, where Marr built his first automobile. Henry Ford was said to have had a shop nearby.

Chapter 5

First Buick automobile

While Buick Auto-Vim & Power Company worked to perfect marine engines for its product line, Walter Marr also focused on the automobile — this was why he had come to Detroit in the first place. Marr, the company's new engine manager, was no doubt encouraged by David Buick — both were enchanted with the horseless carriage.

They were similar in other ways. Like David, Marr was small in stature, about 120 pounds, and at 5-foot-6 a half-inch taller than Buick. Like David, Marr lost his father when he was very young. George Ernest Marr died when Walter was 6, leaving the family with no money. Like David, Marr loved to work with mechanical devices, always looking for ways to make them better and simpler. And also like David, Marr could be quick to anger, and in general was a difficult person to work with.

Still, for Buick, Marr seemed a good catch. Since David had made automobiles a stated element of Buick Auto-Vim's purpose, Marr set out to build one. It would not be his first.

Marr was born August 14, 1865, in Lexington, a small town on the shore of Lake Huron in Michigan's Thumb. Late in the decade the family moved to East Tawas, across Saginaw Bay and up the Lake Huron shore. After his father died, a local man, Sam Anker, took an interest in him and persuaded John Walker, owner of an engineering firm, to hire him in 1882 as an apprentice. Marr was 17 and this was the beginning of his career as a machinist.

Moving in 1888 to Saginaw, a much larger city south of East Tawas, Marr went to work for Wicks Brothers, a company of sawmill and steamboat engineers. There he built his first gas engine, a motor designed by his superintendent. Marr experimented with a variety of carburetors and other devices on that engine. Later that year, when he opened a shop to make and repair bicycles in Saginaw, he learned to use other engines — a Hercules, a Philadelphia Otto and a Sintz — in the manufacturing process.

The bicycle business was booming in this period, so Marr was cashing in on the latest craze. But always, he had his eye on the automobile. "I liked the idea of a horseless carriage from the minute I heard about it up in Saginaw," he told a *Detroit News* reporter in 1939. "So I moved my business into Detroit, opening a bicycle shop at Grand River and Second and began experimenting with gasoline engines." He made the move in 1896.

If he wanted to build automobiles, Marr could hardly have chosen a better time or place to set up his bicycle shop than in 1896 at Grand River and Second avenues in Detroit. This was only several blocks from 58 Bagley Avenue, where Henry Ford built his first automobile, the Quadricycle, that year in a little workshop behind the house. It would be interesting to know exactly when in that year Marr arrived, because in the middle of a rainy night on June 4, 1896, Ford — after famously knocking bricks out of the doorway of his tiny workshop so he could get his machine out the door — motored down Grand River, driving his first automobile for the first time.

As noted, Ford was a friend of Charles B. King, who a few months before had driven the first gasoline-powered automobile in Detroit. There seems to have been a good deal of sharing of information and even hardware among those two and perhaps other early Detroit automobile enthusiasts, such as Barton Peck, who came from a wealthy family, and Charles G. Annesley, about whom more will be said later. Both were reportedly building or trying to build motor vehicles.

How much Marr knew about Ford and his automobile experiments is unclear. He once said that when he first talked to Ford, to his knowledge Ford had not yet built a motor vehicle. That's possible, but most likely he had. Ford shared information only when it suited him. One of his close friends said he did not know until years later that Ford was building motor cars.

But Marr did talk often about his conversations with Ford. And it's hard to believe that if they talked about cars, and Marr's shop in 1896 was so close to Ford's Bagley Avenue shop, that he wasn't aware of Ford's activities. Even if Ford were being secretive, there must have been echoes up and down Grand River about Ford's successful drive of his Quadricycle in the summer of 1896.

Marr continued to use small engines in his bicycle-making business, adding a 6.5-horsepower Olds and a 7-horsepower Cofield to drive the machinery in his Detroit shop. He soon began to meet

Walter Marr (above right) and employee Will Staring with Marr's first automobile, the "motor wagon" with four-cylinder motor, probably in Marr's Detroit bike shop. Marr said he "perfected" this vehicle in 1898. This was before Marr built his first Buick automobile.

horseless carriage enthusiasts such as Annesley and Peck. Bicycle shops were great places to work on horseless carriages — with precision tools, power equipment and finely built components such as wheels, gears, sprockets and chains at hand.

At some point, Marr decided to build what he called a "motor wagon," working in his shop. He didn't say when he started, but boasted he perfected it in 1898. His first motorized vehicle looks in a photo as if it were created from bicycle wheels, a frame and a carriage body. It was powered by a four-cylinder, four-cycle engine.

Using four cylinders was unusual at that time, and would seem especially so for a man building, in a bicycle shop, his first horseless carriage. Bill Close, husband of Marr's granddaughter Sarah, offered an intriguing theory.

When King first drove his horseless carriage in Detroit in March of 1896, he used a four-cylinder engine he had created himself. Close suggested that very engine or possibly just the engine block, may have been used by Marr in his first motor wagon. Close labeled his theory as "sheer speculation" but it sounds possible.

George May, quoting Oliver Barthel, who was King's assistant at the time King made his first Detroit drive, said "a freeze-up" cracked King's engine block later in March of 1896 and he sold the engine together with blueprints and patterns to Charles Annesley. And Annesley became so well acquainted with Marr that he was, within a year or so, building an automobile in Marr's bicycle shop. Close speculated Annesley could have sold or loaned the engine or engine block to Marr, who used it as the basis on which to build his own engine, which he installed in his first motor wagon. We'll come back to this theory. Marr once said he built the car for $1.50, which sounds like a vehicle built from old bicycle wheels and borrowed engine components. Eventually he sold it for $300.

Whatever the source of Marr's engine, he had a lot of trouble with it at first. "When you took it out it would start on four cylinders and you would get home on one; then you'd take the head off and pick out the pieces," he said.

Most of the weight — the engine and water tank — was in the rear. And so, he remembered, the car would sometimes rear up like a "bucking bronco" when he started it. He would be driving in "starts and jerks" while bystanders stood along the road "laughing their heads off." One shouted derisively, "Why don't you get a horse? Who would want a thing like that?"

According to Marr, one bystander didn't laugh. Henry Ford just watched Marr's car and then talked to him about it.

Marr blamed the engine's hot-tube ignition for the trouble. Removing that primitive system, he said he smoothed the performance by fitting the engine with an electrical ignition and a spark advance, or what an interviewer called "novel electric ignition features, arranged to advance the time of the hammer spark production." By

Walter Marr, joined by wife Abbie, drives the first Buick automobile, built in the 1899-1901 time frame, on a Detroit street. Marr built the car, which had a one-cylinder engine, and later bought it from David Buick.

changing the point in the piston's travel within the cylinder where the spark was introduced, he made the engine run more smoothly. In an interview with Charles Hulse in 1934, Marr claimed this was the first use of a spark advance in the country.

Another interviewer reported: "Ford, who had a shop across the corner from Mr. Marr's, saw his car come up the street and make a smooth stop, which was unusual. The next morning Ford was waiting to see Mr. Marr and ask him what he had done to his car."

Compared with Henry Ford, Marr was obviously playing catch-up in his knowledge of automobiles. By 1898, when Marr said he perfected his four-cylinder car, Ford's Quadricycle was already near-ly two years behind him and Ford was at work on his second automo-bile. Ford and his wife Clara had moved from Bagley Avenue in June of 1897. But Ford may well have been in position to talk to Marr. As

Sidney Olson wrote in his excellent book, *Young Henry Ford,* Ford's life from 1898 to mid 1902 "is the despair of biographers" because it is hard to track his activities. "In this period Henry is a real slippery creature…he slides along for a month or two and then pops up in a dozen places at once." And as David L. Lewis, author of *The Public Image of Henry Ford,* observed to the writer, Ford and Marr had some things in common. Each had a mechanical bent, each moved to Detroit to seek his fortune and each was fond of bicycles.

Marr once commented that when he built his first automobile, it was one of only three in Detroit. If true, King must have been between cars, because Marr listed the other two automobile owners as Henry Ford and Barton Peck. Peck no doubt got special attention from Ford because Peck's father was president of Edison Illuminating, where Ford was chief engineer.

There's little to suggest David Buick was interacting with Ford and his group of Detroit automobile and gas engine enthusiasts, though the record is too thin to be sure. It's possible Buick and Ford knew each other from their 1879-1880 work at the Flower brothers' firm. Certainly Marr was talking to Ford, Annesley and Peck and probably to King and others. Marr may have been Buick's best link to Detroit's earliest "car guys." But David Buick was a far more prominent figure than Marr in the late 19th century in Detroit and he was manufacturing engines and engine parts in that period, as well as edging toward plans to build horseless carriages. Notably, David and another auto pioneer, Henry Leland, then head of the Leland & Faulconer engine building firm, were both on the reception committee for the American Foundrymen's Association convention in Detroit in 1897. And a Detroit Yacht Club syndicate, raising funds for a yacht to defend a sailing trophy in 1900, included both David Buick and Henry B. Joy, who in 1902 organized the Packard Motor Car Company. The yacht, incidentally, was named *Cadillac.*

Marr said his bicycle business was successful until a partner ruined it. The unnamed partner gets the blame, but the bicycle craze was ending abruptly about this time and a lot of bike shops were going away. While never discussing the details of his firm's business disaster, Marr made it clear he was devastated. "I was all right with people until a partner ruined my bicycle factory," he said in the 1930s. "Then I didn't trust anybody. Ruined in the bicycle business, with no money and no credit after the failure, I remembered what my first friend [perhaps a reference to Sam Anker back in East Tawas] had said about learning a trade and sticking to it. I wanted to build a machine."

Marr built a motor-driven tricycle in 1899, figuring if he could demonstrate he was a good machinist, he could always get a job. This two-passenger vehicle, he said, "ran to the complete satisfaction of its purchaser." The 118-pound tricycle, according to Marr, was also important because of the configuration of its engine, which will be explained later.

Marr's talents as an inventor and machinist gave him the ability to see a process, borrow it and improve it, as demonstrated several times in his career. In the bicycle business, he heard a nearby factory had an improved process of turning out sprockets. He said he made 14 trips to that factory, trying to slip into the part of the shop where the sprockets were manufactured. Finally he saw the process and was able to copy it — and then improve it. Another quality was his determination to improve his work. He once commented that while other men were at lunch, "I was whittling at some better tool or machine." Bitter about his various setbacks in business, Marr told his brother: "Every dog has his day. I ain't had mine yet, but I will."

After closing his bicycle shop, working at Detroit Shipbuilding and then arriving at Buick Auto-Vim, Marr built his third motor vehicle as part of his job. It was the first automobile to be called a Buick. Pioneer auto reporter Hugh Dolnar, discussing its development in *Cycle and Automobile Trade Journal* in 1903, said Marr built the vehicle in 1900.

Dolnar reported the first Buick car was driven by a single-cylinder, 4-inch bore by 5-inch stroke, horizontal, water-cooled engine with jump spark ignition. This vehicle "had a chain transmission, and in the motor Marr was the first of a group of Detroit experimenters in automobile origination to use the jump spark."[1]

---

1 Jump-spark ignition is the use of high voltage to jump a spark across a gap and ignite the fuel and air charge inside the cylinder. It was a major advance over the old hot-tube ignition, which was simply a tube inside the cylinder that was heated red hot by a candle or alcohol burner or some other external heat source. The red hot tube would start the combustion process within the cylinder. Ransom Olds applied for a patent on his gasoline vehicle on September 18, 1896, that went beyond hot tube to an electric igniter. An electric igniter could be connected to a battery or other power source and would glow red hot, thus igniting the fuel and air charge. When a question arose of whether a car could have a spark advance (the four-cylinder car) without a jump spark, GM engineer Kevin Kirbitz advised one form of early electrical ignition produced a low-tension spark and therefore

Marr later added detail: The car had a three-point suspension, underslung springs and 44-inch buggy wheels. He confirmed a surviving photograph of Marr and his wife Abbie in a buggy-wheeled automobile was of this car and was taken in Detroit — a photo of the first experimental Buick (contradicting published reports the photo was taken in Cleveland, Ohio).

Bill Close said this first Buick's engine probably came off the shelf of Buick Auto-Vim & Power Company. It may well have been designed by Marr, as the firm's engines manager, or even by David Buick. Marr was enthusiastic about his new car. He reminisced: "I remember that when I finished the first automobile that ever bore the name of Buick, I tried it out on the only proving grounds we had — Cass Avenue just north of Grand River. What a day that was!"

There's proof the first Buick automobile existed in 1901 and also reports it was built in 1896, 1898 and 1899 as well as 1900, with the information usually traced to Marr. By the 1930s, Marr had settled on 1898…or maybe '99. And even Dolnar contradicted himself, once reporting Marr and Buick built the first Buick car in 1896 after earlier writing Marr had built it in 1900. Conflicting news articles abound in this period. The opinion here is Marr may have started building his first automobile for Buick by late 1899 but likely did most of the work in 1900. But there are questions. Had David Buick built an earlier car? Did he help build this one? In both cases there is no solid evidence either way.

Most of the debate regarding dates undoubtedly stems from confusion about which vehicle Marr or the writer is referring to — his first motor wagon, with four cylinders, or his first Buick automobile, with one cylinder. In talking to newspaper reporters, he may not have felt it mattered to differentiate between the two for the purpose of whatever point he was making. And probably the reporters — and auto historians — sometimes got things mixed up.

"a spark advance would be theoretically possible even without jump-spark ignition." Indeed, the Buick Manufacturing Company catalog of 1902 or 1903 mentions both types. It says "we use the jump spark and not the mechanical spark, the former being much more simple and not so liable to get out of order and give trouble." So technically Marr's first car could have had the first spark advance and the second car (the first Buick) the first jump spark among the Detroit automobiles, as Dolnar wrote.

On March 25, 1901, David Buick asks Walter Marr to resign.

Anxious for David Buick to see the new Buick car, Marr said he was able to entice his boss to visit his shop only once. Buick and Marr "went for a ride in the Buick car," a reporter wrote in covering a Marr speech in 1934. "The vibrator stuck, stalling the car. Buick was disgusted. A street car was passing and he boarded it."

Marr was furious at the snub. He immediately offered to quit. David Buick, equally mercurial, accepted. Marr kept this letter from David, dated March 25, 1901: "After considering the conversation that we had the other day, and wherein you offered your resignation, I have concluded it is best for both parties to accept the same, and to take effect at once. You will please turn over the keys, and such other articles that you may have to Mr. Sherwood, and oblige."

Buick's note was on old Buick & Sherwood letterhead, the style decorated with a drawing of that firm's most celebrated product — a toilet. Using up that stationery could hardly have left the impression Buick Auto-Vim was an up-and-coming business. (Another clue: No one ever found any Buick Auto-Vim literature or ads beyond the one-liner in the 1900 Detroit phone book and repeated in the city directory). The letter also reveals William Sherwood was still around, at least in control of the shop premises.

One possible reason for David's 1901 split with Marr, other than an angry exchange of words, was money — Buick may have been running out of it. On April 5, 1901, less than two weeks after their split, David offered to sell Marr the Buick automobile (the one Marr built while employed by Buick) as well as engines and carriage bodies.

This is the earliest known written reference to a Buick automobile: "We will sell you the Automobile, known as the Buick Automobile for the sum of $300.00," Buick wrote to Marr. He also offered Marr "all engines" with a few exceptions, and included in the offer all patterns for making them, as well as a delivery body, two new carriage bodies and one runabout body for an additional $1,500. The exceptions were "One known as Stegmeyer's engine, One known as the Noeker Engine, One known as The Double Ended Carriage engine and three of the four cycles."

Students of Buick history make much of this letter. Not only was it the earliest mention of a Buick automobile, it also hinted at the company's other work. With an inventory of carriages and engines, the Buick firm was probably contemplating, if not already working on, another automobile besides the one developed by Marr.

The Stegmeyer and Noeker engines excluded from the offering in Buick's letter were likely being worked on for those customers. Stegmeyer's was probably a marine engine. The Noeker may have been for use at Joseph Noeker's printing company. The "Double Ended Carriage engine"? As Terry Dunham pointed out, that sounds like it could have been a two-cylinder auto engine, though there is no other information about it.

There was no quick response to the letter. Marr, needing a job in a hurry after departing Buick, hired in with the new Oldsmobile plant in Detroit that was being rebuilt after a disastrous fire in March. Marr said he built three of the first curved-dash Oldsmobiles completed as production resumed.

At Olds, he found himself in a situation reminiscent of the one with W.S. Murray and the Buick marine engine. As Marr himself related, the first Oldsmobile he worked on had a problem — it ran

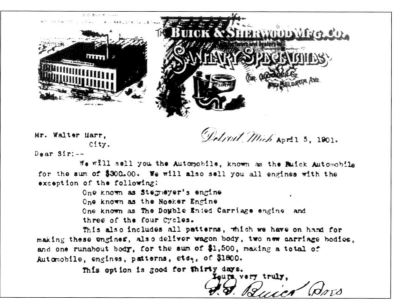

On April 5, 1901, David Buick offers to sell the "Buick Automobile" to Walter Marr, along with engines and carriage bodies — the earliest known written reference to a Buick car.

On August 16, 1901, the first Buick automobile is sold to Walter Marr at a "discount" — $225 instead of David Buick's earlier asking price of $300.

fine when the car was turned to the left but the engine stopped when it was turned right. He and his foreman tore the car down 35 times.

Finally the foreman asked Marr: "What do you think the trouble is?"

Marr responded: "You ought to put a few more staples in the wire." They did, and it worked.

"How long have you known that?" the foreman asked.

"Since the second time we tore it down," Marr replied.

When asked why he hadn't told his boss, Marr replied he hadn't been asked and was hired to do as he was told. When his employer heard of the incident, according to Marr, he fired the foreman and gave Marr the job.

But he wasn't there long. He left on a Saturday night because he had heard there would be a strike the following Monday, and he didn't believe in strikes. (The strike began in late May of 1901). He was out of work six weeks — a rarity for him — and then perfected a bicycle motor for the Detroit Brass, Iron and Novelty Company in a short assignment.

Finally, there was a breakthrough regarding Buick's letter. In August of 1901, Marr traveled to Cleveland, Ohio, following a job opportunity. He said he gave his wife all his money except a dollar and told her he was going to Cleveland to build automobiles "and won't be back until I do." He used the dollar for boat ferry to Cleveland and skipped breakfast because he was then broke. But he was hired shortly after arriving in Cleveland by the American Motor Carriage Company and given $6 in advance pay.

He then returned to Detroit and took up Buick on his April offer. On August 16, 1901, he bought the "Buick Automobile" from Buick — but for $225, not $300. The first Buick car was sold at a discount. He was able to buy it because the purchase money came from the Cleveland firm. Marr took the car to Cleveland as part of his contract to build automobiles for American Motor Carriage. The first Buick car would become the pilot for this company's new automobile.

Meanwhile David Buick was on the move. It's not clear how long he stayed at the Beaubien address (or how long the Buick Auto-Vim name was used), but by mid-January of 1902, according to a *Detroit Free Press* classified ad, the name had been changed to Buick Manufacturing Company, and was now headquartered at 373 Meldrum Avenue — David's home.

That's one indication Buick was using the barn behind his home for his experimental work with engines and automobiles. Outside of the first Buick usually attributed to Marr, David may have built one car or, as the *Detroit Times* noted, "put his entire fortune into a series of cars" until he "finally developed one that he was convinced was commercially practical." That work could well have taken place in the barn. Indeed, the *Times* ran a photo of the barn, noting it was "where Buick built his first car."

However, by late April of '02, Buick Manufacturing had moved to a building at 416-418 Howard Street (now 10-12 Howard) near Twelfth Street in downtown Detroit and at some point David moved his experimental car work there. Although his firm still made several types of engines, David Buick would begin to concentrate on something new.

Somehow, he had discovered a new engine design, with the valves positioned at the top of the combustion chamber. It seemed to have some definite advantages. This overhead-valve design didn't have a name yet, but the company would come up with its own label. For much of the 20th century, Buick would be famous for its "valve-in-head" engines.

47

Charles G. Annesley

Michael W. R. Davis

Chapter 6

Charles Annesley: Finding a missing link

In March of 1901, months before his connection with the American Motor Carriage Company, Walter Marr wrote to an old friend. Marr was then in need of a job after his departure from Buick Auto-Vim & Power Company.

Charles George Annesley, then an executive at the Buffalo (New York) Gasolene Motor Company, replied on March 28, 1901. He told Marr he was "awfully surprised to hear that you had left the Buick concern, as I thought that you were getting along nicely." Annesley said his firm had no openings, but might later. He advised Marr: "My boy, shake the dust of a slow old Detroit off your feet, and go east with some good responsible house where your abilities will be appreciated."

And Annesley added what became a classic paragraph: "What is poor old Ford doing? I feel so sorry for him. He is a good man and perfectly capable, and yet cannot get out of the hole just because he won't leave Detroit."

The letter is also remarkable because it is between the first buyer of a Ford (Annesley, purchaser of Henry Ford's Quadricycle), and the soon-to-be first buyer of a Buick (Marr).

Beyond that, it's fair to ask who is Charles Annesley and why is he important?

Answering the second question first, Annesley is important — or, more accurately, interesting in auto history — because he was one of the very few persons known to have worked in the industry's earliest years, in the late 19th century, with men who helped form the beginning of the two giant U.S. automakers — Ford and General Motors. Annesley was an associate of both Walter Marr (whose abilities helped make Buick a success and therefore led to the creation of GM) and Henry Ford. He was also a friend of Charles B. King, the man who was first to drive a gasoline car in Detroit.

Not only did Annesley buy Henry Ford's first car, he also bought the freeze-cracked engine from Charles B. King's first car — the one that made that historical drive in downtown Detroit. And if Marr's relative, Bill Close, is correct, Annesley may have provided the engine or engine block to Marr for his first motor car — pre-Buick.

An article in the September 4, 1899, *Detroit Tribune* provides solid evidence of the Annesley-Marr relationship and also suggests Marr's bicycle store was becoming a shop of choice for building horseless carriages.

> C. G. Annesley…is building a machine at the establishment of Walter L. Marr on Second avenue, near Grand River. Mr. Annesley has an engine of his own design, a four-cylindered reciprocating motioned affair that is not more than one-sixth the size of a horse and pulls like a 12-ox team. Mr. Annesley has built, when this one is done, six automobiles, and no two alike. Each one was built to order practically. This last one is being prepared for service on heavy sandy roads north of Chicago to Cook county. It will be ready in about two weeks and will be given a speed trial here before it is shipped away.

The article also talks about Walter Marr's motor tricycle:

> Mr. Marr is himself…building a tricycle to be run by a gasoline motor of his own design. His motor is a great source of pride to him and excites general admiration on account of its very small size. He designed it himself, and it sits most inconspicuously in its bracket under the seat on the tricycle. This machine will soon be put out on the road also.

Despite what should have been Annesley's highly visible position in automotive history, he was virtually unknown for many years. George May described Annesley as a "shadowy figure who is best remembered as the man who bought Henry Ford's first car."

The biggest reason Annesley was a "shadowy figure" — or worse, completely unknown — is because his name was misspelled as "Ainsley" in Henry Ford's first book, *My Life and Work,* published in 1922. Ford wrote he sold his first automobile, the Quadricycle, "to Charles Ainsley of Detroit for two hundred dollars." Surprisingly, virtually every auto historian since then picked up the misspelled name and never corrected it.

Finally, two historians figured it out. Sidney Olson in *Young Henry Ford* (1963) spelled the last name correctly. George May in *A Most Unique Machine* (1975) was first to note Annesley had been misspelled as Ainsley all those years.

As Michael W. R. Davis, a journalist, automotive historian and retired Ford public relations executive, once commented: "Because Ford's memory was faulty, he couldn't spell or [his 1922 collaborator Samuel] Crowther was an indifferent researcher, the name of the first purchaser of a Ford-built car went down mis-identified and largely lost from history."

Davis, who took a history course from George May at Eastern Michigan University, decided to further clean up the record by making Annesley the subject of his master's thesis in 1982. It was never published, and Davis had to hunt for a copy among his papers when he learned this writer was working on an account of David Buick's career, which in an oblique way includes Annesley.

The basic connection is that Buick's first chief engineer, Walter Marr, worked closely with Annesley on engines for a period and may have benefited from Annesley's relationship with Henry Ford and Charles B. King. Whatever Marr learned from Annesley, Ford and King, he likely carried over with him to the Buick organization. David Buick and his associates, therefore, were not working totally independent of the other Detroit auto pioneers — which might have been assumed but was never as fully documented.

Unmasking the mystery man, Davis learned Annesley had been born in Bundelkund, India, March 13, 1863, to an Irish mother and English father. He died of a heart attack in Providence Hospital, Detroit, June 10, 1925. His occupation was listed as electrical salesman. His wife, Charlotte Minchener of Detroit, had died two years earlier.

Davis wrote that "Sadly, at the time *My Life and Work* was published, Ford's first customer, Charles G. Annesley, was living (and was soon to die) in obscurity only a few blocks from Henry's office at the Highland Park Plant, home of the Model T."

Looking back at Annesley's career, George May quoted sources as stating Annesley and Barton Peck "each had their cars running before Henry Ford had his out" but they were poorly built and "did not last long." Annesley also took the King engine, which he had acquired from King together with the patterns and blueprints, and, according to May, "formed the Buffalo Gas Engine Company. The

PHILIP DOHN, Vice-Pres.   A. SNYDER, Sec'y and Treas.

Buffalo Gasolene Motor Co.,

Cor. Dewitt and Bradley Streets.

MANUFACTURERS OF

...Motors...

For Vehicle and Marine Purposes.

Telephone Amherst 103.
Cable Address "Fischer."

BUFFALO, N. Y.____Mar.28th.____190/

My dear Walter:-

    I was awfully surprised to hear that you had left the Buick concern,as I thought that you were getting along so nicely.

    We are turning out eight complete engines a week and have put in $5000.00 worth of the latest machinery,we have shipped 24 engines to England,and almost all of our U.S. business is for salt water.

    We are going to put up a line of launches,and have two of our own this summer.

    We have all the help we require at present,but perhaps we will put a good hustling salesman on the road a little later on.

    My boy shake the dust of slow old Detroit off your feet,and go east with some good responsible house where your abilities will be appreciated.

    What the Devil do you think would have become of me if I had stayed there. Here I have the very nicest of a Company,good salary, and Stock in the concern.

    What is poor old Ford doing? I feel so very sorry for him he is a good man and perfectly capable,and yet cannot get out of the hole just because he won't leave Detroit.

    Peck tells me that he got turned down by that puke Whitcombe another sample of what they do in Detroit. Write me soon

                 Sincerely

                    Chas.G.Annesley

Famous letter from Charles G. Annesley (first buyer of a Ford car) to Walter Marr (first buyer of a Buick car) asking, 'What is poor old Ford doing?'

design was used by this company and made in different sizes for marine use."

Bill Close speculated Marr improved the engine Annesley received from King by adding the spark advance for his first motor wagon, then returned it to Annesley. In one interview, Marr said he sold the patent for a spark advance to the Buffalo firm. Close believed Marr actually sold the engine with the spark advance to Annesley, who then patented it on behalf of the Buffalo Gasolene Motor Company. Close had some of the evidence — he owned an early engine from the Buffalo company, and the patent number traces to Annesley.

Davis finally tracked down a nephew of Annesley who remembered him in his mid 50s as "rather bald, but a cheerful, very well-knit little man, about 5-foot-6 and very muscular. My recollection is that he was a broad jumper and a runner — he established a broad jump record that stood for many years at the Detroit Athletic Club."

The nephew remembered Annesley made a living selling electrical components to contractors, and that he was "of such talent mechanically that nothing was ever broken beyond repair around the house." About 1923, Henry Ford contacted Annesley and offered him a job. But he sent him off to see his aide Harry Bennett, who wanted him to start as an hourly employee in the engine plant. "And as far as Charlie was concerned, the hell with that noise," the nephew remembered.

Davis could find no record of what had happened to Annesley at the Buffalo Gasolene Motor Company, or what happened to the numerous automobiles Annesley was said to have built. Davis was able, however, to document Annesley's eventual return to Detroit, the city he had disparaged in his 1901 letter to Marr. But after his move to Buffalo, Charles Annesley — with the exception of one fascinating letter — vanishes from the story of Walter Marr and David Buick. His role had been a small one, an automobile enthusiast who had worked with both Henry Ford and Marr, Buick's first chief engineer, but it deserved to be remembered.

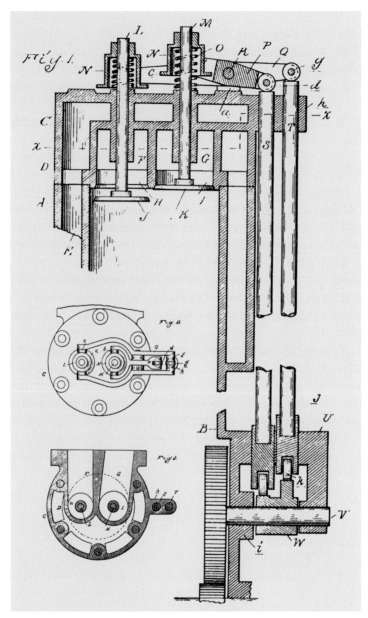

Buick engineer Eugene Richard included these drawings in his valve-in-head engine patent application in 1902. The early success of David Buick's automobile is largely attributed to the "marvelous motor" created by the Buick team, and so described by General Motors founder William C. Durant.

Chapter 7

'Valve-in-head' engines

Overhead valve. "Valve-in-head." Whatever you call it, this advance in gasoline engine design quickly became the big story in Buick's operations. It was a "rare mechanical idea" in the words of an early Buick catalog. Buick can't accurately claim it conceived the idea. But it can reasonably argue it was the first manufacturer to get it right — the first to successfully integrate all of the key elements of the modern overhead-valve engine. Buick was also likely the first to fully understand the significance of the engine, and certainly Buick was the first to aggressively promote the inherent power advantages of that design.

With the valves positioned at the top of the combustion chamber, instead of in the block like most other engines of the time, the Buick design was more efficient than engines with other valve configurations. It was powerful and reliable, and eventually the entire industry would make use of the principle.

To Terry Dunham, writing in *Antique Automobile* in 1995, "the overhead-valve engine was the single most important mechanical factor in the early success of the Buick car. In fact, the ohv engine was one of the most important automobile advances ever."

The Buick people didn't fully understand its importance at first. When Buick began building overhead-valve stationary engines, the company emphasized "ease of manufacture and ease of service" as primary advantages.

The real benefit — the ability of the overhead-valve engine to breathe better and thus produce more horsepower per cubic inch of displacement than other engines — was discovered later. Walter Marr explained it this way to a reporter: Compression in a valve-in-head motor bears directly on the pistons, without any loss in jumping from valve chamber to valve chamber. "It's from 20 to 25 percent more powerful and efficient in performance [compared with other engines]," he told Sam Adkins of the *Chattanooga Free Press* in 1936.

As early as 1917, Buick Motor Company explained it another way. The company advertised that its engine's "small, simple, compact combustion chamber with the smallest possible water-jacketed space" gave it a "more perfect combustion than other types of motors, a quicker ignition of the charge and a smaller loss of heat through the water jackets. The sum of these advantages is more power and less gasoline consumption."

The engine was a key to the early success of Buick automobiles. As William C. Durant, who would save Buick and found General Motors, wrote in the 1930s: "With Buick we sold the assurance that the power to perform was there. Power sold Buick and made it what it is today." Durant (whose major role in the Buick story will be introduced later) knew nothing of engineering. But he knew how to find a key selling point and then promote it. Almost as important as the Buick engine's power was Durant's ability to sell to the public "the assurance that the power to perform was there."

In Buick Motor Company's early days, David Buick was publicized as the company's engine expert. The 1905 Buick automobile catalog refers vaguely to "a rare mechanical idea which found its first inception in the marine engine designed by Mr. D.D. Buick, an engine since adapted to and perfected in an automobile." The catalog says the engine's development of "phenomenal power in relation to size and weight of vehicle has never been approached by any competitor in the field."

But the catalog (probably written under Durant's direct supervision if not by the man himself) says David disclaimed credit for the automobile as a whole. That's because the car "embodies many distinctive features, some of which have been contributed by other men of inventive genius…notably, Mr. Walter L. Marr, who was distinctly a pioneer in this field, having personally built two of the first gasoline engines ever designed in this country. The Buick automobile is, therefore, a composite creature, embodying the results of long years of earnest thought and exhaustive tests…."

David Buick is giving Marr generous credit, but not for the engine and its "rare mechanical idea," which is generally interpreted to mean the overhead-valve design.

Even Durant, who was greatly admired by Marr, described David Buick as "a gas engine expert … very largely responsible for the creation of the marvelous motor which bears his name." Durant's daughter Margery said her father kept the Buick name on the automobile

Durant promoted because he wanted to honor "the man who invented the engine." Once, she said, she and her father and David Buick sat in a shed while David described the workings of the engine.

Occasionally early employees sent their written memories to the company. Frank J. DeLaney documented his 1903-06 employment at Buick with a letter purportedly from David Buick. In a two-page remembrance, DeLaney said, "Mr. Dave Buick conceived the idea of building a stationary single cylinder valve-in-head motor…completed in the early spring of 1903." He credited Marr with later building the two-cylinder valve-in-head engine, which DeLaney said he assembled and tested under Marr's direction. But DeLaney was no doubt unaware of the company's documented work with overhead-valve engines dating to 1901 and also that other sources do not credit Marr for Buick's first two-cylinder overhead-valve engine.

The basic overhead-valve design was developed in Europe. When it came to the United States, Buick was not quite the first to use it in an automobile. It may have shown up first in an automobile in Syracuse, N.Y., where engineer John Wilkinson built an air-cooled, four-cylinder, overhead-valve engine for his experimental car in 1898. His attempt to produce his own car quickly failed. But he soon linked up with Herbert H. Franklin, who headed the H.H. Franklin Manufacturing Company — a Syracuse firm that is said to have invented the term "die casting." In 1902 Franklin and Wilkinson produced the first 219 Franklins. They had engines similar to Wilkinson's original — air cooled, four cylinders, overhead valves (see related article by Kevin Kirbitz at the end of this chapter). The Franklin automobile did well for many years but production ended in 1934 during the Great Depression. Franklin engines were produced for many more years, however, powering helicopters, airplanes and the Tucker Torpedo.

Also, Howard Marmon built an experimental car with an air-cooled engine using overhead valves in Indianapolis, Ind., in 1901 or 1902 and began production with 25 cars in 1905. Marmon abandoned air cooling in 1909. In 1911 Ray Harroun won the first Indianapolis 500 in his Marmon Wasp — but since Marmon left overhead valves from 1909 to 1915, the winning Wasp had a T-head motor. Marmon production ended in 1933, another victim of the Depression — which Buick barely survived.

How the overhead-valve design came to Buick is debated. But the paper trail favors Eugene C. Richard, an engineer who arrived in the United States from France in 1888. Richard was born April

Eugene C. Richard, who may have brought overhead-valve engine design to Buick, with his wife Louisa.

8, 1867, in Savoy, and apprenticed with an uncle in a machine shop before moving to the United States. He then worked in Rochester, N.Y., and in Philadelphia.

In 1898, he moved his family to Detroit but jobs there were hard to find. According to Charles Hulse, who relates details apparently gathered from Richard's close relatives and not found elsewhere, Richard finally caught on as a machinist in Lansing, Mich., at the Kneeland Crystal Creamery, where he worked for two years. While there he designed and invented a cream separator and also helped a local dentist develop a mechanical device for drilling teeth. In the fall of 1900 he returned to Detroit to be with his family and got a job as a machinist at the newly built factory of Olds Motor Works, in the gasoline stationary and marine engine department.

A coincidence changed his career. As previously mentioned, a fire destroyed the Olds plant on March 9, 1901, temporarily stopping production of the Oldsmobile, the first mass-produced U.S. car. As a result, Richard was out of a job. Later that month, Walter Marr, after his rift with David Buick, left Buick Auto-Vim & Power Company. David eventually placed a want ad in the *Detroit News* for a skilled machinist and draftsman, and in May Richard responded and was hired. Choosing Richard to develop his engines was another case of great recruiting by David Buick. Richard (who pronounced it RICH-ard, not ri-SHARD, despite his French heritage) was not only less argumentative than Marr, he was also a knowledgeable and inventive engineer.

Richard provided a rare peek into Buick Auto-Vim. He said he was designer, draftsman, factory superintendent and foreman of a force of about six persons including the watchman and elevator boy, a newspaper reported. Shortly after his arrival, Richard increased the horsepower of Buick marine engines from two to five — considered a big achievement, although it involved only a slight changing of the timing and an increase in the size of the valves.

If money was a reason Marr was let go, why did Buick then hire Richard? Outside of the fact David and Marr didn't get along, a possible reason is David decided to concentrate on engines rather than automobiles – and Richard best reflected the talents he wanted.

According to Hulse, David was at this time experimenting with various types of gasoline engines, trying to perfect one he could make and sell. Richard, after working with Buick's experiments for a few months, decided they were a waste of time. He told Buick he would design a gasoline engine with a new idea that would work. On February 18, 1902, Richard filed for a patent on an overhead-valve gasoline engine, and also for patents on an electric sparker and a carburetor, all assigned to Buick Manufacturing Company.

Dunham, who studied Richard's tortuous path through the patent system, pointed out the application process began by November 29, 1901. The application was rejected by the patent examiner three times (the biggest problem was it originally included a claim for a water-jacketed valve guide that was found in conflict with earlier patents). Patent rights were assigned to Buick Motor Company on April

4, 1904, by Richard, who had temporarily left the firm. The amended patent was granted to the Buick firm on September 27, 1904.

Richard's patent, number 771,095, covers, among other features, "the combination with the cylinder head, of induction and deduction valves having their stems projecting outward through said head." The construction described is "especially designed with a view to simplicity and ease in manufacture and also the facility with which the parts may be assembled or detached when necessary."

Richard's son, Eugene D. Richard, interviewed in his 80s by the writer, said he once asked his father if he had invented the engine. The father replied he could not understand why "everyone was so interested in that" — the design actually came from steam engines in Europe. He said he "just applied it to the Buick engine."

That checks out with Charles Hulse's recollection of talks with Richard's relatives. Hulse said Richard remembered some steam engines in his native France had used an overhead-valve feature and he merely applied the principle to a gasoline engine he was working on at Buick. It appears no one before Richard had ever applied for a patent on an overhead-valve engine. (But there's also no evidence the company ever tried to enforce any claim to overhead-valve technology.)

Another checkmark for Richard is a statement by early Buick financier Benjamin Briscoe Jr. Briscoe, himself an auto pioneer who knew Richard well, described Richard as a "mechanical genius" and said that in his opinion the industry owed credit to Richard for "the original proper application of the overhead-valve principle."

But when Walter Marr was once asked to comment on Arthur Pound's statement in *The Turning Wheel* that Richard was largely responsible for Buick's overhead-valve engine, Marr responded: "What he [Pound] didn't say is that I made the valve-in-head device first because it was the easiest way to make a motorcycle engine."

Motorcycle may be a reference to Marr's motor tricycle. In interviews decades later, he said he made his 1899 motor tricycle with the valves in the head "because it had to be built that way." Marr's claim is supported by his personal credibility and track record and by the 1899 news item, quoted previously, that mentions the engine's "very small size."

Terry Dunham believed Marr designed the one-cylinder engine around the tricycle itself. Positioning valves inside the block would have made it too big. "So he mounted the valve train outside the engine. And in the process he made a smaller engine possible, and he

also made the first overhead-valve engine built here in the U.S.A.,"
Dunham once wrote.

But the reference to Marr being first was made before Buick researchers were aware the air-cooled 1902 Franklin used overhead
valves based on an engine created by John Wilkinson in 1898. Even
if Marr's tricycle did have overhead valves, whether he took that design with him to Buick is not clear. Later, in 1900-01, when Marr
built his one-cylinder automobile for Buick, it almost certainly did
not have an overhead-valve engine. Marr would have said so if it had.

Marr's next car after the first Buick was a model built for the
American Motor Carriage Company (1901-02) in Cleveland. It was
called the "American Gas" and Bill Close believed it was copied from
the first Buick and used a similar engine. While the first Buick does
not exist, an American Gas is in a museum. Its engine has a poppet-
valve intake and its exhaust valve is mounted overhead (above the
piston). It's not a fully overhead-valve design, so Close believed the
first Buick wasn't either.

Marr's relationship with American Motor Carriage lasted only
about six months. Marr had been hired August 7, 1901, as chief designer and superintendent with the purpose of building an automobile. The first American Gas was on the road by December 1901.
Although the first cars performed well, they failed to attract financ-
ing. Production was to be 200 per year but never reached that goal
and the American Gas was out of production by 1904. The number
built is unknown.

During his tenure at Cleveland, Marr once again displayed both
his confidence in his own mechanical ability and his sometimes difficult nature. He was installing a coil in his first American Gas when
his boss told him he had a coil in his office he was going to use in the
car. Marr's response: "Why didn't you build the car then yourself?"

For whatever reason, Marr soon sensed he would be let go once
the car got into production. So he demanded $100 and his car back,
and returned to Detroit in February, 1902.

Meanwhile, as Eugene Richard plugged along in his quest to patent the Buick overhead-valve design, a task that spanned about 2 1/2
years, his boss, David Buick, was reorganizing. After David created
Buick Manufacturing Company in late 1901 or 1902, and moved operations to Howard Street, Walter Marr returned briefly. He told one
interviewer he worked for Buick three times, and each time the com-

pany had a different name (choose from four: Buick & Sherwood, Buick Auto-Vim, Buick Manufacturing, Buick Motor Company).

From Charles Hulse's notes hand written immediately after his 1934 interview of Marr: "[Marr] Went to work for Buick again who was building stationary motors. At the time he started work they were [having] much carburetor trouble, and one day Marr was in the basement and had a carburetor running on the gas and Buick came up to him asking what he was doing and Marr explained that the carburetors were leaky and he was trying to find the trouble. Buick intimated that Marr was wasting his [Buick's] money so after a few words Marr again left Buick's employ."

It may be significant Marr worked briefly for Buick Manufacturing Company upon his return to Detroit in early 1902. That was probably the only time Marr, Richard and David Buick worked together in the formative years — a moment when Marr could have learned about Richard's overhead-valve design. Perhaps he could have even helped improve it.

But there is no record that happened. What is certain is that less than a year after Buick, Richard and Marr worked together, both Marr and Buick Motor Company separately developed overhead-valve engines.

Marr designed an innovative overhead-valve/overhead-cam one-cylinder engine for his Marr Autocar that was running by Christmas 1902. Buick Manufacturing Company displayed overhead-valve stationary engines in its catalog probably printed sometime during 1902. It was not until the spring of 1904, however, that Buick Motor Company began to sell its opposed two-cylinder overhead-valve Model B auto engine — perfected just before Marr returned to Buick for the third and last time.

Incidentally, after his split with the American Motor Carriage Company in February 1902, Marr had successfully demanded the return of his car — the first Buick automobile. He brought it back from Cleveland to Detroit and continued to tinker with it.

The car was apparently one hot horseless carriage in Detroit in the early days of the 20th century. Marr said a policeman stopped him three times in one block for driving 20 miles an hour. And once, after he was ticketed for speeding, the arresting officer told the judge Marr was "doing 16 miles an hour with plenty to spare." How he measured the speed is unknown, but the fine was $25. Marr told the judge "the jig is up" — a fine that size would put him out of business. "Your car

William B. Close

This 1901-02 American Motor Carriage Company vehicle, called the "American Gas," is believed to have been copied almost exactly from the first Buick automobile.

made 16 miles an hour?" the judge exclaimed. "Well, any man who builds something that'll run that fast deserves better treatment." He reduced the fine to $2.[1]

After leaving Buick again, Marr hooked up with J. P. Schneider, a Detroit auto dealer, and began development of the Marr Autocar. Bill Close believed the Marr car (late 1902), like the American Gas, was similar in appearance and many other ways to the first Buick. But it has one major difference, the previously mentioned overhead-valve/overhead-cam engine.

This was an exceptionally fine roadster and a contract was made with Fauber Manufacturing Company of Elgin, Ill., to begin production.

However, Marr walked away in October 1903, disgusted that Fauber could not keep production on schedule, among other concerns. (Hulse said Marr told him the organizers wanted to get control of the patents but Marr had been "smart enough to have patented his plans so the deal was off.") After perhaps 25 Marr cars were deliv-

---

1 In various interviews, Marr seems to refer to different vehicles, usually his first motor wagon or the first Buick, in telling this story. Charles Hulse's interview notes are a clear reference to the first Buick.

63

William B. Close

Marr Autocar of 1902-03 had overhead-valve/overhead-cam one-cylinder engine.

ered, the company was finished off with a fire in the Elgin factory in August of 1904 that destroyed 14 more. By then, Marr was long gone. In fact, he was back building Buicks, although that's getting ahead of the story.

While the Marr Autocar was apparently not the first American automobile with an overhead-valve engine — the Franklin, for one, may have gone into production some months earlier in 1902 — the Marr car likely arrived before the first overhead-valve Buick car. Buick Motor Company first placed its two-cylinder overhead-valve engine in a Buick automobile when it began producing Model B cars in the summer of 1904 (though some of its new engines may have been fitted a little earlier into other makes). Richard probably should be credited for the one-cylinder engine in a prototype auto — the so-called "Briscoe Buick" — built by David Buick in 1902-03. It was most likely an L-head but even if it did have an overhead-valve engine, it was completed after the first Marr car.

Tracking the early development of Buick's valve-in-head engine is fascinating to some because it was so critical to Buick Motor Company's early success, and therefore to the creation of General Motors. But perhaps those who ignore the details and simply spread credit for bringing the overhead-valve design to Buick among David Buick, Eugene Richard and Walter Marr have the most accurate answer.

Certainly David Buick was in charge when the design was introduced at Buick. Marr, Richard and Buick all had strong credentials in inventiveness. They could have worked together, building off each other's ideas — and what they may have learned about the overhead valve design in Europe — to create an extraordinary engine design and then developed it separately. But if they did work on it together, they didn't talk about it.

Bill Close insisted Marr "built a valve-in-head engine before [David] Buick, Richard and the other automobile manufacturers" and contended Marr's "success at building his own car with an overhead-cam, overhead-valve engine in 1902 is proof enough." His position was that Marr's many patents and long and successful career as Buick chief engineer provided convincing evidence of his genius.

GM engineer Kevin Kirbitz offers a different view based on his engineering training as well as his considerable historical research. Kirbitz said that while overhead-valve placement was "a key enabler" in increasing engine horsepower and efficiency, full credit for the Buick engine design cannot be given to any one individual.

"In looking at the early development of gasoline engines, it's almost impossible to credit just one person with the development of any particular feature," he said. "Even when the paper trail of patents exists, there was so much simple trial-and-error experimentation that led to true technological breakthrough that it's hard to say who did what and when."

The development of overhead-valve engines was, he said, "a logical and evolutionary step but certainly not ground-breaking." He noted that when William Davis, who patented a water-cooled valve guide in 1896, used a drawing that clearly showed overhead valves, "he apparently didn't think it novel enough to make a claim." And Kirbitz pointed out that John Wilkinson, the Franklin engineer who designed an overhead-valve engine in 1898, "thought it was the only logical placement for the valves." Walter Marr said he built his 1899 tricycle with valves in the head "because it had to be built that way." And Eugene Richard said he simply applied an existing concept to the Buick engine.

Kirbitz said the question that concerned him was that, given the "nonchalant attitude of these overhead-valve pioneers," why did Buick — and only Buick — so heavily promote "valve-in-head" engines? Finally he decided the Buick engine really was superior, but for other factors in addition to overhead valves. Also, the Buick people — particularly David Buick, Walter Marr and Eugene Richard — came to understand the significance of the design. And once that significance was explained to Durant, the super salesman wasted little time promoting the Buick engine.

Said Kirbitz: "The evidence indicates that Buick, as depicted in the Richard engine patent, was the first manufacturer to successfully integrate all of the elements of what is today commonly regarded as the overhead-valve engine, including valve placement, valve-train operation and engine cooling. It is this combination of ideas which set the Buick engine apart from its contemporaries."

That's a good overall summation. The bottom line: Buick's new engine *was* extraordinary — and it would provide for decades of outstanding success.

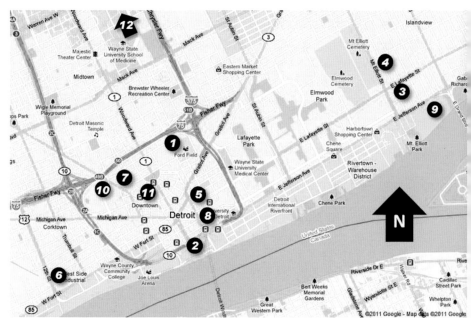

Detroit sites associated with David Buick before moving to Flint include (1) Jane Buick Wilson's home and grocery store where David lived and worked in his youth, (2) James Flower and Brothers, (3) Buick & Sherwood Manufacturing Co., (4) the Buick family's residence from 1887 to 1905, (5) Buick Auto-Vim & Power Co., (6) Buick Manufacturing Co., (7) test site of the first Buick automobile. Other locations familiar to Buick and key to Detroit's fledgling automotive industry are (8) John Lauer's machine shop, where Detroit's first automobile was built by C. B. King; (9) Olds Motor Works, (10) Ford's Bagley Avenue shop, (11) Marr's bicycle shop, and (12) Leland & Faulconer Mfg. Co. (Copyright Google 2011)

Valve-in-Head: Technology in Historical Perspective

Here's a viewpoint on Buick's overhead-valve engine technology from a General Motors engineer who is also a student of Buick history, written especially for this publication.

By KEVIN M. KIRBITZ

Much like today, the dawn of the automotive era was a time of basic technology debates. Would steam, electricity or the internal combustion engine prove superior? Would alcohol, benzene, gasoline or something else be the best fuel? Was air or water the best way to keep an engine from overheating? Where should the valves be located and how should they be operated?

In a four-cycle internal combustion engine, intake valves allow the air and fuel mixture to enter the combustion chamber and, after combustion has occurred, exhaust valves allow the burned gases to escape. When David Buick began experimenting with gasoline engines, several valve configurations were in use. Most valves were set in chambers along the side of the cylinder head and operated in a line parallel to the piston. This arrangement was a predecessor of what became known as the L-head (with valves in chambers along the same side of the cylinder) and T-head (with valves on opposite sides of the cylinder). Engines with valves located directly in the cylinder head above the piston eventually became known as "valve in the head" or overhead valve.

Although the engine and features patented by Eugene Richard for Buick are unquestionably an overhead-valve design, it should be noted overhead valves were not unique to Buick. Such valves were commonly used in steam engines in this period and also in some internal-combustion engines in Europe. There were also a few American overhead-valve engines, like those designed by John Wilkinson and Howard Marmon, which appeared in cars before Buick produced an engine of that design.

The illustration for an 1896 U.S. patent held by William F. Davis clearly shows valves located in the cylinder head. Davis's patentable claim, however, was for a water jacket surrounding the valve stems and valve guides, not for valve placement. In 1902, Davis's company merged with the Waterloo Gasoline Engine Company, which manufactured the now- famous Waterloo Boy tractor, predecessor of John Deere.

In 1898, John Wilkinson, who had attended Cornell University, built a four-cylinder, air-cooled, overhead-valve engine. After an initial deal to manufacture the Wilkinson automobile failed, the talented engineer joined forces with financial backer and industrialist Herbert H. Franklin and in 1902 began manufacture of the Franklin motor car. Unlike Buick, the Franklin firm never said much about overhead valves because, from Wilkinson's point of view, there was no other logical place for valves to be located.

In Indianapolis, Ind., Howard Marmon, a graduate of the University of California-Berkeley, was chief engineer at his family's flour mill machinery business when he built his first experimental automobile in 1902. His engine was an air-cooled V-twin featuring overhead valves. Marmon went on to produce a motor vehicle powered by a V-4 in 1903 and six more with V-4s in 1904. Full-scale production began in 1905 with 25 cars. By 1909, Marmon had abandoned air cooling for water cooling and switched from V-type to inline cylinder arrangements. For a time (1909-1915), Marmon also switched from overhead valves to a T-head design, but returned to overhead valves after that.

Valve placement in these early four-cycle engines had a lot to do with the way the valves were opened and closed. Exhaust valves were typically operated through a mechanical linkage tied to the engine's camshaft through pushrods. This allowed precise timing of exhaust valve operation during the four-cycle process (intake, compression, power, and exhaust).

But intake valves were different. These valves, including those on some early Buick stationary engines, were called "atmospheric" valves. They had no mechanical linkage to other parts of the engine and were opened simply by the suction produced by the downward motion of the piston and closed with a return spring. Because the operation of an atmospheric valve was not precisely timed to the combustion cycle, efficient operation could be sporadic. Atmospheric valves were also sometimes prone to sticking. Further, varying spring tension could also hinder efficient intake-valve operation.

If internal combustion engines were to advance, the problem of the atmospheric valve had to be addressed. Although some manufacturers had experimented with a mechanical linkage for intake-valve actuation, that idea still defied the conventional wisdom of the period. In the 1905 edition of *Self Propelled Vehicles*, author James E. Homans noted "experience has taught that the positive cam-actuating inlet valve is not nearly as efficient as the older [atmospheric] forms." The text continued by saying that in

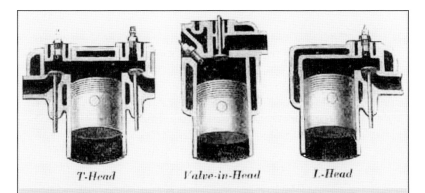

T-Head Valve-in-Head L-Head

"the positive valve type, it is necessary . . . to allow a large compression space in the head, which absolutely reduces compression in itself and causes a loss of power."

Such was the case with early L-head Ford and Packard engines which used positive inlet valves. In these as well as in T-head engines, the additional volume required for the valve chambers reduced the amount of compression the piston could exert on the air/fuel mixture, which lessened the heat output of combustion and resulted in a loss of power. In liquid-cooled engines, larger cooling jacket space typically led to even more heat loss and power loss.

In contrast, the Buick stationary engine, as described in the Richard patent application, employed valves located in the cylinder head above the piston, requiring no additional space for valve chambers. Furthermore, both exhaust and inlet valves were operated through pushrods, driven by a camshaft, so their operation could be consistently and precisely timed. Richard and Buick had very effectively defied the conventional wisdom — the positive cam-actuated inlet valve was actually more efficient than the atmospheric valve, and positive valves did not necessarily require a large compression space in the head.

The design was adapted to Buick's first two-cylinder ohv automobile engine in 1904. Other manufacturers would follow, including Franklin, which abandoned the atmospheric valve in 1905 in favor of the pushrod and rocker arm design.

Richard's patent specifically noted simplicity and ease of manufacture, assembly and disassembly as benefits for locating the valves in the cylinder head. No mention was made of any increase in power due to valve placement. One of the earliest Buick Motor Company catalogs, probably published in 1904, said the company's aim was to "make our engine as simple and as easy to understand as possible, hence our reason for putting all the working parts on the outside."

By 1905, possibly as a result of deductive reasoning and a series of crude dynamometer tests, Buick had discovered that overhead valves allowed the engine to breathe better and the air/fuel mixture to burn faster, resulting in more horsepower per cubic inch of displacement than engines using other valve configurations.

Yet not all early Buick cars used the overhead valve design. In July 1906, Walter L. Marr, Buick's first chief engineer, filed a patent for Buick's first four-cylinder car, the Model D, which used a T-head design. Under Marr's engineering leadership, Buick also introduced the Model 5 in 1908 with a four-cylinder L-head. The 1909 Model 6, 1909-1910 Buick Model 41 limousines, and the diminutive Model 14 of 1910-1911 also had non-overhead-valve engines.

However, based on the solid reputation of the original two-cylinder Buick engine and development of a new ohv four for the 1908 Model 10 — plus an extensive advertising campaign on benefits of "valve-in-head" — it wasn't long until the public began to think of Buick's engines as being among the very best available.

Over time, the overhead-valve engine became the standard for gasoline engines not only at Buick but throughout the world. The Liberty aircraft engine, said to be the United States' greatest technological contribution to World War I, used an overhead-valve design. Though this engine was manufactured by several auto companies and was not a Buick design, the advertising people at Buick were quick to point out it was an ohv. Buick built more than 1,300 Liberty engines during the war and one Buick ad showing a plane, with a pilot shooting, said: "When Engine Failure Means Death, Valve-in-Head Motors Prevail."

Straight-eight "Valve-in-Head," "Dynaflash" and "Fireball" ohv engines powered a generation of Buicks from the depths of the Great Depression to the heights of post-war recovery. Among other notable Buick powerplants were its first V-8 "nailhead" engines of 1953 and the big block 455 of the muscle car era. The 1962 Buick Special was *Motor Trend's* Car of the Year largely because it had the first U.S. mass-produced V-6 engine. That V-6 became the foundation for Buick engines over more than 40 years. Among them were the the turbocharged and intercooled V-6s in the Regal Grand National and GNX of the 1980s, the successful racing engines of the 1990s and a family of supercharged

V-6s that also emerged in the '90s. Nearly three decades of continued engineering improvements led to the 3800 Series II V-6 being named one of *Ward's Auto World's* 10 best engines of the 20th Century.

In 2005, the 3800 Series III became the first automotive engine to attain the SULEV (Super Ultra Low Emissions Vehicle) designation, but the days of the pushrod-operated, overhead-valve Buick engine were numbered. By 1996, pushrod engines were being maligned as old fashioned despite the 3800's compactness, power, versatility and dependability. On August 22, 2008, production of the 3800 officially ended, interrupting 105 years of Buick engine production in Flint.

New ideas and technologies evolve over time, sometimes through trial and error but frequently through lessons learned in one industry being applied to a different industry. David Buick certainly applied his manufacturing process knowledge and experience in casting, machining and finishing metal goods in the plumbing supply business to his pioneering efforts in gasoline engine manufacturing. His technical ideas also found their way from plumbing patents to automobiles. David's first patent was for a stop valve, a seemingly mundane item, used to control the flow of water through a garden hose. Buick's patent addressed a way of achieving a better seal between the valve and valve seat. It's a situation that would arise in designing valves and valve cages for some of the first Buick engines.

In another case, a flush-valve design employed a hollow valve stem with a piston inside. One reason for this was to enable a more compact design that would fit into a smaller space. Nearly 20 years later, when David Buick and Eugene Richard designed an engine for the Wolverine automobile, it too required a compact design. They therefore employed a hollow exhaust valve stem, which housed a smaller concentric intake valve, similar in concept to his plumbing-related patent.

Time and again the problems addressed in David Buick's early plumbing inventions paved the way for concepts employed later in his automotive designs. Based on the various valves he patented for the plumbing business, with levers and fulcrums used for their operation, David Buick's influence on the development of valve mechanisms for overhead valve is apparent. My view is that the overhead-valve idea, as it applied to Buick, was probably Richard's and the valve operation concepts were David Buick's — with further development and detail by Richard.

Although the industries were vastly different, the underlying engineering principles were the same. Instead of controlling the flow of water it was the flow of gasoline and air. Instead of hinges for toilet seats it was hinges for car doors. Instead of brass castings for valves it was brass castings for carburetors. After all, in simplest terms, a carburetor is just another flow control valve.

In looking at the early development of gasoline engines, it's almost impossible to credit only one person with the development of any particular feature. On the question of who brought ohv to Buick, the paper trail of patent applications clearly supports Richard, working for David Buick, with the first patent for what we know as an overhead-valve engine. The historical timeline supports Buick and Richard with the initial development of the Model B engine but Buick and Marr with putting that engine in a successful automobile.

By discovering the benefits of the overhead-valve design in the formative years of the automotive industry, and through years of continued refinement and improvement, Buick gained a crucial competitive advantage in engine development and forever solidified its place in history as the "Pioneer Builder of Valve-in-Head Motor Cars."

Chapter 8

Buick starts a new company

When he offered to sell his carriage bodies to Walter Marr in 1901, David Buick appeared to be giving up on automobiles to concentrate on engines. After all, Marr was the man who could put an entire vehicle together, and now he was gone. But the carriage bodies went unsold, at least to Marr, and by 1902 David was back at it — working on an automobile said to be of his own design.

At the same time, he continued to work on his engine designs, presumably with Eugene Richard. One of his consistent messages was simplicity of engine design, a common theme among engine builders of the time.

Buick Manufacturing's first catalog, probably dating to 1902, also boasts of the best mechanics, the best steel and that "each engine is an advertisement in itself." It makes a big quality claim for the time: "All parts...are interchangeable." It also makes a big claim for fame. Its cover is decorated with a drawing of Uncle Sam pulling a Buick engine on a cart — called "on truck" — across the globe, accompanied with a slogan: "Known All Over the World." (He would keep that design on several future catalogs.)

The catalog discusses overhead valve engines: "The inlet and outlet valves are in the head...so should it become necessary to grind or reseat the valves it would not be necessary to take the entire engine to a machine shop...but simply take the head..." There was no claim of a power advantage.

By late 1902, as he struggled to build an automobile, David found himself in debt for several hundred dollars to Benjamin Briscoe Jr., who operated a big sheet metal business in Detroit and who was learning how to build radiators and other automotive equipment.

Briscoe did not push to collect. After all, he noted, "David Buick and I were old friends from before the automobile business was thought of in Detroit." Buick was "a personal friend and a fine chap generally, and ... I appreciated his having always given me all the business he could in his former company [Buick & Sherwood], which amounted to many thousands of dollars a year."

He explained: "We [Briscoe] were galvanizing and sheet metal workers and Mr. Buick's business of manufacturing plumbers' suppliers required such services as we rendered." Not only that, Briscoe said, after Buick began building stationary engines, he continued to buy a good deal of material from Briscoe "and in that way our business association was maintained."

Buick was undeterred by his inability to pay his debts to Briscoe (and apparently to others). In fact, he was seeking more money so he could complete his automobile. Unwilling to give up that dream, he invited Briscoe to his shop, showed him his unfinished car and asked for more help.

"He told me his troubles and how impossible it was for him to pay me or in fact to pay any one of his creditors at that time," Briscoe recalled. "The reason he gave me was that he had invested most of his capital and 'then some' in a design for an automobile. In fact he showed me that if he could not refinance himself through the medium of this automobile, he would not be able to pay anyone."

Briscoe, intrigued rather than angered, agreed to advance $650 to finish the automobile — but the car would then be his. "I proposed that, as I did not own a car, that I buy the car they were working on, furnishing them money to complete it. I had to furnish a good deal more money that I had anticipated."

When Briscoe planned a long visit to France in the summer of 1903 to study building radiators, Buick became "disturbed," to quote Briscoe. One imaginative source said Buick pleaded: "What am I going to do, Ben?" Briscoe: "I don't know, Dave. You'll have to blow up, I guess. I can't stand any more of this." Briscoe's version is less colorful, merely noting David said he needed more money to "carry on." They finally agreed Buick could survive with $1,500 more for the interim.

So Briscoe proposed a seemingly odd deal. Briscoe would lend the $1,500, which meant Buick's total debt to Briscoe would be about $3,500. In return, Buick would incorporate his company with a capital of $100,000, "mostly represented by patents and inventions," Briscoe suggested, and transfer most stock to Briscoe. Buick could redeem the stock by fall by simply paying Briscoe the $3,500 he was owed, or Briscoe would take over the company. David Buick agreed.

The firm was incorporated under the name Buick Motor Company May 19, 1903. David Buick had 9,499 shares, son Thomas Buick 500, and Emil D. Moessner, Briscoe's son-in-law, one share. Moessner was probably there to keep an eye on Briscoe's interests, because Briscoe was in control (though his name does not show up in the incorporation papers). The incorporation date has been used by Buick Motor Division over the years as its official birth date.[1]

Even after the new company was created, the previous Buick firm stayed in existence for a brief period. Four days after Buick Motor Company's incorporation, Eugene Richard signed a two-year contract with Buick Manufacturing Company as "designer and inventor and head of drafting department" for a starting salary of $100 a month. Under the contract, on January 1, 1904, Richard would have the option of a $25-a-month salary increase or taking $2,500 in stock received from the sale of property and assets of Buick Manufacturing Company to Buick Motor Company.

The contract was probably created to build credibility for Buick Motor Company's $100,000 capitalization by securing the firm's rights to Richard's patents and inventions. The contract stated Richard "further agrees to apply for patents when requested to do so," to apply for patents on all inventions he has already made "in this line" and to assign such applications or patents to Buick. (The original of that document was given by Richard's son to the writer for the Buick archives in the mid 1990s). As it turned out, Richard may not have remained at Buick long enough to take an optional increase — some sources said he left in September 1903, though he did work part time for Buick at least through the following spring.

About the time Buick Motor Company was created, Briscoe began to consider whether he wanted to work with a more experienced auto man, Jonathan D. Maxwell, and clean up the Buick business

---

1 When the writer was privileged to join a small group that previewed a Ken Burns TV special in 2002 at Burns' farmhouse studio in New Hampshire, a coincidence was pointed out. The date of Buick Motor Company's incorporation — May 19, 1903 — is also remembered in automotive history for another event. That very night in the University Club in San Francisco, Horatio Nelson Jackson, a 31-year-old doctor from Vermont, made a bet he could drive an automobile from San Francisco to New York City in less than three months. Four days later, he set out in a Winton in an epic story told in the book, *Horatio's Drive,* by Dayton Duncan and Ken Burns. It was the story of America's first cross-country road trip, which became the television program of the same name previewed in that New Hampshire farmhouse.

This is believed to be the second experimental Buick and the first designed by David Buick. It may have been started in David's barn behind his home on Meldrum, Detroit. It was probably completed in Buick Manufacturing's shop on Howard Street in 1903 and sold to Ben Briscoe, Buick's financial angel. The "Briscoe Buick," as some have called it, was a factor in the sale of Buick Motor Company to Flint Wagon Works directors in fall, 1903. This poor quality photo from a newspaper is the only known possible likeness of the car.

move on. He perceived that Maxwell, who had collaborated with the Apperson brothers, Elwood Haynes, Ransom E. Olds and other pioneer auto designers, was way ahead of the curve when compared with David Buick.

It also helped that Maxwell and Olds had visited Briscoe's office in 1902 with an engine "cooler" (radiator) they wanted him to build. When Briscoe returned with a satisfactory sample, Olds and Maxwell ordered 4,400 of them, along with an equal number of tanks, sets of fenders and other sheet metal parts. This was a big order in the earliest days of the Detroit auto business. If David Buick was a good customer, Maxwell was now an even better one.

Briscoe described Maxwell as a man with "an enviable and successful record" who was also endowed "with a high degree of common sense along with which he had practical knowledge, exceptionally broad at that time, applying to automobiles." Briscoe sent Maxwell to check out David Buick's operations. It's probably fair to say Maxwell was not impressed. Briscoe insisted Maxwell didn't say anything favorable or unfavorable about the Buick proposition.

Benjamin Briscoe, Jr.

But pointedly, Maxwell wondered if Briscoe would like to "hook up" with him in the automobile business.

That sounded good to Briscoe. He shifted gears quickly. By July 4, 1903, he was already backing Maxwell in development of a Maxwell car, and Briscoe would organize the Maxwell-Briscoe Company in the fall of the year. But at the same time, Briscoe was now owner of the second car to carry the Buick name, and the first apparently designed by David Buick.

Although Briscoe would later boast he started Buick Motor Company, which is close to true, he didn't claim much of a hand in the car itself. Writing to the editor of *The Automobile* magazine in 1915, he acknowledged: "As to what part I played in the laying out of the first Buick car, I cannot say I did much of anything with reference to design, except to make general suggestions and recommendations during the progress of the work."

He recalled "the motor had exceptionally large valves, was a single cylinder motor of about 4 x 5...and did develop by brake test about 26 H.P., which was quite marvelous at the time for that size motor, in fact would be a good performance even for today...."

From the Richard family album: Above, Eugene Richard about the time of his marriage (left) and as a young engineer (right). Below, Eugene and Louisa Richard in later years at their Flint home.

Briscoe's recollection is likely wrong. If the engine really was a one-cylinder, it would have generated less horsepower. Charles Hulse states without listing a source that the Briscoe Buick's one-cylinder engine developed 7 horsepower.

If it had been an overhead-valve engine, Briscoe and Hulse most likely would have so noted. The record, however, is not clear. Buick wasn't building overhead-valve engines for automobiles in 1903. However, a year earlier, Buick Manufacturing Company noted its four-cycle stationary engine, which had an overhead-valve design, could "be adapted to automobile purposes, with a few simple changes." Still, as mentioned earlier, the prevailing opinion is David Buick probably used an L-head engine in this vehicle. The overhead-valve Buick auto engine was coming, but not until the beginning of 1904.

The Briscoe company built so many parts for the car they were "too numerous to mention," Briscoe said, but they did include all of the sheet metal as well as machine work on small parts.

Briscoe was adamant about one thing — Marr had nothing to do with this Buick automobile. "I do not recall that I ever saw Mr. Marr there" while it was being designed, he said. Of course he would have known Marr was then developing the Marr Autocar, because Briscoe was also providing many parts for that vehicle.

Briscoe drove David Buick's car for several months and "discovered most of the bugs that were in it...I was part of the experimental department and as such had many strenuous experiences." This automobile was registered as the "Bewick" in Detroit on January 24, 1904, shortly after a city ordinance was passed in Detroit, in advance of the state, requiring that cars be registered. It was assigned license number 365.

Briscoe understood David Buick's passion for automobiles. He was hooked as well, and so could describe the feeling. Buick, said Briscoe, had "gotten the automobile bee in his bonnet, and it is my experience...that when a man became infected with the automobile germ, it was as though he had a disease. It had to run its course. No man in those days would have gone into the automobile business if he had been a hard-boiled conservative business man. It took a man of pioneering instinct, an idealist — of an adventurous nature...."

Briscoe was consistent in his praise of David Buick's abilities. In a 1915 letter, he told D. Beecroft, managing editor of *The Automobile*: "Mr. Buick is a very capable mechanic and I understand he has lately developed a very excellent carburetor."

But Briscoe was quite straightforward in his plans regarding Buick and Maxwell. Briscoe wrote that if he and Buick were unable to sell the firm, and Briscoe was unable to get his money back, he would then "buy out Mr. Buick and have Mr. Maxwell use the Buick shop as a nucleus for a plant in which to produce the Maxwell car."

In the summer of 1903, neither Briscoe nor Maxwell fully understood what David Buick and his team had wrought with Buick's powerful new engine design. Buick Motor Company didn't seem too sure, either. The catalog copy on overhead-valve engines — identified by description because that label had yet to be invented — still boasted only of ease of servicing, not power. And, as noted, the design had yet to be specifically adapted by Buick to an automobile.

Soon that would all change. Jacob H. Newmark, one of Durant's advertising men, commenting from the perspective of 1936, best summed up Buick's No. 1 achievement.

"The Buick Motor Company prospered…almost from the beginning, and all because the company was unusually fortunate in its engine design," Newmark wrote. "Buick, without doubt, had one of the best of the early engines. It would go and keep on going. Roads were of all kinds in those days — most of them sand, clay and what-not. Buick's early valve-in-head motor did have power if nothing else, and the new car would negotiate all sorts of road conditions…The fame of the new motor grew steadily."

David Buick was confident he had good engines. But in the summer of 1903, nobody could have guessed where they would take him.

Chapter 9

Move to Flint

With an incorporated company, a catalog of superior engines and one car to show off, Buick in the summer of 1903 had a package that might sell. And sure enough, it did. The opportunity came from a surprising place — Flint, Michigan, a city of about 14,000, some 60 miles north of Detroit. Dwight Stone, a real estate salesman in Flint, tipped Benjamin Briscoe's brother Frank, who was visiting relatives in the city, that the Flint Wagon Works was looking to buy into an engine company and possibly build automobiles. That's the story as related in Flint.

Ben Briscoe tells it slightly differently, in a magazine article setting up the story in his meandering style that nearly defeats his attempt at drama: "A thing happened which, though trivial in itself, was one of those happenings that measured by the changes it wrought in the lives of many people, and the fortunes of many men, proved to be one of those 'high spot' occurrences that seem as though they are predestined."

During a conversation with a salesman, Briscoe said he learned a Flint vehicle maker — the Flint Wagon Works — was contemplating the manufacture of automobiles.

"I pricked up my ears, and upon my inquiry as to whether they had a car to manufacture, he said he understood they did not, but that they were looking for one," Briscoe continued. "This, then, was my cue for disposing of the Buick car and getting my money out." The next day he and Frank headed for Flint to meet with James H. Whiting, the firm's president and managing director, and other wagon works directors. "I sold the Flint Wagon Works the Buick car on that day. The deal was not closed then to be sure, as they wanted to see the car and talk to Mr. Buick, but for all intents and purposes they bought it that day."

James Whiting, born May 12, 1842, in Torrington, Conn., had moved to Flint at age 21 after serving as an officer in the Connecticut Volunteers during the Civil War. He was a clerk at the William L.

Smith & Company store (which would become Smith-Bridgman's, downtown Flint's big department store for more than a century) before entering the hardware business downtown. In 1882 he joined Josiah W. Begole, later governor of Michigan, and others to convert the Begole, Fox and Company lumber mill in Flint into a successful wagon maker. The Flint Wagon Works became Flint's first incorporated company in 1884. A surviving record book of his expenses paints Whiting as a thoroughly modern businessman, traveling quickly from city to city by train, touching bases with business executives on the road and riding herd on company expenses. In one later entry he notes a need to talk "about tel. bill of DD Buick."

Whiting was also fascinated with automobiles. When he went to carriage shows, he would join fellow carriage executive A.B.C. Hardy in visiting any auto show nearby. And when Hardy began manufacturing his Hardy Flint Roadster automobiles in Flint in 1901, Whiting would visit his factory. (Hardy built 52 cars from 1901-03). The Buick company, not too expensive to buy, not too far away to visit, must have seemed just what he was looking for. Briscoe wrote: "Although there were some discouraging moments during the negotiations and the attempted trial runs of the car, I could see that nothing except some unexpected turn in events could 'unsell them.'" Charles A. Cumings, superintendent of the Flint Wagon Works, told Hulse he went to Detroit with the Whiting group and that David Buick showed them the Buick car he had recently completed.

David himself was the source of a story he had to drive the Buick to Flint to close the deal. That drive is briefly mentioned in a biographical sketch he probably approved. Much later, in his *Detroit Times* obituary, it's said "his car broke down at Pontiac. Horses hauled it back to Detroit. Undaunted, Buick tried again. His masterpiece chugged along bravely and reached Flint – all together." In still another account, an interview in California with *The San Diego Union* (April 3, 1910), found by Kevin Kirbitz, Buick doesn't mention any breakdown.

When I was convinced the machine I built was a success, I interested men of capital at Flint. They wanted a demonstration and I planned a run from Detroit to Flint, a distance of more than 60 miles. They...tried to make the trial run of half the distance, to Pontiac. I said Flint or nothing and started out. After making an excellent trip from Detroit to Pontiac, about 32 miles, I was met by the men... They said, "That's enough. Give the machine a rest."

James H. Whiting: He brought Buick to Flint

You see, those men were in the carriage manufacturing business and thought a machine demanded a rest like a horse. I would not accede to their wishes and finished the trip to Flint, with the consequence a large amount of capital was raised to finance the venture. That machine today is still in use. It is used every day in the year by a rural delivery mail carrier at Lima, Ohio.

Referring to the car as a horseless carriage, he said he designed it in 1893. He misspoke or was misquoted about the year. While it's possible, though unlikely, he may have started work on an automobile by the mid 1890s, the car he refers to was likely the Briscoe Buick of 1903.

Charles Hulse once identified an uncaptioned photo of a car in a largely inaccurate story about Buick in *The Flint Journal* on May 18, 1904, as probably the Briscoe Buick (photo, page 76). Its exterior design had moved farther along from carriage to automobile than either the first Buick or the Marr Autocar.

Buick told the unnamed San Diego reporter he knew when he designed the car that "the automobile was destined to take the place of the horse, but had no idea that the industry would grow to such enormous proportions." He said his organization originally thought the first Buick plant was large enough but every year they had to keep adding floor space.

"The end is not in sight for the possibilities of the automobile," he told the reporter. "I do not look for any decided changes in the mechanism of any of the standard cars, but the various points will grow each year in perfection. We are still using the same engine in our output that was built for the first car. In the manufacture of our cars power has always been our goal...."

When interviewed, David Buick was attending an early aviation meet in Los Angeles, and was photographed there with young son Wynton (news clip, page 157). Buick said the San Diego Buick representative, Byron Naylor, had invited him to visit and the trip was a combination of business and pleasure. His host was so enthusiastic about the area that Buick said he was considering buying a house in San Diego and spending winters there, and was also planning to build a miniature four-cylinder Buick for Wynton. (In early 1910, the business Buick was likely exploring in California was an oil company he was about to start – he was near the end of his relationship with Buick Motor Company. Buick didn't move to San Diego but he did make it to Los Angeles).

If Briscoe's recollections are correct about Whiting's interest in the Buick automobile, then Whiting was hiding his true intentions from others. His public story was he wanted the Buick firm so he could build engines his salesmen could peddle to farmers for stationary use or to wholesale to auto makers. That was probably close to his real position. Marr recalled years later Whiting felt as early as 1904 that the automobile market was almost saturated.

The sale of Buick Motor Company to the Flint Wagon Works directors was completed September 3, 1903. Reportedly the deal was cinched for $10,000, which the Flint Wagon Works directors borrowed on a one-year note from the Union Trust & Savings Bank of Flint, guaranteed by the signatures of its five directors — James H. Whiting, Charles M. Begole, George L. Walker, William S. Ballenger and Charles A. Cumings. As early Flint historian Frank Rodolf pointed out, the bank wasn't gambling money on a shaky automotive concern, but making the loan based on the signatures of five very substantial local citizens.

Flint in 1903 (above), when Buick came to town. Some of the city's famous arches were erected in 1901 but the 'Vehicle City' arch (below) was created in 1905 for Flint's Golden Jubilee. The arches came down just after World War I, but when new ones were erected early in the new millennium, Buick Motor Division sponsored one — though Buick had recently been moved by GM to Detroit.

L.H. Bridgman, an officer of the bank, recalled in 1953 his memory of Whiting walking into the bank with that note signed by the Wagon Works directors. "I can see that note now," Bridgman said. "As the Buick company had been doing business with the Citizens Bank we asked Mr. Whiting why he didn't use that note there. He replied that they had enough notes in that bank. Mr. Whiting's name alone was good enough for our bank, and we gave him the money."

The little city of Flint, incorporated in 1855, could trace its beginnings to 1819 or earlier when a trading post was established by fur trader Jacob Smith on an Indian trail at a shallow crossing of the Flint River. Indians in the Saginaw Valley and northern Michigan who wanted to trade furs could canoe no further south on the river than the site of Flint before they would have to travel 60 miles on foot to the big trading center at Detroit. It was a great place for Smith to set up shop. He could beat the competition and save the Indians the walk. In 1830, John and Polly Todd established a tavern and ferry across the river from Smith's former cabin/trading post (Smith had died in 1825), guarded by a chained pet bear named Trinc. When social observer/writer Alexis de Tocqueville spent the night at Todd's Tavern on July 24, 1831, as he toured the American wilderness, he noted: "What a devil of a country this is, where one has bears for watchdogs."

Soon a government road was cut through the wilderness from Detroit and a land office opened at Flint. Settlers began to arrive in large numbers to clear the land and create farms. But the most valuable natural resource in the area was the white pine. Large stands of pine along the river north of Flint were soon being cut, with the logs floated to the booms in Flint. There, sawmills created great piles of lumber to build Detroit and Chicago and other cities.

One of the area's biggest lumber barons was Henry Howland Crapo (Cray-po), who came from New Bedford, Mass., in January of 1856 to manage timber land for Eastern investors. Crapo built a sawmill and then a railroad. He became mayor of Flint, and then, in the 1860s, governor of Michigan. Twice he met with Abraham Lincoln during the Civil War. Occasionally he sent letters to his young grandson, Willie Durant, who lived with his parents in Boston and would someday move to Flint, save Buick and create General Motors.

By 1903, when Buick came to town, Flint was already known as "The Vehicle City." The name had nothing to do with automobiles. A local judge, Charles Wisner, had built several horseless carriages — the first as early as 1898 — and one former carriage maker, A.B.C. Hardy, was, as mentioned, producing a runabout named the Hardy Flint Roadster in small numbers. But The Vehicle City was an acknowledgment of such carriage and wagon firms as the William A. Paterson Carriage Works, Flint Wagon Works, W. F. Stewart Company and the storied Durant-Dort Carriage Company (which alone produced 50,000 vehicles a year by 1901). When one of the carriage leaders made a decisive step, the banks, the business leaders and local newspapers took notice.

Whiting's announcement that the Flint Wagon Works directors had bought Buick Motor Company was therefore the top news story in *The Flint Journal* on September 11, 1903. (It shared Page One with a story about a state conference of horse shoers —a case of transportation eras passing). Whiting said ground had been broken that morning for a 200x65-foot factory on W. Kearsley Street on the west side of Flint near the wagon works. The newspaper described Buick as a "splendid new manufacturing industry" and it certainly sounded that way. Whiting said the new company had paid-in capital stock of $50,000, would hire 100 skilled mechanics and machinists and would manufacture stationary and marine engines, automobile engines, transmissions, carburetors and "sparking plugs."

Whiting was asked by a reporter to comment on a rumor the company would also build automobiles. He smiled at the question and replied the "broader opportunity" would be considered later.

The Flint Journal in an editorial the next day was both enthusiastic and prophetic. And it pushed Whiting to go further than his announcement:

> Flint is the most natural center for the manufacture of autos in the whole country. It is the vehicle city of the United States and in order to maintain this name by which it is known from ocean to ocean there must be developed factories here for the manufacture of…automobiles. *The Journal* believes that the time is not very far away when every part connected with an auto will be manufactured here and when an immense industry will have been developed.

David said he tried to find money to keep his plant in Detroit but was unsuccessful.

Flint Wagon Works: Its directors bought Buick in 1903, set it up in new factory nearby.

"For two years we have been located at 416-418 Howard Street and the business has grown until orders for $185,000 are on the books which we are unable to fill. It became absolutely necessary to enlist more capital, but no substantial encouragement was made in Detroit."

Discussing the move, he said about 30 employees would move to Flint but didn't sound very excited about personally relocating. "I shall necessarily be compelled to make my home there although Detroit seems to me a very desirable place for a residence."

Buick's departure from Detroit was not unnoticed. *The Detroit Journal* interviewed J. B. Howarth, said to be "one of the most level-headed businessmen" of Detroit, who commented:

> If Mr. Buick has been looking around for additional capital during the last six months, he did so at the wrong time. The banks and those who have the means to invest in such enterprises are now retrenching instead of expanding.
>
> The tightness in the money market has brought about a feeling of conservation. But a year ago, and before that for several years, I heard of no well-organized industry, or any industry that could show a healthy condition, failing to get all the capital it needed in Detroit.
>
> [Flint] is off the main lines of road and is obligated to offer special attractions to individual concerns to induce them to locate there. The fact that we as a city lose an industry to a smaller city in the same state does not appear to me as a very great injury, for the merchants of Flint who will be benefited...depend largely on Detroit wholesalers and manufacturers for their supplies.

88

Howarth's opinion that "Mr. Buick has been trying to do the right thing at the wrong time" revealed ignorance of David's need for quick action to avoid Briscoe's takeover of his company.

Briscoe returned from Europe in the fall of 1903 and learned the sale of Buick Motor Company to the Flint Wagon Works directors was complete. He said David Buick called immediately and "justified my high opinion of his integrity as he 'came through' handsomely, paying me interest on the money and a bonus in addition."

All of this new-found money and the prospect of a new factory emboldened the company. On October 21, 1903, Tom Buick wrote to a boat manufacturer in an unrecorded but presumably far-away city:

> This is no doubt the first time that our name has been brought before you as manufacturers of marine engines…our output was limited, and [we] were able to dispose of all the engines we could manufacture in certain localities…but as we are now building a large and modern plant at Flint, Mich., it becomes necessary for us to extend our territory, and increase our sales to take care of the large output we will have….

He continued that the firm had been manufacturing 2- and 4-horsepower four-cycle engines but was now adding sizes and making a two-cycle marine engine. He boasted Buick's present customers had few complaints and "we are absolutely certain that if you handle our engines your engine troubles will become a thing of the past."

By December 5, when the Flint factory began operations, Arthur C. Mason, formerly of Leland & Faulconer, Detroit, which built Cadillac and Olds engines, was superintendent of Buick production. He had managed the move of the factory to Flint. Later in December, William Beacraft of the same firm was brought in as Mason's assistant. On December 11, *The Flint Journal* reported the plant had 25 employees and had made five engines of three-quarters to 13 horsepower. One model was a four-cycle marine engine that, according to Charles Hulse, was designed by Eugene Richard in 1902 and first produced by Buick Manufacturing Company in 1902-03 and then by Buick Motor Company.

The factory was also starting work on "a huge double-cylinder auto engine," *The Journal* said. This was either a new engine Buick was about to produce to sell retail to any auto maker or a very different powerplant it had just designed for Reid Manufacturing, Detroit, for its planned new Wolverine automobile.

Arthur C. Mason (left) was moved to Flint by David Buick in 1903 as superintendent of the new Flint plant. Mason later worked closely with Billy Durant (below right, with Mason) at both Buick and Chevrolet.

The first mentioned engine, with overhead valves, would become the famous powerplant of Buick's first production automobile, the 1904 Model B. Originally rated at 12 horsepower, it eventually turned out to generate more than 20 hp, astounding experts across the industry and capturing press attention in New York. For clarity, it will be referred to as the Model B engine. Likely being designed late in 1903, it went into production in March, 1904, when Buick still considered building only engines, not cars.

As for the engine for the Wolverine, that's a story in itself. The Wolverine is barely a footnote in auto history. But because Buick brought a lawsuit in 1904 to collect on unpaid bills for engines Buick had built for the Wolverine, testimony survives that sheds light on Buick's engine design and manufacturing activities.

The transcripts indicate David could design engines and transmissions on short notice and get them into production quickly, even before the tooling was fully in place. David Buick at last appears as a bold, resourceful and talented auto pioneer. The transcripts also reveal that Eugene Richard, who sources said had left Buick in the fall of 1903, was still very much involved with Buick — at least part time — through the winter of 1903-04 and well into the following spring. That's worth mentioning because it indicates Richard had a role in designing the Model B engine.

Remaining for a time in Detroit, Richard seems to have operated independently — working for his old employers in Lansing, first the Kneeland Crystal Creamery and then Peerless Motor Company, as well as wrapping up design work on the Wolverine and Model B engines for Buick.[1]

Clues of Richard's work on the Model B engine are two engineering drawings rescued from a wastebasket at Buick Product Engineering by GM engineer Brian Heil during a 1984 housecleaning. One of the saved drawings is of a flywheel, dated September 24, 1903, the other a transmission gear case, dated October 28, 1903, both initialed E.C.R. for Eugene C. Richard. Comparing the drawings with existing 1904 Model B and 1905 Model C Buick engines, Heil and Kirbitz agreed the drawings were likely made for the Model B engine and therefore Richard must have had some role in its design.

---

1 Richard did file for a patent for an engine for the Kneeland firm's cream separator on December 30, 1903, and later worked for Peerless as designer and draftsman. He was promoted to superintendent in 1906 but on June 7, 1908, returned to Buick as designer/draftsman in the engineering department.

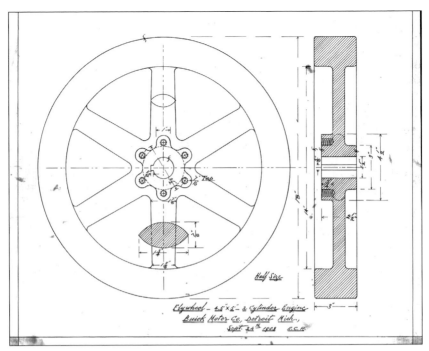

Above is an original drawing of the flywheel for what would become Buick's overhead-valve Model B auto engine. An updated (late 1904) engine, with pushrods on top, is at bottom with plant manager William Beacraft. In the early days he assembled all of the Buick engines. The drawing, by "ECR" (Eugene C. Richard) and dated September 24, 1903, indicates Richard was involved in the design of Buick's early landmark powerplant. (Drawing from Brian Heil collection)

But the genesis of the Model B engine is still not entirely clear. Hulse, assuming Richard had left Buick in the fall of 1903, stated Mason and Beacraft were responsible, incorporating the overhead-valve design that could be traced to Richard. Maybe, but Richard still had his hand in, Mason would have been busy handling the factory move from Detroit to Flint and Beacraft was generally a producer, not a designer. In any event he probably arrived too late to do much design work before he had to start manufacturing engines. It's just as likely Richard created the original design, perhaps in conjunction with his boss David Buick (and who can be sure Walter Marr's ideas were not involved?). Mason and Beacraft may have provided additional design work to get it production ready.

Fred G. Hoelzle, a longtime Buick superintendent who was 15 in 1901 when he became a toolroom apprentice at Peerless, was in his 90s when interviewed by the writer in the late 1970s. At Peerless, Hoelzle recalled working with Richard, apparently in the 1903-04 period on the Model B engine (Buick may have assigned some design work to Peerless because Richard then worked there). Hoelzle remembered Richard was building a two-cycle engine for Peerless and "was also interested in building a motor car for Mr. David Buick in Detroit. I met his Detroit partner while at Peerless, Mr. Walter Marr, and did some work for him. Mr. Richard...was working on an idea of valve-in-head motors. I machined the valve cage with the valve assembly that...could be removed from [the] cylinder for valve trouble, etc., and again assembled with a simple clamp-tightening process. He was very excited about this..."

While the Buick company concentrated on creating its two new engines and producing others as the new Flint factory ramped up, the company was also being reorganized. On January 16, 1904, in a meeting in Flint chaired by David Buick, the board dissolved Detroit-born Buick Motor Company. It transferred assets to Whiting to organize a Flint company, same name, incorporated January 30, 1904. Large stockholders were David Buick and son Thomas (1,500 shares between them), Whiting as president (1,504), Charles M. Begole, vice president (1,068), George L. Walker, director (725), and William S. Ballenger, treasurer (707). The officers were the same as for the Flint Wagon Works, except David Buick was secretary of the motor company.

The purpose listed was as a manufacturer of power machinery, automobile "equipments," pumps, engines, other mechanical appliances — and automobiles. Management was no longer hiding its interest in building cars. The firm was capitalized at $75,000 instead of the $50,000 originally intended, with $37,500 paid in.

Early Buick researcher Charles E. Hulse (left) discusses the Buick stationary engine with William H. Wascher, who was hired as an electrician at the Buick plant when it was built in 1903. The only known stationary Buick Motor Company engine surviving, this one was built in Flint and later sold by Hulse to Harold Warp's Pioneer Village in Minden, Neb.

In what may have been a surprise to Flint investors, David let it be known he could not manage Buick in Flint because he owed $11,000 to creditors in Detroit. He felt he could keep them quiet if he stayed there, but otherwise there might be lawsuits and attachments. It's unclear whether the Flint investors were told this before the sale was complete.

They were certain, however, they needed David's services. So they endorsed a note for his debts, a local bank provided the money and David began work in Flint. The bank reasonably insisted, though, that David not receive his stock until his debts had been paid out of its dividends. Briscoe figured rightly that this would never happen — the dividends would never catch up with the debt. But, Briscoe wrote: "It can be said, however, that as the stock developed its real value, that those who finally secured it gave Mr. Buick a considerable sum of money, although legally not obliged to do so." Carl Crow, in the book *The City of Flint Grows Up,* said the note was eventually paid off but not from earnings of the Buick company.

Reminiscing from the perspective of 1921, Briscoe wrote that with Buick's move to Flint, "thus began that great era in the life of that quiet and pretty town, a town which has produced, it is said, more millionaires than any other place since Cortez discovered the golden temples of Mexico."

94

Arthur Mason: A daughter's recollections

Arthur Charles Mason, born March 30, 1869, in King City, Ontario, Canada, had studied engineering at Toronto University and apprenticed in an uncle's machine shop before co-founding the Mason & Watkins Bicycle Company, Toronto, in 1895. It went bankrupt a year later. Mason then took several supervisor and tool design jobs before landing in Detroit at Leland & Faulconer, the engine manufacturer, as a master tool designer in 1901.

His daughter, Hilda Mason, who recorded these details, said she remembered her father meeting informally around 1902 at the family's Detroit home with David Buick, Walter Marr, William Beacraft, Alanson P. Brush and others as they all discussed ideas for developing automobiles. She said her father had worked with Beacraft in Canada and persuaded him to move to Detroit.

"They put their ideas together and the first Buick automobile was planned," she wrote. But "these young men did not have the money to put their plan into action..." until Buick moved to Flint. "A part of the old Flint Wagon Works was used and here ambitious young men strove to produce a better automobile. Their enthusiasm, hard long hours of work and sincere interest produced the nucleus of the now great General Motors."

Hilda was only 7 in 1902 and her memories were no doubt enhanced by her parents. Maybe the talks she remembered took place later. But it's interesting to speculate that these men with exceptional mechanical minds met together and talked of their dreams before any of them had the money to act on them. It's easy to imagine that when Dave Buick was suddenly bankrolled to build an engine factory in Flint in 1903, he may well have immediately turned to Mason and Beacraft, men he already knew, to manage the new operation — and then soon decided to hire his former employee, Marr, as chief engineer. As for Al Brush, he arrived at Buick a few years later.

Hilda Mason's brief written memories of the very early days of motoring (with spelling and punctuation corrected) capture the atmosphere of the times. Her manuscript, originally preserved by Richard Scharchburg, is now in the collection of Leroy Cole, former president of the Society of Automotive Historians. It was provided for this book by Kevin Kirbitz.

As she recalled, her father and another man had bought a Cadillac together and "all dad's spare time was spent working on that car. The motor was under the seat. A [hoist] in the garage would haul the body up to the ceiling. Many were the evenings mother spent in the garage curled up in her big, comfortable rocking chair while dad added some new improvement to the motor of the car.

"The following evening, this improvement would be 'tried out.' With cushions, baby bottles, warm coats, all would pile into the car and when dad had cranked the motor and it began to spit and roar, all neighbors standing by, we would proudly sail out of our garage, across the field and onto Grand Boulevard at a speed of perhaps four miles an hour, to travel only a few blocks [before an inevitable breakdown].

"We would get out, mother would make the children comfortable and dad would take the motor to pieces in order to find the trouble. Many times the moon would come up and go down before all was repaired and we could travel home again...

"Tires were a constant question. One friend tried filling his tires with oats and then water. Result: Explosion, when oats swelled... Every spare moment of dad's time was spent studying all sorts of mechanical magazines...piles of the *American Machinist* were stored in cupboards.

"The mixer [carburetor] was constantly coming off to be 'improved.' With pliers it was held over the hottest coals in mother's kitchen stove...the sieve in the mixer had to be constantly cleaned. I can remember dad sitting in the garage for hours polishing rods. He would constantly tell mother of the great future of the automobile. The neighbors laughed but the engineers of the day agreed with him."

She described the task of driving the 60 miles between Flint and Detroit. "In these early days of automobile travel, a trip from Flint to Detroit was considered quite an adventure," she wrote. "The roads were only farmers' wagon tracks. On [our] trip down, the water [in the radiator] got too warm for dad's liking. But we finally arrived and dad saw that mother had a comfortable room for us children in the old Cadillac Hotel...He took the car to a machine shop...he must find out why the water was so hot and correct this before leaving for Flint the following day.

"During the night there was a thunderstorm. Dad could think of nothing but the deep slippery clay in the narrow wagon tracks... [Starting out on the trip back to Flint], we decided to start early... All went well until we left Detroit city pavements. The moment we came to the country roads we had to put the car in second gear and here it stuck until we reached Flint — which took us all that day, and all that night, and part of the next morning.

"The yellow clay in Pontiac was a great worry to the few men owning and driving automobiles in these early days. Dad was afraid to stop the motor so he stopped the car and purchased our supper and brought it to us. We started again on our way to Flint. As it grew dark, the sky began to cloud over, and lightning appeared on the horizon with the low rumble of thunder. We were in for trouble.

"Dad did not dare find shelter...as this would mean stopping the motor and he was afraid he would never be able to start it again. But he found a dry place on the road...and dad hauled out great squares of rubberized cloth. These fitted over the back seat, fastening on the top of the seat with small turn buttons. [The cloth] had places cut out for three heads to project out, each opening fitted with a collar and snap fasteners. Each projecting head was supplied with a large rubber hat. In the front seat mother and dad looked like two mounds of black. A hole had to be cut in mother's portion so Roy [the baby] would not smother. We bumped, slid and chugged along hoping to keep on the road. Even with our large goggles the rain was blinding...."

Buick's two-cylinder overhead-valve automobile engine of 1904.

Walter Marr, above with an unfinished Wolverine automobile, worked late in 1903 for Reid Manufacturing Co., Detroit, which assembled the car. An early Wolverine ad is above right. Buick designed and built some engines for the Wolverine (first one below).

Chapter 10

The Wolverine

One distraction for the Buick company in early 1904 was the matter of the Wolverine engine. In late summer 1903, when the sale of Buick to the Flint Wagon Works was almost complete, David Buick, anticipating a large new factory in Flint, had aggressively pursued new engine work.

When he learned Reid Manufacturing Company, headquartered only four blocks from Buick's Detroit operations, was planning to build an automobile named the Wolverine, David tried to win the business of supplying its engines. Harmon J. Hunt, Reid's manager, had already lined up a year's supply of 12-hp two-cylinder engines by October 21, 1903, when Reid formally announced it would build the 1,500-pound car. But when Reid began having problems with its engines, supplied by the Brennan Company of Syracuse, N.Y., Hunt became more open to approaches from Buick. David finally met with Hunt December 1, 1903, bringing along his ideas for an unusual engine to be designed specifically for the Wolverine.

The concept was unlike anything Buick had ever built. Hunt recalled David told him "the engine...would be something different from what other people had, would have more power. He told me it would have concentric valves and that they would be cooled by one being inside the other...his arrangement of the valve pockets in the explosion chamber would give a great deal more compression...that the power of the gas engine depended upon the area of the compression chamber." Hunt was impressed and on December 14 he placed an order with Buick for one sample engine to be delivered by Christmas.

David agreed. In retrospect, there was no way he and his team could have designed an engine and transmission and gotten it out the door in a few weeks — especially with a new plant in a new city. But he was anxious to land that business and made every attempt to meet the schedule — even though it meant pushing his employees to work nights and Christmas day of 1903.

Not only did he miss the Christmas deadline, he didn't deliver the prototype engine until February 13, 1904, with the transmission chasing it six days later. Under the circumstances, that seems a heroic achievement. About eight more engines were ordered by Reid over the next few months, and more after that. But each was delivered late and, according to Reid officials, each displayed numerous quality problems. Regardless, Buick pressed for payment of $1,203 for the engines and transmissions, and when Reid failed to pay, Buick in September 1904 took Reid to court.

The court record reveals new details about David's thinking and operations. It's a mixed bag — sometimes he seems highly knowledgeable and capable. But he also excuses quality flaws in his engines. And it's fair to question David's business judgment. At the very moment he and his company are in a frenetic period of moving from Detroit to a new plant in Flint, David adds to the pressure on himself and his employees by over-promising on a delivery schedule for a new-design engine. On the other hand, it can be argued that this type of reckless abandon sometimes separated the successes from the also-rans in this highly charged period.

The lawsuit transcripts contain historical gems:

"My name is David Buick. I am a manufacturer of automobiles...I have been engaged in the manufacture of motors and gears for automobiles since 1895. I built one of the first cars that ever ran on the streets of Detroit."

And the rarely quoted James H. Whiting is quoted admitting he knew nothing of how a gasoline engine worked: "I could not have explained it if I had tried."

That wasn't true of David Buick. The transcripts reveal David well understood the mechanics of engines and transmissions, including how to design and build them. David claimed he and Eugene Richard — whom he always called "Richards" — together designed the engine for Reid. And he was proud of the work and protective of it. When David offered his engine to Hunt, he was cautious to only describe it verbally and then draw a pencil sketch. He would not reveal details.

"We didn't care to give our engine to every Tom, Dick or Harry that came along," he explained. He had been told one of Reid's employees had designed an engine. Because of that, David said, "we didn't care to furnish them a set of working drawings."

One reason, though, was those drawings had yet to be created. The new engine for the Wolverine was only a concept. "At the time, we had no design of an automobile engine, but we had one in mind," David testified. Quickly those thoughts were translated into a design. David continued: "Mr. Richards [Eugene Richard] and I were designers of this motor...We claimed certain new advantages for our new engine and gear. We claimed that it was a new principle, that the inlet valve would work on the inside of the exhaust valve and would be kept cooler in that construction than it would be under ordinary circumstances."

Kirbitz with his engineering background was impressed with the details of the engine design. "With its concentric-valve design, there is no question that the engine Buick and Richard developed for Reid was novel," he observed. "More than that, it was remarkably innovative."

Buick couldn't have offered its new overhead-valve Model B engine to Reid for the Wolverine, assuming it was ready, because it wouldn't have fit. Reid had already ordered the Wolverine bodies and so a different configuration was required. The Reid engine designed by Buick for the Wolverine was shorter, an L-head.

Discussing the delay in producing the first example, David testified the schedule "required us to deliver the motor within two weeks [which would have been late December], but we didn't start to make it until some time in January. The pattern makers could not finish the patterns in time. We kept Mr. Hunt posted. Every time I came to Detroit I called on him...I was pushing the patterns as hard as I could. We didn't know exactly how we were going to build our engine until after we got our patterns all made. It was a pretty hard matter to make a drawing and not run across some parts that want some slight change...."

David disagreed with a questioner that it would be hard to explain how the engine would perform until the patterns were made. "I don't think it would be very hard for a mechanical engineer to explain and advise what he had originated; there is a well designed principle for figuring horse power from bore and stroke and from pressure."

There was one unusual problem in obtaining the patterns. David said a flood in Flint made it impossible to get the patterns for several days from a foundry there. "In fact, we only got them by building a raft and going after them and sending them to Detroit."

David realized the deadline anticipated showing the Wolverine with its new engine at the New York Auto Show opening in January and he saw the merit of trying to achieve that goal. "I realized... that the number of machines we might sell to the Reid Manufacturing Company would depend upon the number of customers or sales they made. I was interested in getting the trade generally interested in our machine," David testified. "We were working nights, Sundays, Christmas and New Year's, paying double time for it." Then he learned Reid also needed a transmission for the engine. Said David: "We had no idea when we first drew up the engine of making a transmission...this was designed as a new transmission, designed by me to go with the engine..."

Countering Buick's efforts in the lawsuit to collect money from Reid, the Reid attorney painted a negative view of the new engine. "The motors and transmission gears [provided by Buick] were inferior and defective in material, workmanship and construction, and were not made in a workmanlike manner," he alleged. Warming up, he continued that "the connecting rods between the crank shaft and the pistons were not strong enough; and had bolt holes bored in them so deep as to seriously weaken them; that the valves were not uniform in construction, and that the valve connection was a failure; that the exhaust valves were not kept cool; that the valves were continually getting out of true; that the bearings were not made of the best bronze; that the crank shaft connections were made of an inferior grade of Babbit metal...."

The Buick people predictably disagreed. Whiting testified Hunt told him he gave a demonstration of a Wolverine with the Buick engine on a hill and it "passed a machine that was puffing and snorting and went past them in great shape, and he was so pleased that he took the train to come up and tell us what a wonderful engine we had...he urged me to come down to Detroit and just ride in that machine; he wanted to show us what an engine we had, what a beautiful engine."

Buick's lawyer at one point sarcastically asked Hunt, "Your correspondence is constantly calling for more of these awful motors?" Hunt acknowledged he gave Whiting and Buick an order for 25 more motors and transmissions "because I sincerely believed at that time that the motor was a good motor if it was properly made without these defects."

William Beacraft, Buick's master mechanic and production fore-man who in the early days assembled every engine, testified: "I made a test of every engine shipped [to Reid]...Mr. Hunt told me what good results this engine was giving...he said it had all kinds of power, sufficient power to go anywhere. He said nothing to me about any of these motors being wrong." George L. Walker, another Buick officer, said he heard Hunt tell Whiting, " 'Mr. Whiting, that is the best proposition on Earth.' He was very enthusiastic about it." And Whiting himself told the court: "The first time I knew there was any fault with this machine was when we asked them to pay for what they had received."

The testimony reveals the primitive nature of engine manufacturing at the time. In one instance, a lever used to operate the valves was hardened to a point that it broke, dropped into the gearing and caused damage. How could that happen? David replied, "That happens you might say daily in a large factory. You will find pieces that are over-hardened and some underhardened."

One complaint about a spring being too long was also deflected by David, who pointed out his workers "are not spring makers" and had to buy springs. "All that was necessary to do would be simply to cut a little of the spring off; that was undoubtedly overlooked from the fact we were pushing these things as fast as we possibly could." When it was pointed out an oil tube was left out of one engine, David blamed "neglect on the part of the men in the excitement of trying to get these engines to the Reid Mfg. Co. on time." Still, he emphasized, "there was never an engine designed that was more near perfect on the first turning over in the plant than that particular engine."

Responding to a criticism that parts were not being made of a uniform size, David replied: "I knew they were not being made by jigs... Jigs is where a template is made and the hole bored in the proper location and when you get your jigs made satisfactory all parts should come [out] alike." He was then asked if it was necessary to use the jigs in order to make the engines uniform. David replied: "If you could get them out in time. You could not go on and build a new engine and get the jigs out at the same time. We didn't have the jigs. We have been making the engine that we are making today for pretty near three years, and some jigs we haven't got yet."

The Wolverine engine was still remembered when Charles Hulse began interviews with early Buick employees in the 1930s. William H. Wascher, a Flint native hired as an electrician at the plant late in

1903, told him the plant, up and running in early December, was making a few marine, stationary and auto engines, all one-cylinder, and work was beginning on the two-cylinder auto engine for Reid.

And Fred Tiedeman, a part-time photographer, remembered being called to the Buick plant to take a photo of this first Reid engine. Tiedeman was told this was the first two-cylinder auto engine the Buick company had ever made for an automobile. His photo is the only existing illustration of this engine. *Cycle and Automobile Trade Journal* said it "differs from most gasoline engines now on the market in that the engine is placed horizontally under the hood parallel with the axles." The engine, it said, generated 15 hp but that could be boosted to 17.5 at a higher rpm.

On April 30, 1906, the circuit court jury found in favor of Buick for the sum of $1,308.55 plus legal costs. Reid appealed but on September 20, 1907, the Michigan Supreme Court upheld the lower court's ruling. By then, apparently, the Wolverine had long since disappeared and it's unknown if the judgment was ever paid. But the transcripts are a unique source in providing a sense of Buick's early engine work.[1]

As the Buick-Reid drama moved along, Walter Marr was on the edge of events. Apparently on the same day David Buick first met with Hunt in Reid's office, December 1, 1903, Marr was coincidentally hired by Reid to help bring the Wolverine to reality. His employment was terminated barely a month later, on January 5, 1904. Three days after that, Marr would be contacted by a new prospective employer — David Buick.

---

1 According to *The American Car Since 1775* by Automobile Quarterly (1971), the Wolverine automobile was moved to the Wolverine Automobile & Commercial Company in Dundee, Mich., in 1905, absorbed by Maumee Motor Car Works in Toledo, Ohio, in 1906-07 and transferred to Craig-Toledo Motor Company, which went bankrupt in 1907.

Chapter 11

First Flint Buick

On January 8, 1904, David Buick wrote to "friend Marr" that he had heard Marr had just quit another company — Reid Manufacturing, where he worked briefly on its Wolverine touring car.

Walter Marr had moved from company to company after leaving Buick Auto-Vim & Power Company in March of 1901. As described earlier, he built a few curved-dash Oldsmobiles in Detroit in the spring of '01, perfected a bicycle engine for a Detroit firm that summer, spent six months (August 1901-February 1902) in Cleveland with the American Motor Carriage Company, worked briefly at Buick Manufacturing Company in the late winter or early spring of 1902 and then concentrated during much of 1902 and 1903 on developing the Marr Autocar.

His latest assignment, with Reid, started December 1, 1903, and ended barely a month later, on January 5, 1904. No reason was given for the quick departure, which seems puzzling as Reid's Wolverine was about to get an engine built by Buick, a firm Marr knew well. Perhaps his stint at Reid was intended as a short assignment. The firm did assure him in a letter: "Beg to advise, that work which you have done is satisfactory. If we can be of any assistance to you in getting another position, we will be very glad to do so."

Therefore, in early 1904, Marr was ripe for a new assignment. News of his departure from Reid traveled fast — Buick's letter to Marr was written only three days later. In his letter, David Buick asked Marr to phone or visit him at his Detroit home. While Buick spent the workweek in Flint, he lived in his family home on Meldrum in Detroit on weekends. Marr and Buick had a cordial visit there one day. They immediately agreed to work together again.

But Marr made a specific demand. Maybe he had begun to reflect on difficult relationships over the last few years, not only arguments with David Buick but also incidents and disagreements at

THE BUICK MOTOR COMPANY

MANUFACTURERS OF

AUTOMOBILES, STATIONARY, MARINE and AUTOMOBILE GAS and GASOLINE ENGINES

TRANSMISSION GEARS, SPARK PLUGS, CARBURETERS, ETC.

Flint, Mich._____Jan. 8th,_____190__4

Mr. Walter R. Marr,

    C/o J. P. Schneider,

        Jefferson & Bates ,

           Detroit, Mich.

Friend Marr:-

      I have just learned that you have severed your

connections with the Reed Manufacturing Company. If you have

not succeeded in obtaining a position would be pleased to have

you call at my home on Sunday afternoon or call me up on the

phone, East 120.

           Yours truly,

                   The Buick Motor Co.

                Per D.D.Buick

On January 8, 1904, David Buick is ready to invite Walter Marr back.

Oldsmobile, American Motor Carriage, Marr Autocar and possibly Reid Manufacturing. It was time to take a gentler tack.

He told David they must have an enlightened relationship: "I come back with this understanding, Mr. Buick — If I'm hot I'll wait till I cool off to talk; if you're hot, you wait till you've cooled off." Or, as Marr told Charles Hulse, he wanted both to agree that in any dispute they would wait until the next day "when reasoning power has returned to both." By April of 1904, Marr was working with David Buick in Flint (and he would remain at the Buick firm into retirement, and beyond). And, no surprise, by the first week in June, 1904, a new Buick automobile was being driven around the company's yards.

Marr's story is he persuaded Whiting to build automobiles. Whiting was at first disinterested, but agreed to think about it if Marr could drive a car to Detroit and back, touching certain points along the way. While Whiting likely wanted to build an automobile from Day One, he was cautious as a businessman. He may also have feigned reluc-

Arthur W. Hough: Early car builder worked at Buick from 1906 to 1946.

tance so the other directors would believe he was being prudent and conservative.

It's not clear how much help Buick and Marr had. Arthur W. Hough, who claimed in published articles to have built six automobiles in Perry, Mich., between 1900 and 1906, said Buick and Marr were experimenting in Detroit when they heard of the Hough cars. Hough said he used a one-cylinder Buick engine he obtained from David Buick in Detroit for an automobile he built in 1903. In his fifth and sixth cars, built in 1905 and 1906, he used the Buick Model B two-cylinder engines "because they had a lot of power to get up and go." (Hough was also said to have been a test driver for A.B.C. Hardy's Flint roadsters).

According to Hough, Buick and Marr asked him to come to Detroit. But by the time he was ready to drive his car there, he received word to go to Flint instead — Buick and Marr had moved there. Hough sold one of his cars to Buick Motor Company and in May of 1905 David Buick talked him into taking a job in Buick's experimental department in Jackson. He worked at Buick until his retirement in 1946 at age 82.

On one of his first visits to Flint after selling his car to Buick, Hough said he saw it parked at a hitching post on Saginaw Street, the city's main street. He found the owner in a store and asked how the car was working. The man, who had bought it from Buick, said it performed flawlessly and wondered: "Why do you ask?" Hough replied: "Oh, I just built it, that's all. And I was wondering if it was standing up."

It's unlikely Hough had any influence on the development of the earliest Buicks. But some details on building the first Flint Buick are recorded. Bert Calver, a Flint Wagon Works assembler, remembered both the excitement and the difficulty of building it. "All of us were pretty excited to be working on the very first [Flint] Buick," he told Ben Bennett of the *Flint News-Advertiser* in 1953.

"They just came in and told us one day that we were going to work on the Buick. They gave us some blueprints to go by but a lot of the design had to be made up as went along."

First, wagon works craftsmen created a body of wood. (Later, the W. F. Stewart Company made the bodies and the Flint Wagon Works upholstered and painted them.) Then they built the frame and chassis from huge angle irons. Springs and axles were brought from Armstrong Spring and Axle Company across town. They were hauled over in Bert Armstrong's 1902 curved-dash Oldsmobile, remembered James Parkhill, Armstrong's successor as the firm's president.

"Whenever we got stuck," said Calver, "we just did things the way we had done them with buggies. Sounds funny to say that we lined up the wheels with an old pine yardstick and the frame with a piece of string, but that's the way we did it — same as we'd lined up thousands of buggies.

"There was no such thing as welding, so all the parts had to be joined with rivets. And none of the bolts we used were cut to size. We just went to the barrel and hunted around for bolts we thought might fit. And if they were too long, we just cut them off."

The engine was too large for the frame so workers hacked at the angle irons with cold chisels for hours to make room. Then they car-

David Buick (left) and Walter Marr at work at Buick Motor Company, a rare candid photo.

ried the frame and motor to the Buick plant. "It was just across the street," Calver said. "But it was a job."

William Beacraft's notes said the engine was ready for the car on May 27, 1904. On June 4, *The Wolverine Citizen* reported "the first automobile to be made by the Buick Motor Works was finished this week."

But even as this first Flint Buick car was being conceived and created, the Buick Model B engine, already in production, was earning a reputation for power. Companies building the Dolson car in Charlotte, Mich., the Jackson in Jackson, Mich., and the Sommer and Wayne in Detroit contracted with Buick to provide engines though it's unknown when they actually bought and installed them.

Individuals also took advantage of the opportunity to trade up to a Buick engine. Charles Hulse pointed out Flint's automobile culture had not been waiting on Buick. By the spring of 1903, some of Flint's wealthy young men, such as carriage maker William Paterson's son, Will, and William C. Orrell, a cousin of Billy Durant, were buying red Wintons and causing such a nuisance with their noise frightening horses that local citizens called them the "Red Devils." Even Durant, noting his cousin had an automobile, huffed about the "noisy contraptions." The future founder of General Motors said he was "mighty provoked with anyone who would drive around annoying people that way."

About a month after young Paterson bought a Winton in April 1903, four new 1903 Thomas touring cars, all painted bright red, arrived in Flint by train for local citizens William Wildanger, Francis Flanders, George V. Cotharin and Harry W. Watson. The "Red Devils" were growing in numbers as well as notoriety.

By July of 1904, Cotharin had concluded his Thomas's one-cylinder engine was so weak "it wouldn't pull a hen off a nest." Cotharin took the car to the Buick plant and had the engine replaced with a new two-cylinder Buick Model B engine. In 1909 apparently this same car showed up in the St. Louis, Mo., railroad station, serving as a photographer's prop for years. Its 1904 pushrods-on-bottom Buick engine is one of the two survivors from that year, today the centerpiece of a Model B Buick car created with a complete body. (Thomas engines later got better. In 1908, a Thomas Flyer won the famous New York-to-Paris "Great Race").

For a time, David Buick was the company's spokesman with the press. On May 21, 1904, he told the *Flint Daily News* the company was employing a day shift of 90 men and a night force of 50. "This has been a banner week since we began operations," Buick said. "We turned out 22 completed engines this week and have more orders than we can fill."

On June 18, he complained to the same paper about being overworked. "I miss my half holiday on Saturdays since I came to Flint," Buick said. "When I was in Detroit, our factory, the Buick & Sherwood plant, never operated on Saturday afternoons. I am a great believer in the Saturday half holiday, and would like to see it adopted by the manufacturers in Flint."

Whiting and the Flint Wagon Works directors might well have been puzzled to see that quote in the newspaper from the Buick company's leader.

On Saturday, July 9, the first Flint Buick automobile was ready for its big test. It didn't look ready, lacking body and fenders. "One of the new Buick autos was on the streets this afternoon and attracted considerable favorable attention," *The Flint Journal* reported. "The machine was not wholly completed but from its speed it looks as though the Buick will cut quite a figure in the auto world when the company gets to turning them out in greater numbers."

Walter Marr and Buick's son, Tom, were aboard, wearing dusters and caps and goggles. About 1:15 p.m., they left the Bryant House hotel in downtown Flint, with Marr driving, and headed south on a 90-mile test drive to Detroit via Lapeer. A rear bearing failed near Lapeer, so they stayed the night there and fixed the bearing. They arrived in Detroit at noon the next day, Sunday, July 10, "covered with mud and grime," according to Hulse. Since both men were from Detroit, they spent the day visiting relatives and friends. While Marr visited several local auto plants and took notes on Monday, Tom Buick went to city hall and paid $1 to buy car license No. 1024. They headed back to Flint Tuesday.

This ride of July 12, 1904, would be remembered in the annals of Buick. A steady rain deepened the mud in the roads, but the car ran well, averaging 30 miles per hour. "I did the driving and Buick was kept busy wiping the mud off my goggles," said Marr. When an electric car showed up to challenge them in one town, the Buick "showed them the way," Marr said. In another town, "we went so fast...we could not see the village six-mile-an-hour sign," he said. Had he been ticketed? The question was not asked or answered.

"At one place, going down a hill, I saw a bump at a bridge too late to slow up. When I hit it, I threw on all the power and landed over it safely in the road. Buick was just taking a chew of tobacco, and a lump of mud as large as a baseball hit him square in the face, filling his mouth completely. We were plastered with mud from head to foot when we reached Flint."

The route was 115 miles instead of about 90, because Marr missed a turn at Lapeer. They covered it in 217 minutes. Marr declared that was a record. Marr drove directly to the office of *The Flint Journal* and told a reporter: "The machine made the run without a skip. It reached here in the best of condition. We took the hills handily with our high-speed gear and the machine sounded like a locomotive. It simply climbed."

The impressed reporter, noting Marr's words and the mud-caked appearance of the men and car, tapped out this lead: "Bespattered with flying real estate from every county they had touched, but with the knowledge that they had made a 'record,' Tom Buick and W.L. Marr, of the Buick Motor Works, who left for Detroit on Saturday to give the first automobile turned out by that concern a trial on the road, returned to the city late yesterday afternoon. The test of the machine was eminently satisfactory, and, in fact, exceeded expectations."

The two men posed in the Buick for a memorable photo by professional photographer Charles Quay on E. First Street between Saginaw Street and Brush Alley downtown, almost in front of *The Journal* office, and then for another on the mud-rutted roadway at the one-story brick factory. (Quay, writing to Charles Hulse in 1956, said he had known the Buick family since its Buick & Sherwood days in Detroit and also had taken photos of Flint Wagon Works and Durant-Dort vehicles for those firms. "Tom Buick and I used to go out together to photograph the Buick climbing hills," he recalled.)

Upon their return from Detroit, the two found Whiting and his associates waiting with the decision David Buick and Marr had wanted. When Marr told the little group, "We're here," they responded, "So are we," meaning they would finance the beginning of automobile production. The Buick would go to market.

Hulse interviewed Marr in 1934 and asked him why the road test was necessary. Marr replied:

> When I came to Flint in April of 1904, and joined the Buick company, their main line of business was the building of stationary gasoline engines. Mr. Whiting, who had the 'say-so' in the company, carried the thinking that the money was to be made in the engine business. He thought so many firms had got into the automobile business that the market would soon be saturated with cars.
>
> I told Whiting that my interest was in the building of automobiles and that we could make a successful car at the Buick. After several approaches to Whiting on this subject, he finally relented and told me that if I could build up a sample model and prove that it had good possibilities then he would reconsider the idea of Buick building automobiles. After our successful road test run to Detroit, Mr. Whiting gave the go-ahead to build up a few cars to see how they would sell.

In the best known of all Buick historical photos, Walter Marr (above) drives the first Flint Buick back into Flint July 12, 1904, after making a test run to Detroit. David Buick's son Tom (above right) joined him on the round trip. The photo was taken on E. First Street near Brush Alley. The Flint Journal office is in the background at right. Later in the day (below), Marr, Tom Buick and the same car are at the new Buick factory on W. Kearsley.

This license form appears to have been signed in Detroit by Tom Buick on July 11, 1904, during the test run. But it may be just a blank form filled in by an early Buick history buff based on known information.

Like a number of other auto pioneers, David Buick boasted of his vision of the future of the automobile. He probably wrote the biographical sketch in 1913 that noted in a discussion with officers of his company in 1903 or early 1904 "he declared with enthusiasm that the end of twenty years would find only the surface of the business scratched — that in time horse-drawn vehicles would be little more than reminders of a past age. In his mind's eye he could see the immense traffic of the automobile as it is known today...." Buick's comments on cars were now much more bullish than his thoughts of 1910 (Page 84).

More photos were taken later in the summer of the first production Buick automobile alongside the one-story brick Buick factory. These were hardly glamour shots. The car sits in a rutted yard or road with bits of wood and other debris visibly sticking out of the mud. Bicycles are leaning against the factory wall, a man is peering out a plant window and a woman is watching the photographer from the factory porch. Several telephone poles complete the image.

There is one of the unoccupied car, with a sign propped against the running board ("Buick Motor Co., Flint, Mich."). There is one with Marr at the wheel, alone in the car. And still another with the dignitaries — usually identified as Marr and Tom Buick in the front seats, James Whiting and Buick's new president, Charles Begole, in the rear. (One researcher suggests the man identified as Tom may

114

actually be David Buick. Certainly David should have been posed with the other leaders, rather than his son. If so, it would be the only known photo of David Buick with a Buick car. But Tom often filled in for his father and a close look at the photo is inconclusive).

As for the first Flint Buicks, Marr is seen as the expert in putting together an entire automobile correctly. But Hugh Dolnar, who in 1904 wrote the first Buick test-ride report, credited David Buick for the body. David, he wrote, "conceived the happy idea of hinging the side entrance doors in front. This gives two distinct advantages, first, a good substantial door hinge, and second, in connection with the full-length running board, the swinging of the door to the front gives the easiest possible entrance to the tonneau seats." No suicide doors for Buick.

Marr and his engine superintendent were so confident in the Model B that he and Mason each drove one to the track at Grosse Pointe, Mich., on August 27, 1904. For the first time ever, Buicks were in a race. Marr finished third behind Frank Kulick in the famous Ford 999 and W. F. Winchester in a Franklin. Mason was fourth. Not an overly impressive start, perhaps, but the Buick would soon do much better. (David Buick skipped the race, instead taking his wife and younger son Wynton on a weekend holiday). Also that month, David told reporters the original business had grown so much that two stories and a test shed would be added to the one-story factory, which happened in 1905. An ad in *The Implement Age* of September 22, 1904, said the plant was capable of turning out 2,600 engines per year and "we want agents in every town." There was optimism everywhere.

The first Flint Buick to be sold was bought by a 23-year-old Flint physician, Herbert H. Hills. The son of a lumberman from nearby Davison, he bought it for $500 on July 27, 1904, per Dolnar, or August 13, per Hills' diary. As Dolnar noted, Hills had driven it day and night continually without incident up until September 16, when Dolnar arrived at Flint, "and believes he has the best car in the world."

Actually, Hills remembered there were a few problems. He carried a hairpin when driving so he could quickly clean the spark plugs. "There was something wrong with the piston rings, they couldn't keep soot from getting out of the cylinder and covering the plugs," he recalled in a 1953 interview with the *Flint News-Advertiser.*

And once, when he couldn't start the car for an early morning trip, he ran to the railroad station, caught a horse taxi to Walter Marr's house on E. Kearsley Street and called until Marr woke up. As Hills recalled, Marr "leaned out the window and said, 'Hello, doc. What's the trouble?' I told him the car had stopped and he said to give him time to put on pants and a shirt and he'd be right down." Hills took the interurban to his destination, and Marr took the car. It was discovered water had gotten into the gasoline. "It probably isn't as common these days to wake up the chief engineer of Buick to fix your car," Hills commented in 1953.

The doctor was also impressed by the car's light weight. "I could lift the rear end by myself," he said. "That certainly came in handy changing tires. I'd just lift up the rear end and slide the jack in underneath."

Dolnar reported Hills' car was the July 9-12 test car now completed with full body and fenders. But the *Flint Daily News* on July 29, 1904, said the car "that made the fast run to Detroit and back three weeks ago" had been shipped to Chicago the previous day. And years later Marr said that on a visit to Chicago in the 1920s, he saw that Buick's engine being used to pump water.

The company turned out 16 Buicks, Model Bs, in the summer of 1904 by the time Dolnar (pen name for Horace Arnold), writing for *Cycle and Automobile Trade Journal,* arrived in town. Orders for 11 more were on the books. Dolnar was given his test ride the following morning, September 17. This car was a newly built model, not yet test driven.

Tom Buick took the wheel, and Dolnar took notes: "At first, Buick drove with some decent regard for law and prudence. But the road was hard, the clear air was intoxicating, and after one request to 'push her' up one steep hill, which the car mounted at 25 miles speed, Buick began to be proud of his mount and drive for fun...The car simply ran to perfection...the car flew down the hills and flew up the hills, all the same rate, and the engine purred and the wind whistled past and the soft September sun smiled benignly on the fine farms we ran by, and it was all delightful." Even though a policeman stopped Buick, fined him $12 for fast driving, and told him it would be more next time.

The drive was obviously a critical success. Dolnar found the Buick car "thoroughly responsive; had more power everywhere than could be used."

A statement in Dolnar's article that the Buick generated more than 20 horsepower was "very generally questioned," he wrote in

Walter Marr (left) and David Buick: Another rare candid photo of the two at work together.

a later issue. So he ran more tests and concluded "the power of the Buick motor was not less than first stated...and can give about 29 brake horse power at 1320 crank-shaft turns per minute." Chiding his critics, he continued that his account "should be accepted as showing that those reputable gas-engine builders who assert that not more than 16 B.H. P. can be had from a pair of 4 1/2x5 opposed cylinders are more familiar with their own motors than with the Buick model under test, and that while the writer is, unfortunately, compelled to do work in haste, he is not wrong in the stories he tells."

In its 1905 catalog, Buick made much of the notion Dolnar's original report had "startled the whole mechanical world." In October 1904, Buick's first automobile ad stated: "In a class by itself. Actual 21 Brake Horse Power on the stand. Experienced drivers can get the same on the road."

Hugh Dolnar's words of September 17, 1904, would have been a fine birthday present for David Buick, who turned 50 that very day (though the review didn't show up until the October issue). But despite the great publicity of that review, reality had dawned on James Whiting: Starting an automobile manufacturing operation chewed up huge amounts of money compared with the carriage industry. Also, he had discovered, David Buick was no business leader. The directors had invested $37,500 during the startup, and the company had

First Buick Model B in the summer of 1904, with the Flint Buick factory in the background. From left, front seat, are Walter Marr and Tom Buick. From left, rear seat, are Charles Begole and, in a straw hat, James Whiting. Whiting brought Buick to Flint in 1903 and Begole became Buick president later in 1904.

not only exhausted that but owed $25,000 each to three Flint banks. Even the stationary engines, for which Buick salesmen had received large orders, were not being produced fast enough.

On the surface, Buick Motor Company looked as if it were on the brink of success. But that was far from true. In fact, Whiting once admitted, it was insolvent. He figured it needed two things — a younger man to run the business and more money.

During a meeting of carriage makers in Chicago, Whiting discussed his problems with Fred A. Aldrich, secretary of Flint's largest carriage firm, the Durant-Dort Carriage Company. The actual conversation was recalled by Aldrich at age 92 in the *Flint News-Advertiser's* Buick 50th anniversary edition of January 7, 1953. The year is 1904 and Aldrich and Whiting are visiting in the lobby of the Hotel Congress in Chicago:

Dr. Herbert H. Hills, first buyer of a Flint production Buick, with his car. In September of 1904, Hills would use it to give Billy Durant his first ride in a Buick.

"We were sitting on a couch in the hotel and Jim [Whiting] was complaining about [David] Buick and the manner in which he was trying to conduct the new business. I thought Mr. W. C. Durant might be helpful as he was footloose in New York, where he was spending much of his time..."

Aldrich cautioned that Durant was preoccupied with the stock market in New York and he didn't like automobiles much. But he was a booster of Flint, he seemed to have access to money from Wall Street and he had a lot of friends and relatives whose finances were tied up in those Flint banks.

Recalled Aldrich: "I suggested to Whiting that Durant might work out a solution, and that I would like to have them have a talk. When he came to Flint I got them together. This meeting resulted in Mr. Whiting giving Mr. Durant the authority to reorganize the company."

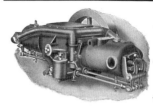

The Buick 12 H. P. Motor

We also Manufacture Transmissions of Planetary and Sliding Gear Type

ARE
YOU SUCCESSFUL?
YOU
WILL BE
IF YOU USE THIS ENGINE
IN
THE CONSTRUCTION OF YOUR CARS
NEED
YOU WAIT?
LET US KNOW YOUR REQUIREMENTS

THE BUICK MOTOR CO., Manufacturers of Automobile, Stationary and Marine Engines

One of Buick's earliest automotive logos was "The Car of Quality," (above). Early ad for two-cylinder valve-in-head engine (above right). First Buick automobile ad, in Cycle and Automobile Trade Journal, *October 1904 (right). Model B ads in same publication in November (below left) and December (below right) of 1904. Note the only major change in the illustration is the wider brass molding over the radiator in December.*

1905 "BUICK" MODEL "B"

In a class by itself

Has no equal

Agents Wanted

Actual 21 Brake Horse Power on the stand. Experienced drivers can get same on the road 1675 lbs. actual weight Climbs all hills on high gear

BUICK MOTOR CO., FLINT, MICH.

BUICK 1905 MODEL "B"

THE CAR OF QUALITY

ACTUAL 21 BRAKE HORSE POWER ON THE STAND

Double cylinder opposed engine lengthwise with the frame. Planetary transmission with cone clutch, two speeds forward and reverse.

Simple in control. Can travel from 4 to 25 miles per hour with high speed clutch in by touching a button with the foot.

PRICE, $950.00 F.O.B. FACTORY

Secure this car now for your next year's business.

Agents wanted everywhere.

BUICK MOTOR CO. Flint, Michigan

BUICK 1905 MODEL "B"

THE CAR OF QUALITY

ACTUAL 21 BRAKE HORSE POWER ON THE STAND

Double cylinder opposed engine lengthwise with the frame. Planetary transmission with cone clutch, two speeds forward and reverse.

Simple in control. Can travel from 4 to 25 miles per hour with high speed clutch in by touching a button with the foot.

Secure this car now for your next year's business.

Agents wanted everywhere.

BUICK MOTOR CO. Flint, Michigan

Chapter 12

The irrepressible Billy Durant

As he studied his options for financial help, James H. Whiting decided he would have no problem reaching out to a competitor. After all, by 1904 William C. Durant was already a magical name in Flint. Grandson of a Michigan governor of the Civil War era, Henry Howland Crapo, Durant was a latecomer to Flint's carriage industry, but he quickly surpassed them all.

On a September evening in 1886, the young businessman hitched a ride in friend Johnny Alger's horse-drawn road cart in downtown Flint. Captivated with the way its patented spring suspension cushioned the bumps, he immediately took a train to Coldwater, Mich., where the cart was manufactured, and bought the rights to build it.

Durant was a very personable young man, about 5-foot-8, slim and often flashing a dazzling smile. He moved quickly and, as a 1931 voice recording reveals, spoke with a clipped Boston accent, a holdover from his childhood. Durant had been about 10 when he moved with his family from Boston to Flint. His actions and speech radiated energy and confidence. He was a natural salesman, trying his hand at patent medicine, cigars and insurance, while running the Flint Water Works on the side.

In 1886, when he needed money to close the deal with the Coldwater Road Cart Company, he avoided banks where his family had influence because "if I make a failure of the venture, I will never hear the end of it." So he went to another bank, Citizens National, where he had no problem persuading its president, Robert J. Whaley, to loan him $2,000 on a 90-day renewable note.

Durant quickly found a partner — friend Josiah Dallas Dort, who put in $1,000 he borrowed from his mother. (In Whaley's restored home in Flint, the original Citizens National bank book of the Flint Road Cart Company is displayed, with the first entries of September

28, 1886, being deposits of $1,000 each by Durant and Dort — the first document in a series of events that led to the creation of General Motors).[1]

Then he shipped the best of his two road carts, which had been built by the Coldwater firm, to a big fair in Wisconsin, and began to work. To Durant, the road cart was a "self-seller," and he was confident nobody could match him in selling a genuinely appealing product. His self-confidence was not misplaced. Even though his sample road cart showed up very late at the fair, Durant took orders for an astonishing 600 carts, at the fair and during train stops on the way home, before he had built one. Back in Flint, he contracted with the best local carriage maker, William A. Paterson, to build 1,200 carts at $12.50 each. He figured he could sell them for nearly twice that.

By the turn of the century his Flint Road Cart Company, renamed in 1895 as the Durant-Dort Carriage Company, was said to be the leading volume producer of horse-drawn vehicles in the United States. Durant had pulled together suppliers from across the country and had created what automotive historians would someday label "the General Motors of the carriage era." It was a giant concern and Dallas Dort called Durant "easily our leading force and genius."

In 1904, Durant, though only 42, was semi-retired from the carriage industry and playing the stock market in New York. Like most carriage leaders, he was no fan of automobiles. A.B.C. Hardy, who had been president of the Durant-Dort Carriage Company before building Hardy Flint roadsters, remembered going to a carriage convention in New York along with about 350 other participants, including fellow Flintites Whiting, Durant and Dort. They were all offered an opportunity to take a side trip to ride in a horseless carriage. Hardy said only he and Whiting jumped at the chance "to see and ride in those strange contraptions." When he asked Durant why he didn't try them out, Durant said banker friends had told him automobiles "were

---

1 While Durant would always be the promotional genius of their carriage businesses and then their early automobile ventures, Dallas Dort was his anchor — the leader who handled the overall job and details of managing the financial and manufacturing operations, including labor and Flint civic duties. As Arthur Pound once quoted Durant's lawyer, John J. Carton: "Billy never thought that GM would become the big manufacturer it did. What he desired, most of all, were large stock issues in which he, from an inside position, could dicker and trade. After Billy left Durant-Dort for Buick there were always too many yes men around him for his own good. Dallas Dort and Charlie Nash and Fred Aldrich and the rest of them in Durant-Dort could bring Billy down to earth. Away from them he just soared, high, wide and handsome."

Famous portrait of Billy Durant was pulled from candid photo (right) of Durant greeting John O. Heinze, president of Lowell (Mass.) Automobile Club in 1909, probably during a "speed festival" at Lowell which included Buick racing team. Buick's Bob Burman won one major race there, the Vesper Cup for light cars. Burman also won a class event and Buick's Louis Chevrolet won three class events.

to be sold to rich men for their foolish sons, and that some doctors were buying them."

Hardy went to Europe, learned of the bustling automobile industry there, and came back to Durant with a warning he should get out of the horse-drawn vehicle business. "Billy, there is something coming that will sweep it away," Hardy said. "Get into this horseless carriage field...."

Durant, always polite and patient, listened carefully, and then said: "We have more business than we can handle. Ours is a permanent business, and we are going to add another factory."

But enthusiasm for automobiles was beginning to take off, even in the carriage capital of Flint, and even among relatives of the carriage king. Arthur Jerome Eddy, who had grown up in Flint and mar-

123

A.B.C. Hardy (left), Flint's first car manufacturer, with W.C. Durant and wife Catherine.

ried Durant's cousin, Lucy Crapo Orrell, was a Chicago lawyer when in 1901 he wrote a book, *Two Thousand Miles on an Automobile,* using only the pen name "Chauffeur." It was an account of his incredible long-distance trip in an unidentified car (it was a one-cylinder, 8 ½ -horsepower Winton). Eddy drove out of Chicago on August 1, 1901, and on to Boston, New York City and Albany. He then returned through Canada to Sarnia, Ontario, and on to Flint to visit his parents. The roads, he reported, were best in Canada, worst in Michigan. He then drove to Montreal and had the car shipped back to Chicago. For 1901 it was a stunning adventure, said to be the longest auto trip yet taken in the United States.

Eddy's conclusion: "Any woman can drive an electric automobile, any man can drive a steam; but neither man nor woman can

One of the first 16 Model Bs of 1904 on the road, here with William Beacraft, Buick engine production foreman, and his family. Beacraft bought it in 1907 from E. E. Edwards, a Flint wholesale grocer, the second person in Flint to buy a Buick.

drive a gasoline; it follows its own odorous will and goes or goes not as it feels disposed."

In 1902, Eddy, by then the owner of a Panhard and visiting his parents again, gave rides to a number of Flint citizens, notably Dallas Dort. Durant's daughter Margery also got a ride in the car. When she raced into the house to tell her father of her exciting adventure, Durant scolded her for taking a foolish chance.

Clearly, the prospect of selling an automobile concern to Durant would be daunting for Whiting. But if he wanted to save Buick Motor Company, he needed to be persuasive with his case. Durant was not only a great salesman but he also had no peer as an organizer and promoter. And with his connections, he could put Wall Street money behind a product. As Fred Aldrich, the Durant-Dort secretary, remembered, he advised Whiting: "William C. Durant is the man who can put Buick on its feet." Whiting, working through Aldrich and Durant's partner, Dallas Dort, asked him to come home and take a look at Buick.

So Durant returned to Flint in the fall of 1904. Although he was admittedly dubious about automobiles, he was loyal to Flint and

Billy Durant (left) and Dallas Dort talk outside Buick headquarters in Flint, with Imperial Wheel in background. The building below is the Durant-Dort Carriage Company headquarters in Flint. It is now a National Historic Landmark, its offices tied to the birth of General Motors.

liked a good business challenge. Possibly more important, he was concerned Flint banks, where he and his many relatives and friends did business and had ownership, were being made vulnerable by their loans to Buick. And so he would check out the Buick proposition.

Dr. Herbert H. Hills gave Durant his first ride in a Buick on September 4, 1904, per Hills' diary. It's a story remembered by Hills himself in an interview shortly before his death in 1953. "We started off with Durant and me in the front seat, and Mrs. Durant and their daughter in the rear. We drove out East Kearsley Street, then one of the few paved streets in Flint, and Durant kept firing questions at me about how the car ran and if I liked it or not. We didn't talk about anything else the whole time." (Hills joined Buick as assistant sales manager in 1906 and left Buick for Packard in 1909).

As Donald E. Johnson, husband of Whiting's granddaughter, Alice, told the writer in the 1970s, Whiting then drove Durant around Flint, and they pulled up in front of Whiting's house and talked for an hour. When Whiting walked into his house, he told his family: "Billy's sold!"

Sam McLaughlin, longtime chairman of GM of Canada, told several versions of a different story. In his recollections, Durant revealed no intent to study the Buick proposition when he arrived back in Flint in the fall of 1904. McLaughlin said Marr drove one of the first Buicks to Durant's office, but Durant refused to ride in it. "Then later, Walter and Dave Buick drove it up and down past Mr. Durant's house all that evening, and then the next day induced Mr. Durant to go out in it for a ride."

Although the elderly McLaughlin, recalling this story to Buick General Manager Ed Rollert in a 1964 letter, wrongly remembered Marr came from Lansing with the car, he had known Durant from the carriage era and presented the anecdote as a well-known fact. He had provided more detail to Eric Hutton in *MacLean's* magazine 10 years earlier, relating that after Durant refused to even look at the car, Marr taught Dallas Dort how to drive it.

Dort returned to the office and said excitedly to Durant: "Come on out! It's great. They taught me how to drive. I've been driving a car!" To which Durant replied, "I want nothing to do with it."

But Marr kept driving the car back and forth in front of Durant's house, that evening and then the next morning (along with David Buick, according to McLaughlin's letter to Rollert). Durant, finally impressed with Marr's persistence if not the car, agreed to go for a

Durant lines up every Buick available at Saginaw and First streets in downtown Flint November 3, 1904 — his first publicity event after taking control two days earlier.

ride. According to McLaughlin, Durant then learned Marr was not trying to sell him a Buick car, but the Buick company!

All of this could be at least partially true, starting with Durant's first ride with Hills, coaxed into a second ride by Marr and Buick, and the clincher meeting with Whiting (though McLaughlin's memory, like Durant's, was at least occasionally more creative than entirely accurate).

There are also oft-repeated accounts of Durant taking the Buick out himself, test driving it around Flint. Durant put the Buick "through swamps, mud and sand and pitchholes for almost two months," wrote Arthur Pound in *The Turning Wheel.* Others are doubtful, characterizing Durant as a super salesman, super promoter and super organizer of big business, but no test driver.

But he should have driven the car and probably did. He was about to make an important decision. The master salesman needed to persuade himself this was indeed a great product. The roads around Flint were poor but the Buick engine was always up to the challenge. Durant became convinced. This car performed.

Dort once said Durant would have gotten into automobiles sooner or later because he was a gambler — he would have been in the thick of the California gold rush, or in railroads, in earlier times. Perhaps, but he certainly wouldn't have chosen such an unlikely enterprise as Buick had he not been persuaded by his friends and relatives in his adopted home town of Flint.

Now that he was enthusiastic about the product, Durant needed to find out how serious the stockholders were about placing the business on a sound financial footing. There was money in Flint — fortunes had been made in lumbering, carriages and even cigar-making. But it now needed to be invested in the new business in town. Buick

129

Buick factory on W. Kearsley after being expanded from one to three stories.

was important to the city's economy and it could not survive under-capitalized and heavily in debt.

Durant said his investigation of the firm in the fall of 1904 "ascertained that it was practically insolvent," agreeing with Whiting's assessment. However, he said in a 1911 legal document, he believed that if the business were "properly conducted and vigorously prosecuted, there was a fair prospect of bettering such condition."

Under Durant's prodding, Buick's stockholders agreed to increase the capital stock to $300,000 on November 1, 1904, and to raise it again to $500,000 on November 19. Of this, $175,000 would go to the stockholders and the remaining $325,000 would be turned over to Durant "as his sole individual property to be used by him in his sole judgment he deemed for the best interest of said company…," according to the legal document. Coincidentally (or maybe not), at virtually the same time, owners of the Flint Gas Light Company sold that firm to other interests for $325,000 and it is reported Durant persuaded the sellers to invest much of that money in Buick stock.

With the financial details agreed upon, finally the decision was made. On November 1, 1904, Durant was elected to the Buick board. He was now in charge but declined the presidency in favor of Charles Begole, a Flint Wagon Works director and son of a former Michigan governor, Josiah Begole. Whiting resigned to devote more time to the wagon works, but he would soon be working with Durant again.

General Motors celebrates its birth date as September 16, 1908, when the company was incorporated — but the real beginning of GM was November 1, 1904, when Billy Durant took control of Buick. This was the spark. Once Durant held control of Buick and properly capitalized the company, the great success story was launched.

The decision of the stockholders to agree to Durant's proposal is both a tribute to his reputation and a sign of how desperate they were to keep the company solvent. Their money and their trust were well placed. Durant quickly turned Buick around and made each share of stock a fabulous investment. The decision also quickened David Buick's long slide from power and influence.

As an immediate example of his showmanship, Durant created a Buick event on November 3, 1904, two days after taking control. He paraded eight Buicks — all he could find and several not yet completed — through downtown Flint "with tooting bugles...[creating] a great deal of attention and much favorable comment," *The Flint Daily News* reported. Another historic photo bearing Charles Quay's imprint captures the Buicks lined up at Saginaw and First streets, one of the city's main intersections.

Durant avoided one sticky problem by quietly obtaining a license late in the year so Buick could join the Association of Licensed Automobile Manufacturers. This was the organization that tried to control the industry under the patent of George B. Selden. The ALAM was blamed by A.B.C. Hardy for forcing his Flint Automobile Company out of business in 1903. Durant realized he would have to deal with the ALAM so he bought the failing Pope-Robinson Company and obtained its license. The ALAM's control was eventually ended thanks to the legal fight of Henry Ford, to the general relief of the industry as a whole.

1905 Model C with William C. Durant's daughter Margery. This was the first model Buick to combine the expertise of David Buick, Walter Marr and W.C. Durant.

Buick produced only 37 cars in 1904 (forget the incorrect old accounts that 16 were made in 1903; the first 16 were made between June 1904 and September 16, 1904). With Billy Durant aboard, the small number was meaningless. After all, local people still talked about how he had started in road carts, when he shipped one cart to a Wisconsin fair. There, he talked the judges into giving him a blue ribbon. He then took 600 orders for his "Famous Blue Ribbon Line" of carts before he had even figured out how to build them.[2]

2 Production numbers for Buick in 1903, 1904 and 1905 have often been confused. Here is the writer's version: Beyond the one experimental Buick built in Detroit by Walter Marr (1899-1901) and the second built in Detroit by David Buick for Ben Briscoe (1902-03), the first group of Buicks were 16 1904 Model Bs — the first production Buicks — built in Flint between early June and September 16, 1904, all but one built after mid July. No Buick was ever advertised as a 1904 model, but those cars were clearly 1904s. Among the 16 was the July 9-12 test car, later fitted with a body and sold. By the end of calendar 1904, 37 Buicks had been built, including those 16. At least some of the last 21 cars built in 1904

With Buick, he followed the same pattern. With fewer than 40 Buicks under the company's belt, Durant shipped a car and a chassis to the New York Auto Show of January 1905 and within a few days had accepted orders for 1,108 Buicks. As his wife Clara wrote to a friend: "The Buick certainly is a success." To Durant, the Buick, like his first road cart, was a "self seller" — a product so good it could sell itself. David Buick and Walter Marr had produced an automobile that was not only mechanically and cosmetically pleasing, but could navigate mud and steep hills like no other automobile he had ever seen.

Just as Durant had done with the road cart, he had backed a vehicle with a unique attribute (spring suspension with the road cart, overhead-valve engine with the Buick), emphasized the asset and made a large number of sales, largely because of his own engaging personality and relentless energy.

Durant immediately promoted engine performance. The company noted in a catalog, "the first conspicuous event that impressed the general public…was furnished on Thanksgiving Day (November 24, 1904) at Eagle Rock near Newark, New Jersey. That day marked America's greatest and severest hill-climbing contest."

The Motor World told the story: "In the class for cars between $850 and $1,250, the new Buick car made its initial appearance, and in a twinkling stamped itself as a wonder. It easily carried off the first honors in its class by a wide margin…the clean-cut and businesslike appearance of the car and its quiet running caused much favorable comment."

The Buick company pointed out the car was "not specially built or geared for hill climbing or for racing; it was a regular stock model" and driven by "a gentleman [dealer H. J. Koehler] who is in no sense a professional" whereas many of its competitors "were specially built or specially geared and driven by factory experts."

---

were advertised in the first Buick car ads as the 1905 Model B. In 1905, Buick built in Jackson, Mich., 750 Model Cs according to official records, but only 729 according to William Gregor, a later owner of a Model C who saw the official records before they disappeared. But if the 21 from late 1904 (assuming they are assigned as 1905 models) are added to the 729, the total is 750. According to official records, there was no 1905 Model B, but clearly such a model was advertised and presumably sold late in 1904. The designation was changed so quickly from Model B to Model C that the total may have just been folded into 1905 Model C production. It's also possible the number 750 was created merely by rounding off the numbers built in Jackson in 1905.

1905 Model C Buick, the official factory photo.

1905 Buick Model C owned by Elmer E. Souley family in downtown Flint, Mich.

Durant took David Buick with him to the New York show, and it became apparent other automobile writers had been reading about the Buick engine. The overhead-valve engine was news in New York.

134

Dealer drive-away of Model C Buicks in downtown Jackson in 1905.

The Motor World reported in its discussion of the show: "There is one newcomer which must command the attention of the public, the Buick, already famous for claims of wonderful development of horsepower from a relatively small engine...Twenty-two guaranteed horsepower from two 4 ½ by 5 cylinders is equal to, if not in excess of, the best performances by a motor of any kind."

The publication also interviewed the reticent David Buick. It reported: "Mr. Buick...very generally and in a very nice way explains why he is certainly getting more horsepower than engines of similar size." It followed with this explanation:

In the first place his valves, 1 7/8 inches in diameter, are at the end of the cylinder; the diameter given is generous. The gas as it enters, enters the piston clearance at the end of the piston immediately. His spark plug is on the side of the cylinder about midway between the pistons (should have said valves), at the top of the stroke and under the cylinder head. This puts his ignition point directly in the cylinder proper. Compare this with the fashionable type of valve chambers,

135

sometimes two or three inches from the cylinder pipe, and it is easily seen that quick burning of the gases is arrived at, with the pressure exerted quickly and immediately upon the pistons, and that all these points tend to give better efficiency. The fashionable type is good for a lot of things, but it is perfectly sure that the quicker you burn the gas the quicker you fill your cylinders, the better the horsepower achieved.

David and Tom were enthusiastic upon their return to Flint from New York on January 23, 1905. "The Buick car was the sensation in its class," said David. The car was to be exhibited that very week at the Philadelphia auto show.

Decades later, when an elderly Durant was attempting to write his autobiography, he unfortunately did not get around to writing the Buick chapter, though his outline did lay out plans for one. But he did manage to record one Buick anecdote — and it was about the engine.

Durant said a respected friend went on record opposing Durant's move into automobiles in general and Buick's two-cylinder valve-in-head "high-speed" motor in particular. So Durant hired an engine expert named Simmons who studied the Buick engine and came back with a report it was "basically unsound and extremely dangerous and was likely to explode." Trying to be funny, Simmons suggested that anyone who bought one of the engines should also buy a bushel basket to pick the pieces.

Durant noted the high-revving engine was "the product of Arthur Mason," Buick's production manager. Durant recalled Mason became annoyed as he listened to Simmons. Finally Mason responded: "This motor is the culmination of long study, experiments and sleepless nights and I have the utmost confidence in it." Mason then started the engine and put his head alongside. "If it explodes," he said, "I might as well go with it." Simmons left in a huff.

Durant concluded: "Needless to say Mason's work was crowned by a great success and was largely responsible for Buick's quick recognition as a leading motorcar, and his theory adopted by automobile manufacturers all over the world."

The story is repeated as one of Durant's few written Buick remembrances, but its accuracy is questionable. Mason appears to be now getting too much credit for the Buick engine. Whatever happened to the earlier work of David Buick, Walter Marr and Eugene Richard? The story also has a made-up quality that sounds like a shortened version of Dolnar's claims and critics. Further, Durant named the respected friend who first warned him as Col. William McCreery, a prominent local figure who was a hero for escaping the Confederate Libby Prison during the Civil War. Durant was a young admirer of McCreery, and no doubt wanted him in his autobiography. But in fact McCreery had died on December 9, 1896 — nearly a decade before he could possibly have talked to Durant about Buick engines.

By 1905, David Buick and his family were getting settled in Flint. The family had moved to that city in September of 1904, leasing a house from businessman Flint P. Smith at E. Kearsley and Stevens streets, and selling his place on Meldrum in Detroit by year's end.

In June of 1905, Flint's civic leaders created a big celebration in honor of its 50th anniversary as a city. Tom Buick was on the Committee on New Flint along with James H. Whiting, William S. Ballenger and Charles W. Nash. (The event's Reception Committee included Billy Durant, his attorney, John J. Carton, carriage maker William A. Paterson and Flint banker Arthur G. Bishop).

A highlight of the Golden Jubilee was a parade down Saginaw Street with U.S. Vice President Charles W. Fairbanks waving to the large crowd from a carriage. Carl Crow, in *The City of Flint Grows Up,* pointed out "one of the features of the parade was a new car driven by a daughter of Dave Buick, one of the first women in the United States to drive a car."

Crow added a personal observation: "A local reporter was so excited by this unusual spectacle that he described the car as being filled with yellow chrysanthemums. This does not appear probable for the parade was held in June — some months before chrysanthemums were in bloom. The reporter's error was unimportant…" The reporter's error was nonexistent. A photo of the parade unmistakably shows two 1905 Model C Buicks covered with the flowers.

Indeed, Buick's elder daughter, Frances Jane, won an award for her decoration of the car. Her younger sister, Mabel Lucille, drove the Buick in the parade. Frances Jane was a passenger along with Miss Jennie Dullam and a Miss Fenton. The second flower-bedecked Buick, just behind Mabel's car in the photo, was driven by Flint P. Smith, who had bought it in April.

But David's time in the sun in the Buick organization was growing short. Before the end of 1905, it became apparent Durant was beginning to lean more on Marr than on David for mechanical expertise. Late in the year, Durant and Carton needed to list the assets that would justify a boost in Buick's capitalization from $500,000 to $1.5 million. Finding himself $60,000 short when he added them up, Car-

David Buick's daughter Fanny won an award for her decoration of this Buick Model C (above), covered with chrysanthemums for the 1905 Golden Jubilee parade celebrating Flint's 50th year as a city. Her sister, Mabel, at the wheel, was the driver in the parade (below). Behind Mabel's car, another Model C, this one covered with roses, is being driven by its owner, Flint P. Smith. The parade featured U.S. Vice President Charles W. Fairbanks.

138

ton assigned that amount of value to contracts between Durant and Marr for "the exclusive use by said W. C. Durant of improvements in explosive engine construction, invented by said Walter L. Marr, but on account of business reasons not patented..." Carton's use of Marr's name, rather than David Buick's, made it clear Marr was now recognized within the company as its mechanical innovator.

(The language for such intangible assets, by the way, was questionable. But Carton's excellent connections in Michigan government allowed the explanation to stand. Carton had been speaker of the House in the state Legislature in 1901 and 1903 and would be president of the state Constitutional Convention of 1907-08.)

There was also no question about who was in charge at Buick Motor Company. William Beacraft remembered the situation when he arrived in Flint in late 1903 as Arthur Mason's engine foreman and master mechanic, at a time the company had only 40 employees: "We were just struggling along then, and it was not until the second week of my arrival that I hired an assistant. In the spring of 1904 we put out our first cars....Our first thought then was whether we could sell the cars when we made them, but this soon reversed itself to: how can we get them out fast enough to supply the demand?

"It was when W. C. Durant took hold that the company was reorganized and took on new life.... In those days we were so busy that I used to sleep in the shop, but we never could keep up with the demand..."

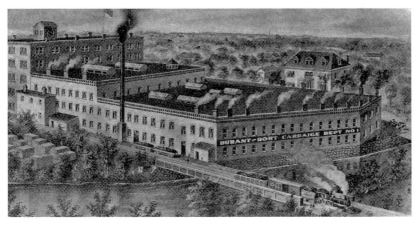

Durant-Dort Carriage Co., Flint, 1904 view, where GM founder Billy Durant first built vehicles (horse carts) in 1880s and had his office (dormered building background, now a National Historic Landmark) when he took over Buick in 1904. In 2013, surviving Durant-Dort plants at right, including Flint Road Cart Co. factory (adjacent to tall smoke stack), were bought by GM for development as GM's historic birthplace (page 225).

139

Building on the success of the Model C of 1905, Buick introduced a slightly improved version, the Model F, for 1906 (top). Other noteworthy Buick models of the next several years were the Model D of 1907 (middle), one of four new Buicks that year with four-cylinder engines, and the popular Model 10 of 1908 (bottom).

Chapter 13

Buick thrives, but where's the founder?

With Billy Durant in control of Buick Motor Company, the next few years were charged with energy. As Ben Briscoe wrote in 1921, the period after Durant's 1904 takeover was "so fraught with romance that it made the Arabian Nights look commonplace."

As for David Buick, it's ironic he was overshadowed by Durant and virtually becomes lost in the historical record, because his name would hardly be remembered at all if Durant hadn't built the company into a giant.

Though engine production remained in Flint, Durant moved Buick's assembly operations in early 1905 to a large and vacant plant owned by the Durant-Dort Carriage Company in Jackson, Mich. About 750 Model C Buicks were built in Jackson that year.

Durant used some of the $325,000 in stock he had been given by the shareholders to finance the move to Jackson. He transferred $101,000 to Whiting and $22,000 to Begole in exchange for their personal management of the Buick company. Whiting took charge of Buick in Jackson and Begole helped manage the Jackson and Flint operations.

(Whiting was later criticized by Ballenger and several other stockholders who filed a legal complaint in 1911 contending Whiting had cut a secret deal with Durant at the time Whiting was helping Durant raise capitalization to $500,000. Both Whiting and Durant denied it. Durant said it was only after he gained control of Buick that he realized he needed management help and in December of 1904 arranged with Whiting to go to Jackson to manage operations there and with Begole to help manage the firm in Flint as well as Jackson).

Durant turned over some of his Buick stock to the Durant-Dort Carriage Company, partly in payment for use of the Jackson plant, and partly because, as he pointed out, he was promoting Buick on the carriage company's time. According to the respected auto writer W. A. P. John, Durant used the rest to get Buick out of debt. "When the banks were extricated and all obligations settled, only $75,000 of the

$500,000 remained. And it was from this specific picayune sum that the whole of General Motors, with its countless millions, sprang," John wrote in *Motor* magazine in January 1923.

Early in 1905, after the move of Buick assembly to Jackson, Durant raised another $500,000, mostly from his business associates in Flint, to build a gargantuan complex of factories on Flint's north side. Most of the financial supporters, Durant pointed out, had never ridden in an automobile.

They came up with the money to assure Durant would move the whole Buick business back to Flint – and not leave it at Jackson or move it to Bay City, a serious contender. "I walked all over Bay City," Durant told a friend. "I talked with business men I had once sold cigars to. I talked with men who were working in lumber mills and in small factories. I visited the waterfront and determined that the harbor was available for shipping in raw material...and that finished automobiles could be shipped to distant places by barge and boat...I made an offer to the town that if the citizens would raise $100,000 I would match it and move the Buick Motor Company to Bay City. That was in the winter of 1905. But the money was not raised and Bay City lost the Buick company."

Some of the Flint investors were Durant's wealthy uncles and cousins. Money generated decades earlier by Henry Crapo's lumber operations would now help finance the big new opportunity of the early 20th century. Others included Flint banks and even Durant's partner, Dallas Dort. Among the big investors was the Durant-Dort Carriage Company itself, which pledged $100,000.

Workers poured into Flint by the thousands, first building the complex and then building Buicks. The new Buick complex, called the Oak Park Plant, was situated on the 220-acre farm of lumberman William Hamilton, a combination of open farm land and scrub oak, with railroad access, which Durant had bought for $22,000 for expansion of the Durant-Dort Carriage Company around 1900 and which was sold to Buick Motor Company in 1905.

When the first phase of the complex was completed by 1907, it encompassed an office building, three factories and a garage, some still under construction and all owned by the Buick firm, situated in the center of a group of 10 factories. The others were owned and operated by companies manufacturing bodies, springs, wheels and castings — "a part of the product of each outside factory being purchased by the Buick Motor Company," an auditor reported. The

"Buick City" idea of a main plant to build the entire car, with supplier factories closely aligned, arrived with fanfare in Flint in 1984, but Durant had first demonstrated the concept on the same site about eight decades earlier — and very successfully.

The auditor, J. W. Wellington, checking the property for Ben Briscoe at a time Briscoe wanted to join Durant in a consolidation of companies, said in 1908 that all the buildings "complete what is probably the finest equipment in the Country for the manufacture and sale of automobiles." Wellington's conclusion: "The business as a whole is in excellent condition and can be developed to give magnificent results with an extremely large factory output, a great volume of sales and excellent profits."

The factories quickly ran two and three shifts as production soared. Starting with 37 Model Bs built on W. Kearsley in Flint in 1904 and 750 Model Cs assembled in Jackson in 1905, Buick production rose to 1,400 in Jackson in 1906, to 4,641 after the new Flint complex opened in 1907 and to 8,820 in 1908. By 1910, production reached 30,525. The Model B of 1904, Model C of 1905 and Model F of 1906 were essentially the same and no doubt featured more of David Buick's input than any other production Buick.

The valve-in-head Model B engine was the product of David's team, which was said to include, besides the earlier work of Richard and/or Marr, major engineering and design by Mason and Beacraft. Marr, having persuaded Whiting to consider building cars according to his own recollection, took charge of planning the total vehicle. David was said to have designed the body, which was built of wood by the Flint Wagon Works. Perhaps it was David who found those quirky steel front fenders that show up only on the models B and C.

The Model B was classified as a light touring automobile, weighing 1,675 pounds. The five-passenger side-entrance body was finished in dark blue. The engine was a two-cylinder valve-in-head of 4.5 by 5 bore and stroke developing up to 21 horsepower at 1230 rpm. The price was $950.[1]

---

1 A notable aspect of the 1904 engine was the location of its pushrods. They were positioned on the bottom of the engine. Some customers complained that the pushrods' location caused trouble — dirt collecting on the rods would foul the engine. For 1905, the Model C engine was turned around so the pushrods were on the top, which allowed less oil to drip out and less dirt to creep in. Said Mason: "We just flopped the old engine bottom-side up." Only two of the 1904 Model B pushrods-on-bottom engines are known to exist.

By the time Buick automobile production was transferred to Jackson and the 1905 Model C moved into production, Buick was claiming it "has more speed, more power, more room and style and less vibration, and makes less noise and trouble than any other car in its class on the market."

On May 10, 1905, when David again gave a production report to the *Flint Daily News,* it described his duties as "in charge of the Jackson end of the Buick Motor Company" (although Whiting actually had that job). Said Buick: "We shipped 53 machines last week, and the output this week will be 70 machines." By then, the decision to build the new Flint complex had been made. "The Jackson plant will be kept in operation until the enlarged Flint plant is in readiness for operation, probably about the first of next January," he said.

By 1907, there were more new models. Besides the Model F, which was the Model C successor, and the G runabout, both of which debuted in 1906, there were now the models D, H, S and K. These four were all four-cylinder 1907 models.

The big product news for 1908 was a nicely styled newcomer — the Model 10. This sporty car was officially described as "a gentleman's light four-cylinder roadster." It was set on an 88-inch wheelbase and powered by a new 3 ¾ by 3 ¾ 165-cubic-inch, overhead-valve engine that generated 22.5 horsepower. The three-passenger car was often referred to as the "White Streak" because it was painted an off-white color called, for some odd reason, Buick gray. It featured bold brass accents, a long and low profile, acetylene headlamps, two-speed planetary transmission, jump-spark ignition and a price of $900. The car quickly grew in popularity because of its appearance, smooth power, ease of control, eventual racing success and price tag.

The Model 10 evolved from Durant's attempt to find a use for the Jackson plant after Buick operations returned to Flint. Durant brought to Jackson a naval armaments engineer named P.R. Janney, whose Janney Motor Company was organized to produce a light four-cylinder engine. The engine proved unsatisfactory, so the business was absorbed by Buick. Walter Marr and his assistant Enos DeWaters redesigned the motor for the Model 10. The Jackson plant was used to build Buick trucks for several years after Buick returned to Flint.

When production of all models totaled 8,820 in 1908, Durant could claim Buick was now the No. 1 producer in the industry — surpassing the combined total of its closest competitors, Ford and Cadillac. Being on top didn't last long because Henry Ford began

Billy Durant (light cap in front seat) in a 1906 Buick Model F. This was during the 1906 Glidden Tour, two years before Durant used Buick as the foundation when he created General Motors.

production of his legendary Model T in the fall of 1908. But for the moment Buick was king. Durant had made the leap from top producer of horse-drawn vehicles to top producer of motor cars.

"Never was there such a man [as Durant]," wrote C.B. Glasscock in *The Gasoline Age* in 1937. "Beside him Henry Ford was a plodding, insignificant, colorless mechanic utterly lacking in romance or drama, without distinction, without charm — the tortoise beside the hare." Glasscock and others credit Durant for linking the auto industry to Wall Street, bringing in much more money as well as stock promotion.

Thanks to the financial success of Buick, Durant was in position in early 1908 to pull together a group of auto and supplier firms under one umbrella. Durant first met with Ben Briscoe, Buick's original financial angel and at that time head of Maxwell-Briscoe Company, over breakfast at the Dresden Hotel in Flint and then at Buick headquarters there, to discuss a consolidation of car companies in the low-price field. Such a merger had been suggested by George W. Perkins, a J.P. Morgan partner and a financial backer of Maxwell-Briscoe.

For a time the talks also included Henry Ford and Ransom Olds, who by then had left Oldsmobile and was in charge of the REO Motor Car Company. One afternoon in 1908, Durant, Ford and Olds were invited to meet with Briscoe in the old Penobscot Building in Detroit. As Durant recalled: "In the public reception room were gathered the principals, their close associates and advisers. The room was small, no place to discuss business. I sensed, unless we ran to cover, plenty of undesirable publicity in the offing. As I had commodious quarters in the Pontchartrain Hotel, and as the luncheon hour was approaching, I suggested that we separate and meet in my room as soon as convenient. I had the unexpected pleasure of entertaining the entire party until mid-afternoon."

The discussions eventually foundered when Ford and then Ransom Olds demanded cash instead of stock in a new company.

When those talks collapsed, Durant set out on his own. He created a company which he called General Motors, incorporating it September 16, 1908, using unknowns as officers to avoid attention. First he had General Motors buy Buick for $3.75 million, mostly in an exchange of stock, and then Oldsmobile for a little more than $3 million, again mostly in an exchange of stock. After Buick and Olds, Durant then brought in Cadillac, Oakland (Pontiac predecessor), a group of truck firms that would eventually form GMC, and altogether more than 30 automotive and supplier firms.

Durant even backed a young spark plug maker named Albert Champion, whose initials would eventually form a brand name — AC Spark Plug (his name was already on the Champion spark plug from his previous firm). Champion's first base of operations for Durant was in a corner of the new Buick factory on Hamilton Avenue in Flint (and not the Buick office building, as sometimes reported).

The car that launched GM was Buick and specifically two models. The first was the original Flint Buick that was introduced as the Model B and evolved into the barely changed Model C (1905) and Model F (1906). The second was the Model 10 of 1908. The models B/C/F were powerful and reliable light touring sedans equipped with two-cylinder valve-in-head engines (with the Model G, introduced for '06, a runabout offshoot). These were the cars created under David Buick's direction by Buick and Marr (with additional engine design credits to Richard, Mason and maybe Beacraft). Of 6,828 Buicks produced from 1904 through 1907, most of them — 6,187 — were the models B/C/F and G. And in 1908 — the year GM was created — there were 3,281 Model Fs out of 8,820 total Buicks.

In 1908, the Model F relinquished Buick production leadership to the new Model 10, of which 4,002 were built that year. Just as the Model F gave Durant the early confidence, momentum and money to create General Motors, the Model 10 — sometimes called the first General Motors car — provided a big boost during the year of GM's creation. (Model 10 production doubled to 8,100 in 1909 and jumped to 11,000 in 1910 before the post-Durant leadership unac-

Model 10 waits for an earlier mode of transportation to pass near Liberty, N.Y.

countably killed it off as Buick production fell from 30,525 in 1910 to 13,389 in 1911).

During his early period of assembling companies to form GM, Durant almost bought Ford Motor Company, too. But in 1909 he couldn't persuade banks to loan the $8 million price tag for a firm that was already producing the Model T and would be worth $35 million a few years later. Durant expressed no regrets. He said later he never could have succeeded with Ford to the extent Henry Ford did.

In 1910, Durant was forced from control of General Motors by bankers concerned he was expanding too recklessly. How he dramatically reprised the Buick story to set the stage for his creation of the Chevrolet car, and how he then regained control of GM, is told in a later chapter.

Durant surrounded himself with plenty of high-powered men in this period. Among them were Louis and Arthur Chevrolet and Wild Bob Burman of the great Buick racing team, super salesman Charles Howard, one of Teddy Roosevelt's Rough Riders who became Buick's western distributor (and was later famous as the owner of the race horse Seabiscuit), and such leaders as Charles W. Nash and Walter P. Chrysler, both of whom headed Buick before creating marques of their own.

Fred Smith, Oldsmobile's leader at the time Durant bought Olds for General Motors, observed in 1928: "I had at least the intelligence

147

to see in him [Durant] the strongest and most courageous individual then in the business and the master salesman of all time…It would be a poorly posted analyst who failed to list W. C. Durant as the most picturesque, spectacular and aggressive figure in the chronicles of American automobiledom."

So where, in all this, is David Buick?

Durant's daughter, Margery, recalled in a privately published memoir her father's relationship with David. She described Buick as "an inventor he [Durant] had met and liked, and whose invention had interested him." While some of his friends urged him to change the name of the car from Buick to Durant, he declined. She recalled her father musing: "Buick…Buick. Wonder if they'd call it 'Boo-ick?'" But finally he decided he thought the name had appeal, and it honored "the man who invented the engine."

Margery also remembered her father, under a gaslight, drawing a rectangle and then writing the name Buick diagonally, slanting upward to the right.

"Margery, I think that's the name we want," Durant said to his daughter. "And I think that's the way we want to use it." She was defining the creation of the early Buick script logo.

This would have been entirely in character. Durant not only liked to name his products, he particularly relished working on the graphics. For example, the famous "bow-tie" Chevrolet emblem he chose was virtually a copy of a symbol he saw in an illustrated Sunday newspaper in 1911 in Hot Springs, Va., his second wife, Catherine, told the writer. That refutes an old yarn he saw it on wallpaper in Paris, a city he never visited until many years later. "I was with him," said Catherine. "We were in a suite, reading the papers, and he saw this design and said, 'I think this would be a very good emblem for the Chevrolet.' I'm not sure he said Chevrolet, because I don't think he had even settled on a name yet." After seeing this quote in a Durant biography by the writer, Ken Kaufmann, an authority on early Chevrolet history, checked out Catherine's recollection by going through Sunday newspapers that would have circulated in Hot Springs at the time. He found a symbol almost the same as the bow-tie in an advertisement for "Coalettes" — processed coals — in the *Atlanta Constitution's* Sunday rotogravure section of November 12, 1911, nine days after Chevrolet Motor Company was incorporated. In the same ad, Durant was attracted to a circle icon containing the words, "the Little Coals with the Big Heat." He used that icon — the circle and word Little — as the logo for the Little automobile, which Durant later folded into Chevrolet.

When Durant bought a fledgling refrigerator company in 1918 and later turned it over to GM, he himself thought up the firm's brand name — Frigidaire. Durant also claimed to have created the name General Motors, one of several suggestions he was said to have placed on a list for his lawyers to check out.

Margery noted that when her father defended keeping the Buick name, "perhaps…there jumped into his [Durant's] mind the picture of the little shed where he and I went and listened to Mr. Buick explain the mechanism; just a little outhouse with shelves full of tools and metal parts, greasy and cramped and dark. Just the kind of place you'd think might be the cradle of a great invention. And he'd feel the justice of perpetuating the name…" [2]

Despite such sentiments and amidst all the excitement of rapid sales increases, numerous racing victories and the beginnings of General Motors, David Buick quickly got lost. He almost disappears from the record. This tough little Scotsman, who had so carefully controlled and nurtured his tiny businesses, must have been way out of his league in this new environment. There were too many big personalities. There was too much going on. (According to one report, David's reduced stature is indicated by the fact he owned 1,000 shares of Buick stock on March 10, 1904, but only 110 shares on September 9, 1905 — though he may have sold some to help son Tom finance his share of a new brass foundry).

Then, in early 1906, David's leadership role in the company officially ended. According to Buick's board of directors minutes of February 13, 1906, "Mr. D.D. Buick presented verbally his resignation as General Manager of the Company, same to take effect at once. Upon motion the resignation was accepted."

The minutes continue:

Mr. W.C. Durant was elected General Manager to succeed Mr. Buick. The vote was unanimous. The conditions under

---

2 The words reflect the talent of Fitzhugh Green, Margery's ghost writer, who became her husband. The "little outhouse" may have been the test shed adjacent to the original Flint Buick plant on W. Kearsley Street.

which the Buick Motor Company was being operated were talked over quite generally and it was discussed when to take some steps to try to overcome the troubles and to bring into harmonious action all the efforts of the entire force.

All this appeared in such Florida newspapers as the *St. Petersburg Times* and *Tampa Tribune* on February 8, 1925, in an advertisement by Buick Motor Company, at that time chastising David Buick for not so subtly trying to connect the Buick automobile name with a land deal David was then promoting. The ad is a remarkable case of a company attacking its founder in print. It also raises as many questions as it answers. What, for example, were "the troubles" and "the conditions under which the Buick Motor Company was being operated"? But the ad certainly makes it clear for the first time when and how David officially lost control of the company he created.

David, though replaced by Durant as general manager, was not yet finished. He was pushed aside but not banished. Indeed, the company seemed to try to enhance his image. After all, his last name was everywhere — on the product, on the building, in the ads. In February 1907, *The Flint Journal* in describing the Buick firm said "the experimental department is one of the most important in the entire factory, and the one over which D.D. Buick himself has personal supervision. The men of this department are among the highest paid of any in the company."

Also, on November 6, 1907, *The Flint Journal* reported the Buick stockholders' annual meeting was held the previous day in the Buick offices. The story said it had been a remarkable year for Buick, and there were predictions of an even better one ahead. It said 50 stockholders were introduced from Chicago, New York, Boston, Detroit, Owosso, Flint and elsewhere. David Buick was listed as among those elected to the board.

But in general, David was shrinking from the limelight, apparently contenting himself with experimental work. What evidence exists suggests he busied himself with inconsequential projects, building a reputation as a dreamer. Maybe that was because the company's founder and namesake was no longer its leader.

The Buick family's status within the company continued to slip. Tom Buick left the company in 1906 after a dispute with Durant and became more involved with a brass foundry, Auto Brass & Aluminum Company, of which he was part owner. It provided the

Buick company with brass parts. When the foundry was organized in 1904, Tom was its secretary. It went bankrupt when the Buick company couldn't pay its bills in a later financial crisis, sending Tom Buick's finances spiraling out of control. In early 1909, Tom was listed as president of Genesee Tire Company in Flint, but later that year he was bankrupt.

Another of David's children was at the center of an unhappy situation. In July of 1905, Buick Motor Company was sued for $5,000 by a woman slightly injured in a car accident in Jackson involving a daughter of Buick. Rachel Beadle claimed she was knocked down by one of the company's automobiles which was being shown to a prospective purchaser. The car was driven by an "inexperienced woman," the Buick daughter.

Catherine Durant, second wife of General Motors founder William C. Durant, was Durant's secretary in 1905 when he was taking control of Buick's fortunes. They were married in 1908.

The incident took place on April 10, 1905. Fanny, 25, David's elder daughter, whose first husband was a Dr. John L. Estabrook, 26, was driving a Buick Model C with her husband of two months a passenger, and Buick employee Ed Crankshaw in the back seat, when she slowed almost to a walk to avoid a woman arguing with a streetcar conductor. The woman, Mrs. Beadle, was upset because the streetcar had missed her stop. As Fanny drove past the scene at about four miles per hour, she honked the horn twice. Mrs. Beadle stepped out of the way, but then, unaccountably, walked back into the path of the car and was hit by it. She was dragged about five feet. Fanny's doctor husband treated her at the scene. Fanny was described as "reasonably familiar with the handling of an automobile, having driven a car a great many times." Also, several witnesses placed all the blame on Mrs. Beadle. Nevertheless, months later, Mrs. Beadle filed a lawsuit against Buick Motor Company.

The suit was dismissed as without merit, but John Carton, who was Durant's attorney (and sometimes acted as the Buick company's attorney), had trouble collecting a $92.58 legal bill charged to David Buick after David said he would handle it personally.

Carton insisted on this payment from the man who had given his name to the Buick automobile. Finally Durant stepped in, sending the check, and this note: "Mr. Buick wishes me to say that until a few moments ago this was more money than he had in the world. He disliked very much to make this admission…."

This was apparently in jest — or was it? Durant's letter to Carton continued: "All joking aside, and in fairness to Mr. Buick, I wish to say that the fault is not entirely his. Some time ago we had an understanding with him as to his compensation for the present year and I have only just learned that Mr. Whiting failed to put this into effect on the lst of October. Mr. Buick wishes me to express his regret that he has been unable to meet this matter earlier and to offer his apology for his neglect for which he feels he has been justly scolded."

So we're left with this picture of Whiting failing to pay David Buick, of Carton harassing him for a minor bill, of Durant stepping in and calling it all a joke. The only thing clear is that David Buick's relationship with Buick Motor Company was strained virtually to the breaking point.

Fred Hoelzle, interviewed at age 92 by the writer in 1976, worked at Buick when the founder was there. David Buick, said Hoelzle, "never seemed to fit himself in with others. Nobody seemed to take to him. I think he was most interested in finances. He was quiet and we didn't see him very often. Finally, he just kind of faded away. Nobody seemed to notice." That judgment may not be worth much as Hoelzle was probably not often in position to cross paths with David Buick. And he incorrectly remembered David as a tall man. It's ironic, though, that by 1908, when Buick Motor Company claimed to lead the industry in production, Buick the man had disappeared into the bureaucracy.

His name did surface occasionally. In January of 1906, a fire wiped out the barn of Flint businessman Flint P. Smith. The newspapers reported two cars parked there, each worth $1,200, were destroyed. One was Smith's car, believed to be a 1905 Model C Buick, likely the car bedecked in flowers he had driven in the Golden Jubilee parade. The other car destroyed might have also been a Model C parade vehicle — it had been temporarily parked in Smith's barn by David Buick.

Chapter 14

David Buick hits the road

At some point, it all became too much. David Buick figured it was time to do something else — although that would turn out to be not such a good idea, either. As for the timing, the 1925 newspaper ad previously quoted provides the most authoritative answer. The ad says Buick Motor Company's own files "show that Mr. Buick ceased to be Secretary on November 6th, 1906, and a director on November 3, 1908, after which time he has had no official connection with the Buick Motor Company and his name does not appear on the payroll as an employe after September 30, 1910."

After he was re-elected to the Buick board in November 1907, the evidence is slim. A 1930s Buick magazine article describes an early scene in which racing reports were telegraphed to a machine shop at the Buick factory. David was said to be in the shop, nervous, pacing the floor constantly and chewing his cigar as news clattered over the wire. Like most early auto men, David was said to be a big racing fan.

Terry Dunham found enough information to identify the above-mentioned race as the 232-mile Cobe Trophy won by Buick racer Louis Chevrolet on June 18, 1909. So David could have still been with the company then.

If so, it's easy to see how he could have gotten lost in the highly energized Buick organization. This was an incredibly busy period. The automobile was being perfected and there was a virgin market. With Billy Durant leading a sales surge, the factories were pushed to their limits and beyond. This was the period David recalled when he complained to Bruce Catton: "There wasn't an executive in the place who ever knew what time it was…I tell you, the automobile business was a tough one in those days."

If that wasn't enough, Durant, using Buick as the foundation, energetically scooped up more companies as he created the nucleus of a General Motors that would become unbeatable in size in the 20th century and into the early years of the new millennium. He bought so many companies because, he said, he was afraid of missing out on some hot new technology. As Durant explained to A.B.C. Hardy: "How could I tell what these engineers would say next? …I was for getting every car in sight, playing safe all along the line."

The Buick organization was running at top speed at all levels. Its racing team led by Wild Bob Burman and Louis Chevrolet was hitting its stride as it won 500 trophies from 1908 to 1910.

As the *Detroit News* reported in 1909: "One must see for himself; one must get into the atmosphere of the tremendous undertakings; one must himself walk over the literal miles of factories in process of construction before one begins to grasp the immensity of the manufacturing undertaking that has made Flint, next to Detroit, the automobile center of the world."

A sense of Durant's reputation at this time is revealed by author Arthur Pound. He said lawyer John Carton "wanted me to realize that Billy Durant put no value on money for its own sake; that the founder of General Motors was an unconventional soul who soared high above ordinary humanity, that the one and only Billy…was almost a prince among mortals, enjoying first of all power, then excitement, then the affectionate adulation of his friends."

Evidence of the time of David Buick's departure from all this is an advertisement in the *New York Herald* dated November 6, 1910, in which Buick is quoted: "One year ago my health broke down and I was a physical wreck — so the doctor said. I went to California but I seemed to get no better. I lived in Los Angeles and while I was trying to recover my health I made a study of the oil business.…"

That seems a clear statement Buick became ill in late 1909 and then went to California. But another David Buick ad, undated, says he "went to California in April, 1910, in search of health." Somehow, David got the idea he should get into the oil business. In a lawsuit filed in 1914, it was said he made that decision in answer to an advertisement from a man seeking a wealthy partner to invest in California oil properties.

David incorporated Buick Oil Company in California in March of 1910. Either Buick was setting up the business from long distance or the April date for his arrival in California is wrong. Fall of 1909 seems a more likely date for his departure from Buick Motor Company, though he may have left earlier before traveling to California.

David Buick after he left Buick Motor Company, a rare profile from the album of his grandson, David Dunbar Buick II.

David is telling his story in advertisements because the ads are soliciting investors in his oil properties.

In his interview with Bruce Catton, Buick reiterated he left the Buick company because his health had broken. Although he did not specifically blame Durant, several men who worked for Durant were driven to the brink of health breakdowns — or over the brink. One was Durant-Dort President A.B.C. Hardy in the carriage era. He resigned at the point of collapse and took an extended trip to France. Another was Walter Marr, who said he was working 22 out of 24 hours a day, ruining his health. And still another was early Frigidaire executive Alfred Mellowes, who said he may not have quit had Durant allowed him a vacation in the north woods.

But this could be unfair to Durant. David would surely not have been the only man who worked to the point of exhaustion just because of the frenetic, exciting challenges of the times — instead of being driven to illness by some unforgiving boss. David Buick was apparently being made to feel unwelcome at Buick Motor Company for unrecorded reasons. Perhaps it was nothing more complicated than an inability to get along with the new leadership under Durant, or a loss of interest since he was no longer in charge. At the same time he was being lured by the potential profits in California oil and an opportunity to be boss again. Those combined forces may have been a bigger reason than any health problems for David's decision to leave the company and head west.

When David left, Durant reportedly gave him $100,000 — about $2 million in early new millennium dollars — for his stock, though a contradictory report indicates David still had considerable GM stock after his departure. Buick's grandson, David II, said his father, Tom Buick, claimed stock that should have been given to David, and never was, would have been worth $115 million at the time of David's death. Briscoe seems to confirm this, but David II said it may only be a family story. "My father was very bitter about this, but Grandpa [David Buick] never seemed to be."

David gave his version to Catton: "I had a good block of stock. The directors held a meeting the day I left. I was told that they'd voted to pay me my salary the rest of my life. I thought I was all set. But they only paid it for three years. After that, I never got a cent."

According to the grandson, David "didn't hold much animosity toward the Buick company for the way he ended up. I remember that he did own a Buick once…"

The most revealing judgments about David's career at Buick Motor Company come from A.B.C. Hardy and from Durant himself.

Hardy's take was that David was a dreamer who kept experimenting with some new gadget without applying his talents to the business of manufacturing a marketable motor car.

And Durant gave his view to George H. Maines, a prominent public relations executive whose father developed property near the Buick factory into homes for the workers and their families.

"David Buick was a likeable fellow," Durant told Maines. "But he was a dreamer, and he couldn't be practical…We did everything we could at the plant to make it easy for him. We arranged for his

THE SAN DIEGO UNION: SUNDAY MORNING, JANUARY 16, 1910

Prominent Automobile Manufacturer Coming To San Diego Soon

Has Heard So Many Favorable Reports of City that He Plans to Make Lengthy Stay

D. D. Buick, the well known automobile manufacturer, and his young son viewing the aviation meet in Los Angeles

"I have head so much of Southern California, and especially San Diego, that last summer I made up my mind that I would spend the winter on the Pacific coast. And here I am. Enjoying the aviation meet just now, but next week, when the aeroplanes are packed up and the aviators are on their way to their several homes, I am coming to San Diego, and I expect to have an even better time there."

D. D. Buick, the prominent automobile manufacturer, was the speaker. Mr. Buick was found on the aviation field by the special representative of The Tribune. His presence there was known only to a few of his intimate friends, as he had sent no advance word of his coming to the coast and was endeavoring to prevent his visit from becoming generally known.

"My trip to the Pacific coast is mainly for pleasure," said Mr. Buick to the Tribune man. "At the same time I expect to combine some business, for while out here I might as

David Buick is with son Wynton at Los Angeles aviation meet in clipping from San Diego Union *January 16, 1910. Several months later, David would form Buick Oil Company in southern California.*

son, Tom, to be on the payroll, and to try to keep his father settled, but after some years he just drifted away."

Whatever the reasons, David Buick's relationship with Buick Motor Company was over. Now, with the reported settlement money from Durant, David might well have gone home to Detroit – or even to California – and taken up boating again, enjoying a comfortable early retirement at age 55. But David Buick seldom took the easy path.

Chapter 15

Oil in California

In his first 55 years, David Buick seldom displayed much appetite for personal promotion. Indeed he was so quiet he largely disappeared from everyone's radar screens, including those of the leaders of Buick Motor Company.

But by the time he arrived in Los Angeles after half a century of living in Detroit and Flint, Mich., he was virtually being marketed as David Buick — Superstar! Advertisements soliciting investors in his new-found oil properties suggested this was a successful and very wealthy businessman who had stepped away from thousands of admiring workers in Flint only because his health had failed and he needed a warmer climate.

The ads, appearing in late 1910 in newspapers in New York, Chicago, Toronto and probably elsewhere, were big and sensational. One, displaying a portrait of David Buick, was headlined, "Buick Makes Fortune in Oil." It sought "conservative investors" willing to back David's dollars with theirs. "He is not a poor man with a promising future," the ads assured. "Buick is a rich man, with a lifelong list of business successes to his credit.... As a businessman who does not let his enthusiasm run away with his common sense, he...knows he will get it all back many times over."

One of the ads was a virtual "advertorial," several pages in *The Strand Magazine,* in what looked like a magazine article, complete with a byline, except with a coupon for more information at the end. After praising the character and the successes of David Buick, the "article" described Buick's old plumbing supply business, Buick & Sherwood, as at one time "the largest plumbing supply house in the world." David was "now heavily interested in the General Motors Co., the largest corporation of its kind in the world." Furthermore, "to the automobile trade he has always been known as a practicer of the Square Deal...."

Buick Oil Company solicitation ads starting 1910.

In Flint, though Buick Motor Company was driving the economy, the big names linked to the company were Durant, Whiting, Mason, Begole and maybe the new general manager, Big Bill Little. Buick the man was hardly a public personality. But the magazine ad proclaimed: "15,000 workingmen in Flint, Michigan, know this man and his business ideals."

David Buick's automobile had finally made him famous about the time he left it. Now he was either being surrounded by people who saw his name as a ticket to success, or he himself was deeply involved in building his image and creating aggressive oil promotions. Probably some of both.

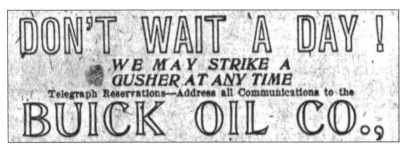

Most information about David's California years comes from those who were either promoting or attacking him. In one lawsuit, it was alleged Buick Oil Company "from the beginning was impregnated with fraud...." On the other hand, Buick Oil Company officials loyal to David stated he and his associates strongly opposed "reprehensible" advertising.

The basic facts were David Buick incorporated Buick Oil Company March 4, 1910, with four Californians – J.B. Lehigh, Stacy C. Lamb and Walter Rose, all of Los Angeles, and John M. Herndon of South Pasadena – and that firm quickly acquired an option on 640 acres of oil-rich property, the "Buick Midway Holdings," in Kern County, north of L.A.

According to a 1914 lawsuit, Herndon and Lehigh were promoters of oil and mineral lands. Herndon advertised for a wealthy partner to invest in oil lands and David responded. Together they put up $20,000 for an option to buy the Kern County acreage.

By 1913 David was boasting of big successes, and no wonder. If you wanted to be in oil, Kern County was a good place to be. Oil had been oozing to the surface there from ancient times. In the 1700s, Indians used tar from local pits for trading, waterproofing and as an adhesive. In the mid 1800s, entrepreneurs were digging shallow pits and refining tar into lamp kerosene. Next came tunnels and mines, then wells. A new chapter began in 1896 when the Shamrock gusher blew, sending 1,300 barrels of oil flowing per day, according to the San Joaquin Geological Society. This was good timing as the gasoline engine was a very important — and very thirsty — new arrival on the world industrial scene.

If solicitation ads were accurate, one Buick Oil Company well produced 900,000 barrels of oil in 10 months. Another came in as a gusher and produced 500,000 barrels in four months. David called it "one of the most sensational gushers in the history of California oil."

News stories supported some of the claims. An article in the *Los Angeles Times* on January 14, 1912, that was headlined "Buick Gusher is Beyond Control," reported the well was "shooting a stream of oil high over the derrick," an awesome sight captured in a photograph. But a few months later, another article reported Buick Oil Company was trying to deny this well was "ruined by water infiltration of the rich gusher sands."

Such reports were not true, according to the Buick firm. Standard Oil Company, which had a contract with Buick Oil Company, said the percentage of water and other contaminants in the Buick oil was acceptable — from 1 percent to not more than 3 percent. At the same time this was reported, Buick Oil Company announced a 4 per cent dividend, which reportedly placed it "in the front ranks as a dividend payer." (There must have been something to the rumors about the wells, though. In 1915, the company acknowledged its first well "sanded up" in January of 1912 and two others in April 1912 and February 1913.)

At one point, David described himself as president and chief stockholder of a successful gold mining company "operating on the mother lode" in Tuolumne County, Calif. That firm was not recorded by the California secretary of state, but overall, Buick painted a picture of success. David Buick wanted very much to be seen as wealthy. "Since locating in Los Angeles, Mr. Buick has built a handsome home in one of the fashionable residence sections of the city and his family has taken an active part in the social life in California," his 1913 biographical sketch revealed. It also noted:

> While he is distinguished for having made a success in all his ventures, Mr. Buick's greatest success came to him late in life, for he was forty-nine years of age when he organized the Buick Motor Company; but since that time all of his ventures have been attended with extraordinarily large rewards.

When David first went to Los Angeles in 1910, he lived at 3016 S. Western Avenue. By 1911, he and his family lived in a house at 446 S. St. Andrews Place, near Wilshire Boulevard and Western. Apparently he liked the neighborhood, because a year or two later, David built a house at 350 S. St. Andrews.

Buick's younger daughter, Mabel Lucille, lived with her parents until she married James Duryea Coyle, a native of San Francisco and president of James D. Coyle Realty Company of Los Angeles, on April 9, 1912. Miss Buick "formerly resided in Detroit and Flint, Mich., where she was well known in society circles," said a notice of an engagement party given by Mr. and Mrs. Buick at their Los Angeles home (at that time 446 S. St. Andrews). The couple planned to live in Los Angeles after a honeymoon in Honolulu.[1]

As for the oil business, David's ads soliciting investors described his observations and experiences at some length. David had learned, one ad said, the oil business didn't take much labor — three men were working nine wells and could handle many times that number. He became as fascinated with oil as he had earlier with engines and automobiles. "The question of oil was so interesting and so absorbing to me that I could not think of anything else," he was quoted as saying. It was explained he was spending all of his time in the oil fields, using his engineering experience to direct operations first hand.

In some ads, potential investors were warned to act quickly if they really wanted to make money: "One week from today may be too late."

---

1 The elder daughter, Frances Jane, after an early divorce married Frank Patterson, a one-time shoe salesman from New York who was eventually involved in the oil business. They had one daughter, Caroline Louisa Patterson, who married Warren Boes. Their son, Doug Boes, remembers his grandmother, Frances Jane, lived with them for a time. The only family treasures that came down to him were a set of silverware from a Flint firm, decorated with the letter "B" stamped on each item, and the small brass cannon David had used as a starting gun for regattas in his early Detroit days.

Terry B. Dunham

Buick Oil Company hits a gusher in California in 1912.

And then came the headline in the *New York Times* on November 22, 1910.

"Postal Raids Show Vast Stock Frauds."

U.S. Post Office inspectors and police detectives had raided two of the largest sales agencies of unlisted stock in New York City and arrested four men "prominently identified with the distribution of stock in oil companies, wireless concerns, mining and other enterprises...." The raids were part of a crusade "with the approval of President Taft" to wipe out swindling operations through the mails "which in the last five years...have filched from the public more than $100,000,000," the newspaper reported. One raided outfit was Burr Brothers, a firm

Buick Oil Company stock certificate.

whose president, Sheldon C. Burr, was arrested along with two other company officials.

Buick Oil Company was only one of a large number of companies listed in the article, with postal authorities noting Burr Brothers had recently been advertising its stock. David Buick, however, managed to stumble prominently into the story:

> Yesterday afternoon while Inspector [T.M.] Reddy was in the office of the Burr Brothers, there came a long-distance call on the telephone for S.C. Burr. The man at the other end announced that he was David Buick, head of the Buick Oil Company and that he was at Flint, Mich.

> "What's all this I hear about Burr Brothers getting into trouble?" he asked. Inspector Reddy told him. Mr. Buick asked that a telegram be sent to him at once telling him what had happened and stating whether the Buick Oil Company had been drawn into the matter in any way.

> "I'm not here to send you any telegrams," said Inspector Reddy. "If you want information you had better come here and get it."

David Buick's involvement was hardly ignored by the automotive press. A week later (November 30, 1910), *The Horseless Age* weighed in with a story headlined: "Buick's Oil Venture Gets Black Eye"

When the postal authorities swooped down upon the get-rich-quick scheme of Burr Brothers, of New York city, David R. (sic) Buick, of Flint, Mich., whose name one of the General Motors Company's cars bears, and head of the Buick Oil Company, was considerably annoyed, especially when he heard of the arrest of the members of the Burr Brothers' outfit. This company, which has promoted a number of great schemes for separating the public from its money…were selling agents for the Buick Oil Company. Upon learning the state of affairs, Buick started for New York, and the morning after the raid, had a long talk with Assistant United States Attorney Dorr. To the latter Buick declared that he was quite ignorant of the business records of the men he selected to sell his stock, and that picking Burr Brothers was an error of judgment.

The episode has no bearing on the automobile business, save that the prosperous condition of the industry and the name "Buick" were used as capital by the oil agents to interest "come-ons." The latter were somewhat falsely led to believe that David Buick was the big man of the Buick Motor Car Company, and that he was a great factor in the automobile world. Also that great quantities of refined Buick oil would soon be consumed for lubricating and fuel purposes, not only by owners of Buick cars, but by motorists generally, which naturally would yield enormous dividends. Thousands of "easy" ones bit at the bait.

Just why Buick permitted his name to be connected with such a wildcat scheme without first investigating thoroughly has caused much talk in automobile circles. Just what effect the arrest of the agents will have on the oil concern itself has not yet been determined.

That was far from the end of it. David's oil ventures were becoming more widely noted for legal entanglements than for oil gushers. A geologist, Ralph Arnold, filed suit in Superior Court in Los Angeles on January 26, 1912, alleging he had been promised a one-quarter share of the company for his work in finding oil reserves but had received nothing. He was seeking $375,000 plus other damages.

Arnold was not your average geologist. He was the son of a famous Pasadena scientist (the late Delos Arnold) and, according to a news story, "had played with mastadon bones in his nursery." When he went to Stanford, Arnold was said to have known more about fossils than the professors — and almost as much about geology.

Later, as a member of the U.S. Geological Survey, he made maps for the government and wrote bulletins describing all of the oil lands in California. "He has defined the limits and determined the zones of all the oil country in California and has written enough oil and mineral bulletins to fill several five-foot shelves," the article reported.

Arnold was touted in Washington as the leading oil expert on the Pacific Coast and "is busy every minute at $100 a day, according to his attorneys, and is on the staff of the Mexican Petroleum Company, the Union Oil Company and a dozen other large corporations, including an English syndicate which has taken him to Europe twice within the last year."

And now Ralph Arnold was a victim of Buick Oil Company, a story recounted in Los Angeles under the headline: "His Reward a Freeze-out?" One of the subheads: "Automobile King Is Among the Defendants."

This did not look good for Buick, but untangling the Arnold problem created another. A federal lawsuit filed in 1914 by disgruntled Buick Oil Company shareholders complained about the way Buick and John M. Miner, who was described in the suit as "Buick's alleged attorney," settled with Arnold. Buick and Miner agreed, according to the suit, to pay him $10,000 in cash from the company treasury and transfer to him 100,000 shares of Buick Oil Company stock. The stockholders' attorney, Alfred E. Case of Chicago, contended Buick and John Herndon had entered into the agreement with Arnold before the oil company was organized, and therefore the decision to use company assets to settle the Arnold claim was fraudulent. The attorney argued the stock transfer should be voided and the $10,000 returned to the oil company's treasurer.

There is no file on what could have been Buick's obvious answer — that Arnold's work had probably led to the Buick Oil Company's early successes.

Arnold's was one of several lawsuits attacking Buick Oil Company. Also in 1912, a suit was filed by Benjamin F. Moffatt, demanding the return to him of a large block of the company's stock. And on April 15, 1914, the complaint filed by Case on behalf of the disgruntled stockholders demanded — besides action in the Arnold case among other things — a receivership for the company.

Buick Oil Company responded aggressively. In the Moffatt case, Fred Van Orman, company secretary, alleged Moffatt and the Burr Brothers (one of the firms raided in New York) had secured allotments of the company's stock and were selling it "in the most reckless and unwarrantable manner, realizing profits ranging from 100 to 600 percent."

Said Van Orman: "Their methods were so reprehensible that in the Moffatt case, the company took extreme measures to put a stop to his methods by refusing to make further transfers of stock for him until he had promised the company that he would desist from further questionable advertising."

And in the case brought by the disgruntled stockholders, Buick Oil Company lawyers persuaded a federal judge the complaint had little merit. A news report said the judge issued "a stinging rebuke" to those filing the complaint. The judge held that 70 pages were filled with "scandalous, redundant and impertinent matter" that should be stricken from the record. But he did grant attorney Case time to prepare a new bill of complaint.

This amended bill was filed by Case on April 21, 1915, in federal court in Los Angeles. The stockholders he represented, who had formed the Buick Oil Association to pursue the legal action, lived in 20 states and three Canadian provinces, as well as Australia and Scotland, and represented 500,000 shares of the company's stock.

In summary, Case alleged David Buick had devised a scheme to control valuable oil properties in California without having to pay for them himself, had falsely represented himself as far more wealthy than he was, and that, after incorporating Buick Oil Company, had worked with his "cronies" to manipulate the company's stocks and improperly spend the company's money. The attorney, listing company officers David Buick, John Herndon, John Miner and Fred Van Orman among defendants, alleged no reports of many sales were made and that false and fraudulent statements were made in regard to the value of the stock.

Case told the association that after Herndon and Buick optioned the Kern County property, Buick organized his own company with $5 million capitalization. This firm, Buick Oil Company, issued to David Buick and Herndon three million shares of stock in return for the option on the property. Each took one million shares and transferred one million to J.B. Lehigh, another of the company's directors. They planned to sell a sufficient amount of the other two million shares to the public "to bring in the wells and for other purposes."

Case's numerous letters and telegrams to representatives of the association focused on three subjects: (1) David Buick and his associates had engaged in illegal activities; (2) Case's legal actions against them would assuredly lead to victories that would boost the value of Buick Oil Company stock; and (3) Case needed more money from the association if he were to continue the fight. As time went on, it appeared No. 3 rose to the top of Case's concerns.

In reply, Buick Oil Company said its actions were legal, that the stockholders had failed to complain about alleged illegal actions by normal routes, and it was untrue that Buick, Miner and Van Orman had a scheme to wreck the company "and stop the flow of oil."

Meanwhile, the negative news about Buick Oil Company did not play well back in Flint, at Buick Motor Company. William C. Durant had been temporarily pushed aside in 1910 as bankers took over two-year-old General Motors (he would make a triumphant return to power at GM five years later) and one of Durant's old subordinates at the Durant-Dort Carriage Company, Charles W. Nash, was in charge at Buick. On December 19, 1912, Nash responded in a letter to a question about Buick and the oil venture from Fred Warner, head of Buick operations in Chicago. Nash stiffly replied that any reference to David Buick or his oil company in connection with Buick Motor Company "is too absurd to hardly deserve thought."

Nash described Buick as a man "without means" who had persuaded the Flint Wagon Works to invest in a two-cylinder automobile motor designed by Walter Marr. "After they got in quite a ways and needed money Mr. Durant came upon the scene and properly financed the proposition, and the outcome of that has been what you see in the Buick Motor Company of today."

Nash continued: "After two or three years Mr. Buick, who had received some Buick Motor Company stock for what he had done in the matter, disposed of his stock and all his relations with the Buick Motor Company to promote this oil deal of which you read so much. Mr. Buick has had no connection whatever with the Buick Motor Company for the last five years. In fact, I think it is safe to say that he never has entered the Buick Motor Company's office or plant during that time. Therefore, you can see what connection he has had with the Buick Motor Company."

Despite mounting troubles, David himself seemed affable in a long letter to Walter Marr in 1913. He described himself as a booster of Los Angeles. "I like both the warm days and the cool nights for the reasons you can go to bed and sleep every minute; something that you can't do in the east when you have a very hot day," he wrote.

At that time Marr was working on his Cyclecar, a concept compact car of the times, the idea being to create an economy model. It was a narrow vehicle with the passenger seated behind the driver. "I have talked to a great many people," Buick wrote. "And without a single exception they all prefer the seats along side of each other and claim that the tandem seats would not take at all. Of course you will understand all of this is for your information as I do not wish to influence you in any way…." Marr ignored the advice. He built his Cyclecar in 1914 with one seat behind the other. It still exists. But the concept never went anywhere.

Neither, for that matter, did the Buick Oil Company. Case, the attorney representing the disgruntled stockholders, engaged in a long court fight with the company, which battled back with "eight or ten of what are supposed to be the best lawyers in the city," Case said. One newspaper article said an upcoming hearing "promises to furnish a fine display of daylight fireworks if the predictions of the attorneys are verified." Another reported: "The affairs of the Buick Oil Company are a fruitful source of trouble in the local Federal Court, and every time the matter is brought up, it requires the efforts of all the peace conservers concerned to keep the attorneys from each other's throats."

Beginning in early 1914 and continuing into the spring of 1915, letters and telegrams flew back and forth between Case and the representatives of the association of disgruntled stockholders. Most were between Case and the association's secretary, George Kyles, who, like Case, lived in Chicago. Some were between Kyles and the stockholders.

Some letters from Case attacked Buick Oil Company and David Buick. Sometimes Case predicted victory in the courts. April 16, 1914, Case to Kyles: "I have them [Buick Oil Company] on the run." April 22, 1914, Case to Kyles: "Criminal matters under consideration." May 27, 1914, Case to Kyles: "I know I can win and clean the pirates out root and branch… The policy of the law is 'to the diligent litigant belongs the spoils.'"

Walter Chrysler (left) and Charles Nash (right) with Walter Marr and his Cyclecar, a 1915 Buick concept. David Buick criticized its configuration in a letter to Marr.

But often, Case was looking for more money from his clients: May 22, 1914, Case telegram to Kyles (punctuation added): "Can't pay hotel bills...court costs...expenses...keep two families six horses two dogs...make millions from defunct corporations for stockholders on blue sky for the glory of it...cash exhausted...hotel bills due Sunday...money was to be here Tuesday... if Association can't raise funds must quit." June 9, 1914, Case to Kyles: "Money almost gone, bills are overdue." June 10, 1914, Case to Kyles, predicting it is "practically assured" the Buick Oil Company officers will be indicted "but I will or must have money."

By September 15, 1914, Kyles was pleading with the stockholders to send more expense money to Case: "Mr. Case must be back in California in three weeks. You are not so cheap that you would ask him to walk out there, and then sleep in the parks after he gets there. He is fighting your battle...."

On January 8, 1915, Case told A. H. Wolyn, a stockholder whose complaint originally triggered the lawsuit: "I have assured you we

*Another view of one of Buick Oil Co.'s
California derricks.*

will win and we will if you don't drive me from the field." And on
February 2, Case informed Kyles he had been told "Buick has quit
and that Miner is really the only one in the game. I can assure you I
am confident his days are numbered."

David Buick had apparently reacted at Buick Oil Company almost as he had at Buick Motor Company. When things began to go
wrong, he became quiet, and then he disappeared from view, and
then he left.

The whole show was about over anyway. By then, events were
coming to a head between Case and the association. On February 16,
1915, Case wrote to Kyles: "I hope the sheckels are coming in as I
am about three weeks behind in my hotel bill...If the Court does not
do something pretty soon I am liable to start something, as I become
very active when aroused. Everything seems to be working for our
advantage but it is too slow for my nerves."

Too slow for the association's, too. Perhaps under pressure from
stockholders, Kyles asked for an accounting of Case's expenses.
Case's response, on February 17, was explosive: "Do you imagine
that I am a slave of yours, to be dictated to and through you, of how

and what I shall do, how I shall spend my money, what I shall eat, where I shall stop, where I shall sleep? By reason of your letter I feel that I am relieved from looking after the affairs of the Association any further...."

Case hung around long enough to file the amended bill of complaint on April 21, 1915, but again there was no quick action. A. H. Wolyn decided he had seen enough. In a motion to dismiss the suit, Wolyn revealed numerous letters from Case, including the quotes above, noting they were merely examples of many on the subject of Case's continual demands for expense money.

Wolyn noted Case had given the association "profuse promises to win for them some substantial returns for the outlays of money they were sending to him" and had often threatened to abandon his efforts if funds were not forthcoming. In total, about $2,200 was provided to Case by the association, Wolyn said. It seems not overly expensive, even in 1915 dollars, for a Chicago lawyer working a case for more than a year in California, but it was more than the association — which had seen none of the promised results — wanted to spend.

On September 25, 1915, Wolyn told the association Case had been discharged as its attorney and that the association had directed that the lawsuit against Buick Oil Company be dismissed. With both sides agreeing, the case was officially dismissed on December 28, 1915.

But the damage was done. With all of the expensive litigation, the company was wrecked.

CONDENSED STATEMENT OF THE CONDITION

OF

General Motors Company

September 30, 1909

ASSETS

Cash and Cash Items	$1,365,235.24
Stocks Owned	16,288,048.59
(Valuations Based on Inventories Sept. 30, 1909)	
Other Investments	690,571.96
Other Assets	37,512.07
Total,	$18,381,367.86

LIABILITIES

Companies and Individuals		$11,593.14
Dividend		237,173.79
(Due Oct. 1, 1909)		
Capital Stock		
Common,	$4,211,630.00	
Preferred,	6,782,493.89	10,994,123.89
*Surplus		7,138,477.04
Total,		$18,381,367.86

* After charging off $1,040,000.00 for Depreciation, Patents and Questionable Accounts.

9 mos operation.

GENERAL INFORMATION

Volume of Business	$34,000,000.00
Number of Motor Cars Produced During Fiscal Year	28,550
Number of Employees	14,250

OFFICERS

President	W. M. Eaton
Vice-President	W. C. Durant
Vice-President	W. J. Mead
Secretary	Curtis R. Hatheway
Treasurer	Curtis R. Hatheway

BOARD OF DIRECTORS

W. M. Eaton	Curtis R. Hatheway
W. C. Durant	H. G. Hamilton
W. J. Mead	John T. Smith
Henry Henderson	

See Statement Jan 1" 09
Profit in 9 mos
$10,000,000

First GM annual report, two small pages and a title page covering nine months of operations, carries this note in Durant's handwriting: "Profit in 9 mos. $10,000,000."

Chapter 16

Buick sets pattern for Chevrolet

While David Buick was fighting lawyers in California, back in Michigan his successor as head of Buick Motor Company was engaged in a bigger drama — the struggle for control of Buick's parent company, General Motors. By the time it ended, William C. Durant had presided over a remarkable chapter in business history — one that would see two future automotive titans, Charles W. Nash and Walter P. Chrysler, become successive presidents of Buick, and a Buick racing star, Louis Chevrolet, become the namesake of another iconic American automobile. Durant, by creating the Chevrolet Motor Company and by regaining GM and turning it into an ever-expanding giant, would become a legend among auto pioneers.

Even in summary, it's a story not told quickly. As Durant recalled, it started when GM made $10 million in its first year but he needed $15 million more to boost production. With his new corporation doing well, he didn't expect a lot of problems in raising the money.

But late in 1909, a prominent financier at a bankers convention loudly declared that the financial demands of auto companies were excessive. Durant described the results as devastating. He said that by May 1, 1910, "our bank loans were all called and we were deprived of every dollar of working capital — the life-blood of our institution — which brought about the complete stoppage of our business with a loss to us of more than $60,000 a day."

Eventually, helped by well-connected friends, he did find two firms, Lee, Higginson & Company of Boston and J. & W. Seligman & Company, New York, that would fund GM — but the terms, Durant said, were "outrageous."

Under the terms I received $12,250,000 cash (not $15 million) for which I gave $21,600,000 of the best securities ever created — the enormous commission to the bankers of $9,350,000. And listen to this — it took seven months to secure the money at the frightful price paid for it to start the wheels in motion and put thousands of men back to work.

I refer to this situation because ...the bankers reported that at the time they became interested, General Motors was a "scrap heap," which statement I have always resented.

There was one more detail. The bankers demanded control of GM — a voting trust for the five-year term of the loan. Durant had no choice — nobody else would lend the money. And so on November 11, 1910, a group of 11 directors, friends of Durant, left the board. Durant would stay. His friends were replaced by five financial men from New York, four from Detroit and Boston banker James J. Storrow as interim president of General Motors.

In Durant's view, the new directors couldn't make quick decisions, knew nothing of how a business should be run and were "trained in banking rather than practical lines." And there were other problems. He was also unhappy to observe some of his close associates cozying up to the bankers.

I discovered that some of my own organization "weak sisters," so to speak, men who felt that they could lift themselves up by catering to the "powers that be," were not quite 100 percent...I saw some of my cherished ideas laid aside for future action, never to be revived. Opportunities that should have been taken care of with quickness and decision not considered. The things that counted so much in the past which gave General Motors its unique and powerful position were subordinated to "liquidate and pay." Pay whom and for what? The people that took control of the business and received $9,350,000 in cash and securities as a commission for a five-year loan of $12,250,000.

As Durant handed control to the bankers, he did persuade Storrow to install Charles W. Nash, vice president and general manager of his Durant-Dort Carriage Company, as president of Buick.

Durant and Nash went back 20 years, to 1890 when Durant met young Nash working in a Flint hardware and offered him a job at his carriage company. Nash was thrilled to get the job at the Flint Road Cart Company (which in 1895 would become the Durant-Dort Carriage Company). His childhood had been impoverished, financially and emotionally. At age seven, he was "bound out" by his father to a farmer. He was to work for his keep until adulthood, but when he was 12 he ran away to sell his labor to other farmers. He also was hired part-time in the W.C. Pierce hardware where Durant found him. Working for Durant and Dort, Nash was not only a prodigious laborer but a good student on improving quality and cutting costs. He eventually rose to vice president and general manager of Durant-Dort.

Meantime Durant, after taking over Buick, was ignoring carriage company business to the chagrin of Dort and Nash. As Dort once said, Durant was "easily the firm's leading force and genius." One day, Durant remembered, the two showed up at his Flint home to persuade him to become more actively involved with the carriage company again. They found him happily pumping a player piano, and then talking with enthusiasm about the future of automobiles. Nash, reacting to Durant's excitement, turned to Dort and said, "Dallas, I think Billy has gone crazy."

Yet in 1910, when Nash succeeded Durant as president of Buick, he was quickly transformed into an automotive executive, impressing Storrow and the new GM banker board. In late 1911, they elevated him to president of General Motors, while retaining him as Buick president. They also recruited important help for Nash. At Storrow's suggestion, Nash hired an assistant manager of American Locomotive as Buick's works manager. Storrow felt Nash needed a good manufacturing man at GM's most important operation. Actually Nash was cool to the idea at first, and he offered only a modest salary to the new recruit. The man's name? Walter P. Chrysler. And even though Chrysler would lose money by taking Nash's offer, he accepted anyway. Chrysler was determined to get into the automobile business.

Walter Chrysler turned out to be an exceptional manufacturing leader. When he first toured the immense Buick factories in late 1911, he saw men skilled at working with wood, a holdover from carriage days — which was temporarily acceptable as automobile bodies were still made of wood. But Chrysler saw they had little knowledge of metallurgy. He thought to himself, "What a job I could do here, if I were boss."

Once he was hired as Buick works manager, Chrysler made daily decisions to cut costs, build quality and speed production. He improved assembly lines, working conditions and paint processing and made countless other accommodations. Arriving in February 1912, he took leadership in continually improving the product. One notable example was working with Nash to finally clear the way for equipping Buicks with Charles F. Kettering's electric self-starter for 1914 (two years after Cadillac and over the objections of insiders whose criticism had killed this much-desired feature for 1913 Buicks). He supported his workers with improvements in lighting, ventilation and on-site medical help, while also encouraging company sponsored baseball and soccer teams.

This was all very helpful to Nash, who was enjoying his new career. Buick's Flint complex became so famous that Theodore Roosevelt, the former U.S. president campaigning for a return to office, toured the site with Nash October 8, 1912, surrounded by crowds of workers. It was chilly and rainy and Roosevelt had a cold, so there was no speech. But Teddy turned to the crowd as he walked into Nash's office and proclaimed he had just learned Nash had started 22 years earlier working for a dollar a day. "That is what I believe in — equal opportunity for every man."

Durant was having less fun. Though still a GM vice president, he saw himself with little power in the company he had founded. When he made suggestions, no one listened. Or so he said.

Durant wouldn't accept that for long. Noted for his ability at card games, he began to play the new reality like a poker hand, sometimes coolly, sometimes with dizzying and unpredictable moves. At times his actions were clearly calculated; at other times he must have been feeling his way along. But he knew where he wanted to go. As he wrote:

> With no idea of being disloyal it seemed to me that it would be better to let the new group handle the business to suit themselves and if I ever expected to regain control of General Motors, which I certainly intended to do, I should have a company of my own, run in my own way. In other words another one-man institution, but taking a leaf out of Henry Ford's book — No Bankers.

Durant, still on the GM board, began to work. At no time was his nickname "the little wizard" more appropriate than in 1911-1912, when he created five firms with seemingly a wave of his magic wand. One of them was named Chevrolet Motor Company.

The beginnings of Chevrolet are particularly relevant to the Buick story because Durant used his Buick experiences as a pattern for his new company. And not just his experiences — but the same city, same people, same factories.

Also, in his autobiographical notes, Durant stressed the importance of telling "the true story of the early history of one of the greatest units of General Motors Corporation — the Chevrolet Motor Company...I am placing this recital ahead of at least 20 stories of lesser importance because I want this story preserved before it is too late. If the other 20 are never written, it will make no material difference." Indeed, it can be argued that GM was not fully launched until it was combined with Chevrolet.

Helping Durant in one way or another as he created Chevrolet Motor Company were former Buick presidents James H. Whiting and Charles M. Begole, former Buick treasurer William S. Ballenger, former Buick plant manager William H. "Big Bill" Little and former Buick engine builder Arthur C. Mason. Reaching deeper into his past, Durant tapped A.B.C. Hardy, onetime president of the Durant-Dort Carriage Company and in 1901 Flint's first automaker, for his manufacturing expertise. And Dallas Dort, Durant's old carriage partner, was for a time scheduled for a major leadership role.

Of all the Buick men now on Durant's Chevrolet payroll, the most notable was Louis Chevrolet, that former member of Buick's elite racing team. Born in Switzerland, raised in France, the 210-pound six-footer was physically strong, energetic, determined, with large intense eyes and a bristling mustache. He was flamboyant, courageous and successful, with an instinctive knowledge of automobiles. Louis Chevrolet was a big name among those daring pioneer auto racers.

Chevrolet and his fellow members of the Buick racing team — notably his co-star, Wild Bob Burman — had won 500 trophies from 1908 to 1910 under Durant's enthusiastic sponsorship. But by late 1910, with Durant no longer in charge, the racing team was starved for funding from the new banker-led regime. So Chevrolet was agreeable when Durant tapped him on the shoulder. As Louis himself remembered: "He was planning a comeback and told me, 'We're going to need a car.' So I built it.'"

The wizard moved on several fronts. Working with old associates Arthur Mason and Bill Little, Durant helped create two new companies in Flint, Mason Motor Company July 31, 1911, and the Little

Motor Car Company, which would build the Little automobile, October 30, 1911. Turning to Detroit, Durant worked behind the scenes to create Chevrolet Motor Company November 3, 1911. Besides Louis Chevrolet, the incorporators were Bill Little and Dr. Edwin R. Campbell, Durant's son-in-law.

Durant also launched two other firms, Republic Motor and Sterling Motor. He envisioned Republic, announced in July 1912, as his super company, sort of a new GM, capitalized at $65 million. Under Durant's grand plan, Republic would be the mother of 10 other corporations in as many states that would have the same name and handle sales (and maybe regional manufacturing) of the new Little and Chevrolet automobiles. Sterling Motor, with Durant and Dort as its top officers, had been incorporated August 29, 1911, originally to build six-cylinder engines for Chevrolet and Little cars in Flint. Both Republic and Sterling became dead ends. Durant's whole elaborate Republic plan was soon scrapped in favor of making Chevrolet the dominant company. As for Sterling, it was defunct by November of 1913.

Chevrolet historian Ken Kaufmann relates this sequence of events. Durant and Louis began planning a Chevrolet car company shortly after the Buick racing team was mostly disbanded by GM's management team early in 1911. Durant agreed to sponsor a new Chevrolet racing team and to finance a Chevrolet motor and car. Louis rented a second-floor shop at 701-707 Grand River in Detroit and hired French designer Etienne Planche, who he had worked with earlier, and machinist Henry Winterhoff to help create a high-powered sporty "raceabout." Kaufmann called this "the first Chevrolet car built in Detroit" and described its engine as a very powerful twin-cam T-head that Kaufmann estimated generated 75 horsepower. It was fast and noisy. Once, while Louis was testing it in the middle of the night, a policeman stopped him and asked his name. When Louis responded, the unbelieving officer ticketed him for impersonating a famous race car driver!

Louis's hot "raceabout" never got into production but by May, 1911, *The Flint Journal* was reporting Durant was planning to organize the Chevrolet Motor Company in Detroit. In June the Flint Board of Commerce protested it wanted the factory in Flint. On July 15, newspapers reported that Bill Little was saying a Chevrolet car company was about to be organized and that a plant of the Corcoran

Top: Louis Chevrolet at the wheel of a Buick race car. Center: Louis (in tie) working with fellow Buick racing team members on a Marquette-Buick engine. Below: Louis in white coat with the first Chevrolet automobile, a Classic Six, in Detroit. Others include William C. Durant, GM founder and creator of Chevrolet Motor Co. (standing nearest windshield); A.B.C. Hardy (just behind Durant); and Big Bill Little (tall man in cap next to Louis). Durant's son Cliff is at the wheel, with wife Adelaide.

Detroit Lamp Company on West Grand Boulevard was to be leased August 1.

Meanwhile, Louis and his team turned to development of what would become the first badged Chevrolet, the Classic Six or Type C. Progress was slow. Three to five prototypes were built from late 1911 into 1912. The famous photo of the first Chevrolet Classic Six, positioned with Billy Durant, Louis Chevrolet, A.B.C. Hardy and Bill Little, and with Durant's son Cliff at the wheel, was first published in the *Detroit Free Press* December 15, 1912. Production versions were finally on the market in the summer of 1913, apparently as 1914 models.

Up in Flint, Durant took control of the Flint Wagon Works. It was winding down, making only a few horse vehicles and a small car named the Whiting. The wagon works' owners, Whiting, Begole and William S. Ballenger, were happy to work with Durant again, selling the wagon works to him for almost no up-front money on a promissory note. Durant put his old associate A.B.C. Hardy in charge of turning wagon factories and the Whiting tooling into a modern automobile operation.[1]

In August of 1911, Bill Little began design work on a small four-cylinder roadster and six-cylinder touring car — which would become the Little Four and Little Six — in the leased former lamp factory in Detroit. Actually, A.B.C. Hardy confirmed that the Whiting — scrapped by Durant after he took over the wagon works — was simply "revamped and improved" to create the 1912 Little Four (which was updated with a stylish torpedo body after about two dozen were built, according to Kaufmann). After the enhancements were made in Detroit, the resulting Little prototype was sent back to Flint November 9, 1911, where production would begin at the wagon works. On March 2, 1912, *Automotive Topics* reported Little had stopped using the Whiting company's name. The first production Little left the Flint plant in mid-April 1912. Durant arranged for Bill Little to work with Louis Chevrolet to get production started in

---

1 Besides the Whiting and its apparently close cousin, the Little, there was one other barely known marque. Hubert K. Dalton, James Whiting's son-in-law, was in charge of Whiting production when, with Whiting's backing, he developed a small roadster called the Dalton around 1911. After Durant bought the Flint Wagon Works, where the Whiting was built, Dalton and Whiting announced plans to build the Dalton at another Flint location. However only three were ever made. In 1970, the writer interviewed Carl Prahl, 84, a Buick retiree who had designed the Dalton's engine, which he said was similar to the Whiting's.

Evolution of vehicles built at the former Flint Wagon Works factory include (from top) 1911 Whiting, 1912 Little and 1913 Chevrolet Royal Mail roadster.

Detroit on the Classic Six, though Durant was none too enthusiastic about the car's size and cost.

Durant also arranged for Mason, who left Buick in 1911, to move his new company in the spring of 1913 from a corner of the Flint Wagon Works into the original Flint Buick factory, part of the wagon works property. (One report said Mason had designed a new engine but that Buick leaders, backed by Beacraft, had opposed any change, so he quit and started his own company). Buick engine production had moved in 1909 to a huge new factory in the north Flint Buick complex, with Randolph Truck briefly occupying the original Buick building. Mason, who had begun building Buick engines in that very plant starting in 1903, would now make motors there for Durant's newest automobiles, the Chevrolet and the Little.

One of Durant's best decisions was to place A.B.C. Hardy in charge of getting the Little car into production in the old Flint Wagon Works buildings. Hardy, bald and plump and one of Durant's best friends, was a strong hands-on leader. He rolled up his sleeves, sold off the remnants of the wagon business, cleared out the buildings and quickly converted the old Whiting assembly operations to production of the Little.

In the meantime, Louis Chevrolet and his car struggled in Detroit. The oft-quoted Chevrolet production number of 2,999 cars built in 1912 is actually total production in Flint of the Little Four in 1912-13. The 2,999 are listed as Littles in a Chevrolet memo of April 14, 1917, made available by Ken Kaufmann. Don Williams, president of the Vintage Chevrolet Club of America, also provided information on this period. (Whether cars badged as Littles should also be counted as Chevrolets is an auto-historian issue that will largely be avoided here — though it's hard to see the 2,999 as anything other than Littles. Adding to the confusion, in an undated but probably summer 1913 ad of Chevrolet Motor Company, a model is titled the "Chevrolet Special Little Six.") In June 1913, it was announced Chevrolet had purchased the entire business of the Little Motor Car Company and that the complete line of cars formerly made by both companies would hereafter be known as Chevrolets. One Chevy historian suggested it would be more accurate to say Durant merged the Chevrolet company and the Little company into a single entity, because he controlled them both.[2]

---

2 The 1917 memo also says 494 of the Little Six were produced in 1913 and 402 of the Chevrolet Type C (Classic Six) were built in 1913-14. A few of the Classic

While Durant and his associates worked through various production scenarios in Detroit and Flint, as early as fall 1911 rumors were circulating that Durant was considering moving the whole Chevrolet operation to Flint.

Flint civic leaders, giddy about the possibility Durant might visit another great industry on the city, held an appreciation dinner for "the Man" on November 28, 1911, in the local Masonic Temple. It was gala event, sold out, headlined "The Wizard's Banquet." Old friends paid Durant lavish tributes and cigars were passed out labeled "El Capitan de Industria." Durant wrote to Catherine from a hotel in Detroit: "It was a great tribute and I can never forget it. Truly the event of my life."

Durant struggled to find the right product for his comeback. He said one of his cars, apparently Louis Chevrolet's Classic Six, was "from the standpoint of cost, impossible." He felt it was too big and too expensive. He wanted a product just a little upscale from Ford's Model T. Also, he said, the first car built in Flint, which would be the Little, was "a disappointment — it did not stand the grueling test to which it was subjected — driven to its death in 25,000 miles." Still, a small and inexpensive car was closer to what he wanted. Finally Durant made his decision. In early 1913, he moved Chevrolet production to Flint, soon folded up the Little car (Hardy told him the obvious: the Little name alone made it hard to market) and began making newly designed Chevrolet cars on the Little assembly line at the wagon works.

So, in the summer of 1913, the 1914 Chevrolet Royal Mail roadster and Baby Grand touring car – the first cars to wear the Chevy bow-tie logo – were in production in Flint, in the old wagon works buildings (bow-tie logo story, page 148). Durant had also bought the old Imperial Wheel plant, which was situated in the growing Buick complex, and assembly began there of the Chevy Classic Six and possibly Light Six. Reportedly 3,500 Chevrolets were built there the first year.[3]

Sixes were built in Detroit, but most were built in Flint. The only known Chevrolet Classic Six in the United States is in Flint's Sloan Museum; an older one has been identified in Canada.

3 In 1914, this plant, known as Chevrolet No. 2, was sold to Monroe Motor Company, for a time closely associated with Chevrolet. Buick took control of the building in 1916. It was razed in 1939, according to Don Bent, the leading authority on the history of the Flint Buick complex.

Charles Begole, who had been Buick's first president under Durant, was by then Chevrolet's president. Hardy was Chevrolet's vice president and general manager and also a vice president of Mason Motor.

Flint, the old Vehicle City of carriage days, which got its original impetus as a boom town under Durant's grandfather, the lumber baron and governor Henry Crapo, was now booming as never before as thousands came looking for work and finding it in Buick and Chevrolet factories sprouting everywhere.

But before 1913 was out, Louis Chevrolet was gone. Unhappy to see his Classic Six about to be dropped in favor of smaller, cheaper models, he decided to resign — but the trigger was a quarrel over Chevrolet's smoking habits. Catherine Durant told the writer it wasn't so much that Louis smoked — Durant himself had smoked cigars for a time — but that Chevrolet's habit of having a cigarette hanging off his lower lip "used to annoy Willie to tears." Chevrolet told Durant: "I sold you my car and I sold you my name, but I'm not going to sell myself to you...I'm going to smoke my cigarettes as much as I want. And I'm getting out."

Another dropout was Dallas Dort, Durant's old carriage partner and a behind-the-scenes force as Durant took control of Buick and then founded GM. Dort had been considered for a major role in what was to become Chevrolet. But in 1913 they split — Dort decided to create his own auto firm, Dort Motor, out of the vestiges of the Durant-Dort Carriage Company. Durant concentrated all his plans under the Chevrolet name and resigned from Durant-Dort. The parting of these two partners has puzzled local historians for decades. It's likely Durant's son-in-law, Dr. Edwin R. Campbell, played a role. In recently discovered letters to Durant from that period, Campbell expressed at some length his view that Dort looked too old "and will be a damn nuisance to you." Whether Durant agreed, the parting did not destroy their relationship. Durant and and Dort remained friends until Dort's death in 1925.

With the right Chevrolet models now in production, Durant once again headed east in search of money to boost production. He violated his "no bankers" rule when he found one he could trust — Louis J. Kaufman, president of the Chatham & Phenix Bank of New York City. Durant made that connection through a mutual friend, Nathan Hofheimer, and was so concerned about their first meeting that he

The ever-changing signage on this Flint, Michigan, plant shows how local industry evolved from carriages to automobiles and then how ownership changed from one brand to another. Built in 1901 as a factory of Imperial Wheel Company, a Durant-Dort Carriage Company subsidiary, it was used first to make carriage wheels. In 1912-14 it was an assembly center for the Chevrolet Classic Six and then briefly (1915) for assembly of Monroe Motor Company cars. Finally it became part of Buick's vast Flint operations, once one of the world's largest manufacturing centers (above in 1916 and below, circled, around 1938 in air view shortly before demolition).

took A.B.C. Hardy with him to Kaufman's apartment in New York's Ritz-Carleton Hotel. The meeting was a success — Kaufman became Chevrolet's leading financier and persuaded a major brokerage house to underwrite a Chevrolet stock issue that generated $2.75 million for the company. Durant said this financed tooling of a Chevrolet assembly plant in New York City, the purchase of a former Maxwell plant at Tarrytown, N.Y., and the beginning of Chevrolet's "magnificent growth that has not stopped since."

Durant arranged with old friend Sam McLaughlin to build Chevrolets in Canada, as well as the McLaughlin Buicks he was already producing. The nucleus of GM of Canada was being formed.

By 1915, having built Chevrolet Motor Company into a prosperous, fast-growing player in a booming industry, Durant was primed to wrest control of General Motors from the bankers. Thanks to Kaufman's connections, he got help from top executives of the powerful DuPont Company, first treasurer John J. Raskob, and then president Pierre S. du Pont. Durant could make GM stock available at the right price. Kaufman persuaded the DuPont interests to support Durant's return to power at GM, although they apparently didn't realize they were walking into a dispute over control.

Durant, more bullish about the future of the automobile than GM's own banker board, believed the corporation's stock was very much under-valued. When the price fell to $25 a share — at a time Durant figured it was worth $1,000 — he began to buy aggressively. He persuaded his friends to buy as well and began trading Chevrolet stock for GM stock. Quietly they built their collective stake in GM. And they were willing to part with shares at an apparent loss in order to bring in the powerful DuPonts.

For a time, the bankers on the GM board seemed oblivious to Durant's plans. Most of them appeared uninterested in buying GM shares. They may have felt satisfied. The years of banker control had yielded positive results in their minds. They had pulled the corporation through retrenchment and into a period of advancing sales. Charles Nash had proved a solid leader. But this was a virgin market, the automobile was being greatly improved and Ford was pulling far ahead. As one unnamed GM vice president told author Lawrence H. Seltzer in *A Financial History of the American Automobile Industry*, "The bankers were too skeptical about the future of the automobile industry...Under Durant, the company might have had a little finan-

WILLIAM C. DURANT IS FEASTED BY FRIENDS AS FLINT'S 'WIZARD'

"El Capitan de Industria" Is Title Conferred Upon Him by 150 of City's Leading Business Men.

Banquet at Masonic Temple a Tribute to Man Who Put Vehicle City on the Map of the World.

Honored Guest Tells of Beginning of His Industrial Activity and His Hopes for the Future of Flint.

William C. Durant, "the wizard," "El Capitan de Industria," was the guest of honor at a banquet tendered by about 150 of his friends and associates in the Masonic temple Tuesday night. It was named "the wizard's banquet," and its purpose was to evidence in a public way the appreciation of his personal acquaintance and business associate for the things he has done for Flint. It was designed as a recognition of his efforts to place Flint on the map through the medium of the largest automobile plant in the world, due directly to his genius for organization and development. Further, it was an appreciation for the interest he has taken in Flint institutions, his philanthropy in assisting movements which are now industrial...

WILLIAM CHAPO DURANT.

PATTERSON JURY OUT

DELIBERATES ALL NIGHT WITH-OUT REACHING VERDICT.

Counsel in the Case Do Not Expect

El capitan de industria

A memorable dinner, "The Wizard's Banquet," honored W.C. Durant at the newly built Flint Masonic Temple Nov. 28, 1911. Durant wrote wife Catherine: "It was a great tribute...truly the event of my life." There has been speculation it may have helped persuade Durant, Buick's ex-leader and GM's founder, to move Chevrolet production to Flint. Local car historians gave the manager of the 102-year-old Masonic a framed document including this clipping in June 2013.

cial difficulty now and then, but it would have grown much faster and its earnings would have been much greater."

At the GM stockholders' meeting of September 16, 1915, only weeks before the bankers' voting trust was to expire, Durant struck. He dramatically claimed he and his associates owned enough stock to take control of the company. Durant had informed Nash of his plans, and Storrow and the banker board were ready for him. After heated discussions, there was a short-term compromise, with DuPont executives, just learning of the dispute, agreeing to be a buffer between the banker and Durant interests on the board. One important new director was Arthur G. Bishop, president of Flint's Genesee Bank, who had helped bankroll Durant's developments from those early days in the carriage business and his start with Buick.

Durant stopped his take-over plans long enough to support a sensational $50 dividend for holders of GM stock that had sold for $25 two years earlier because no dividend had ever been paid. Then he stepped up his stock-buying spree. By the spring of 1916, with help from friends, Durant had gathered enough GM stock to take full control. His Chevrolet company held the controlling shares. Chevrolet, in effect, owned General Motors. (In 1918 Durant untied what Alfred P. Sloan Jr. called this "odd knot" and placed Chevrolet under the GM umbrella).

When he started his comeback in 1915, Durant had asked Nash to remain as GM president. Nash was less than enthusiastic — he knew Durant would make all the decisions. While he still had some affection for his long-time friend and former boss, Nash was now closer to Storrow and others on the bankers' board. On one hand, Durant respected Nash's abilities and valued their old friendship. But he also remembered Nash's long-ago comment to Dort that maybe Durant was crazy to become so excited about the auto industry. It was a joke, but still it contained a truth. By the time Durant had finally jumped into automobiles, Nash was still a horse-and-buggy man. And the reason Nash was president of GM was because Durant had gotten him placed as president of Buick. There was no question Nash was a fine man and a talented executive. But GM was Durant's "baby" and he didn't want a lot of advice on how to raise it.

For a time Nash stayed on, wavering. "I am fast becoming discouraged and losing interest in the whole proposition," he told Durant at one point. Durant, put off by what he saw as Nash's lack of loyalty, began to turn on him. Storrow, a major adversary of Durant, had predicted Nash's departure in a letter to a business associate on September 24, 1915, that showed no appreciation for Durant's role as GM's founder.

> If a good opportunity comes along...I shall resign [from the GM board]. If things do not seem to be going smoothly or well, Mr. Nash undoubtedly will resign also. I felt obliged to make the fight [his unsuccessful effort to keep the bankers in control of GM] because it seemed to me we could not permit the Company to be turned over to Mr. Durant to wreck again. I feel reasonably confident that the new Board will not allow Mr. Durant to be the dictator of the Company.

Durant was certainly a mesmerizing figure. He was usually charming. Even Storrow's biographer, Henry Greenleaf Pearson, was impressed. He quoted one New York banker: "Durant is a genius, and therefore not to be dealt with on the same basis as ordinary business men. In many respects he is a child in his emotions, in temperament and in mental balance, yet possessed of wonderful energy and ability along certain other well-defined lines. He is sensitive and proud; and successful leadership, I think, really counts more with him than financial success."

In the 1916-20 era, William C. Durant (6th from left, front row) was at the peak of his power at GM. Among others here are Walter P. Chrysler (directly behind Durant), president of Buick and then GM vice president of operations; Pierre S. du Pont (just to the left of Durant), chairman of GM's board; A.B.C. Hardy (just to the right of Durant), general manager of Chevrolet; John J. Raskob (second from right in rear), chairman of GM's finance committee and later builder of New York's Empire State Building; and Charles Stewart Mott (second from left in rear), who would serve on GM's board for 60 years and become Flint's great philanthropist.

But Durant could turn cold if crossed. Aristo Scrobogna, Durant's last personal secretary, generally praised the man he called "the boss" — even referring to him as "Christ-like." But he admitted to the writer: "Once he decided he didn't like something or someone, he could be quite mean."

Durant wrote in the spring of 1916 to Dr. Edwin R. Campbell, not only his son-in-law but by then his closest confidant: "Nash ...appears to have gotten himself in bad and I am to be a reception committee of one to meet him on his return from California [a business trip]. I am through with the side-stepping and four-flushing and expect...to have the atmosphere cleared once and for all." After a confrontation, in which Durant allegedly told him, "Well, Charlie, you're through," Nash submitted his resignation April 18, 1916. In June, Durant finally took formal charge of his "baby" — he became GM president.

Durant valued loyalty. He never forgave Charles F. Kettering for a perceived affront. "Boss Ket," inventor of the automobile self-starter, would become GM's — and maybe the world's — most famous engineer. In 1916, on the day GM completed purchase of Kettering's companies in Dayton, Ohio, Kettering didn't show up at Durant's office, instead sending his business partner, Edward Deeds, to complete the sale. Decades later, Durant admitted to Deeds he was "very surprised" by Kettering's absence. Durant was even angrier after he had Deeds sign a statement that day promising not to sell stock received in the transaction for four months, only to discover a large offering of the stock immediately went on the market from Kettering's broker.

Kettering would never discuss the incident at any length with Durant, who still pressed for an explanation about all this a quarter-century later. Kettering in a letter to Durant December 5, 1940, said, "I cannot give an intelligent answer to your questions. Am just a mechanic as you well know." Durant never bought that argument. In 1943, he wrote to Deeds that Kettering "has always been too busy to pay any attention to me."

In 1916, Storrow tried to get Chrysler to follow Nash out the door, to join Nash and Storrow in the purchase of the Thomas B. Jeffery Company of Kenosha, Wis. (which would become Nash Motors Company). But Durant, using both his salesmanship and a great deal of money, persuaded Chrysler to stay and become president of Buick Motor Company. Chrysler became an admirer of Durant (As Chrysler once famously remarked: "He could charm a bird right down out of a tree"). But as Nash predicted, their business relationship would not last long.

Durant and Chrysler did have a few successful years together. In 1917, during World War I, Chrysler personally landed a contract for Buick to build 3,000 Liberty engines for aircraft (it built 1,338 by war's end). He expanded the huge engine plant to assure all Buicks would have six-cylinder engines by 1919. That year, when Chrysler had moved up to GM vice president of operations and a member of its executive committee, he persuaded Durant and the GM board to buy 60 percent of Fisher Body, a great addition to the corporation.

In his second tenure at GM, Durant expanded the corporation greatly. He brought in such iconic figures as Alfred P. Sloan Jr., who became a legendary GM leader in the post-Durant decades, as well as the brilliant Kettering. Durant also personally backed a small company that was struggling to make refrigerators. Durant, excited about this latest benefit to humanity, this wonderful new "self-seller," provided personal funds to develop the product and he himself came up with the brand name — Frigidaire. Once Frigidaire was up and running, he placed the company under the GM umbrella without taking a personal profit. Frigidaire became a huge success. Said Sloan: "I'd bet my life he did not make a dollar for himself in that or any other similar deal...W.C. Durant habitually behaved unselfishly."

In Flint, the Buick complex on the city's north side was a monument to the efforts of both Durant and Chrysler. When Durant was putting that complex together, he called it "one of the largest and best equipped automobile factories in this country, with a capacity of 25,000 cars a year." Twenty years later, the complex had 68 buildings with 4.6 million square feet of floor space. That included the engine plant, built by Durant in 1909, expanded by Chrysler a few years later, and said to be the largest manufacturing building in the world, with more than six acres under roof.[4]

In early 1920, John J. Raskob, then chairman of GM's finance committee, sent Durant financial statements pointing out that in 1915, the year the voting trust matured and Durant regained control, the company had about $58 million in assets, and by October 31, 1919, the latest balance sheet showed total assets at $452 million. "In other words," Raskob wrote, "the General Motors Corporation of today is eight times as large as the company which the bankers were managing. This is indeed a fine tribute to your foresight."

But things began to unravel. Chrysler quit late in 1919 after a series of disputes with Durant over control of Buick decisions — though the two repaired their relationship and became close friends for life. "The automobile industry owes more to Durant than it has yet acknowledged," Chrysler said years later. "In some ways, he has been its greatest man. Sometimes we found ourselves in arguments but we also had a lot of fun." In the 1920s, Chrysler would take over what was left of Maxwell operations as the basis to form Chrysler Corporation.

---

4 The complex continued to expand over the decades, notably under two of Buick's best general managers. In the late 1940s, under Harlow Curtice, later a GM president and 1955 *Time* magazine "Man of the Year," the complex grew by two million square feet of floor space. Fortune magazine said Buick estimated it could then build 500,000 cars a year on that site. In the 1980s, Lloyd Reuss, who would also become a GM president, set the stage for the complex to be reconstructed into a state-of-the-art assembly operation named Buick City, which for a time produced world-class quality LeSabres. Assembly at the complex ended in 1999, after which the buildings were razed.

At Buick, he was succeeded by Harry Bassett, who had been president of Charles Stewart Mott's company that had moved to Flint from Utica, N.Y., in 1906-07, at Durant's invitation, to build axles for Buick. When Weston-Mott was absorbed by GM in 1916, Bassett became assistant general manager and then general manager of Buick under Chrysler's Buick presidency. So he was perfectly positioned to take over for Chrysler. Bassett, though a quiet man whose name is barely remembered compared to his predecessors, was nevertheless an effective leader. Under his direction, the Buick automobile was continually improved until his untimely death at age 51 on October 17, 1926, when he contracted pneumonia while traveling in France.[5]

In late 1920, the Durant era at General Motors ended rather abruptly. Billy Durant, the savior of Buick, Cadillac, Oldsmobile and Oakland, the creator of Chevrolet Motor Company, the founder of General Motors and finally its president, was removed from power — again — when he became heavily indebted in the stock market. Whether his departure was solely the result of his own stock speculations or a plot by others as his widow and last secretary insisted — or a combination of both — is still debated.

Alvan Macauley, president of Packard Motor Car Company, remarked in a letter to U.S. Sen. Truman H. Newberry on December 9, 1919: "There is still a clique in Wall Street that hasn't forgiven Durant for his coup in regaining control of General Motors. I have always understood they intend to get him ultimately, and there may be opportunities for them to do so, if things should not continue to break handsomely."

Durant landed on his feet. He promptly created Durant Motors and became the "bull of bulls" in the stock market in the Roaring Twenties.

---

5 For the record: When Durant reorganized the General Motors Company as the General Motors Corporation, Buick Motor Company disappeared as a company as GM turned its various companies into divisions. On December 30, 1916, Buick Motor Company filed a notice of dissolution. The document was recorded January 3, 1917, and Buick was no longer a separate corporation. Another event to note: In September 1917, during a reorganization of Buick, Durant became president of Buick for one hour, with Chrysler then re-elected president.

Chapter 17

David Buick's final years

As Billy Durant alternately won and lost battles as he created a giant industry, David Buick drifted from one misadventure to another. His last name, however, was marching on to great success. Despite the considerable turmoil at General Motors, its Buick automobile had become ever stronger under brilliant successive leaders — William C. Durant, Charles W. Nash, Walter P. Chrysler and Harry H. Bassett.

By the early 1920s, the Buick marque was one of the world's elite automobiles — in terms of power, reliability, value and style. Beginning about that time, all kinds of leaders were driving Buicks over a 20-year period — from the king of England to the last emperor of China to the sultan of Johore. This was no accident. As Alfred P. Sloan Jr., who became GM president in 1923, once commented, Buick succeeded because "it had the management of stars."[1]

Discussing the state of the business in the early 1920s, Sloan observed: "It was Buick that made any kind of General Motors car line worth talking about." In 1921, Sloan wrote to GM Chairman Pierre du Pont: "It is far better that the rest of General Motors be scrapped than any chances taken with Buick's earning power."

By this time, Enos DeWaters had succeeded Walter Marr as chief engineer, though Marr still worked until 1923 on special projects for

---

1 Pu Yi, last emperor of China, was forced to abdicate as a child in 1912 but returned to at least partial power during turbulent political times. Pu Yi bought a six-cylinder Buick on May 8, 1926, from an American agency in Tianjin, according to Wang Qingxiang, a researcher with the Academy of Social Sciences in Jilin Province. He writes in his book, *Extraordinary Citizen*, that Pu Yi took the car, which was painted red, to Changchun and often drove it at the palace there. He even had the national flower of Manchuria painted on the car. Also, Sun Yat-sen, first provisional president of the Republic of China, was photographed in a Buick in Shanghai in 1912. A 1941 Buick similar to one owned by the widely respected postwar president of China, Zhou Enlai, was seen by the writer in a Shanghai museum in 1997. A postwar Buick often used by Madame Chiang Kai-shek, wife of the generalissimo, is displayed in another museum.

the company from his retirement home at Signal Mountain, Tenn. Marr's career had been eventful. He helped create Flint's first airplane, the *Flint Flyer*, which had a Buick engine, in 1910. He designed an experimental tank for Buick during World War I. Seldom leaving Signal Mountain, he often commented on, and sometimes solved, engineering problems sent to him from Buick headquarters.

His interest in aviation was such that an early airport near Marr's retirement home was named Marr Field (Marr chose the site and even helped clear the land). While he didn't like to venture far from his treasured home, he did reminisce about his life in speeches before clubs in Chattanooga and in newspaper interviews during infrequent visits to Flint. There he would visit the Buick plant and such old friends as Charles Stewart Mott. Marr died in 1941.

Eugene Richard also remained at Buick until his retirement. The man who patented the Buick overhead-valve engine (he held seven patents during his first period at Buick) had continued to be an important contributor after rejoining the company in 1908. He was issued 12 additional patents between 1912 and 1931, all pertaining to various aspects of engine performance — intake manifolds, carburetors, fuel systems, valve springs and pistons. During that period he was often called upon by chief engineers DeWaters and later Dutch Bower to weigh in on engineering decisions until he became ill in 1931. Richard died in 1938.

James Whiting, 76, died June 9, 1919, at the home of his daughter, Mrs. Hubert Dalton, in New York City. He and his wife Alice had gone East to a resort the previous summer. He was called from there to New York on business in September and had a paralyzing stroke there. He hoped to return to his home in Flint but never recovered enough to travel. His funeral was in Flint.

As for David Buick, when he went to California he was still trying to make money using his inventive abilities – and his now famous name. In 1913 he patented a well-boring tool designed to improve the efficiency of drilling in the sandy oil fields. In 1914, he patented an automobile carburetor and licensed the rights to the Jackson (Mich.) Carburetor Company, owned by his old associates Ben and Frank Briscoe. That year he also briefly considered establishing an auto factory, brand unnamed, in Monrovia, Calif.

In the fall of 1919, David was joined by his two sons in a new firm, the David Buick Carburetor Company, headquartered in Wyandotte, Mich. That firm built and sold the "Buick Hi-Power Carbure-

In this circa 1920 photo discovered in a news service archive, the only person identified is David Buick at left. There's no other information but the timing and background suggest it may have been taken during a test of his new carburetor somewhere in the west. The wild flowers appear safe.

tor" which, it was advertised, could improve a car's power 30 percent and its mileage 25 percent. One ad said, "dealers and agents offered big opportunities — write quick."

A 1920 product review said a Briscoe car equipped with a Buick carburetor averaged 28.8 miles per gallon in a Los Angeles-to-Yosemite economy run. Later, in more ideal conditions, it was said to average an amazing 51.2 mpg. Ads continued to appear into 1923 but not much more was heard of it.

In June of 1921, David appeared as president of Lorraine Motors Corporation in Grand Rapids, Mich. The announcement, published in *Automotive Industries*, said David "has designed a new car that will be put on the market shortly." The car would be marketed as the Lorraine but would be different from that which the company had been manufacturing. The new model, it was announced, "will be equipped with a valve-in-head engine, Buick being credited with having brought out the first engine of that type." (George Ferris of Grand Rapids, who once wrote an article on the Lorraine for *Antique Automobile*, told the writer the overhead-valve engine for Lorraine never happened. The Lorraine was powered by an L-head motor.)

Automotive Industries said a "strong organization" had been created. David's associates included A. H. Wyatt, who was "well known

The New Dunbar Car, Roadster Model.

Keith Marvin

Ad for Dunbar automobile.

in automotive and financial circles in Michigan," and John H. Larkin, former sales manager of the Haynes car of Kokomo, Ind. According to one published report, about 350 Lorraines rolled off the assembly line in the brief period Buick headed the firm, probably in name only, before it folded.

The Lorraine car had barely hit the rocks when a story was floated about a new David Buick automobile venture — to build a car named the Dunbar (his middle name and his paternal grandmother's maiden name). *Automobile Topics* of August 12, 1922, reported: "It is understood that negotiations are pending for the purchase of a plant. Production is expected to begin, in five models, early next year. Financial plans are not shown as yet but it is understood that a capital of $5,000,000 will be set upon. The project has been hatching for some little time."

Walden, N.Y., a village of 5,000 people about 85 miles northwest of New York City, would be its location. The local hat factory had just closed, and so had the Borden Company's milk processing plant. The Borden plant, a sprawling brick structure dating to 1884 and with 70,000 square feet of floor space, was being peddled by the Dairymen's League. Walden was clearly in the market for jobs.

According to the late auto historian Keith Marvin in *Special Interest Autos* in December 1980, the key promoter of the Dunbar car was Harry C. Hoeft, whose top assistant was J. L. Dornbos, who in

May-December marriage: David Buick and Margaret Harrington

turn had the titles of vice president and treasurer of the newly formed David Dunbar Buick Corporation, headquartered in New York City.

At a mass meeting in Walden on February 1, 1923, Hoeft outlined the company's plans. The corporation would indeed be capitalized at $5 million. Common stock would be available at $10 a share — or $5 if you were a citizen of Walden. Attractive stock certificates were printed.

Enough money was raised to purchase the former Borden factory, and David Buick himself arrived in Walden on February 15, apparently to oversee the purchase details. On April 26, 1923, *Automotive Industries* confirmed the corporation had bought the plant and said operations were expected to begin in May. Plans now called for building four models of the Dunbar automobile, with the open cars listing for around $1,100 and the closed models at about $1,400.

In August, the corporation opened part of the factory so hundreds of investors and other interested persons could tour the building and see the one Dunbar car, said to have been built for $500 and shipped in from Detroit. A party atmosphere, with picnic tables and refreshments, was created inside the plant.

199

The car looked good and, with its Continental engine, it ran well. The Walden *Citizen-Herald* said it was painted "in a beautiful maroon with battleship red wheels." The newspaper's editor was given a ride. "The engine works beautifully and the furnishings of the car were first class," it was reported. But when the party was over, the car disappeared, the factory doors closed and nobody even cleaned up. When someone peeked into the building 10 weeks later to see how the factory was progressing, it was discovered, as Marvin wrote, "the site was exactly as it had been when the picnic ended. Plates, napkins and glasses still graced the tables, the room was still festooned with the red, white and blue bunting and the well-fed mice had long since disappeared."

There were only token, futile attempts to sue the backers. Decades later, people were still wondering about whatever happened to that beautiful maroon Dunbar roadster, with its sleek styling and red disc wheels. "I don't think anyone knows where it was built or where it went," Marvin told the writer.

Marvin's story was headlined: "The Dunbar Deception: Was David Buick a schnook or a sharpie?" Interviewed by the writer, Marvin pointed out he didn't write the headline. "David Buick was a bad-luck guy," he said. "He had a series of problems [in his business ventures] after he got out of the plumbing business." Marvin said he believed David was ignorant of any fraud plans and was basically "played for a sucker."

David took time out from all these failed business ventures to remarry. His first wife, Carrie, had died of pneumonia June 8, 1916, and his mother, Jane, died on January 4, 1917. He then lived with Tom and his family for some years. On August 21, 1923, he married Margaret T. Harrington, 31, a native of Ireland who was about 37 years his junior.

In 1924, David was back at work, lending his name and his time to a land promotion in Marion County, Fla. He was among a number of speculators who jumped into the Florida land boom about that time. The property he promoted is along Lake Weir about halfway between Ocala to the northwest and Leesburg to the south. Rather than merely trying to flip property for a quick buck, Buick and his associates apparently chose the site after a serious search and began an ambitious development effort. The *Tampa Morning Tribune* of December 3, 1924, described the 1,750-acre site as "on the western shores of Lake Weir, the highest point between the Gulf and the Sea.

David Buick's ad promoting Florida property in Tampa Tribune *in December, 1924. Note slogans: "When Better Cities Are Built Buick Will Build Them" and "In the Kingdom of the Sun." Also note the development name, "Buick City."*

As its main arteries of travel the property has the national and Dixie highways and the Seaboard and Atlantic Coast Line railroads." (The site is today almost adjacent to The Villages, an impressive modern development).

The *Tribune* helpfully noted "Lake Weir, for many years, has been the pleasure resort of Ocala and one of the most popular centers in the state for lovers of aquatic sports and beautiful country." The newspaper quoted the Buick development's representatives as saying the lake property "will be converted into a model city with boulevards, fine homes and elaborate bathing facilities." Lots were being offered at pre-development prices of $250.

It's easy to see why this site appealed to David Buick. For years in Michigan, he was attracted to water, sailing the Great Lakes and testing marine engines on the Detroit River. He later fell in love

Veteran Buick engine experts Eugene Richard (right) and William Beacraft (next to him) join a future Buick chief engineer, Ferdinand A. (Dutch) Bower, in admiring Buick's one millionth car, a 1923 Model 23-55 Sport Touring. The celebration consisted of a quick photo opportunity on a snowy day near the Flint Buick factory.

with balmy southern California. In Florida he found both water and weather, plus other assets. Besides the two railroads, there were those major highways. With roads and automobiles being continually improved, he could offer attractive property to the newly prosperous population centers of the East and Midwest.

Buick toured the area with Joseph N. Pugh, Buick Realty Company's vice president and general manager, as Pugh gave talks in small cities and gained the support of such leaders as the mayor of Leesburg and the editor of the *Summerfield Chronicle*. One newspaper reported "three long avenues have been graded and sidewalks are being laid...Five miles of streets will be started immediately. Plans are also under way for the construction of ten homes...."

Once again Buick Motor Company became incensed, an echo of Buick President Charles Nash's anger back in 1912 after David formed Buick Oil Company. This time, the Buick automobile people were understandably angry that David played off a famous Buick ad slogan, "When Better Automobiles Are Built, Buick Will Build

Them." David Buick, in a large ad for his Florida real estate, playfully proclaimed: "When Better Cities Are Built, Buick Will Build Them."

(David had an interesting name for his development — "Buick City." Decades later, in the mid 1980s, that name was given by Buick Motor Division to Buick's home complex in Flint when its tooling was totally replaced — then a takeoff of "Toyota City" in Japan.)

The 1924 real estate ad included this statement, likely generated by David Buick, identified as "founder of Buick Motor Company" (which he was) and president of the Buick City Realty Corporation:

David Buick in 1928, at the time he was interviewed by Bruce Catton.

> Millions and millions and millions of dollars have been spent advertising the name BUICK. In every nook and corner of the Globe, people who speak hundreds of languages know of BUICK and his wonderful achievements. The man who is responsible for the magic name being known the world over is now the active head of a development company that will make it mean more than ever before. Can you comprehend the value of this name Buick? It stands for Excellence. It means something and now it is attached to a city.

Clearly, David was determined to reclaim his name as a valuable property, even though he must have expected the likely reaction of his old company.

He didn't have long to wait. Buick Motor Company created its own ad, signed by its vice president, H.J. Mallory, headlined in large print, "All Buick Dealers and Distributors," and printed in some Florida newspapers February 8, 1925.

It is obvious that the name 'Buick' is being capitalized to the fullest extent in connection with the advertising relative to the development known as 'Buick City,' and we feel that it is only proper for us, in justice to you as our dealers as well as to the public, to state the facts regarding Mr. Buick's connection with the Buick Motor Company.

Our records show that D.D. Buick was one of a number of organizers of the Buick Motor Company on February 20th, 1904, and he became manager and one of the five directors at about the same time. [Documents show the reorganization took place January 30, 1904]. He ceased to be manager approximately two years after its organization, to wit, on February 13, 1906.

The ad then quotes from the minutes of the Buick board of directors about David's resignation as general manager and the "troubles" and "the conditions" under which Buick was being operated at the time of his resignation, as noted in an earlier chapter.

The ad says the board minutes were quoted "solely for the purpose of indicating the conditions that prevailed at the time Mr. Buick ceased to be General Manager of the company...so that you might draw your own conclusions as to the propriety of his now claiming that he is the founder of the Buick Motor Company and responsible for its achievements."

The word 'Buick' and the name of Buick Motor Company, as well as the paraphrasing of its slogan, are not only being used, as stated, without our consent or authority, but very much against our wishes. We do not know anything about the real estate which is being offered for sale at Buick City, but we wish it distinctly understood that the Buick Motor Company has no connection with it whatsoever, and we would esteem it a favor if those who are backing this promotion, as well as the newspapers which are carrying any of the advertising, would discontinue using the name of the Buick Motor Company, its slogan or any of its trade rights in reference thereto in any form, shape or manner.

Buick Motor Division's concern was understandable, but the facts were that David was indeed the founder of the company. And, thanks in part to his hiring of such men as Walter Marr, Eugene Richard and Arthur Mason, he was responsible for its early achievements, including its superb engine and impressive first production automobiles.

Criticism could cut more than one way. In 1924 a Buick dealer ad read: "Two decades ago, in the town of Flint, U.S.A., David Buick installed his valve-in-head engine successfully in what was then called a horseless carriage...." Yet, about a year later, Buick Motor Company sharply criticized David for using his own name in a real estate development. Recently, one observer wryly noted: "So, while the Buick Motor Company was still using Dave Buick's name to promote cars, Dave Buick shouldn't use his own name to promote real estate?"

The Florida land speculators hoped to make big profits by selling dreams of a tropical paradise. They created a real estate bubble that burst around 1925 when not enough buyers showed up. Like Buick Oil Company and the Lorraine and Dunbar ventures, David's Florida land promotion turned sour, though his financial losses are unknown. What is known is that David Buick was then an aging man who was experiencing hard times mostly caused by his own poor decisions. He had tried hard to turn his now-famous name into a profit, but none of his dreams panned out and he was becoming desperate to survive financially in an era before the government provided safety nets.

The Buick family suffered through years of real poverty. During the rich years, Tom Buick spent $100,000 to improve his $75,000 house in a suburb of Detroit. But his son, David Dunbar Buick II, remembered other times — the family so impoverished it was evicted from 13 apartments for nonpayment of rent. The stress sent his mother to hospitals with migraine headaches before her early death.

Even though Tom had accompanied Walter Marr on the test drive of the first Flint Buick and given Hugh Dolnar the first Buick press ride, he oddly never drove a car in the memory of his son. "It was explained to me that some kid threw a firecracker in our car when I was a baby and dad would not drive again, though I don't know how much stock you can put in that," said David II.

When Tom criticized GM in published interviews for not doing better by his father, Tom's son felt the negative reaction caused him to lose a job as an office boy at GM. David II had landed the job, but

David Buick descendants include son Wynton Rodger Buick (left in left photo) as a race boat mechanic with driver Kaye Don after winning the Gold Cup on Lake George, NY, July 25, 1936; daughter Frances Jane "Fanny" (top right); and grandson David Dunbar Buick II (bottom right), son of Thomas D. Buick.

was told not to report to work for his first day. David II did once buy a Buick when his name got him on a dealer's preferred list immediately after World War II, when cars were hard to get. He received the car in five days and paid full price.

But eventually David II, grandson of the auto pioneer, got a job in the export department of Chrysler Corporation, where he worked for 25 years before retirement. When the writer interviewed him at his Detroit home in 1980, a Plymouth was in his garage. His only mementos of his grandfather were a few never-published photos (one a profile with a cigar, another with his second wife), a small corroded set of drafting tools (which eventually were sold to Flint's Sloan Museum) and a book of typed minutes from the David Buick Carburetor Company.

Tom Buick, a small but tough man who David II said had been a strike breaker before his Buick Motor Company years, never found a good job after the years with his father's businesses and his brass foundry. He was a Fuller Brush salesman when he died July 4, 1942.

In 1926, David Buick was featured in ads for the Detroit School of Trades in Popular Mechanics *magazine. The school was at the base of Woodward Avenue.*

Wynton, David's younger son, at one point joined his father and brother in the carburetor business. He also was a riding mechanic on champion racing boats in the 1930s and '40s.[2]

In 1946 Wynton was awarded a patent for a safety device for supercharged engines. The patent was assigned to George and Earl Holley of Holley Carburetor Company, where he was employed. In 1960, Wynton retired to Lake City, Fla. When he died in 1966, he was survived by his wife Leona, their only child, Wynifred Buick Holland of El Paso, Texas, and two grandchildren.

Following the Lorraine and Dunbar non-starters and then the Florida real estate venture, David was back in the news in 1925 when his new job with the Detroit School of Trades was announced by the school as a major event. In ads in such magazines as *Popular Mechanics*, David appears in photos apparently making a speech and then shaking hands with a student. One ad proclaims graduation diplomas would be signed by David Buick. Another is headlined: "Now! Let BUICK himself train you quick for big pay auto jobs." And still another: "For 2 Cents Buick Himself Will Show You How to Earn More Money."

While his record of earning money was a little weak, that record was not widely known. For one final moment, David was again being promoted as an automotive superstar. And once again, it didn't last. David's grandson told the writer there were complaints from GM that David's position with the school was an embarrassment to the corporation. The ads did quickly disappear but the Detroit School of Trades kept David on staff, apparently until his death.

It was 1928 when Bruce Catton found him at the Detroit School of Trades. He and Margaret were living at that time in a flat at 17140 Third Avenue in Detroit.

While Buick was usually upbeat during his conversation with Catton, once he let his guard down. "You know, I've been to practi-

---

2 In 1935, the *Notre Dame*, driven by Clel Perry, won the President's Cup on the Potomac River. *The New York Times* reported: "Alongside Perry sat Winton [sic] Buick, son of one of America's best known pioneer automobile men and himself a mechanic as good as they come." The next year, Wynton rode alongside Englishman Kaye Don in *Impshi*, owned by Horace Dodge, to win the Gold Cup race on Lake George in New York. He would go on to race in two other Dodge-owned boats, *Delphine IX* in 1937 and 1938, and *Miss Syndicate* in 1940. Both boats were powered by a massive V-16 engine designed and built by Harry Miller of Indianapolis 500 fame, his associate Leo Goosen, who had earlier worked with Walter Marr, and J. Paul Miller, a supercharger expert.

cally every one of the friends of the old days — millionaires now, every one — and asked for a job; and none of them had anything for me. I wouldn't want to be president, or treasurer; all I'd want would be security — a feeling that I was all set for the rest of my life. Damn it, I'm not after charity or pity. I'm still strong and able. But you know, it's kind of hard for a man of my age to be uncertain about the future. I've got to have a job."

Catton's article, which included nothing of Buick's business promotions after he left Buick Motor Company, was widely printed. And from it came expressions of sympathy. An engineer in Saskatchewan wrote to Buick in early 1928 that he realized "a man of your type craves neither charity or sympathy" but nevertheless offered him "a home and my care at any time you feel that you would like to quit your present vocation and take things easier."

David was disappointed when the 25th anniversary of Buick Motor Company was celebrated in August, 1928, and nobody invited him to the festivities in Flint — hardly surprising, given the company's battles with its namesake over the years. And apparently the company under General Manager Ed Strong's leadership was keeping things local. Organizers of the event didn't invite Marr or Durant either.

By the start of 1929, it was apparent David Buick would not live much longer. A newspaper described him as "emaciated" from cancer. For a few weeks in the new year he "worked doggedly" at the Detroit School of Trades, though in consideration of ill health he was assigned to an information desk while still holding his title as an instructor. By early February he could no longer continue, and was confined to his home.

The Buick family, though lacking in money, was fortunate in one regard — the family was close knit and would gather in one apartment or another for card games. But one night in February, as the auto pioneer and his wife Margaret tried to join other family members in son Wynton's apartment on Epworth Street in Detroit, Margaret called to say David was too ill to travel. Tom, the older son, rushed him to Detroit's Harper Hospital. An operation for a bowel obstruction revealed the extent of the cancer. A grandson suggested his decline was hastened when he caught pneumonia after a nurse left a window open.

David Buick, 74, died at 8:15 p.m. on March 5, 1929, "leaving only his name on a car," as one newspaper article phrased it. Surviving besides wife Margaret were his sons, Thomas D. and Wynton

R., daughters, Mrs. James (Mabel) Coyle of Detroit and Mrs. Frank C. (Fanny) Patterson of Los Angeles, and David's half-sister, Mrs. Jane Kutz, also of Detroit. Services were at the Henry J. Hastings funeral rooms. Burial was in Woodmere Cemetery in Detroit. The standup tombstone is engraved with a Buick script.

Buick's death was the Page 1 banner-headline story in the *Detroit Times* on March 6, 1929. The article emphasized his hard times in recent years. Under the DAVID BUICK IS DEAD banner was a sub-head, "Buick Founder Dies in Poverty." The *Times* noted Buick had recently said, "I'm not feeling sorry for myself." The lead paragraph:

> David D. Buick, who spent a fortune on his dream of "horse-less carriages" for all and reaped poverty in return, is dead to-day at the age of 74.

His obituary was widely published. Some of the articles were severe: "Mr. Buick, whose name appears on the gleaming front of approximately 2,000,000 automobiles, died a penniless, forlorn, bitterly disappointed man. For years he lived and worked in the very shadow of the wing of fortune. At his finger tips danced millions. Around the corner waited uncounted and almost unaccountable wealth. Time after time he saw the doors of Midas swinging before him, but always, just before he could enter these golden realms, they swung shut in his face and left him on the outside, bewildered, puzzled, disappointed."

With that kind of publicity, inevitably letters arrived at Buick head-quarters wondering why the founder and namesake had been allowed to die in poverty.

A doctor in New Jersey wrote: "Countless thousands have read with horror and disgust of the distressing circumstances attending the death of David D. Buick...the reaction of the general public against the Buick Company is most unfavorable."

A man in Cleveland observed "the passing of David Buick appears to be a pretty sad affair...I have been the proud owner of six Buick cars, but I do not feel quite so proud this morning...We pension the old soldiers, and have homes for the indigent, but David Buick, founder of the company which builds the magnificent car bearing his name, has to die in poverty."

A man in Grand Rapids, Mich., offered to be the first to contrib-ute "a small sum of money" to erect a monument in David Buick's memory. From Pinehurst, Ga., came a suggestion that the company set

Buick's death was big news in the Detroit Times *March 6, 1929. Note photo of barn in Detroit where Buick did experimental car work. The inset, however, appears to be of the first Flint Buick, which was not built there. That actual barn print is reproduced on Page 26 of this book (the newspaper's editing marks once visible).*

aside $1 for each Buick sold "during the present year if not longer" for a fund for Buick's family.

In some cases, Ed Strong, the general manager, sent dealers and others to visit the writers and try to explain the company's relationship with its founder. The facts were that David Buick had left on his own, had been given a substantial amount of money on his departure and had been gone for 20 years. And for those who still doubted, the Buick firm could point to a *Time* magazine article of March 18, 1929, that basically put most of the blame for David's plight on the man himself.

The company might have pointed out that upon arriving in the California oil fields after leaving Buick Motor Company, David had described himself as "a very rich man," even if that was an overstatement. The founder's later financial problems were of his own making, an opinion David Buick never denied. As *Time* pointed out: "He left the

211

company with a block of stock which would soon have made him an exceedingly rich man. But David Buick seemed to have no affinity for money. He could not make it himself and he was not content to let abler business men make it for him."

Certainly David was not alone in running into hard times — the Great Depression would soon put many others in similar circumstances. Indeed, at the time of Buick's death, GM founder Billy Durant was also headed for big trouble. His Durant Motors empire, so promising at first, had fallen apart and he was about to be devastated in the stock market. In 1936, Durant would declare bankruptcy.

David Buick II once wrote to Sloan, asking if he had any information regarding his grandfather's departure from Buick. "He sent back a hand-written note saying he had no recollection — it had all happened before his time," the grandson recalled.

But not all connections between the Buick family and former colleagues were severed. David II remembered that years later Durant sometimes came to his father's house for Sunday dinner and once gave the boy a beautiful blank diary.

Almost a decade passed after David's death. And then GM began to resurrect his name. The corporation's design staff wanted a Buick family coat of arms to decorate the front of automobiles. That inevitably would bring attention to the man. The name had already adorned more than 2 million vehicles (by the time of Buick's centennial, the count had reached nearly 37 million).

So a design was created, based on a reference found by GM designer Ralph Pew in the 1851 edition of *Burke's Heraldry* he found in the Detroit Public Library (for an unknown reason the reference was dropped in later editions). The Buick crest debuted as an emblem on the nose of 1937 Buicks.

As Howard E. O'Leary, assistant director of GM's Styling Section, wrote to Buick Manufacturing Manager Edward T. Ragsdale on September 23, 1937: "Back in 1935 and 1936, the idea of using the Buick crest was thought of by Mr. Earl [Harley Earl, GM's legendary first design chief] and the writer. We discussed it many times." He discussed sending Pew to the library in search of a Buick crest.

"I might add that our thinking of using the Buick crest was an outgrowth of the fact that it has been a custom on automobiles, where the name of the car is the name of a family, to employ the crest if one exists," O'Leary wrote. "I am only adding this so that you will not get

The Buick crest as it first appeared in 1937 (left) and the now highly styl-ized Buick "tri-shield" used in 2011.

the mistaken idea that we had an idea in the Styling Section, as they are coming so damn few and far between I would hate to mislead you."

The coat of arms is a red shield with a checkered silver and azure diagonal line running from the upper left corner to the lower right, an antlered deer head with a jagged ("erazed") neckline in the upper right of the shield and a gold cross in the lower left section, the cross pierced in the center. It's likely David Buick had never heard of it.

Today, it's greatly changed, three shields instead of one (starting in 1960 to symbolize LeSabre, Invicta and Electra introduced for '59). The details have been removed for clarity, the colors dropped for what marketing folks call "edge." The so-called "tri-shield" decorates the grilles of Buicks more than 100 years after incorporation.

Very subtly, the man is still part of the car.

Rare Buick stock certificate

This is the only known example of a Buick Motor Company (BMC) stock certificate. Shortly before William C. Durant created General Motors in September 1908, he reportedly called in all shares of BMC stock and later replaced them with certificates of the new GM stock. There are other kinds of existing, but scarce, Buick stock certificates -- for Buick Oil Company, David Dunbar Buick Corporation and David Buick Carburetor Corporation for example. But it was believed no BMC certificate survived – at least none showed up in known collections of stock certificates or in the private papers of Durant or other auto pioneers. However this BMC certificate, a blank example, was discovered in a book of samples created by the Calvert Lithographing and Engraving Company of Detroit. At this writing it's in the collection of Lawrence Falater, who revealed it to Kevin Kirbitz. The certificate, mentioning Buick factories in Flint and Jackson, Mich., was possibly created in mid 1905. This example is published here for the first time. It was added to this updated edition in 2013 – more than a century after all of the issued shares apparently disappeared from view.

Chapter 18

Celebrating the past; a peek at the future

Not long after David's death, Theodore MacManus and Norman Beasley in their book, *Men, Money, and Motors*, observed: "Fame beckoned to David Buick — he sipped from the cup of greatness... and then spilled what it held." The passing of decades didn't improve on that assessment. In 1968, Beverly Rae Kimes in *Automobile Quarterly* weighed in with: "Seldom has history produced such an unrecalled — or misrecalled — man." In 2000, Vincent Curcio in his biography *Chrysler* brought a new-millennium perspective: "The General Motors Corporation was founded on a tragedy whose name was David Dunbar Buick."

There was no relief in his native Scotland. When the *Glasgow Sunday Post* pointed out on September 15, 1974, that the 120th anniversary of David Buick's birth was that week, the headline read: "But who remembers David Buick?"

That was too much for Buick General Manager George Elges. He fired back: "I would like to answer your question, 'Who remembers David Buick?' We do — all 18,000 of us employed here at Buick, plus a community of some 200,000 people in Flint, 3,200 Buick dealers in the United States, not to mention the 5 ½ million around the world still driving Buicks."

Elges, in a letter probably written by Buick PR Director Jerry Rideout, noted "it just so happens that yesterday [September 26, 1974], a new highway was opened here and dedicated to your Scotland native. The new Buick Freeway now provides a faster and more convenient link between the Motor City, which is Detroit, and Buick town, which is Flint."

Not for long. A state legislator, cozying up to a United Auto Workers official, persuaded the Legislature to change the name of the expressway to the UAW Freeway. The UAW man was not impressed. "I feel by taking away from Buick, the honor to the UAW is a little tarnished," he told the writer at the time. To make amends, the state renamed another local freeway, which was to have honored Louis Chevrolet, as the Chevrolet-Buick Freeway on a small, obscure sign. Buick couldn't even get top billing on a freeway in Flint. Not only that, a home of the late James Whiting, the man who had brought Buick to Flint, was razed to make way for the Buick (now UAW) Freeway.[1]

So honoring the Buick name has not always been easy.

In the early 1980s, when Flint boosters created a downtown theme park named AutoWorld, it was an opportunity to give some attention to David and other local auto pioneers, such as Durant, Dort, Nash, Chevrolet, Chrysler, Mott and Champion. A big dome housed buildings representing Flint pioneer days back to Jacob Smith's trading post and Todd's Tavern. It also featured a rushing river, ferris wheel, a couple of theme park rides and a garish wooden creation in the shape of a giant auto engine. The adjacent old IMA Auditorium was cobbled into an IMAX theater featuring an auto-themed film. While AutoWorld had a beautiful dome and some impressive features, its backers, carried away by hometown enthusiasm, misread the market. Flint might have done better with a strong auto museum rather than a weak theme park. AutoWorld, over-hyped and underfunded, could not draw enough paying customers to sustain profits for its backers. An opportunity for the city to promote its impressive automotive heritage was fumbled. Several years after its gala grand opening, AutoWorld closed in a sea of red ink and disappeared in the dust of the imploded auditorium.

In 1994, at Buick World Headquarters in Flint, a state historical marker was unveiled, an impressive free-standing sign with brass words on a green background, describing David Buick's career, the development of the Flint complex and the beginnings of General Motors. But four years later, the headquarters staff moved to Detroit,

---

1 Some people in Flint have expressed concern about how auto pioneers are honored locally. When the Flint College and Cultural Center was being developed, nothing would have been named for Billy Durant had not Flint's great philanthropist, Charles Stewart Mott, intervened. "I wouldn't have been where I was, or where I am, if it hadn't been for Durant," Mott told the writer in an interview for his 95th birthday. So a large marble base for flagpoles and a grassy area between the new museum and auditorium were named for Durant, with appropriate words and ceremony. Even so, Joyce Cook, a retired *Flint Journal* women's editor who had grown up with the families of Flint's industrial pioneers, was unimpressed. Standing in front of the flagpoles in Durant Plaza, she looked around. "Whiting got the auditorium," she said. "Sloan got the museum. And Durant got the shaft."

followed inevitably by the razing of the impressive white marble and glass administration building — barely 35 years old. And hundreds of acres of bleak, vacant land now marked the site of Buick City, the storied Buick home plant. Miles of buildings had been scraped away. There were no factories, not even scrub oak as in 1905 — just flat bare clay. Oh, and the state historical marker had disappeared. No one bothered to replace it.

In his late 80s, the retired Jerry Rideout lamented in a letter to *The Flint Journal* that this "hallowed plot of land" had been the home of Buick for virtually all of the 20th century and had "housed the cornerstone upon which Billy Durant founded General Motors in 1908. It was the product of this site that put the city of Flint on the global map. Now it is to be razed, to become just a plot of land in a city already overrun with vacant lots."

Some efforts to preserve and recognize Buick's heritage fared better. In 1976, volunteers at Flint's Sloan Museum created a replica of the original Flint Buick car that David Buick and Walter Marr had built in the summer of 1904 — a U.S. Bicentennial local history project. The replica — looking like the original in 1904 photos when it had no body, no fenders — used many parts from a 1905 Buick and was fitted with one of two existing 1904 Buick engines. Local car buff Charles Hulse's idea had won support from the museum's director, Roger Van Bolt, and Buick enthusiasts Greg Fauth and Jack Skaff. The museum's Jim Johnson led the project.

No sooner was it completed than Johnson, his father, Gerald, and the volunteers drove it to Detroit, just like in 1904. They met the news media over lunch at the Detroit Press Club, coincidentally located on Howard Street, the street where Buick had operated before the move to Flint. The next morning they left the GM Building for the return to Flint, retracing the original route through Lapeer.

The vintage replica's trip took 12 minutes longer in July of 1976 than the original did in 1904. Problems with fuel, spark plugs and cotter pins created difficult moments. The writer remembers helping push the car through the turn at Lapeer. But the 1904 engine kept running and the trip ended triumphantly before a small crowd on E. First Street near Saginaw Street in downtown Flint, at the spot where the original car was photographed in 1904. Today the car is displayed at the museum.

Also in the 1970s, a newspaper campaign led to saving the decrepit Durant-Dort Carriage Company office building from the

Commemorating David Buick's birthplace in Arbroath, Scotland, on June 9, 1994, are (from left) Eric Buick of Arbroath (no relation); Bob Coletta, Buick general sales and service manager (and later general manager); Larry Gustin of Buick PR, who with Eric arranged for the plaque, and Brian Milne, who as head of the Angus District Council was Arbroath's top elected official.

wrecking ball. The 19th century three-story brick building held Billy Durant's office at the time he began building the Buick organization. Today it's considered virtually GM's birthplace. Pete Kleinpell, a prominent local businessman who was then city administrator (acting anonymously at the time), reacted to the publicity by agreeing to personally buy the building and turn it over to the city. It was named a Michigan Historical Landmark, which led to recognition as a National Historical Landmark. Then Richard Scharchburg, curator of the archives at General Motors Institute (now Kettering University), took the lead in raising funds for its eventual restoration.

In another heritage event, in June of 1994, Buick officials on an European business trip detoured to Arbroath, Scotland, to unveil a plaque at David Buick's birthplace after an Arbroath resident, Eric Buick (no relation), expressed regret that local residents didn't know Buick's founder was born there.

The gesture played well in the news media in Great Britain. The BBC even sent a television crew to Flint to retell the story of the Scotsman who had such an impact on the industry, a feature telecast in 23 countries.

At the plaque unveiling, Robert E. Coletta, Buick's general sales manager and soon-to-be general manager, observed: "Buick has been one of the great names in American automobiles through virtually all of the 20th century. It is certainly appropriate for us to honor this

218

man, not only because his name identifies our automobiles, but because his genius and hard work formed the beginning of an unsurpassed automotive success story — that is still being written."

Those words were heard first hand by the writer, who introduced Coletta to the gathering on that brisk morning in Arbroath. The scene included five vintage Buick cars (1939 to mid '50s) driven by their owners who had heard of the planned event, plus a new Buick Park Avenue brought in from Europe to shepherd Coletta's party to the plaque site. Other speakers included Eric Buick and the writer. The point was made that while David Buick was ultimately not financially successful, his name by that time had appeared on more than 32 million automobiles — including 9 million still on the road. About a half million Buicks a year were being built. "How many of us," the audience was asked, "would like that kind of legacy?"

A letter to the mayor of Flint from Brian Milne, Arbroath's political leader, said "the bonds of kinship and friendship between our two countries are very strong and the link between Arbroath and Flint through David Dunbar Buick strengthens these bonds in a more personal way."

On November 10, 1998, an addition to Flint's Sloan Museum, named the Buick Gallery and Research Center, was dedicated. Completed just before Buick's main office was moved to Detroit to join other GM marketing divisions, the gallery, in a warehouse near the museum, was designed to be a living legacy of Buick operations that had been headquartered in Flint since 1903. Coletta told a crowd the gallery would "remind future generations that this company and this city together stood for something very important...[they] helped create a great industry...that changed the way people live and brought both mobility and undreamed financial rewards to workers throughout the 20th Century." (See related article at the end of this volume).

Buick's 100th birthday celebration in 2003 was a time to recount stories about the founder and his company. Buick and Sloan Museum developed a touring heritage exhibit of vintage cars, photos and other artifacts and sent it to selected museums across the country, hosting centennial press/VIP receptions in Los Angeles, Reno, St. Louis, Saratoga Springs, Detroit and Flint.

A large and memorable celebration in Flint combined with the Buick Club of America's national meet, orchestrated by Dennis Meyer of the club's Flint "Buicktown" chapter, included an impressive 1,800 vintage Buicks. Nicola Bulgari, international jeweler and the world's leading collector of vintage Buicks, brought 10 of his cars and donated full-size and model cars to the Buick Gallery.

As a centennial project, Buick Motor Division proposed restoring a 1905 Model C, assembled in Jackson, which had been in Flint longer than any other Buick — from August 1905. Charles Hulse left a handwritten note stating it was built April 17, 1905 — which would likely make it one of the two oldest existing Buicks.[2]

Whatever its rank among the 14 surviving Model Cs, the Flint car is particularly significant as it had been rescued years earlier from the property of Fred Aldrich, where it had almost rusted away. Aldrich — the man who put James Whiting and Billy Durant together in a 1904 meeting that led to Durant's takeover of Buick — had bought it new for $950 in August 1905.

In 2004, in time for the 150th anniversary of David Buick's birth, another Michigan historical marker featuring Buick, the man and the company, was installed at GM World Headquarters at Detroit's Renaissance Center. It points out his first engine shop, Buick Auto-Vim & Power Company, had been located just a few blocks up the street (Beaubien). It was in a building that at this writing still stands. The marker also states that David's fledgling auto company, after the move to Flint and its takeover by Durant, eventually became the foundation for GM's birth.

On September 17, 2004, the actual 150th birthday, Eric Buick hosted a luncheon for local officials at Buick's birthplace in Arbroath.

---

2 The centennial project gathered funds from Buick, the Buick club's Buicktown chapter, the Sloan Museum's Summer Fair and the estate of Greg Fallowfield, a Californian who held the BCA's No. 1 card as the club's founder. Hulse may have found the production date by seeing the first production records before they disappeared in the 1950s or by talking to the car's original owner, Durant-Dort Carriage Company executive Fred Aldrich, who lived into his 90s in the mid 1950s. If the date is correct, the car is no doubt one of the oldest existing Buicks, though its engine number (3076) would appear to place it as seventh oldest survivor. The car often referred to as the oldest Buick, in Harold Warp's Pioneer Village in Minden, Neb., was probably also built in April of 1905. But the ranking of surviving Model C Buicks assumes the engines were actually installed in order by engine number, instead of randomly, as the frames were. Since it's unknown if that assumption is true, any ranking system for the Model C is suspect. On another subject involving that project, it's notable that the job of restoring the Model C required taking some parts back from the Model B replica, and then making replica parts for the Model B. So both cars were being rebuilt at the same time.

In Birmingham, Mich., the founder was recognized at a dinner tied to the Ryder Cup golf tournament (being held nearby) and Buick's involvement with golf. Centerpieces at dinner tables were miniatures of the Buick state historical marker. In Detroit, David Buick was remembered with a toast by a small group at that marker.

In Flint, where the Sloan Museum and Buick Gallery offered free admission that weekend, a storied past is celebrated with the Durant-Dort headquarters; the restored home of Charles W. Nash in his Durant-Dort days; the restored Flint Road Cart Company plant; statues of Durant and Dort; Charles Stewart Mott's home, "Applewood,"; another elegant home, that of Durant's early banker Robert Whaley; the venerable Durant Hotel restored with upscale apartments; and the Sloan Museum and its Buick Gallery and Research Center. New-millennium replicas of downtown Flint's famed arches, including one sponsored by Buick, have been erected in a project headed by Flint history activist David White. At the nearby Historical Crossroads Village, a 19th Century village of restored buildings with a steam railroad, one of those buildings is a small horse barn that had once belonged to Durant. It came from the property of Durant's Flint home and was identified as a Durant building by its onetime owner, Ernest Gardner, father of the writer's closest childhood friend, Janet Gardner (now Mrs. Gerald LeVasseur).

In the summer of 2008, Flint celebrated another centennial — this one GM's 100th birthday — by again hosting a national meet of the Buick Club of America. The Buick Model B updated replica and Fred Aldrich's restored 1905 Model C — the 2003 Buick centennial projects — made their debut together at the Sloan Museum's Buick Gallery. The Durant-Dort building's board staged a centennial ceremony at the landmark building and hosted a meeting there of the Buick Heritage Alliance, an organization of vintage Buick enthusiasts. The BHA, then led by Terry Dunham and Jeff Brashares, promotes historical research on the origin and development of the Buick car and the individuals who contributed to it.

Finally, in the summer of 2011, plans were advanced in Flint for a statue of David Buick. The man behind the Buick automobile would at last receive public recognition — in the Buick company's old home town. The inspiration came from Al Hatch, a Flint native and retired senior account manager at Rockwell Automation. Hatch in 2005 was the force behind "Back to the Bricks," basically an impressive array of vintage car displays and a community celebration on the brick pavement of Saginaw Street in downtown Flint. Even though it was staged annually on the same weekend as the Woodward Dream Cruise a few miles to the south, Back to the Bricks became a huge success, spawning a week of related events and drawing hundreds of thousands of people downtown. Hatch's next idea was to plan a series of statues of Flint auto pioneers (there were already statues of Durant and his carriage partner Dallas Dort near their old Durant-Dort headquarters on W. Water Street). Life-size bronze statues were soon unveiled downtown: Louis Chevrolet (August 2012), David Buick (December 2012) and a second one of Durant, positioned between Louis and David (August 2013). Civic leaders in Buick's old home town of Arbroath, Scotland, also planned a David Buick statue. The prospect of two statues being created of a man who had been ignored for about a century became the subject of a *New York Times* online feature. Also intriguing: Joe Rundell, sculptor of the new Flint statues, was a retired Chevrolet machine repairman. He was primarily — and internationally — known for his sideline of creating elaborate engravings on expensive firearms until, at age 71, he turned to this new creative activity.

In 2009, GM fell briefly into bankruptcy as a result of the financial crisis that started a year earlier. When it emerged, only four GM domestic brands were chosen to survive under the corporate logo. One was Buick, GM's historic foundation marque, thanks in large part to its success in China — which a few years earlier would have been unimaginable. The others were Chevrolet, Cadillac and GMC Truck — Chevy created by Durant using many of the same people and buildings he used to build Buicks, and Cadillac and GMC, which he saved.

Fritz Henderson, who as GM president led the corporation through its bankruptcy in the summer of 2009, is the son of retired Buick sales executive Bob Henderson but said his personal affection for the brand was not a factor in his determination to save Buick. In a 2010 interview with the writer, the younger Henderson, no longer with GM, said any other executive probably would have made the same decision, driven by business considerations. It didn't hurt that Buick's new products in this period — Enclave, LaCrosse and Regal — were getting high marks from auto writers who saw the vehicles as world class in quality and overall appeal. As GM's vice chairman, Bob Lutz, told the writer: "For Buick, Enclave is a game changer!"

Henderson elaborated on Buick's survival and what he sees as its potential future.

First, Buick was immensely succesful in China and I knew we would continue to develop beautiful, sculptured Buicks for China. So we could get all of the engineering for Buicks in the North American market for free — we'd have to pay for the tooling but not the engineering. Great, but not a reason alone to continue with the Buick brand in the U.S.

Second, it makes a great business case to pair uplevel Buick cars and GMC trucks in U.S. dealerships. We needed to put them together to make successful dealerships — profitable for dealers and profitable for GM. In effect, we knew we needed a truck and car brand in this channel, and without a brand like Buick we had real concerns regarding the viability of a stand-alone GMC truck brand.

Third, we learned with Enclave we could move the needle. Good volumes, great transaction prices and consumer demo-graphics, and attractive profitability. Enclave gave us confi-dence that the Buick brand could be successful if we could get the product right. It's an extremely important brand — a move up from Chevy — and we've followed Enclave with the new LaCrosse and Regal.

The fourth consideration was we felt there was a market for this type of uplevel car (and truck with GMC), a segment be-low true luxury, which could provide attractive profit contribu-tions to GM while meeting a specific market need. I do think the final chapter hasn't been written yet, but if GM continues to bring forward great models, I expect Buick will be a success.

Edward H. Mertz, a retired GM vice president and general manager of Buick for 11 years (1986-97), agreed that "without the success in China, Buick likely would have been dropped during the latest bank-ruptcy."

While China has been the most recent success, it's only the latest example of events and leaders that over decades resulted in Buick's pe-riodic recovery from crises that threatened its existence. The flamboy-ant Harlow Curtice, an unusually powerful leader, took over Buick in the depth of the Great Depression and in a long career there (1933-48) introduced stylish and powerful new models, made its manufacturing center a huge supplier of World War II military goods and then, quickly converting to peacetime production, built the division into a postwar powerhouse. He also ordered up Buick's best-known styling cue — portholes.

Moving into the '50s, Curtice became GM's chief executive and *Time* magazine's 1955 Man of the Year (another former Buick leader, Walter Chrysler, had received that honor in 1928). Even after leaving Buick to preside at GM, he kept his home in Flint and his hand in with his favorite marque. When the mayor of Flint bought a Cadillac, Curtice quietly suggested to him, "I think that's too much car for you." The mayor turned in the Cadillac and bought a Buick. And when GM celebrated its 50th anniversary in 1958, in Curtice's last year before retiring as GM president, Buick made a notable contribution. It created the Buick Open golf tournament, which ran (with an interruption) at Warwick Hills in the Flint suburb of Grand Blanc for another half century.

In the early and mid 1960s, another general manager, Ed Rollert, restored Buick's quality reputation and introduced the U.S. industry's first mass-produced V-6 engine. Starting as chief engineer in 1975 and serving as general manager from 1980 to 1984, Lloyd E. Reuss (pronounced Royce) promoted turbocharging at Buick while also leading the division's short but highly successful return to racing. He brought back the convertible (1982-85 Riviera) and — working with factory leaders and UAW members — created Buick City, a state-of-the-art manufacturing center built in the shell of Buick's original home complex. Reuss set the course for a series of legendary Regal Grand Nationals and provided the momentum for two record million-car worldwide sales years, while sowing the seeds for the two-place Reatta coupe and convertible. Eventually he became a GM president.

In the late 1980s and 1990s, Ed Mertz earned the respect of auto editors for articulating Buick's "premium American motor cars" image and providing products to match. Buick became the industry leader in sales of supercharged cars under his watch and won so many high-quality rankings in independent studies that Buick sold itself as "the new symbol for quality in America." Mertz improved Buick's profitability and market share, keeping the marque viable in critical years. Fritz Henderson was the right person, at the right time, to assure Buick survived the GM bankruptcy. And you could add many others to the list of those who gave Buick momentum, including such talented engineers as Charlie Chayne, Joe Turlay and Cliff Studaker and such creative designers as Henry de Segur Lauve, Ned Nickles and Bill Porter.

Mertz told the writer: "Had it not been for Buick's success in increasing market share while other divisions like Oldsmobile were losing, it's possible Buick would have been dropped instead of Oldsmobile in 2000. The strong Buick product line, the recognized J.D. Power quality ratings and the division's profitability all served to protect Buick while Oldsmobile was having trouble. Later GM diminished the Buick product while enhancing that of Oldsmobile, but it was too late. The China project was already under way and that card was strong enough to provide long life to the Buick brand."

In 2010, Motor Trend's *first Buick cover in 28 years signals "Buick Is Back!"*

One sign of Buick's new reputation in 2010 was an edition of *Motor Trend,* which for the first time in 28 years featured Buick on its cover. Along with an arrangement of new models was the headline, "Buick is Back!"

After Henderson resigned as GM president late in 2009, a young engineering executive named Mark L. Reuss became president of GM's North American operations. He is the son of Lloyd Reuss — whose reputation, even in retirement, among vintage Buick buffs was so well remembered that he was named recipient of the prestigious Buick Heritage Trophy at the 2010 Buick Club of America national meet.

Mark Reuss got off to a fast start — Buick and overall GM sales soared. Like his father, he also displayed an enthusiasm for GM/Flint history. Mark had begun his GM career in Flint. After touring the old Durant-Dort headquarters (the National Historic Landmark recognized as virtually GM's birthplace), he arranged for a substantial donation by GM in 2013 for upkeep and operation of the building, and he said support would continue. He also led an initiative for GM to buy the 133-year-old former Durant-Dort carriage factory nearby -- a combination of buildings including the original factory of Durant and Dort's Flint Road Cart Company. This was where GM founder Durant first built vehicles, even though they were horse-drawn carts. Reuss called these buildings "Factory One," described them as "the center of GM heritage" and said, "we're going to do everything we can to see that [Factory One is] recognized and treated as such." He said that when Factory One is reborn, plans for the site include technology related activities, an automotive history archives and library as well as vintage car (and possibly road cart and carriage) displays and meeting rooms.

As Henderson noted, the final chapter hasn't been written yet for GM and specifically Buick. But for Buick's founding fathers it has been.

The story of David Buick's final years has been covered. As for Durant, after he went bankrupt in 1936, he eventually returned to his adopted home town of Flint — to work, though he and Catherine kept their New York apartment. In 1940 he opened an 18-lane bowling center, North Flint Recreation, in the refurbished former center of a trucking firm. A year later he added Flint's first drive-in restaurant, the Horseshoe Bar, which he promoted as a swanky "hamburger heaven." He saw the bowling center as a prototype for recreational facilities he might promote across the country — wholesome places, with no beer or liquor sold, for the family.

Reporters saw the irony: North Flint Rec was only a few blocks from the giant Buick complex Durant had created decades earlier — and he was now renting bowling shoes to the children of Buick workers he had brought to Flint by the thousands. Also at least one local car dealer liked to take his salesmen to the Horseshoe Bar so the founder of GM could serve them hamburgers.

Durant was nevertheless enthusiastic about his bowling/restaurant business. Sometimes he closed the restaurant to the public and held private dinners there for such old friends as Charles Stewart Mott, who had become Flint's great philanthropist. Durant often stayed at the downtown Durant Hotel, named in his honor when it opened in 1920. The management now would rent him a suite for the price of a small room. (The eight-story hotel closed in 1973 but was completely restored 37 years later in a multi-million-dollar project. It reopened in 2010 as The Durant, an upscale apartment building in a downtown area newly crowded with students from the University of Michigan-Flint, Kettering University, Mott Community College and Baker College).

Durant's business career effectively ended when he had a stroke in the Durant Hotel on Oct. 2, 1942. His wife Catherine got special permission — these were the World War II years — to travel by aircraft from New York to Flint to be with him. He spent his 81st birthday in Flint's Hurley Hospital, composing replies to congratulatory telegrams and letters. The governor of Michigan had declared his birthday as "W.C. Durant Day" in Michigan. A week later, on Dec. 15, 1942, he was taken by ambulance to Detroit and then by train to New York.

Catherine confirmed to the writer that Durant had no money left. "Yes he did die broke," she said. "Not only was the money gone but I was compelled to sell all my jewels for a fraction of the cost...." There was, however, a support group. Apparently in response to a letter from Catherine in 1943, Alfred P. Sloan Jr. wrote to her: "I have given a good deal of thought to the problem that presents itself to you, and altho I do not want to make any promises at this time, I will see what might be done whereby you might reach the same objective along a different route...."

In other words, Sloan wasn't interested in purchasing valuables but would try to help the Durants financially. At some point, Sloan worked out a plan for Sloan, Mott and others to provide regular contributions to allow the Durants to live out their last years in dignity. It's believed Walter Chrysler, who died August 18, 1940, had earlier made even bigger contributions to Durant, who called Chrysler his best friend. Durant, age 85, died in his sleep March 18, 1947, in his apartment at 45 Gramercy Park, New York City. His widow lived to tell his story to this writer 25 years later, the first interview taking place in that Gramercy Park apartment.

David Buick was named to the Automotive Hall of Fame in January 1974. Billy Durant got there a little earlier, in 1968. But the Buick name is certainly more widely recognized, thanks to the name on the product. It's fair to believe David would have been pleased.

"Success is mostly hard work," Buick had told Bruce Catton during that 1928 interview. "It's work and it's stick-to-it-ive-ness... I'm not worrying. The failure is the man who stays down when he falls — the man who sits and worries about what happened yesterday instead of jumping up and figuring what he's going to do today and tomorrow. That's what success is — looking ahead to tomorrow." The reporter noted a sign on Buick's desk: "No trials, no triumphs."

Catton was impressed. Summing up his interview with the man, he came to the conclusion David Buick was a heroic figure. Catton's impression: "This man, whose name is world famous, but whose purse is thin, is neither discouraged nor unhappy…His eyes, that have seen the company he founded go on to greatness without him, are bright and cheerful. He does not seem defeated.

"The giants of the automobile world are true giants, that cannot be crushed; and David Buick, if you will, is one of them."

Giant? Maybe not. Maybe you reserve that descriptor for Durant and Ford and a very few others. When the Society of Automotive Historians created a list of the industry's 30 most significant figures, it ranked Henry Ford No. 1, Billy Durant No. 2 and Walter Chrysler No. 3. Charles W. Nash placed 10th. Three one-time Buick people had made the top-10 list. David Buick didn't make the top 30.

David Buick and Billy Durant hardly operated in the same dimension. Whereas David tried to build a Buick car by borrowing $1,500 from Ben Briscoe in 1903, Durant tried to build General Motors by borrowing $15 million seven years later — and was upset when he had a hard time raising it. David could invent an elegant carburetor. Durant painted in vivid strokes, creating a corporation that would become the world's biggest.

But certainly you could credit David Buick with tenacity. Coming out of the 19th century with little more than an idea of how to build gasoline engines, he attracted such brilliant mechanical minds as Walter Marr and then Eugene Richard and Arthur Mason, and hired them. He presided over the development of superior engines. He found just enough money to stay afloat. And he held his tiny company together long enough to get the Buick automobile into production.

Whatever business talents he had left him early, but David had a clever mind when it came to mechanical devices. Richard's son, Eugene D., told the writer, with a laugh, "David Buick was a businessman — he didn't know anything about automobiles." But David's track record, including his patents and even his 1904 court testimony, says otherwise. This was a man who could design engines and transmissions and an automobile, and he hired talent when he found it. How much David himself contributed to Buick's significant engines and the first Buick automobiles is still elusive, but one thing is clear: He was the boss when they were developed.

It took others — Durant and his associates — to make the Buick marque great, and to use it to create General Motors. But David Buick set the stage, from before the turn of the century to 1905. Marr, Richard and others wandered in and out of the spotlight, but only one was always there, David Buick, chasing a dream that he could build a motor car.

Boydell Building (foreground), still standing at Beaubien and Lafayette (previously Champlain) in downtown Detroit, housed Buick Auto-Vim & Power Company in 1900. The building today is within sight of Buick Motor Division's marketing headquarters in Renaissance Center (background), which is also General Motors headquarters.

This overhead-valve 4-horsepower stationary engine in the Smithsonian Institution was built in Detroit by Buick Manufacturing Company, predecessor of Buick Motor Company, and is likely the oldest surviving engine produced by one of David Buick's companies. It was probably built in 1903.

229

From the Marr family collection: Above, portraits of Abbie and Walter Marr in retirement in 1930s at 'Marrcrest' at Signal Mountain, Tenn. The rest are photos of the 1903 Marr Autocar, a link between the first Buick completed in 1900 or 1901 by Walter Marr, and the 1904 Buicks he returned to build. Below (left) are Marr's great grandson, Barton Close, and his wife, Cindy, and (right) Bill and Sarah Close at Amelia Island Concours d' Elegance after winning best-in-class trophy. Sarah is a granddaughter of Walter and Abbie Marr.

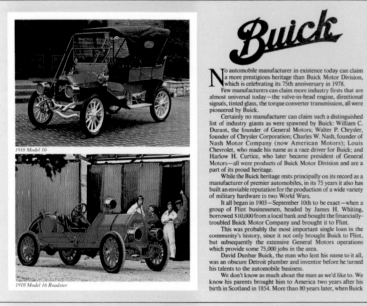

First Flint Buick is being completed in June or early July of 1904 in this fine illustration by an unidentified artist. It was used for the cover of a Buick Motor Division brochure produced in honor of Buick's 75th anniversary in 1978. The artist's setting looks more like David Buick's barn in Detroit rather than the factory on W. Kearsley in Flint where the vehicle was actually built.

1910 Model 10

1910 Model 16 Roadster

Buick

No automobile manufacturer in existence today can claim a more prestigious heritage than Buick Motor Division, which is celebrating its 75th anniversary in 1978.

Few manufacturers can claim more industry firsts that are almost universal today—the valve-in-head engine, directional signals, tinted glass, the torque converter transmission, all were pioneered by Buick.

Certainly no manufacturer can claim such a distinguished list of industry giants as were spawned by Buick: William C. Durant, the founder of General Motors; Walter P. Chrysler, founder of Chrysler Corporation; Charles W. Nash, founder of Nash Motor Company (now American Motors); Louis Chevrolet, who made his name as a race driver for Buick; and Harlow H. Curtice, who later became president of General Motors—all were products of Buick Motor Division and are a part of its proud heritage.

While the Buick heritage rests principally on its record as a manufacturer of premier automobiles, in its 75 years it also has built an enviable reputation for the production of a wide variety of military hardware in two World Wars.

It all began in 1903—September 10th to be exact—when a group of Flint businessmen, headed by James H. Whiting, borrowed $10,000 from a local bank and bought the financially-troubled Buick Motor Company and brought it to Flint. This was probably the most important single loan in the community's history, since it not only brought Buick to Flint, but subsequently the extensive General Motors operations which provide some 75,000 jobs in the area.

David Dunbar Buick, the man who lent his name to it all, was an obscure Detroit plumber and inventor before he turned his talents to the automobile business.

We don't know as much about the man as we'd like to. We know his parents brought him to America two years after his birth in Scotland in 1854. More than 80 years later, when Buick

Terry B. Dunham

(Above) Buick Manufacturing Company catalog, circa 1902. (Right) Rare 1904 Buick stationary engine.

Replica of the first Flint Buick is shown here on E. First Street in Flint, at the site where the original was first photographed in 1904. The replica, which has an original 1904 Buick motor, is positioned with last Buick built in Flint – the last car off the Buick City assembly line June 29, 1999 – a 1999 Buick LeSabre, which Buick donated to the Sloan Museum.

Above: A 1905 Model C valve-in-head two-cylinder automobile engine, from Fred Aldrich's car that was restored as a centennial project.

A 1905 Model C, the first Buick to go into serious production. Of about 750 Buicks built that year, 14 are known to exist. This one, owned for decades by early West Coast Buick dealer and distributor Charles Howard (later famous as the owner of the great race horse Seabiscuit), is believed to have been the first Buick sold on the West Coast.

Flint Wagon Works, whose directors bought Buick Motor Company and brought it to Flint.

Buick's assembly operations were moved to this plant in Jackson, Mich., in 1905.

Early view of Flint Buick complex at shift change.

More colorized postcards of Buick's north Flint complex.

Buick headquarters offices at north Flint complex. 235

Early Buick racer on track in New Jersey (top); the complete Buick complex in north Flint (center); shipping day around 1910 (bottom).

236

Top: Painting of W.C. Durant originally for cover of author Gustin's 1973 biography, Billy Durant: Creator of General Motors. *Dresden Hotel in downtown Flint where W.C. Durant met Ben Briscoe in 1908 to start talks that eventually led to the creation of General Motors. Right: Buick's second Administration Building, opened in 1917. Below: Buick home complex in late 1960s, with the third Administration Building (at bottom) just completed.*

One of the few surviving personal artifacts of David Buick is his drafting set, donated by his grandson, David Dunbar Buick II, to the Buick Gallery and Research Center of the Sloan Museum in Flint.

Walter Marr's experimental Cyclecar, circa 1915, with his grandchildren (from left) Anne Ballard, Sarah Close, Joan Williams, Richard Marr and Walter (Skip) Marr III.

Douglas Boes, a great-grandson of David Buick, displays a small brass cannon used by David to start regattas in Detroit in the late 19th century. In 2012, Boes attended the unveiling of David's statue in Flint and donated the cannon to the Buick Gallery and Research Center.

1913 Logo

1920 Service Sign

1942 Crest

1947 Crest

1960 Tri-Shield

1990 Tri-Shield

239

Celebrating Buick heritage: Top, a gathering views the unveiling of a plaque at David Buick's birthplace in Arbroath, Scotland, in June 1994. Above, Bob Coletta, Buick general sales and service manager, and Brian Milne, Arbroath's top elected official, with vintage Buicks and the plaque on the building at the birthplace site. Below left, Coletta, Buick PR Director Jack DeCou and Buick General Manager Ed Mertz unveil a state historical marker in Flint in 1994. Below right, the marker at GM Headquarters in Detroit, created in connection with Buick's 100th anniversary in 2003 and installed in 2004 in time for the 150th anniversary of David Buick's birth. The marker is on Jefferson at Beaubien in downtown Detroit, a few blocks from the original site of Buick Auto-Vim & Power Company.

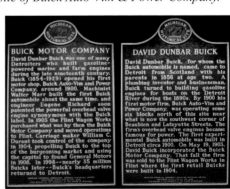

David Roman

Buick's centennial celebration in Flint in July of 2003. Top row, from left: Harold Calhoun's truck that transported the Buick Blackhawk show car was a traveling centennial ad; closeup of David Buick's family crest on Blackhawk, a highly stylized car based on a 1939 design. Second row: Early Buicks on display; Buick history enthusiast Greg Fauth with his 1911 Model 26 Runabout. Third row: A lineup of Buick Reatta two-seaters (1988-91); Buicks from the late '40s and early '50s with portholes and carnivorous grilles. About 1,800 vintage Buicks were displayed.

Below, Nicola Bulgari, international jeweler and vintage Buick collector, visits statues of Durant and Dort and is interviewed while sitting in one of his cars at the centennial event.

Above: Buick World Headquarters in Flint, just before the move to Detroit in 1998. By 2006, the building had been demolished, along with most of the huge factory complex. Below, Buick marketing's new home at GM headquarters in Renaissance Center in downtown Detroit – several blocks from original site of Buick Auto-Vim and Power Company.

Above, sculptor Joe Rundell, who created statues of David Buick and Louis Chevrolet, was working on a new statue of Billy Durant in 2013 when he brought its head to the writer's home to compare it to Durant pictures (visible on wall). Here the head sits on Durant's personal desk in the writer's home office, where grandchildren Grant, Ava and Olivia Gustin admire the work. Rundell (right) made several minor changes in Durant's expression. Below, the first (1988) statue of Durant and one of carriage partner Dallas Dort (both by Derek Wernher) appear to admire a 1908 Buick Model F during Flint's celebration of GM's centennial in 2008. Buicks of 1908 were the first GM cars.

Kevin M. Kirbitz

Preserving the past, promoting the future – Above: Inside the Buick Gallery and Research Center at Flint's Sloan Museum. In the photo at top, the replica of the first Flint Buick of 1904 is in the foreground, the Buick Bug racer of 1910 is in the background. Above, the Buick concept XP-300 of 1951 is in the foreground at the Buick Gallery. Below: GM Vice Chairman Robert A. Lutz introduces the 2005 Buick LaCrosse to the news media at Bay Harbor, Michigan. LaCrosse is displayed with a 1905 Model C from David Buick's time of 100 years earlier, and a 50th anniversary Buick, the classic 1953 Skylark.

Buick Gallery and Research Center, Alfred P. Sloan Museum, Flint, Mich.

The Buick Gallery and Research Center of the Alfred P. Sloan Museum in Flint, Mich., was dedicated November 10, 1998, in a ceremony headed by Steve Germann, then director of the museum, and Robert E. Coletta, then Buick general manager and a General Motors vice president. The gallery was designed to be a living legacy of Buick operations that had been headquartered in Flint since 1903, as well as a repository for Buick artifacts, photographs, documents and other papers. Buick's main office was being moved late in 1998 to join other GM marketing divisions at the corporation's world headquarters in Detroit's Renaissance Center.

"The Buick Gallery is a stake in the ground that makes a forceful statement that Buick and Flint will always be together," Coletta said at the ceremony. "It is one thing to say the heart and soul of Buick is in Flint — for many people that will always be true — but another to have a facility you can touch and tour...to remind future generations that this company and this city together stood for something very important.

"Together, the city and the company helped create a great industry. It was an industry that changed the way people live and brought both mobility and undreamed financial rewards to workers throughout the 20th Century."

Coletta said he hoped the gallery would continue to grow, to "help researchers tell the story of Buick and Flint, to help restorers preserve the great Buicks of the past and to be a link that always ties Buick headquarters to Flint."

Today, the Sloan Museum and Buick Gallery together house one of the world's best Buick collections. About 40 vintage Buicks are displayed, including two 1905 Model Cs, the famous 1910 Buick Bug racer, the 1951 XP-300, 1954 Wildcat II and 1956 Centurion concept cars and even a World War II Buick-built Hellcat Tank Destroyer. Several well-restored Buicks from the late 1930s and early '40s, as well as model Buicks, have been donated to the gallery in recent years by Nicola Bulgari, international jeweler and holder of one of the world's largest private Buick collections.

A replica — created by museum staff and volunteers — of the stripped 1904 Model B, first Buick built in Flint, is powered by a

Fred Aldrich (left) shows his 1905 Model C Buick to A.B.C. Hardy, Flint's first auto manufacturer and later a leader of Chevrolet. Aldrich, who persuaded James Whiting to bring Billy Durant into Buick, bought the car in August 1905. One of the oldest existing Buicks, it was restored as a Buick Centennial project and is now displayed at Sloan Museum's Buick Gallery and Research Center in Flint.

rare original 1904 Buick Model B engine, in working condition. Also displayed are horse carts built by the Coldwater Road Cart Company and Flint Road Cart Company, the products that brought William C. Durant into the vehicle business — the first vehicles in his career that resulted in the creation of General Motors. Among other artifacts is the personal drafting set of David Buick.

One of the 1905 Buicks, restored in 2003-2005 as a Buick centennial project, has been in Flint since it was delivered new to Fred Aldrich, secretary of the Durant-Dort Carriage Company, in August 1905. Aldrich was the man who put James Whiting and Billy Durant together in the fall of 1904 in a meeting that led to Durant taking control of the fledgling Buick firm.

The Buicktown (Flint) Chapter of the Buick Club of America donated funds generated by the 2003 Buick centennial celebration in Flint to create a paint shop within the Buick Gallery where vintage Buicks and other cars are continually being restored by volunteers working under the museum's staff.

Inquiries about the Sloan Museum and Buick Gallery and Research Center collections, the Merle Perry Archives and the Lawrence R. Gustin Archives, as well as contributions of artifacts (including vehicles), photographs and documents, should be directed to Jeremy Dimick, Sloan curator of collections (jdimick@ sloanlongway.org, phone 810 237-3434). Financial contributions to support preserving Buick history and the maintenance of the museum's automobile collection should be directed to Todd Slisher, Executive Director of Sloan Museum and Longway Planetarium (tslisher@sloanlongway.org, phone 810 237-3445). Main address: Sloan Museum, 1221 E. Kearsley St., Flint, MI, 48503.

Acknowledgments

Terry B. Dunham, who was my good friend for 40-plus years and my co-author of *The Buick: A Complete History* in six editions (1980-2003), continually pushed for improvement in this volume. He asked the right questions, closely examined the answers and provided thought-provoking opinions. Terry commented on various drafts of this third edition, offering ideas and encouragement almost until the time of his death in November, 2012. Terry's enthusiasm, his personal contributions and the historical materials from his files were critical to the success of all three editions. Without his encouragement, this book would not have been attempted; and once started, may never have been completed.

Many thanks are also due William Close, the late husband of Walter Marr's granddaughter, Sarah. Bill Close carefully studied the early years of Walter Marr's career. He even bought and completely restored the only existing Marr Autocar — which is a link to the first Buick automobile ever built. Bill offered information and his own fascinating thoughts on those pioneering days when David Buick and Walter Marr were creating the early history of the Buick automobile, and he filled in many of the blanks in this barely documented period.

Kevin M. Kirbitz, who is helping create a new generation of Buicks and other General Motors vehicles as a GM engineering manager, provided a large amount of historical material from his research, some of it internet based, that made these updated editions necessary. As Terry Dunham once wrote, "With the patience and determination of the GM engineer that he is, Kirbitz has approached the research of Buick's earliest days in Detroit like no one else before him." His research included sifting through old plumbing industry publications, city directories, legal transcripts, newspapers, census reports and other documents. The result has been new information on David's life and on his early career as a builder of automobile engines. Among other contributions, his research led to a new chapter on Buick's work on an engine for the Wolverine automobile in 1903-04 and to a detailed report on David's Florida real estate venture of the 1920s.

Special thanks to Bob Lutz for the message at the beginning, to Fritz Henderson for granting me an interview about the reasons the Buick marque survived the 2009 bankruptcy, which occurred while he was president of General Motors, and to former Buick general manager Ed Mertz, for his observations about Buick in the 1980s and '90s.

The late Charles E. Hulse deserves thanks from all of those interested in the early history of Buick and of Flint (and of Oldsmobile, as well). Hulse was personally helpful to me, and assured that after his death all of his research on Buick's early years would be preserved. The Hulse collection includes notes on his personal interviews with Walter Marr and others and on the news articles he discovered by spending countless hours looking through microfilms of early newspapers. Hulse's Buick material is now available at the Sloan Museum's Buick Gallery and Research Center in Flint, the gift of his daughter, Susan Kelley.

For original material on William C. Durant, appreciation goes to the late Catherine L. Durant, his widow; the late Aristo Scrobogna, who was Durant's last personal secretary; and Scrobogna's daughter, Estelle Roberts. Catherine spent many hours over several weeks discussing her husband's career in 1972 and 1973. Aristo and Estelle preserved and gave me Durant's personal letters and other documents, including drafts of his unfinished autobiography. Aristo also gave me a treasured gift, Durant's personal desk, complete with the GM founder's brass lamp, inkwell and letter opener. Many others were also helpful on Durant, particularly the late Roger Van Bolt, Clarence Young and Richard Scharchburg and Durant business colleagues Archie Campbell, Charles Stewart Mott and Durant's secretary for 30 years, W.W. Murphy. Shortly after I wrote a 10-part series on Durant's life for *The Flint Journal* in 1972, Scharchburg made available GM internal papers that helped document Durant's career for my 1973 biography of Durant and also notes from his interviews with W.W. Murphy and others.

GM engineer Brian Heil offered 1903 engine component drawings made by Eugene Richard and salvaged by Heil from a wastebasket at Buick Product Engineering in the 1980s, as well as his interpretation of early Buick engine history. Don Bent sent a copy of his excellent 2005 book, *A Place Called Buick,* which describes in words and pictures the colorful history of the Buick home plant in Flint. In Arbroath, Scotland, where David Buick was born, another man with the Buick name, Eric Buick (no relation), shared information on the village and on Buick genealogy — and he and his wife Amy provided gracious hospitality to my wife Rose Mary and me on the occasion of our visit to Arbroath in 1994. Another resource was Michael Dixon, a student of early Detroit engine and marine history, who provided several specific pieces of information on David Buick's life, including facts about his involvement with sailboating and powerboats. At the Sloan Museum and Buick Gallery and Research Center in Flint, director Tim Shickles; Jeff Taylor, former curator of collections; and Jane McIntosh, former assistant curator, strongly supported the research effort. Through Shickles, Sloan and its Buick Gallery became the publisher of this book. Thanks to Todd Slisher, Shickles' successor, and Jeremy Dimick, the new curator of collections, support for this book has continued.

Leroy Cole, former president of the Society of Automotive Historians, kindly opened up his vast collection of automotive books, documents and other papers and photographs and was always available with guidance and encouragement. Michael W. R. Davis, a veteran of automotive journalism and auto public relations, provided access to his unpublished master's thesis on one of the early industry's mysterious figures, Charles G. Annesley. In Flint, Jim Johnson, Jack Skaff and David White, along with the late Merle Perry and Greg Fauth and others mentioned previously, were always helpful with advice and information. All of them shared an appreciation for the auto pioneers and the dramatic events they created in the Vehicle City. For information on the Wilkinson and Franklin cars, both of which featured overhead-valve engines, thanks to Frank Hantak, trustee and treasurer of the Franklin Automobile Museum in Tucson, Ariz. For information on the Marmon automobile, which also featured overhead-valve engines, thanks to Chic Kleptz of Dayton, Ohio, owner of more than 20 Marmons.

For information that resulted in saving Billy Durant's horse barn, thanks to the late Ernest Gardner and his daughter, my childhood best friend Janet Gardner (now Mrs. Gerald LeVasseur). The barn, which was on Gardner's property, is now preserved at Historical Crossroads Village, a recreated 19th Century village tourist attraction near Flint, thanks in large part to the efforts of local historian Clarence Young.

During many years of research on Buick history (covering more than four decades), I interviewed several people who had personally known David Buick, all of whom have since died: His grandson, David Dunbar Buick II; Fred G. Hoelzle, a longtime Buick employee who knew David Buick as early as 1904; and the above mentioned Charles Stewart Mott, a 60-year member of the GM board of directors, and Catherine Durant. Also helpful have been members of Walter Marr's family, including grandsons Walter L. Marr III and Richard A. Marr, the previously mentioned granddaughter Sarah (Mathes) Close and her late husband, William B., and Dan N. Williams, husband of another Marr granddaughter, Joan (Hays). I also appreciate the help of Eugene C. Richard's son, the late Eugene D. Richard, and grandson Robert MacRae. An important source for anyone writing about Flint's early industrial development is Frank M. Rodolf's manuscript, "An Industrial History of Flint," in the editorial library of *The Flint Journal*, where he worked in the 1930s and early 1940s. On an evening in New York in 1972, after a meeting with Catherine Durant, I discussed with Rodolf his personal interviews of Billy Durant in the days when Durant owned a Flint bowling establishment near the Buick complex he had created decades earlier. George S. May, author of *A Most Unique Machine*, was also helpful with advice in the early 1970s on Buick history. Also, Thomas J. Pyden, one of the most talented PR executives while at GM, was always helpful in providing access to key executives.

George H. Maines, a widely known personality in Flint who handled public relations for such national figures as Huey Long and numerous entertainment and sports stars, spent hours talking about Flint pioneer automotive figures he had known from his childhood. "In the early days of this (the 20th) century, Flint had a group of men of unusual ability," he once told me. "There was probably not a more lively bunch anywhere else in the country. And the spark plug of them all was Billy Durant." Maines, whose father was a business associate of Durant's, was among a number of people who lived in Flint during the 1950s and '60s who helped bring to life the almost-forgotten days when Buick, Chevrolet and General Motors were created. Thanks also to Tom Klug, associate professor of history at Marygrove College, Detroit, for the reference to C.B. Calder of the Detroit Shipbuilding Company, and to Michael Dixon for pointing out its significance. Kim Crawford, formerly of *The Flint Journal*, who has written a fine and detailed book, *The Daring Trader*, the first biography of Jacob Smith, the fur trader who founded the Flint settlement, helped in checking Flint facts. Bob Gritzinger, who became an editor at *AutoWeek*, helped me research information for Buick's state historical marker in Detroit. In trying to flesh out David Buick's years in California and the legal battles of Buick Oil Company, researcher George J. Fogelson of Redondo Beach was particularly helpful, as was Gwen Patterson in finding records at the National Archives and Records Administration in Laguna Niguel, Calif. At GM, John Cortez was helpful in my work with Bob Lutz. In trying to unravel the intricate beginnings of Chevrolet, special thanks to Ken Kaufmann, a veteran Chevrolet historian; Don Williams, president of the Vintage Chevrolet Club of America, and Jim Miller, retired auto writer of *The Flint Journal*. And in finally constructing this manuscript and all of the photographs into a coherent package, many thanks to Heather Shaw, who put it all together, and to *Ward's Auto World* editor emeritus David C. Smith, for recommending her.

Thanks also to the gracious staff of the Old Course Hotel at St. Andrew's, not far from Arbroath, Scotland. At 4 a.m. on the day we unveiled the plaque near David Buick's birthplace, I sat alone in a little den/library/dining room, looking out on the historic golf course and the North Sea beyond, and composed a small story on the unveiling for my old newspaper, *The Flint Journal*. Without asking, a staff member brought me tea and a plate of cookies. As the day dawned gray and then orange and blue on that historic setting and the warm room where I sat, I remember thinking it was a fine day to honor the founder of The Buick.

Among those who were kind enough to read drafts of this manuscript and offer advice were Charles K. Hyde, professor of history at Wayne State University; David L. Lewis, professor of business history at the University of Michigan; two former Buick PR directors, Jack DeCou and Margaret G. Holmes; Mark Patrick, then curator of the National Automotive Historical Collection at the Detroit Public Library; and Roger Van Noord, retired managing editor of *The Flint Journal* and biographer of the Beaver Island (Mich.) Mormon king, James Jesse Strang.

David Buick had two sons, Thomas D. and Wynton R., and two daughters, Frances Jane (Fanny, Mrs. Frank Patterson) of Los Angeles and Mabel Lucille (Mrs. James Coyle) of Detroit. I interviewed David Dunbar Buick II, Thomas's son, and Doug Boes, who is the adopted grandson of Frances Jane Patterson. Fanny's daughter, Caroline, married Warren Boes. Others interviewed include Sally Buick of Birmingham, Mich., and William Walcott Buick of Bryn Athyn, Pa. William said his grandfather, Detroiter William Dunbar Buick, was a "first cousin, twice removed" of David Dunbar Buick. Sally's late husband, Henry Wolcott Buick, was William's brother. Sally has two sons, Jeffrey and David Dunbar Buick.

Finally, I want to thank my wife Rose Mary, our sons Robert L. Gustin and David M. Gustin and their families, and my late parents Robert S. and Doris M. Gustin, for their support over a number of years of research on Buick Motor Division and its personalities. My father was a supervisor at AC Spark Plug. His father, Edward M. Gustin, began working for Walker-Weiss, an axle-making subsidiary of the Durant-Dort Carriage Company, around 1899 before becoming an executive at the firm as it evolved into Flint Motor Axle Company on the Buick complex's Flint site (it was on the north Flint Buick site before Buick arrived there and built axles for the Dort automobile, among others, but unfortunately not Buick). My mother's father, Thomas E. Irving, moved his family to Flint from Barrow-in-Furness, England, where he had been a shipwright with Vickers, in 1928. He went to work at Buick, from which he retired as a wood patternmaker in 1952. My mother's pride in Flint and Buick no doubt influenced my interest in Buick's historical importance.

Books

Solid and original information on David Buick is found in only a few automotive history books. The most informative for this effort were *A Most Unique Machine* by George S. May, *The Turning Wheel* by Arthur Pound, and *My Father* by Margery Durant. Several Henry Ford biographies were also helpful. Allen Nevins' *Ford: The Times, The Man, The Company,* and Sidney Olson's delightful *Young Henry Ford* were particularly useful because they best described the times and the people in Detroit at the very time David Buick and Walter Marr were trying to perfect automobiles, although they rarely if ever mention Buick or Marr.

Bent, Don, *A Place Called Buick,* Flint, Mich.: Bent, 2005.

Crawford, Kim, *The Daring Trader,* East Lansing, Mich.: Michigan State University Press, 2011.

Crow, Carl, *The City of Flint Grows Up,* New York: Harper, 1945.

Curcio, Andrew, *Chrysler: The Life and Times of an Automotive Genius,* Oxford University Press, 2000.

Dammann, George H., *Seventy Years of Buick,* Glen Ellyn, Ill.: Crestline, 1973.

Dixon, Michael M., *Motormen and Yachting: Waterfront Heritage of the Automobile Industry,* Detroit, Mervue Publications (www. mervuepublications.com), 2005.

Dunham, Terry B. and Gustin, Lawrence R., *The Buick: A Complete History,* sixth (Centennial) edition, Automobile Quarterly, 2002.

Durant, Margery, *My Father,* New York: Knickerbocker Press, 1929.

Glasscock, G.C., *The Gasoline Age,* Indianapolis and New York: Bobbs-Merrill, 1937.

Gustin, *Billy Durant, Creator of General Motors,* Grand Rapids: Eerdmans, 1973. Expanded and updated third edition, Ann Arbor, Mich., University of Michigan Press, 2008.

Gustin, editor, *The Flint Journal Centennial Picture History of Flint,* Flint, Mich.: The Flint Journal, revised third edition, 1977.

Hyde, Charles K., *The Dodge Brothers: The Men, The Motor Cars, and the Legacy,* Detroit: Wayne State University Press, 2005.

Lacey, Robert, *Ford: The Men and the Machine,* Boston-Toronto: Little, Brown, 1986.

Lewis, David L., *The Public Image of Henry Ford: An American Folk Hero and His Company,* Detroit: Wayne State University Press, 1976.

MacManus, Theodore F. and Beasley, Norman, *Men, Money and Motors,* New York: Harper and Brothers, 1930.

Maines, George H., *Men, A City, and Buick,* pamphlet, Flint, Michigan: Advertisers Press, 1953.

May, George S., *A Most Unique Machine: The Michigan Origins of the American Automobile Industry,* Grand Rapids, Mich.: Eerdmans, 1975.

May, *R.E. Olds: Auto Industry Pioneer,* Grand Rapids, Mich: Eerdmans, 1977

Nevins, Allen, *Ford: The Times, The Man, The Company,* New York: Charles Scribner's Sons, 1954.

Olson, Sidney, *Young Henry Ford,* Detroit: Wayne State University Press, 1963.

Pearson, Henry Greenleaf, *Son of New England, James Jackson Storrow,* Thomas Todd Company, 1932.

Pound, Arthur, *The Turning Wheel, The Story of General Motors Through 25 Years,* Garden City, N.Y.: Doubleday, Doran, 1934.

Seltzer, Lawrence H., *A Financial History of the American Automobile Industry,* Boston and New York: Riverside Press Cambridge, 1928.

Sloan, Alfred P., Jr., *My Years With General Motors,* New York: Doubleday, 1964.

Therou, Francois, *Buick "The Golden Era" 1903-1915,* Brea, Calif.: Decir, 1971, primarily early catalog reprints.

Articles

This is a partial list of newspaper and magazine articles that would be helpful to researchers.

The Plumbers' Trade Journal, various 1894, 1896 and 1899 editions with articles, photos and ads about David Buick, his plumbing career and The Buick & Sherwood Manufacturing Company. Kevin M. Kirbitz collection.

The Detroit Tribune, September 4, 1899, *Local Automobile Makers Busily Hustling Things.* Small story with important message about Walter Marr's tricycle engine and his relationship with Charles G. Annesley.

The Motor Vehicle Review, October 1899, first reference to "Bruick" experimenting in "the manufacture of motor carriages."

Buick Manufacturing Company, catalog circa 1901-1903, Terry B. Dunham Collection.

The Automobile and Motor Review, December 20, 1902, a brief account of Marr Auto Car Company being formed.

The Motor World, May 21, 1903, on Buick Motor Company incorporation.

The Motor World, September 29, 1903, on Buick moving to Flint.

Cycle and Automobile Trade Journal, October 1903, Hugh Dolnar, *The Marr Autocar.*

Buick Motor Company, catalog, 1904, Dunham collection. Copy in Buick Gallery and Research Center, Sloan Museum, Flint, Michigan.

Cycle and Automobile Trade Journal, March 1904, Buick ad; November and December 1904, Buick car ads.

The Automobile, July 30, 1904, discusses first drive (Detroit-Flint-Detroit July 9-12).

Automobile Review, September 10, 1904, *Buick 20 H.P. Tonneau.*

Cyle and Automobile Trade Journal, October 1904, Dolnar, *The Buick Motor Company's Side Entrance Tonneau,* one of the best early account of Buick's beginnings, plus the first test ride of a Buick by a journalist.

Auto Trade Journal, October 1904, first Buick car ad.

The Motor World, November 24, 1904, *Buick Gets License,* explaining Buick took over the Selden license of Pope-Robinson and would therefore become a full-fledged member of the Association of Licensed Automobile Manufacturers.

The Motor World, undated, probably February 1905, a brief interview with David Buick on his engine while at New York Auto Show.

Cycle and Automobile Trade Journal, December 1905, *Buick Motor Brake Horse Power,* Hugh Dolnar defends his statements on Buick's power.

New York World, November 2, 1910, Buick Oil Company advertisement.

The Horseless Age, November 30, 1910, *Buick's Oil Venture Gets Black Eye.*

Los Angeles Times, January 27, 1912, *His Reward a Freeze-out?* Ralph Arnold's lawsuit against Buick Oil Company. There are several articles on Buick Oil Company in this newspaper in the 1910-15 period, including *Accusations in Rebuttal,* April 17, 1912, Benjamin F. Moffatt, who demands return of large block of Buick stock, is criticized by firm's secretary; *Busy Day for New Tribunal,* October 27, 1914, reference to Buick Oil Company case, and *Too Much of It,* April 23, 1915, judge criticizes complaint against Buick Oil Company.

Press Reference Library: Notables of the West, International News Service, Volume 1, 1913. David Buick biographical sketch.

Buick Weekly, March 19, 1920, *Beacraft Helped Make '1st' Buick.*

Detroit Saturday Night, Benjamin Briscoe Jr., *The Inside Story of General Motors,* January 1921. An excellent historical account by one of David Buick's most important early associates.

Automotive Industries, June 1921, announcement on David Buick's design for a new car to be marketed as the Lorraine.

Buick Bulletin, October 1921, *Men You Should Know About: Walter L. Marr.*

Motor, January 1923, *That Man Durant,* W.A.P. John.
Automotive Industries, April 26, 1923, on David Buick's plans to build Dunbar automobile.

St. Petersburg (Fla.) Times and *Tampa Tribune,* February 8, 1925, ad placed by Buick Motor Company attacking David Buick on David's Florida land promotion; contains rare excerpts from Buick Motor Company board of directors' minutes of February 1906.

Newspaper Enterprise Association, April 28, 1928, Bruce Catton, *David Buick, Founder of Buick, Lives in Poverty at Age of 74.* This is the only extensive interview of David Buick by a professional journalist, a year before Buick's death.

National Cyclopedia of American Biography, David Buick, undated, but after David Buick's death in 1929.

The Buick Magazine, September 1937, *Buick in the Beginning.*

Chattanooga Free Press, October 5, 1937, Sam Adkins, *"Walter Marr Came Here to Die…"*

Old Timers News, August 1952, W.H. Wascher, *Buick and Mustachioed Workers Build a 'Better' Engine in 1904.* Memories of a worker who started at Buick in 1903.

Flint News-Advertiser, August 11, 1953, Ben Bennett, *Pine Yardstick, Piece of String ,* early Flint Wagon Works workers reminisce about building first Flint Buick.

Flint News-Advertiser, Buick 50th anniversary issue, 1953, small article quoting Fred Aldrich on how he helped bring James Whiting and Billy Durant together, leading to Durant's takeover of Buick.

MacLean's, Oct. 1-Oct. 15, 1954, *My Eighty Years on Wheels,* by R.S. McLaughlin as told to Eric Hutton.

Elgin (Illinois) *Courier-News,* August 11, 1964, Edward F. Gathman, *Fire Wrote End to Elgin Car Manufacture Venture,* Last Marr Autocars go up in flames in August 1904.

Automobile Quarterly, Summer 1968, *Wouldn't You Really Rather be a Buick?,* Beverly Rae Kimes.

The Flint Journal, October 2, 1980, Lawrence R. Gustin, *Mr. Buick drives a Plymouth,* interview with grandson of David Buick.

Special Interest Autos, December 1980, Keith Marvin, *The Dunbar Deception: Was David Buick a schnook or a sharpie?*

The Flint Journal, August 9, 1981, Gustin, *'The Thing': Michigan home of 1880s car can call itself first 'auto city.'* Tracking down the story of Thomas Clegg of Memphis, Michigan, and Michigan's first automobile – a steam-engine vehicle.

Automobile Quarterly, Summer 1993, Gustin, *The Buick Flint Would Really Rather Have.* A 1905 Model C returns to Buick.

Antique Automobile, March-April 1995, Dunham, *Cobwebs and Overhead Valves,* an account of work leading to the first Buick valve-in-head engine.

Buick Bugle, a publication of the Buick Club of America, December 2003, Dunham, *Searching for Mr. Marr.*

Buick Bugle articles by Gustin in May and August 2007 (David Buick's plumbing career), April and May 2008 (on Buick's first two-cylinder valve-in-head auto engine) and June 2008 (on recreating 1904 Buick replica and restoring Fred Aldrich's 1905 Model C).

Buick Bugle, November 2007, Kevin M. Kirbitz, *Exploring Detroit with David D. Buick.*

Automotive History Review, Spring 2008, Kirbitz, *David D. Buick and the Wolverine.*

Michigan History, September 2008, Gustin, *Flint, Billy Durant and the beginning of General Motors.*

Automotive History Review, Summer 2010, Gustin, *Sights and Sounds of Automotive History,* collecting film and audio of auto pioneers including Durant and Marr.

Various newspaper articles in the Charles E. Hulse collection at Sloan Museum's Buick Gallery and Research Center are not listed separately. There are also others, some undated and unidentified as to source, in the files of William Close, Terry Dunham, Kevin Kirbitz and the author, as well as in the files of the Sloan Museum and its Buick Gallery and Research Center in Flint, Mich.

Letters, Manuscripts, Audio-Video

- Fred G. Hoelzle, manuscript, undated, discussing early role with Eugene Richard, Walter Marr and David Buick.

- Various letters between Walter Marr and several associates, including David Buick, author's collection.

- Michigan Supreme Court record filed September 20, 1907, Buick Motor Company vs. Reid Manufacturing Company, containing transcripts of Wayne County Circuit Court testimony filed September 27, 1904. David Buick and James Whiting discuss early engine design, manufacturing and marketing.

- Michael W. R. Davis, master's thesis on Charles G. Annesley, author's collection.

- Legal depositions by W.C. Durant and James H. Whiting, 1911, author's collection. These were in response to a complaint by William S. Ballenger and other Buick stockholders that Whiting had reached a secret agreement with Durant in which Whiting would receive a substantial block of Buick stock after helping Durant sell a stockholders' agreement to the other shareholders. Durant and Whiting denied the charge, with Durant contending he did not decide until later that he needed Whiting's help to manage the company.

- Charles W. Nash, letter to Fred Warner, manager of Buick in Chicago, December 19, 1913, almost dismissing David Buick's role in the company's past. Buick Gallery and Research Center, Sloan Museum, Flint, Mich.

- Frank J. DeLaney, manuscript, *A History of the Buick Motor Company,* undated. Early employee relates history as he remembers it. Author's collection.

- Charles E. Hulse, hand-written notes on interview of Walter Marr, 1934. Author's collection. Copy in Hulse collection, Buick Gallery and Research Center, Sloan Museum, Flint, Mich.

- A.B.C. Hardy, recollections, 1946. Sloan Museum, Flint, Mich.

- *Legend of Buick,* Buick Centennial DVD, Lawrence R. Gustin, director; Bill Harris, narrator. Work incomplete but viewing copies available. Motion pictures of auto pioneers including Ransom Olds, Henry Ford, Louis Chevrolet, Charles W. Nash, Walter P. Chrysler, Henry Leland, Sam McLaughlin and Walter Marr (Olds, Chrysler, Leland and McLaughlin with their voices); voice recording and brief motion pictures, William C. Durant. Includes video of David Buick birthplace commemoration, Arbroath, Scotland, 1994, and sound film of Dutch Bower, Charles Chayne, Harlow Curtice and more recent Buick executives. Copies at the Buick Gallery and Research Center, Sloan Museum, Flint, Mich.; in the University of Michigan Library; Flint Public Library; and Detroit Automotive History Collection.

- R. Samuel McLaughlin, letter to Buick General Manager Ed Rollert, October 27, 1964, gives his version on how W.C. Durant first rode in a Buick (at least partly inaccurate). Author's collection.

- David Buick, letter to Walter Marr, December 11, 1913, discusses Marr's Cyclecar. Buick Gallery and Research Center, Sloan Museum, Flint, Mich.

- Buick Oil Company lawsuit documents dated 1914 and 1915 filed under Equity Case A121, National Archives and Records Administration, Laguna Niguel, Calif.

- Original letters, manuscripts and other documents from the estate of William C. Durant, first used by the author for his biography, *Billy Durant: Creator of General Motors,* in 1973 and since sold by Catherine L. Durant's estate to the General Motors Institute Foundation, are now in the Richard P. Scharchburg Archives at Kettering University in Flint. Additional Durant documents given later to the author by Aristo Scrobogna, Durant's last personal secretary, and by his daughter, Estelle Roberts, are now in the author's collection.

- Birth records of David Buick in Arbroath, Scotland, are courtesy of Eric Buick of Arbroath. Eric Buick also provided information about David Buick's early life in Scotland.

- Thomas D. Buick, letter to a boat manufacturer, J.C. Schmidt, October 21, 1903. Discusses Buick marine engines and the company's upcoming move to Flint. Terry B. Dunham Collection. Copy in *The Buick: A Complete History,* sixth edition.

Gustin Archives at Sloan Museum

Lawrence R. Gustin, author of this book in association with Kevin M. Kirbitz, and of a biography of Billy Durant, as well as creator of a picture history of Flint and co-author with Terry B. Dunham of a history of Buick automobiles, has donated his 50-year collection of files to Sloan Museum. They are managed as the Gustin Archives under the direction of Jeremy Dimick, curator of collections. These include some of Durant's personal records, including two copies of Durant's autobiographical notes, one with his original marginal memos, plus photographs, news clippings and numerous automotive books. Also included are video tapes, many of which were used to create the *Legend of Buick* DVD and documents related to David Buick. Gustin made the donations to help preserve Flint's automotive heritage for new generations.

By 1925, most of the main figures in Buick's early history — David Buick, Billy Durant, Walter Marr, Charles Nash, Walter Chrysler, Louis Chevrolet, etc. — had long been gone from the Buick scene. But Harry Bassett, a onetime assistant to C.S. Mott who had been Buick general manager under Chrysler and then Buick president starting in 1920, was still in charge. Five Buicks were entered in the Soviet Union's 1925 National Test Motor Run and won most of the major awards for general excellence, fuel economy and speed against automobiles from around the world. Here a Buick Master Six, Model 49, is cheered in Moscow's Red Square at the finish of a Leningrad-to-Moscow endurance and reliability run it won. The successes didn't translate into a bonanza of Buick sales in Russia — but the Soviets were said to have copied some of the Buick engines.

Index

Photo Index

About the Author

Lawrence R. Gustin, a native of Flint, Mich., was a writer/editor from 1960 to 1984 at *The Flint Journal* in what was then Buick's headquarters city. He was from a General Motors family, his father a supervisor at AC Spark Plug, one grandfather a wood patternmaker at Buick, the other once a supervisor at Flint Motor Axle, a former Durant-Dort Carriage Company subsidiary on Buick's north Flint site. While Larry covered such events as the launch of Apollo 11 that sent the first men to the Moon, the first Ali-Frazier "fight of the century" and the inauguration of President Carter, he also became auto editor and then assistant metro editor in charge of the auto/business/labor writers.

In 1973, he wrote the critically acclaimed first biography of William C. Durant, *Billy Durant: Creator of General Motors*, re-issued in an expanded third edition by the University of Michigan Press in the GM centennial year of 2008. For the first edition, he received the Antique Automobile Club of America's Thomas McKean Memorial Cup for exceptional use of history, among other Michigan and national awards. In 1976, Larry created *The Flint Journal Centennial Picture History of Flint* in the first of three editions. He also launched a newspaper campaign to save the Durant-Dort headquarters, which was about to be razed. That three-story brick building, closely tied to the birth of GM, is now restored and a National Historic Landmark.

In 1980, with Terry B. Dunham, he co-authored the award-winning book, *The Buick: A Complete History*, updated in five more editions from the mid-1980s to Buick's centennial in 2003. Larry, who became Buick assistant public relations director, launched another award winner, *Inside Buick* magazine, and helped create the Sloan Museum's Buick Gallery and Research Center. He received a Distinguished Service Citation for his historical work from the Automotive Hall of Fame in 1999. A 1959 graduate of Michigan State University, he was elected in 2007 to the Hall of Fame of the MSU daily, *The State News*.

In 2003 he directed Buick's centennial activities – including a national heritage tour of Buick exhibits at auto museums, an award-winning poster and brochure, Michigan historical marker and *Legend of Buick* DVD – that earned the top overall award in that year's International Automotive Media Competition. At Buick PR (1984-2005), he was the official Buick representative at the 1997 groundbreaking for the plant in Shanghai that would produce the first Chinese-built Buicks, and two years later he walked down the Buick City assembly line with the last Buick built in Flint. He worked with Buick events and people in Beijing, Paris, London, Mexico City, Rome and

274

Rio de Janeiro — and in David Buick's home town of Arbroath, Scotland. Both the Durant and David Buick biographies were translated into Chinese and published in Shanghai in 2008. Larry was awarded the Buick Heritage Trophy by Buick Motor Division and the Buick Gallery in 2005 and was honored again with the first Buick Heritage Alliance Award in 2012. He received silver medals in the International Automotive Media Competition for the first two editions of *David Buick's Marvelous Motor Car* (2006 and the 2011 update) and for an article in a Society of Automotive Historians magazine on searching for film and voice recordings of auto pioneers. Larry and his wife Rose Mary live in Michigan's Oakland County (after more than 60 years in the Flint area) and have two sons and five grandchildren.

Kevin M. Kirbitz

Kevin M. Kirbitz, born in Flint, Mich., has lived in the Flint area most of his life. He grew up in a General Motors household (his father retired from Buick after 42 years; his mother retired from GM Public Relations' Flint office after 20 years, his brother worked for AC Spark Plug) and he earned degrees in mechanical engineering and manufacturing management at General Motors Institute (now Kettering University). Starting at GM in 1979 at Buick Motor Division in Flint, he worked five years in planning, implementation and production of the Buick City project. He was then assigned to product engineering in several GM operations in Flint. In 1998, Kirbitz began three years with GM of Canada in Oshawa, Ontario, during which time he received a GM Chairman's Honors award. Since 2001, he has been an engineering manager in Advanced Vehicle Development at GM's Warren (Mich.) Technical Center.

Kirbitz has long been involved in research on and preservation of local and GM history. In 1974 he designed an award-winning logo for Historical Crossroads Village, a project of Genesee County's Parks and Recreation Department to recreate a mid 19th century town with historic buildings relocated from throughout the county where Flint is located. In 1983 and 1984, he was recognized for his historical research on Buick's foundry and on Oak Park Industries, a forerunner of modern industrial parks and home of Buick's mammoth Flint manufacturing complex. He has contributed to books on Buick and GM history and his work has appeared in the Buick Club of America's Bugle and the Society of Automotive Historians' *Automotive History Review*. For his writing skills and contributions, he received the Buick Club of America/Terry Dunham Literary Award in 2008. That year, he was awarded Buick Motor Division's prestigious Buick Heritage Trophy for his original research and new findings on the early life and career of David Buick. Kevin and his wife Denise (whose father, grandfather and great-grandfather all worked at Buick in Flint) live in Grand Blanc, Mich., and have one son and one daughter.

A window from the past frames Buick's 21ˢᵗ century home

This view is from a second-floor window in downtown Detroit's Boydell Building, probably the exact location of David Buick's first motor shop, Buick Auto-Vim & Power Co., in 1900. The window frames a view of Renaissance Center, today the world headquarters of General Motors and its Buick offices. The photo was taken at the time of Buick's centennial in 2003. Between 1900, the year Buick Auto-Vim arrived, and 1998, when Buick marketing offices moved to RenCen, Buick Motor Division was headquartered for 95 years (1903-1998) in Flint.

Also by Lawrence R. Gustin

Billy Durant: Creator of General Motors

Updated and expanded third edition

Available from the University of Michigan Press

Reviews of Billy Durant:

"Gustin has done tremendous research and his new book is a masterpiece." —*Road & Track*

"A fascinating book...a sympathetic look at the man who glued General Motors together and in the process made Flint one of the great industrial centers of America." —*Detroit Free Press*

"It is refreshing to report that *Billy Durant* is one of the best researched books dealing with an automotive giant."
—*Antique Automobile*

"*Billy Durant* fills in a masterly way the only important void remaining concerning the work of the motorcar pioneers."
—Richard Crabb, author of *Birth of a Giant: The Men and Incidents that Gave America the Motorcar*

"Excellent biography"
—Bruce Catton, Pulitzer Prize-winning historian